Liz
I hope you
enjoy my book
Thank you
Gary Benassi

il Dottore

Gary Benassi

il Dottore.

Produced and printed
by Stillwater River Publications.

Visit our website at
www.StillwaterPress.com
for more information.
First Stillwater River Publications Edition
Paperback ISBN: 978-1-952521-76-8
1 2 3 4 5 6 7 8 9 10
Written by Gary Benassi.
Published by Stillwater River Publications,
Pawtucket, RI, USA.

To all of the victims of Nazi and Fascist oppression,
may they rest in peace.

Prologue

Peering from their hiding place, two men lay in wait for a particular individual. One of them was Special Agent George Sloan of the British Judge Advocate General's Office: the other was a young man named Luigi Ferraro, a local from the town of Nettulo. Actually it was little more than a village between Mt. Pelocalati and Mt. Nebrodi, in northeastern Sicily. It lay less than ten miles from the gorgeous and picturesque city of Taormina.

The two men were waiting for the expected arrival of one Leonardo Goncalo. Dottore Goncalo if one so pleased. A physician, a man with a dark and evil past.

As Sloan spied his watch he noticed it was approaching 10 pm. Darkness had settled into the pleasant night in their present location of Ottavino. Fireflies dotted about in the humid, fetid air. Sloan and Ferraro paid them no mind.

"Perhaps he is not going to show," whispered Sloan, as disappointment lay hidden in his voice.

"Do not worry Capitano, he will show," replied Ferraro with unwavering certainty. "If I know the good doctor, he will make his nightly appearance."

Sloan wasn't so sure. In fact, he had had a hard time believing that a personage such as Leo Goncalo would have anything to do with a flyspeck of a town as Ottavino was almost beyond belief.

George Sloan had been assigned to the Goncalo case by his superior, Colonel John "Black Jack" Thomas in their Hamburg Germany headquarters. What Sloan had been told was nothing short of stupefying. The only known Italian to have performed grisly and ghastly surgeries at the Auschwitz concentration camp. Not only that. Leo Goncalo hadn't been forced or coerced into the camp, he had willingly volunteered. Goncalo had specifically requested to be allowed entry, so as to enable him to work and study under the infamous and notorious Doctor Josef Mengele, the "Angel of Death."

Sloan could not imagine what kind of mind, what kind of perversion of soul, what degree of inhumanity Leo Goncalo must have possessed to willingly, if not eagerly, enter the realm of the devil.

"Sppp," hissed Luigi Ferraro to Sloan. I do believe our quarry is approaching."

Sloan squinted his eyes into the brooding Sicilian night to take in a man of medium height, perhaps 5' 10" tall, average build, walking toward their position. The man gave no hint or air that he was aware of being watched. About 20 feet away from the two men, Goncalo stopped and turned toward a doorway and inserted a key into the doorknob. A metallic click sounded in the night air. Goncalo paused for a moment or two and glanced in both directions. Apparently satisfied, Goncalo turned the door handle and entered the apartment building. The address read 25 Via Nicadimo.

Moments later, Sloan and Ferraro quickly left the hiding place. "Well, what do you think my friend?" asked Ferraro in a voice.

"He certainly seems to fit the description of the man from what my superiors have told me and from what you have said," replied Sloan in a cautious, pensive tone. Their soft-soled shoes left no echo as the men walked along the deserted alley.

"There is someone who lives not far from here. Someone who may be able to provide you with more and direct assistance," continued Luigi Ferraro.

"Who is he?" asked Sloan.

"It is not a he, Capitano, it is a she. And her name is Rosalie Donato. Meet me at the cantina at 10 am in the morning. I will provide you with some additional details." And with that Luigi Ferraro went silent.

George Sloan turned to him and merely nodded. This was turning into a more intriguing case by the moment. The two men bid goodbye to one another and departed. Sloan made his way to his pensione, where he would jot down some notes on what had just transpired.

Clear blue skies, broken by an occasional puffy cloud, lingered over Ottavino on this Saturday morning. Sloan was seated across from Luigi Ferraro in the small café owned by proprietor Georgio Mancuso. It was an old establishment frequented by many of the locals. Today saw a crowded venue, it being the weekend. Customers patiently waited for their espressos or café lattes. Some even bought rolls and croissants.

"Did you sleep well, Capitano?" asked Ferraro pleasantly. He was dressed in a slightly upgraded peasant style of clothing: white shirt, black baggy pants, and knee-high jackboots.

George tilted his head slightly to the right, as if trying to clear earwax. "Eh, not too bad, not too bad."

"Bene, bene, that is good," said Ferraro, whose English was nearly flawless. It was surprising to Sloan, something he had not expected. "As I said to you last evening. This woman lives not far from here, near Taormina. She may be able to help you to apprehend this Leo Goncalo. I believe Rosalie Donato has direct knowledge of the Goncalo clan.

Sloan was now looking straight into the eyes of Ferraro. "That is most interesting Luigi. What does she know...that you think may be of help to me?"

"Signora Donato lost her father and her mother to the Fascists during the war. And the good doctor and his Fascist father, Carlo, played a direct part. Mostly, the father," said Ferraro, his gaze level with that of Sloan's.

George leaned back in his chair, which elicited a slight groaning sound as if it might suddenly give way. He brought his espresso to his lips and sipped. One of his favorite things about Italy, and Sicily, was the superb espresso coffee offered just about anywhere. When George was feeling especially expansive he would frequently order a double espresso, or doppia. How so, Luigi?"

"I do not know all of the particulars, but I do know that Carlo Goncalo had it in for Rosalie's father, Umberto, especially about some of the land he possessed. Goncalo senior has always coveted this land, and he wanted to add it to his own holdings. When his Fascist connections provided his opportunity he pounced. Goncalo saw to it that Umberto Mancini would languish in jail. It would be a sentence from which he'd not escape from. Mancini died in his prison cell."

All of this information had the full attention of George Sloan.

"That is most interesting Luigi, most interesting. Only, how does that pertain to the son, the doctor?" asked Sloan.

"Ah, well, you see, Carlo, or Gaetano, his given name, but he preferred using Carlo. Anyway…where was I? Oh, well, Carlo Goncalo apparently thought he might be a matchmaker. He had the idea that Rosalie would make an excellent match for his son and…"

Goncalo senior had the resources to have Rosalie's husband removed?" filled in Sloan.

"Ah, no, not exactly. Her husband, Franco, served honorably during the war. He passed away a short time ago from cancer. But I do believe Rosalie can help you bring Goncalo the younger to justice."

"Tell me, Luigi, how do you know of these things?" asked Sloan conspiratorially as he looked about the café. It had become more crowded as the hour approached 11 am.

"Capitano, Rosalie Donato is my cousin."

Chapter One

The Young Fascist

"Leo, *viene qui?* Where are you?" shouted out his mother, Marcella Goncalo, to her ten year old son. In exasperation she muttered to herself, "Honestly, I sometimes simply do not know what to make of Leo. He is always disappearing."

Leo Goncalo had indeed heard his mother calling after him and he knew why. Undoubtedly, his mother wanted him to go to his father he knew was with some of his Fascist cronies gathered in the family living room. His father would want to show off his incredibly bright and loquacious young man. Almost as if he were a hand puppet for his domineering father.

But for now, young Leo was engrossed in something far more important. Set down before him and scattered around his bed lay numerous photographs of young women in varying stages of undress or wearing nothing at all. He did not know how his friend Matteo had procured them, and, frankly, he did not care. Some of the pictures were of young women who were simply exquisite: displaying large, rounded breasts or long, long legs. A few were of blond-haired girls; undoubtedly German. Some pictures showed a young woman gently fingering herself, while looking directly at the camera.

Young Leo Goncalo had not yet reached the age of puberty, but he was pretty sure he had felt a gentle stirring within his loins. And now, of all times, his mother was looking for him.

Leo quickly gathered together the pictures of the naked women and placed them in an accordion paper folder. He then carefully placed them between the mattress and the box spring of his bed. He would have to remember to relocate them before the maid, Lucinda, did the beds in two days' time. Leo well knew that if Lucinda found the folder she would immediately inform his parents, and then, holy hell would descend upon his head. The woman was an inveterate busy body. Leo then crept out of his bedroom and called out to his mother down the hall.

"Ah, Leo, there you are. Your father wants you to join him and his friends," said his mother, as she looked down at him and saw the frown on his face. A knowing half-smile was on her face.

"Yes, mama," responded Leo, foreboding building up within his body. A nervous trembling also began to manifest itself as well. He desperately hoped his father would not try and turn him into his own personal puppet toy and have him recite some silly poem or, perhaps, expectorate upon some speech il Duce had given to thousands of his followers in Rome.

Down the stairs the young man plodded to his certain doom. How he had always hated these staged events. Leo loved his father, but in a guarded way. He also feared him and he knew that if he did not appear or disappoint his father by pouting, he would later face a whipping from the old man's leather belt. Getting this was usually reserved for his older brother, Mario, but he, Leo, was not immune by any means from receiving a taste of the leather.

At the foot of the stairwell, Leo could hear his father and the other men assembled in the living room. The gist of their conversation had been something about Mussolini and his Black Shirts and the wonderful things they were now doing for Italy. The country was responding with alacrity and verve to the Duce's call for new and dynamic action. Italy had to move away from its pedestrian and previously backward thinking if it wanted to take its rightful place with the other nations of Europe, especially France and Great Britain.

"Ah, my Leo," exclaimed his father proudly, as the boy stood silently in the doorway. "Leo, come in, come in my son," continued Carlo Goncalo as he gestured for Leo to come in and join him and the other men.

Leo dutifully strode over to where his father was seated.

"Leo, you know Don Antonio," said Carlo as he cast an open hand to the large and frightful looking bear of a man seated nearby in an overstuffed armchair. The furniture piece looked as if it would shatter at any moment. Leo knew of the man's reputation as the local Mafia don. Many men who had dared to cross the man in the past had not lived for long. Sometimes their demises had been of a most unpleasant nature. Don Antonio gave the slightest of nods to the boy, while he puffed away on a large black cigar. In the other massive hand a glass of brandy sat cradled.

Carlo Goncalo resumed the introductions as he pointed to Gianni Simone, Gugliemo Cardi, and Roberto "Bobo" Moncado.

These were men of lesser rank than Don Antonio, and, in a way, to his father. Nevertheless, they were men who should be afforded great respect and deference.

Leo remained standing by his father's chair, sweat beads forming around his forehead and behind his ears. Hardly a breeze stirred through the large and suffocating room. It was absolutely stifling to the boy. He hoped that whatever his father now had planned would be concluded quickly so that he could escape and go back to his room. Perhaps he would be able to ogle the pictures once again. He had been particularly enamored with one red-headed woman. But it had not been her hair color that had caught his attention. The woman had a pair of the largest breasts he had ever seen mounted firmly upon her chest.

"I tell you comrades, il Duce is the best. He will prove to be the greatest leader ever. Perhaps there with Caesar himself," Carlo Goncalo expostulated, his white-maned head enveloped in a cloud of his cigar smoke.

"You think so, Carlo?" questioned Don Antonio. He shifted his great bulk, making himself appear even more intimidating, if that were possible. The don had become increasingly concerned as to rumors that Mussolini would soon turn his Black Shirts loose upon the Mafia. This would spell doom for Don Antonio and for his like-minded brethren across Sicily and the Naples area on the mainland.

"I know what you are thinking Don Antonio. But do not concern yourself as to what I consider idle and unfounded rumors. I have had personal assurances from some of Duce's top people that you and your other colleagues will not be touched," further exclaimed Carlo Goncalo.

Young Leo had remained standing close to his father. It made him feel like a ventriloquist's dummy, waiting to be manipulated. Only now Leo was not being asked to say anything. Perhaps he was fulfilling the role of a mute.

"Ahh Leo, why don't you just take a seat and listen to some of these wise men. You can learn much from them."

"Si, papa," replied Leo in a barely audible voice.

"Eh, Carlo, we will have to clean up our acts. No cursing is to be allowed," joked Gianni Simone. At that, all of the men chuckled. Simone owned a large number of rental housings throughout Ottavino and also in Taormina. Most of these units could only charitably be considered slums. Naturally, Simone was always required to kick over the requisite tribute to Don Antonio.

"Indeed, indeed gentlemen," chimed in Goncalo senior. "In any event, these are new and exciting times for our nation. But this is only the beginning," continued Carlo Goncalo, his enthusiasm building.

"How long do you think the Duce will require until Italy is a vibrant manufacturing state again?" asked Bobo Moncado.

"Ah, I would estimate about…about five years. I have been in touch with some of the top economic ministers in Rome, and in Palermo, and they have assured me that no more than five years is realistic and feasible. Remember, gentlemen, a vibrant industrial base will be essential if Italy is to develop and maintain a dynamic war machine. A machine developed for conquest."

Little did any of the men present realize that within months Benito Mussolini would begin a deadly crackdown on the Mafia, and especially so in Sicily. Don Antonio Navarona would be forced to go underground, eventually escaping the island and making his way to New York where he would join his brother, Marcantonio. The pair would become the linchpin in the New York underworld, and would become among the first mafia families to court and promote the sales of drugs.

Leo was dismissed by his father, as the men had some important topics still to discuss. Topics beyond the ears of a ten year old boy. Joyfully, Leo practically ran from the room, but he decided he would linger for just a moment just outside it. The men were now engaged in the subject of the land, or rather, the acquisition of more of it.

The boy had never been quite sure as to what his father did for a living. Most days, when Goncalo senior, was not laying about he would be found locked in his study for hours on end. Leo and his brothers always had to remain very quiet while in the house when their father was closeted in his office. One time Leo and his brother Franco were engaging in some horse-play when they both lost their balance and slammed into the double doors of the study. All of a sudden, Carlo Goncalo violently opened the doors and angrily confronted the boys. With no warning, Carlo Goncalo struck each one with the back of his left hand, the hand that contained a large university ring. Leo received a cut across his right cheek which would require three stitches. Seeing what he had done prompted Carlo to threaten Leo and Franco if they informed their mother. Both were told to say they had fallen in the garden just outside the house.

Men, important men, said his father, were constantly coming and going at the home. It was more like a villa with more than a dozen rooms, and three lavatories. Most Sicilian homes lacked even one. And there was Manolo, his father's driver and personal bodyguard. Manolo, who hardly uttered a word, and with his slick mustache and cold, sinister glare looked as if he could snuff out a man's life and not even bat an eye.

***

Leo Goncalo's upbringing could best be described as unremarkable, punctuated by an occasional moment of brilliance. The boy did develop into a brilliant student, especially concerning the subjects of biology and chemistry. Carlo Goncalo had always envisioned the boy might well become a lawyer, who might one day matriculate up to the level of magistrate. But it was his mother who had noticed signs pointing in another direction, another path. The path to the field of medicine.

Leo also displayed a passion for soccer, and he especially liked playing goalie. He liked the fact that a goalie was a team's last line of defense against the opposition scoring a goal. Besides, a goalie played a rather sedentary position, at best, relative to the forwards and mid-fielders who were always in motion across the soccer pitches, oftentimes at a frantic pace.

***

The year turned to 1929 and for Italy, and much of the world, an economic cataclysm would soon place its iron grip on virtually every nation. The Great Depression in the United States, and the ripple effect it created throughout the rest of the world would severely retard any economic progress the Fascist nation had been making. Benito Mussolini urged and encouraged Italians to tighten their belts. This was easy enough to say, but in southern Italy and Sicily it must have sounded like a cruel joke. Ever since the Italian Republic had come into existence the people of these regions had experienced almost nothing else but a grinding poverty . Many had gone hungry, and for such a gastronomic people it had proven to be a cruel and bitter irony. Many simply gave up and made plans and preparations to emigrate to foreign shores, such as the United States and Canada.

One day Leo was summoned to his father's study where he found Carlo seated behind his massive oaken desk. Papers were scattered about its tabletop. Leo could not imagine what his father wanted. Carlo had already lectured the boy on the facts of life and how some young girls might try to tempt him into formal activities. How this would bring shame and humiliation upon the family name and stain Leo as well.

Leo cleared his throat and tentatively approached his father. "You asked for me, papa?, he asked. Leo could feel his knees begin to knock together.

Carlo Goncalo slowly looked up and nodded his gray-coiffed head, his brow slightly furrowed. "*Si, Leo,* I did. It has come to my attention that you have not yet become a member of the Young Pioneers. You do realize that this a most important organization, one that the Duce is behind 100 per cent. "

Leo was somewhat startled . The Young Pioneers were to Leo nothing more than a glorified boy scout troop, marching about and playing around campfires. They acted as if they were real soldiers on maneuvers. To Leo, these boys were clowns. But obviously, not to his father. "Leo, if you want to move forward in life you may, from time to time, have to make certain sacrifices. And one of these is joining the Pioneers. Do you understand what I am saying?" his father had continued. The large and imposing grandfather clock tick-tocked in a corner of the room.

Leo nodded his head in understanding.

"Leo, do you understand?" Venom coated each word as Carlo persisted.

"*Si, si, papa,* I understand," said Leo in a soft, trembling voice.

"*Bene*, then I expect you to report to the local headquarters of the Fascist party here in town first thing in the morning and to enlist. Eh?"

"*Si*, papa, I will do as you command me to do," answered Leo. Since it was summer and school was out, he could go and enlist on any day of the week.

"Leo, I just want to say that your mother and me were very proud to see your last report card. It was very impressive, excellent grades. We think you will develop into an excellent young man who will be able to go far in life. Perhaps it will be a vocation in the law, or perhaps something else…like medicine. You know we are living in an exciting time and there is no telling how far the Duce can lead Italy forward. Ah, that will be all Leo. You are dismissed," concluded Carlo Goncalo, who then returned to his paperwork.

Leo quickly shuffled his way out of the study. "Damn!" he thought to himself. He had already made plans to join his friends for a round of soccer at the nearby pitch. "Those damned Pioneers, always strutting about, why, they resembled geese with that ridiculous march. Leo thought the Pioneers were trying to imitate the Italian Army's famed Bersaglieri troops. Out loud to himself, Leo muttered, "Oh well, I suppose there could be worse things I could be forced to join."

***

Leo Goncalo had just turned 16 years old. He had clearly become smitten with a young girl in Mettuno, one Rosalina Cardi. He dreamt and thought of her each and every day, fantasizing about her cherubic and full face, her pouty lips, her dark and curly hair, and, the shape of her chest.

Young Leo knew that his father was quietly trying to direct him toward another young woman in town. Carlo Goncalo had resigned himself to the fact that his younger son possessed hormones, perhaps raging ones. So why not provide the lad with some parental guidance in the selection of a suitable mate. Enter one Rosalie Mancini, daughter of Umberto Mancini, a minor land baron in the region. Not as powerful as Carlo, but a formidable man in any case.

Goncalo junior did not share the same opinion of Rosalie as his father. It was true the young woman of 16 herself was very attractive from her frizzled blond hair to her hooded eyes to her alluring figure.

And yet there was something about this Rosalie Mancini that did not sit well with Leo. He had to acknowledge that the young woman was most attractive, and she was bright and vivacious. No, for Leo, Rosalie Mancini was just a little too full of herself, too confident in the way she carried herself. In short, Leo was simply intimidated by the Mancini girl. He was afraid she would overpower him, both in the emotional sense and in the physical one.

One night during the summer of 1931 the life of Leo Goncalo took a turn he never would have imagined. He had finally been able to lure Rosalina Cardi to an abandoned farmhouse on his father's property. No one ever bothered to go there. It would be the perfect spot for what Leo had in mind for Rosalina. The pair had been fencing around one another for quite some time: attending church socials and occasionally dancing together. Of course, this all had to be done very carefully and properly. After all, various townspeople would be in attendance and would surely have frowned upon any unseemly behavior. Not to mention what his father's reaction would have been.

On this sultry July evening, Leo Goncalo carefully guided Rosalina Cardi into the barn, whereupon the two virtually assaulted one another. Rosalina, or Lina as she preferred, quietly divested herself of every stitch of her clothing. When she unhooked and dropped her bra, Leo's breath caught in his throat. The girl was more than he had ever imagined. He stood stark-still, staggered.

"Leo, I think you can begin to disrobe, don't you think?" Lina teased sarcastically. She knew she was more than enticing him as she noticed his penis stiffening. Undoubtedly, this was probably his first time. It would not be hers, but who was counting.

Goncalo slowly began to remove his checked shirt, pants, and underpants. But he continued to stay rooted to the ground. "Was this really going to happen?" he asked himself. "Should I just take off?" No, he would have to go through with it. Leo had been bragging about his conquests with his friends for a while. Word might well get around amongst these same friends and he would become a laughingstock.

"Did you remember to bring protection?" lured Lina as she slowly advanced on Leo, she lasciviously licked her lips, while she cupped her breasts.

"*Si, si*, I remembered. I have one here," said Leo as he began rummaging through his pants, stumbling about the clothes.

"Let me see it," commanded Lina. Clearly she would be in charge of the night's activities. "I guess this will be suitable," she said while she looked the packet over as if she were a company inspector. "Do you want to put it on now or would you prefer to wait until we are both aroused and then I can place the condom on your manhood?"

Leo stood there dumbfounded. He did not know what he should say, so he merely nodded.

At this, Lina became impatient. "Well, which do you prefer? Maybe I made a mistake. Maybe I misjudged you. Maybe you are not yet ready to experience something wonderful with a beautiful and willing partner. Maybe you are still a little boy, and not a man," said Lina as she bit off her words.

The words stung and wounded Leo. Each comment was as if he were undergoing a knife wound. He had to get a grip on himself. He had to. "No, I mean, why don't you just place the condom when we are ready. You seem to have the experience."

"*Bene*, then I will do so," replied Lina, seemingly satisfied. She then took the packet and tore off one end, revealing what looked like a rubberized ring. Lina took hold of the condom and began to stretch it out. She then took hold of Leo's rigid shaft with her long, cool fingers of her left hand and then slowly unsheathed the prophylactic and brought it over the head and rolled it along the shaft.

"Oh, one more thing," said Lina as she took hold of the end of the condom between her thumb and forefinger slightly away from the penis. She then pinched the end, creating an air pocket. "There you are, just right. Now we are ready to commence in some love-making."

Leo couldn't believe what he had just seen, Lina, his lovely and sweet Lina, was an expert in this…this type of thing. At the least, she was more of an expert than he was.

Lina once again advanced on Leo and whispered in his ear. "Do not be afraid. Lina knows that you desire her, you want her, you must have her. Is that not true?"

Leo nodded his head dumbfoundedly, but it was clearly spinning and might well topple right off. Before he knew it, Lina's tongue was within his mouth and his was soon in hers. The girl then took hold of his penis with her right hand and began stroking it. Slowly, at first, but then at a faster pace. Leo was becoming totally aroused. He could not control himself .

Lina sensed this and then dropped herself to the ground and onto her back. Bales and strands of hay lay about and it scratched at Lina's body, but at that moment she did not care. She wanted Leo inside of her and so she guided him down to her. She took hold of his manhood and guided him into her. Lina then decided to shift positions and told Leo to place himself on the ground.

The boy took in the full measure of Rosalina Cardi as she slowly started to hump away above Leo. He became mesmerized as the girl's large breasts swayed as she cupped them. Lina continued to hump and grind herself for a few minutes, desperately hoping Leo would be able to ejaculate. At last, Leo could no longer contain himself and he fired into Lina. That was the last thing he remembered as he immediately passed out.

Some time later, Leo awakened to find himself sitting up, some straw hung down from his tussled hair over his eyes. Lina was brushing away straw and sawdust from his back.

"What happened?" he mumbled.

"You passed out, silly," said Lina in a jovial tone as she continued to pick out straw from his back and head.

"I guess…I, wow," said Leo, his head encased in a fog.

"Wow, indeed, my young prince," said Lina. She had now seated herself beside Leo and was fully dressed. "You won't need this anymore, my love," she continued and then proceeded to peel away the condom from his limp penis. "Now, why don't we get you cleaned up a little and get you dressed."

Leo, assisted by Lina, slowly got to his feet. He proceeded to clean up as best he could. He would have to do a better job later so as not to allow his father to notice that Leo may have been engaged in anything so scandalous.

"It was pretty good for your first time, Leo," said Lina. Her soft gray green eyes scanned over him, but he thought they appeared softer, more tender, than before they had made love.

"How did you know it was my first time?" burst out Leo. Lina's comment had insulted him.

"Well, I just kind of knew. We girls are rather intuitive."

"Was this …was this your first time?" implored Leo, desperately hoping it was so. Inwardly he realized it hadn't been.

"That is something a girl should not be forced to reveal," said Lina as she looked away. "Anyway, what's done is done. Perhaps next time it will be in more suitable surroundings."

Leo said nothing as he slowly finished dressing. He desperately hoped that the condom had performed as it had been designed to do.

July turned to August and with it Leo was hit with the news he had secretly been dreading. One Saturday morning he suddenly ran into Lina while strolling through Mettuno. They were approaching one another near town marketplace. The sun was blazing down upon them, not a cloud in the sky.

As Leo neared Lina he noticed that she was looking down at the ground. She did not appear happy in the least. Somehow Leo knew he was about to be greeted with the words he, nor did any young man, want to hear.. "Lina, how nice to see you," he greeted her, trying desperately to put on a good face. "Lina, is something wrong?"

Lina stood before Leo. She was dressed in a plain, unflattering peasant dress. Undoubtedly, it was only something her austere parents would have approved of.

"Yes, Leo, something is wrong," she muttered to him, still not being able to look him in the face.

Leo waited patiently, he knew what was coming, but he had to hear it in the flesh. "Well?" he stammered, unable to withstand the building tension.

"I'm late...with my period," cried the girl as tears began to trickle down her tanned face.

"Late? Late? Are you sure?" he grunted.

"Don't you think I know my own body. Yes, I am late. What will we do? My parents will kill me when they find out. They will absolutely kill me, and probably you as well," she went on.

"I don't know what we'll do, but something will have to be done," implored Leo, as he began guiding Lina away and out of sight. It would do no good to have some passersby pick up any of the gist of their devastating conversation.

The pair made their way to a secluded spot away from the heavy foot traffic.

"But I thought the... the protection would be sufficient," said Leo as he fought to maintain his equilibrium.

"Those things are not foolproof, you realize." Lina now raised her head and met Leo's anguished face. There was a softness, a desperate softness upon it. She began to resemble a little girl. "Well, right now we can do nothing. But sometime in the near future you and I will have to come to a decision. I know what my parents will say and I am pretty sure I know your parents will react in the same way," Lina said levelly, her gaze never leaving Leo.

"Yes, you are right, of course. Let's meet in a few days and then we can decide. How does that sound?"

"I suppose you are right, Leo. Alright, a few days. Now, I have to pick up a few things for my mother. I will see you soon," Lina finished, her tears receding. She then turned abruptly and left Leo, nearly sprinting to be as far away as possible.

***

The few days ran past to the end of August. School would be resuming soon. Leo could not find Lina anywhere, he certainly could not go to her house to seek an audience. Panic began to build within him again; what would he do?; go to his older brother, Mario? No. Go to his father? Not if he wished to keep his head.

Simply put, he would be ruined. His father would, in all probability, take care of things in his Sicilian way, that is take care of things with Lina and her family, But he, Leonardo Goncalo, would be forever stained, his dream of going to the university destroyed.

Just after school opened again he saw his chance to corner Lina. It happened on the outskirts of the nearby town of Ottavino where Leo saw Lina walking alone. Books were resting upon her bosom. Moving as surreptitiously as possible, Leo approached from behind the girl unnoticed.

"I've been looking for you, Lina. You seem to have made yourself scarce for the past couple of weeks," said Leo with a firmness in his voice he did not actually feel. But he had passed the point of fearfulness, he had arrived at the point of being very angry with the girl.

I don't know what you are talking about. Get away from me, or I'll scream," Lina boasted, but it was not a bluff. Inwardly, she knew she had been exposed.

"Oh, don't you? You know my darling Lina, I have begun to think that you were never pregnant, or with child as some people prefer. No, I think that for some reason you made the whole thing up. Perhaps you thought this could have been a way to worm some money out of my family. I know that your father has had some... some money problems of late," said Leo as he stopped in the path while he took hold of Lina's elbow. He then twisted her around until she was facing him. No one was within earshot. "That was it, wasn't it Lina? You were not late, there would be no baby."

Lina looked down, tears fell from her eyes. Leo was unmoved. He knew he had struck the right chord, he had gotten to the truth "*Si, si*, you have figured things out. And that had been my stupid plan. I am sorry, Leo. I never meant to cause you any harm," her voice was just above a whisper.

"Didn't mean to cause me any harm? Do you realize how many sleepless nights I have been through? But you didn't care, you never did," Leo flared with an anger that was slowly growing. If he wasn't careful he thought he just might strike the girl.

"I'm sorry, Leo. Do you or could you ever forgive me?" Lina pleaded.

Leo Goncalo thought for a moment and when he turned to Lina. He said, "I can't believe I am going to say this, but...but...yes, I do forgive you. However, I never want to see you or speak to you ever again. Is that clear?" Leo had never spoken before with as much conviction.

***

"I do not think the Duce is exactly thrilled with Herr Schickel-gruber," said Bruno Calvi, the erstwhile business manager of Carlo Goncalo. Calvi was more reminiscent of a consigliere, but Goncalo was not a mafia don.

The men were seated in Goncalo's study. In the background, thunder and lightning crackled and boomed in the doom laden sky.

"No, I agree with you, Bruno. The Nazis have come up short this time, but everyone should keep an eye out for them, and for Adolf Hitler," said Goncalo, using the correct name for the Austrian rabble-rouser.

"*Si*, you have a point there, Carlo," mused Calvi as he lounged back in his chair, sipping on anisette.

"Now, Bruno, I asked you here now not to discuss the political machinations of Europe, but for another specific purpose," replied Carlo Goncalo in a serious tone. "I have been thinking about some of that land that Umberto Mancini possesses out near Ottavino. It is land I have had my eye on for quite some time."

Bruno Calvi remained silent, Inwardly, he thought he knew what Goncalo was about to propose. He had witnessed this type of thing numerous times over the years.

"However, I do not want it to seem like this is an outright land grab, if you know what I mean. No, I want to procure some fifty acres that are now in Mancini's possession. But I have to come up with the right front man."

Calvi steepled his long, arthritic fingers into a shape that resembled a tent. He was a sober looking man with an impressive mane of flowing white locks. He looked younger than his 60 years. Bruno Calvi possessed penetrating blue eyes, a narrow nose, and a somewhat wide mouth. It was a mouth that always spoke carefully and guardedly. The man did not look Sicilian, because he was not a Sicilian. Bruno Calvi hailed from Milan, in the northern region of Italy. And he was a man in whom Carlo Goncalo trusted implicitly.

"That is the question, but why, may I ask, do you need a front man or stooge? Why not just make your play?" asked Calvi, his eyes even with Goncalo's.

"I have my reasons, Bruno. And I cannot reveal them to even someone as close to me as you. I hope you understand and will not take this as an insult," replied Goncalo.

Calvi hunched his shoulders as he said, "I do not feel insulted Carlo, I was only asking."

"Of course, but I was thinking of Alberto Cardi. He is a greedy and oily individual. At times I do believe he would be willing to sniff my shorts. He has, at times tried to get too close, to insert himself too much into my affairs. However, I understand that he has recently come into some monetary problems. And for that reason, he may be receptive to what I have planned."

Carlo Goncalo would not reveal his motive to Calvi because this was still a closely guarded secret of his. And it was something which had nothing to do with money or power. It could best described as a matter of the heart. Carlo had long desired that Leo should become romantically involved at some future point in time to Umberto Mancini' s daughter, Rosalie. And Goncalo could not openly swindle Mancini of some of his land and then expect the man to be amenable to a coupling between his daughter and his son.

No, it was a matter which had to be handled more discreetly and more smoothly. Goncalo might be forced to have Mancini consigned to a Fascist prison to completely effect his plan.

***

"I tell you Maria, something is up. I can feel it, and what is more I can smell it with my fine Sicilian nose," thundered Umberto Mancini as he pointed to that very nose to his wife of more than 25 years.

"Oh, Berto, you always suspect that something is up. You always have. You and that Sicilian nose of yours.

"No, I tell you. I have heard rumors of late about Alberto Cardi and his supposed desire for more land, our land to be specific," continued

Mancini, his powerful fists now clenched, sweat poured out down his unshaven face on this rather steamy August night.

Maria was seated nearby, continuing to listen patiently to her agitated husband, as she performed some needlepoint work with her nimble fingers. The woman had long been a master of the craft. How many times had she sat and listened to her husband lambaste someone or some group and their attempt to steal the Mancini acreage.

"It was a good thing that our two families joined forces years ago and put together this partnership. Only this, I tell you, has allowed us to ward off the filthy clutches of swine like Don Antonio and his ilk. Now the don has had to leave Sicily because of Mussolini's crackdown on the mafia. But this had, in turn, led to some individuals like Carlo Goncalo to increase their own power and wealth."

"But you have said Alberto Cardi was making a play for some of our land," said Maria in a plaintive voice. She had now put down the needlework and was paying close attention to Berto's rant.

"Cardi is just a pimp, a front man. No, the one behind this scheme can only be none other than Goncalo. And with the Don out of the way his task has been made that much simpler."

"Then why doesn't Goncalo just come right out and make this land buy himself?" asked Maria.

"Because not only is Carlo Goncalo a slippery and slimy snake, he must also have something else up his sleeve," continued Berto, who by now was becoming more worked up.

"What could that be, dearest?" asked Maria, clutching his hand.

"I do believe that Goncalo secretly thinks that his son, Leo, should be matched up with or daughter, Rosalie."

"No, I don't believe it. Not for a second," lamented a now thoroughly alarmed Maria.

"I do believe that I am right. Don't ask me how I know, but it is a feeling have right here in my gut," rambled on Mancini as he pointed to his mid-section.

"I do not know about this. All of this maneuvering…this posturing… this…."

"You do not understand men like Carlo Goncalo or Don Antonio. To them it is all a game, a chessboard. They move people around, acquire other people's land and possessions as if they were moving knights and rooks on a board."

Overhearing her parents' conversation was Rosalie, the Mancini's youngest of five children. She had been passing by the kitchen when she observed her parents huddled in distressing talk. She had been able to discern what the topic of discussion was, and it had unnerved her.

"Leo Goncalo to be matched with her, ridiculous!" she thought, not that the 18 year old Goncalo wasn't bad" what with his handsome face, good body, and his family's wealth. But Rosalie did not care for the fact that Carlo Goncalo was Leo's father. She thought him to be, unlike her father, a wicked man. It was not a family she would ever want to marry into. Despite the fact that nearly all Sicilian marriages were arranged by parents, Rosalie Mancini was determined that she would marry a man of her choice, and only hers. Not one arranged for her by others. She felt her parents, whom she loved deeply, would always back her up. There had been too many girls of her age, some of whom she knew, who had already married. Married themselves into lives of grinding and abject poverty.

***

He could not say as to exactly when the light was turned on for him as to the relative merits of Fascism, but if Leo Goncalo had to put a finger on it he would have said that it came when he had just graduated from high school. He was now set to enter the University of Palermo, on the far side of Sicily. It would be as far from home as he had ever been. It would be his entry into a new and different world from the one he had grown up in in Mettuno. At long last, Leo would be free of the dictates of his father. True, he would miss the love and kindness of his mother. The woman simply did not possess a mean bone in her body. She had always been a counterweight to the often overbearing ways of his father.

Leo Goncalo had been elevated to manhood; he had honed his body to the point where he could be viewed as quite a specimen. Leo Goncalo, through the use of weights and athletics, was now in possession of wide shoulders, formidably developed arms, and a near six-pack abdomen. He now had to literally fight off the young women of the town. In the back of his fertile mind were the warnings and lectures of his father, and the near fatal episode with the young girl, Lina.

By his 18th year, young Leo Goncalo had begun to immerse himself in the themes and beliefs of the Fascist creed. He had begun to see the Duce, Benito Mussolini, in a new light. Much of what the boisterous dictator spouted had now begun to make more sense to him. Maybe, in a strange way, his father had been right all along. Until just recently, Leo had viewed the Black Shirts as nothing more than thuggish goons who went around terrorizing those Italians who could best be characterized as non-believers, those not committed sufficiently to what the Duce and Fascism had to offer.

One day, Leo would find the time and the opportunity to travel to Rome. He would see Benito Mussolini in the flesh as the Duce addressed a vast crowd of thousands. He would stand spellbound as he listened to the stirring oratory of the great man as he expounded on how Italy was moving forward, ever forward, and would now be able to take its rightful place among the great nations of the world. She would become worthy of being addressed with the same respect and reverence and, yes, fear of Britain or France. Mussolini would transform the Italian nation into the second coming of the Roman Empire. She would gain conquered territories beyond those of Libya and Eritrea.

Chapter Two

The Swindle

Eighteen year old Rosalie Mancini found herself facing a quandary; what to do with her life. True, she was an attractive woman who possessed a keen and intelligent mind, and she had a quick wit. She was never one to suffer fools gladly.

Rosalie still lived at home with her parents. Her five brothers and sisters were already married, mostly by way of arranged affairs, as was the Sicilian custom. But this young woman was determined to find a man on her own. There was no way she would submit herself to any type of arrangement where she would not have a say.

The family business was largely farming and winemaking. The Mancini farm contained some 30 head of dairy cattle, a number of pigs, and some sheep. Prancing around the farmyard were some scattered chickens. Rosalie had always detested the sheep; a strange and unpleasant odor seemed to cling to them. And she thought them to be simple-minded and unintelligent creatures. Her brothers Aldo, Paolo, and Alberto basically ran the operation.

The winemaking was strictly within the domain of Berto Mancini. All in all, it could well be considered to be a rather profitable enterprise. Annual output was usually around 7,000 to 10,000 bottles of chianti, vin rose, and pinot grigio. The Mancinis had always been conscious of the lurking presence of Don Antonio and his Mafia associates. And now Carlo Goncalo could be added.

Rosalie was not sure as to where she was supposed to fit in, or if she ever could, into the family dynamic. Her options were limited, but she desperately wanted to be able to go it alone. Her schooling had ended two years before, and she could attend the few technical schools that were available. The thought of college could be forgotten. It was 1933 and Sicilian women were not expected to be well educated. Their place was within the home and to bear children. This was a fact practically ordained by the Fascist government of Benito Mussolini and the Catholic Church.

***

"Will you be attending the dance in the village center this weekend, dear? asked Maria Mancini, as she and Rosalie ironed some clothing in the gathering dusk. The approaching night air still contained a cloying heat, despite the arrival of September.

Rosalie shrugged her shoulders as she gripped the solid block that was the iron. The implement had been previously heated on the wood-fired stove. She was pressing a pair of her father's dress pants. "I think so, mama. I don't see why not."

"That is good. Just a reminder for you to behave yourself, not that I have to. You have always been a good girl, of whom your father and me have been very proud of," continued Maria.

Rosalie could feel herself begin to blush, although it was good to hear an occasional compliment from her parents. She maintained her ironing, head down.

"Do you expect to see anyone you know? Perhaps someone special," her mother continued.

Rosalie started to blush once again, she knew where her mother's dialogue was heading. Again she shrugged her shoulders. During the past few months she had been assisting her family with some of the farm work: hoisting and carrying bales of hay and straw. It gave definition to her arms and legs. It was not the kind of work any Italian girl was supposed to do.

"Just the usual people from the village," she murmured.

"Well, I do believe that Franco Donato might well be attending. You know he is a good looking young man."

"Mother, I am well aware of that. It does not have to be pointed out to me," Rosalie bit off the words, instantly regretting them. But her mother had struck a nerve.

For the past few months, Rosalie and Franco had been secretly meeting in various locations: abandoned barns, derelict houses. Most of the time they had spent in hand holding or talking. Of late, their relations had progressed to the point of heavy petting, and eventually to kissing. Just recently the couple had engaged in some French kissing. Rosalie could always feel a heat burning within her body, and she was sure Franco felt the same. They were getting close, very close, to the sharing of their young and developing bodies.

Rosalie knew she had to be very careful and circumspect, lest she be found out and exposed. It would ruin her reputation, and, in turn, that of her family's. Sicilian women were believed to be temptresses of the most wicked kind, from the very devil himself. They were to be viewed warily by any Sicilian male. Some in Sicily said women were more dangerous than the shot-gun.

***

The University of Palermo was founded in 1806 and organized into 12 faculties. Its earliest roots dated back to the year of 1498, just six years after Columbus's discovery of America. At one time, the Jesuit fathers had granted degrees in Theology and Philosophy. In 1767 they were expelled by King Ferdinand.

Following the unification of Italy in 1860, the university was modernized under the direction of chemist Stanislao Cannizzaro and the Director of Arab Studies, Michele Amari.

Leo Goncalo's entrance into the venerable institution was, at first, with some trepidation. The young man may have thought of himself as somewhat worldly, but truth be told, he had never ventured outside of Mettuno or Ottavino. Inwardly, Leo felt himself to be a rube. He only hoped he would not stick out like the proverbial sore thumb.

Goncalo's first two years were largely occupied by the study of basic subjects, such as chemistry, calculus, and biology. He easily excelled in all of the subject matter set before him by the faculty. At times. Leo hardly had to crack a book.

Exams had just been completed in early June of 1935 when Leo Goncalo found himself once again engaged in an amorous affair. Lilliana Gentile was a tall, raven-haired beauty, hailing from Reggio di Calabria on the Italian mainland directly across from Messina. The girl was studying art at the university and resided in the women's wing of dormitories. It was most unusual, and somewhat odd, that a woman could be found enrolled in any university in Italy at that time. Lilliana did not, in any way, see herself or her enrollment as being out of place.

The couple had been quietly fencing around one another for the better part of the spring semester: engaging in small talk, flirting, or meeting for a coffee or drink. Finally, in June, on a Friday evening after both had imbibed a little too much of alcohol Leo and Lilliana conducted some animated lovemaking. This, despite the fact that Lilliana had known she was at a danger point concerning her period. She would be cutting things pretty close.

Leo had been home for about a month when he received a telegram from the girl informing him that he was to be a father. There was no mistake. She would be sending him definitive proof in the ensuing days to back up her claim. A sense of impending doom and dread swept over Leo. This time, he was sure, there would no lucky break coming his way. No lucky break which would allow him to go merrily on his way. This time he would have to go to his father and lay bare his soul and seek the old man's influence and power to help rectify the situation.

Less than a week later a large manila envelope , marked Palermo arrived in the morning mail. At least the girl had had the good sense to not place a return address.

Leo sat down with the envelope in his shaking hands, sweat poured down his perspiring face. At first, he could not bring himself to open the package, but after awhile he knew he had to. Slowly, he tore it open and began to remove the documents it contained. There was a letter from Lilliana's father explaining, or more accurately, threatening him as to what had happened to his daughter, and that he expected some form of remuneration from the Goncalos. Leo then found himself staring at a document prepared by a physician, one Dottore Mancuso, attesting to the fact that Lilliana Gentile was, in fact, pregnant, and that Leo was the father.

Goncalo was left with the impression that Enrico Gentile was expecting him to go to his father and have him take care of the matter, or else. Enrico Gentile would make the problem public and he would ruin the name of the Goncalos.

"You fool, you stupid fool, did you think I would not find out?" screamed Carlo Goncalo to his downcast, trembling son.

Leo stood mutely silent, seemingly rooted to the floor of his father's study How Carlo had come to already know about his problem he had no earthly idea It didn't matter. Now that he would have to go begging on his hands and knees to his father.

"Well, my son, you have really stepped in it this time. And, this time, it is true. This…this Gentile tramp is pregnant, or should I say is with child so as to make it more palatable?" continued Carlo.

"What do you mean this time, father?" asked Leo in a timid voice that he somehow managed to find.

"Ha-ha-ha, what do I mean by this time you ask? What I mean is that I already knew about your other little peccadillo with that other tramp. What was her name? Lina…Lina something."

Leo looked downward, wishing he could permeate into the floor, but then looked quickly back at his father. He was stunned that Carlo knew about this other snafu of his.

"Do you not think that I have my sources of information? Do you not know of my many connections?" senior went on. Slowly, ever slowly, Carlo Goncalo was regaining his equilibrium. His tenuous blood pressure was beginning to subside. "Well now, in consideration of your dear and sainted mother, and to spare her further shame, I'll take care of things with the Gentile family. But believe me, my dear son, if this type of situation ever occurs again, then I will personally cut off your manhood. Do I make myself clear?" thundered the elder Goncalo, as his right hand swept the air.

Leo had a lump in his throat that could choke a horse. Perhaps that would be a better fate than to what he would now be consigned to. He gave off little more than a grunt.

"What was that? I couldn't hear you," asked Carlo Goncalo as he leaned forward onto his massive oaken desk. In the background loomed the oversized grandfather clock giving off the hour of 1:00 pm.

"*Si, si*, father. It will not happen again. I..." lamented the crestfallen Leo Goncalo. He thought his shaking and buckling legs might well give way and he would collapse to the floor.

"That had better be the case, my boy. Leo..." the older man paused, "Leo, you are a gifted young man. A most handsome man, I implore you, to not throw it all away over some flings with young women who do care for you. You can have a brilliant future as a lawyer or perhaps as a doctor. Fascism and the Duce, and me, are all there for you. From this day forward there will be no second chances. I hope I have made myself clear."

"*Si*, father, you have," Leo responded, now wishing he could sprint out of the room.

"*Bene*, then you are dismissed."

In the forthcoming days Carlo Goncalo would take the required steps to alleviate the problem of Lilliana Gentile's pregnancy. The Gentiles would be quietly and discreetly paid off with a handsome sum of money. And as to the young woman, well, Lilliana Gentile would be quietly dispatched to a convent somewhere on the mainland where her baby would be carefully and taken care of discreetly.

***

In the meantime, Benito Mussolini had been in the process of expanding and consolidating his power within the central government. Given the bold manner in which he had seized power in 1922, he had seemed somewhat restrained as he clutched at the instruments at hand. Of the 14 ministries in his cabinet he had appointed only three Fascists, beside himself.

Still, the Duce retained for himself the key posts of Minister of Foreign Affairs and Interior Minister. He also managed to find places for some of his key allies. Men such as Cesare De Vecchi at the Military Pension Bureau and Italo Balbo at the downtrodden air force ministry.

Together with two other key figures. Mussolini created what was called the Quadumvirate. He then set about revamping the internal structure of the country. If Italy were to move forward in the 20th century, then things could not remain in the status quo. A moderate approach was taken with the Chamber of Deputies, which gave off an appearance that Mussolini would rule things through the parliamentary system.

In the following years, Benito Mussolini managed to still the babel of voices in the chamber by adapting such measures as the silencing of all political opponents of the party. He neutralized the press by the seizing of opposition newspapers throughout the country. He had uncooperative journalists arrested and jailed. He also formed a national state militia outside the realm of the military establishment. Mussolini snuffed out any kind of civil disorder by decreeing capital punishment for any attempt at insurrection. He ordered that all boys aged six to 21 belong to Fascist youth groups, in which they were to be trained in the use of arms by military officers.

Mussolini's grip over the nation also took in what Fascist theorists called the "corporate state" whereby all business and industry would fall under the aegis of the central government. Companies, trade unions, and the professions were to be made responsible to a Minister of Corporations, who, in turn, would appoint executive officers who would rule on contracts, labor disputes, and apprenticeship programs. That was the plan, on paper.

Mussolini also geared the country for war by an increase in production of materiel for the armed forces. In 1933, he placed himself in charge of the Ministries of War, Air, and Navy. Appearing in full-dress uniform he addressed 2,000 officers to inform them: "We are becoming, and we shall become, a more military nation. And, since we are not afraid of the words, let us add: and in the end a more militant nation."

Eventually, the army received a small amount of modern equipment, largely in the form of artillery and transport. The navy launched an ambitious shipbuilding program for new cruisers and battleships. These were sleek, fast new vessels which would help promote Mussolini's dictum of the Mediterranean Sea being a lake to be dominated by Italy. Great attention was paid to a refurbishing of the air force under Italo Balbo. Sadly, though he had been an intrepid and superb flier, Balbo turned out to be a poor administrator.

Benito Mussolini was soon to win plaudits from all over the world. Such luminaries as the Archbishop of Canterbury and Winston Churchill all had words of growing praise for the Italian Duce. Even his protégé to the north gave Mussolini the sincerest form of praise: imitation. Italy's youth programs became the model for the Hitler Youth. All industry was placed under state control.

***

"I do not know, Carlo. Do you really think it can work?" asked a pensive Alberto Cardi as he sat in front of an imperious Carlo Goncalo.

"Am I sure? Of course I am sure, why else would I have even broached the subject with you," thundered Goncalo. He was beginning to think that Cardi might be getting cold feet and would lack the nerve to carry out his part in Carlo's grand plan. The goal was for Goncalo to get his hands on nearly 75% of Berto Mancini's land.

"Well, if you are that confident, then I suppose I will agree to having me play part. It's just that I am a little surprised that you need this much of *Mancini's* land."

"Alberto, I have the feeling that you have been having second thoughts about my plan."

"Eh, *si, si*, I have been. It's just that why do you require to obtain this much land?" questioned a vexed Cardi.

"I don't, I just want it. It is as simple as that. Alberto, there is no need for you to know. But I will make it well worth your while, I can assure you." In the back of the study the big clock chimed on. He never let on about the truffles.

Alberto Cardi had always despised the clock, as it always seemed to portend a deep and oppressive gloom. He prayed that one day it would simply cease to function; death by natural causes or otherwise.

"Mmmm," Cardi mused, not quite being able to feel fully confident in Goncalo's grand scheme.

"Cardi!" boomed Carlo, no longer addressing his so-called friend by the man's first name. "Listen to me. You will make the denunciation of Umberto Mancini and I will tell exactly how to do it. Is that clear?"

"*Si,* I will do as you ask."

"*Bene.* You are to go to the prefect in Ottavino and you are tell him that have overheard Mancini speaking ill of the Duce, and in no uncertain terms. In fact, you felt as if Mancini is planning bodily harm on the man. But, and this is most important, you'll have to be most convincing. Don't be fretful or the Prefect may smell a rat. He is a good fascist, but we can't take any chances. Do you understand?"

Alberto Cardi remained silent for the moment as to what Goncalo had just instructed him on.

"Cardi, do I have to remind you of the great favor I once did for you and, by extension, your son two years ago?" asked Carlo in a malevolent and sinister voice.

Cardi knew he was beaten down and well-remembered what Goncalo had brought up. His son Federico had impregnated a young woman. Alberto had gone to Goncalo and desperately asked for his help. The problem was solved by having the girl's father "sleep with the fishes" and the girl having to submit to a backroom abortion performed by an old, evil-eyed woman. The girl would never be able to conceive again. But, at the least, she had survived. Not all of the abortionist's clients had always been to be able to tell about it.

***

Rosalie Mancini and Franco Donato began seeing one another more frequently in the ensuing year from the night of that village dance. The chaste, safe kisses soon escalated to more passionate ones involving their tongues. It was Rosalie who had been the first to offer hers to Franco. He had been slightly startled, but more so to the rapid hardening of his penis. And yet, he eventually responded with his own tongue. Things progressed no further, at least, for a while.

Rosalie began to think of Franco on a daily basis. She could not seem to get him out of her head: his ready and friendly smile; his well-proportioned body; his dark, curly hair; his soft, brown eyes. But most of all, she could not get over the feeling that came over her when they kissed passionately. Her nipples would harden, and the mound between her legs would moisten. And, one time, she reached down into Franco's pants and taken hold of his penis. She began to stroke it, gently, at first, until she increased the pressure. Rosalie could not control her hand until Franco could with- hold himself no further. His release flew off, startling Rosalie and himself.

Moments later Rosalie was startled as to what she had just done. There she was, a good Catholic girl, once so prim and proper, and, now, what had she just done to her boyfriend? Perhaps what had surprised her even more had been Franco's reaction to it all. As if it had been the most natural thing.

Despite all of what Rosalie Mancini had believed or, at least, had told herself, she and Franco married in the spring of 1936. She had just turned 19, Franco 20. She had become just another young Sicilian housewife, possessing virtually no skills, other than domestic ones, and having some rudimentary knowledge of winemaking.

In the weeks following the couple's brief honeymoon in Catania, Rosalie couldn't bear another fish market for a while, as they settled back into Mettuno. It had been nothing short of a miracle that Franco and Rosalie had been able to make their own arrangements as to their pre-nuptials and wedding. After all, Sicilian custom still held, by and large for parents. It had usually been them who had decided their children's futures.

Franco Donato had promised his new bride that he would do his best to see that Rosalie could read as much as possible, be it the classics, or books on history or the sciences, whatever. He was not, nor ever had been, much of a reader himself and had not been much of a student, he would not deprive his wife any of these things.

For her part, Rosalie deeply appreciated what her husband was doing. The mere fact that Franco wanted his wife to learn and to become more knowledgeable about the ways of the world, was breathtaking. One might have said that in his own simple Sicilian way Franco Donato had evolved into a Renaissance man.

All of this would stand Rosalie Donato in good stead in the ensuing years.

***

"I must say Alberto that I was surprised to hear you state that you had a most urgent matter to discuss with me," said Prefect Stefano Fanti, as sat down heavily into his office chair. The instrument groaning beneath his weight.

"Well, when you hear what I have to tell, you will see why," said Alberto Cardi.

Fanti had been appointed prefect of Ottavino upon Benito Mussolini's ascension to head of state. An inveterate Fascist from the beginning, it had been part of the natural order of things for Fanti to have assumed his position. The policeman was a veteran of the Great War where he had served in a staff position, rising to the rank of captain. Stefano Fanti liked to regale his friends with stories of his heroism at the front, especially his involvement in the disastrous Battle of Caporetto where Italian forces had been routed by the combined armies of Austrians and Germans. Truth be told, Fanti had been no closer than 50 miles from the front lines. He had never tossed a German grenade from a trench he occupied with several other soldiers. It was a complete fiction. Of course, no one in Ottavino would dare try and question the prefect and hero. To have done so might well result in someone being consigned to a jail cell. Such was Italian jurisprudence in Mussolini's Italy.

"Well then, Alberto, what is this matter of such great importance," asked a now perplexed Fanti, who knew of Alberto Cardi as being a personage of intrigue and duplicity.

"Well, you see...ahh Prefect," stammered a slightly shaking Cardi, who was now wondering if he could go through with his part of Carlo Goncalo's plan. *How had he allowed himself into this sordid and duplicitous scheme?* "Uh, as I was saying, yes... as I was saying...the matter," rambled Cardi, now looking down at the floor and wishing he could disappear under it. "It has to do with Umberto Mancini and...and..."

"Mancini, you say?" asked Fanti as he arched his bushy, graying eyebrows and twitched his bristled moustache. "What has Umberto Mancini done as to warrant your visit here today?"

"It isn't what he has done, but what he has said and...and, in fact, has been saying. And, I might add, what he has been saying for quite some time now." At this, Alberto Cardi was beginning to calm himself down. He was growing into his role. Perhaps he would be convincing enough to Stefano Fanti.

"So, Alberto, what has comrade Mancini been saying that is apparently so egregious as to bring you here?"

Alberto Cardi then came straight to the point. "Umberto Mancini has been uttering some rather and demeaning words about... about...the Duce." Cardi was now looking up and as he did so he found himself looking about Fanti's office. There was the obligatory portrait of Mussolini hung directly behind the prefect's desk. This one had the great leader mounted on the back of gleaming white stallion. A bold black helmet rested upon the man's head. The Duce's prominent chin was thrust outward in an imposing manner. Mussolini wore the expression of a great and conquering hero. The left side of his military uniform was fully bedecked with an array of medals. Not that many of them had any great worth or meaning. As he scanned further, Cardi noticed two of the walls contained posters, proclaiming the greatness of Fascism. He also noted a number of photographs, most likely of family members and friends of Fanti and, perhaps some were unknown dignitaries.

"Can you list some specific things that he said? And, how do you know this, Alberto? Did you, in fact, hear these things in person?" asked Stefano Fanti, who had now begun to jot down some of Cardi's testimony, using a quill pen, occasionally pausing to dip the metal nub into a bottle of blue ink.

"*Si*, uh yes, I did hear these denunciations directly. I mean he did not say them to me personally. I overheard him speaking to some men in one of the cantina's."

"Who was he speaking to? Do you know the person?," questioned Fanti, by now completely engrossed in the tale Cardi was weaving.

"I cannot say, as I did not get a good look at this person," responded Cardi, who had be now nearly completely regained his confidence. *Yes,* he thought, *I can fulfill my role. Carlo Goncalo will be extremely grateful when I tell him about what happened during my visit to the prefect.*

"Was this person a woman?"

"It was a man, but I only saw the side of him. This man did have a rather thick walrus type moustache. That I do remember. And, there was something else," Cardi paused for a moment as if in deep thought.

"And...and this something else? What was it?" pressed Stefano Fanti, who was now leaning forward as if he didn't want to miss a word. Only Alberto Cardi was drawing things out, as if were a Shakespearean actor on the grand stage. Fanti could hardly stand it. "Out with it, man!"

"This man had a speech impediment, a kind of lisp and a... a slight, very subtle stutter. It was quite imperceptible. But it was there."

"I see, I see. You also said that Mancini has been speaking badly of the Duce for quite some time now, is that correct?" resumed Fanti, in a prosecutorial manner.

Alberto Cardi was taken somewhat aback. *What had Goncalo told him to say?* Should this type of question arise. *What was it?* A cold and clammy sweat had now broken out as the poor man felt he might be on his way to blowing it. Carlo Goncalo would be very disappointed, very disappointed. Men like him did not at all like to be let down, and the price could be quite painful. At last, at long last, the light went on Alberto Cardi's brain. "Well you see, Prefect I started asking around. And it seems that others also heard Mancini speaking quite ill of the Duce…"

"Others? What others? Can you provide some name?" asked Stefano Fanti as his dark brown eyes bored into the skull of Alberto Cardi.

"Well now, let me think," said Cardi as he pretended to go through a mental card file. "Oh yes, there is Vicente Borrelli and… and… but, let me think," continued Cardi his slow lugubrious manner, which was absolutely killing Fanti. "Yes, there was Federico Ferri. Yes, yes," said Cardi as, at last, he finally finished, a slightly crooked smile crossed his visage.

"Mmm, well that is something to go on, Alberto. All right I believe that will be all for now, but should you happen to remember some new details about anything come to me straightaway. Do you understand?" questioned Fanti, as he now pretended to make a show by stretching out his tie and smoothing out the sides of his hair which gleamed in the paling sunlight.

"*Si, si*, Prefect, I will do so now. You know I really didn't want to have to come here and…denounce a fellow citizen, but I felt compelled to do it as part of my own civic duty. After all, I am still a dedicated Fascist."

Stefano Fanti rose from his chair and presented his right hand to Cardi, but at the last second he withheld it. Alberto Cardi had the distinct impression that Fanti really just saw him as an informer, a snitch. "I can assure you, Alberto, you have done the right thing and I will take it from here." And with that, Cardi was summarily dismissed. Alberto Cardi stood mutely and took his leave.

Now, Stefano Fanti would have to begin a discreet surveillance of Umberto Mancini, and he would have to forward his findings to Rome.

***

The calendar on the wall of Leo Goncalo's dormitory wall indicated that the day was 10 Oct 1936. It was 7:15 in the evening and Goncalo had his radio tuned in to the government owned station. Over the cracking airwaves came the imperious and commanding voice of Benito Mussolini.

At that moment, Leo's roommate, Mario Del Bonis walked in and upon hearing the Duce's voice he winced. The leader was not a particular favorite of Del Bonis, but he had always kept his tongue in check. He would never utter a word of criticism or crack a joke that could remotely be interpreted as critical or at odds with Mussolini, or his Black Shirts.

"Leo, must you have the volume on so loud?" asked Del Bonis as he set some books down upon his bed. The roommates had just commenced their junior years at the university.

"What's that you say? The Duce is too loud for you?" mimicked a feigning Goncalo.

"No, no, of course not. It's just that the volume is a little high, don't you think?" asked a chastened Del Bonis.

"I know Mario. I was only teasing you. You know, breaking your balls a little. You know me by now, don't you?" said Leo, not bothering to turn away from the radio as he raptly listened to Mussolini bellow on.

"Today, my fellow Italians, Italy is on the march. A march that will end in our forces entering Addis Ababa, Ethiopia!" Mussolini crowed. The crowd, estimated at more than 100,000, roared its approval with echoing shouts of: "Duce! Duce! Duce!" in the background. The great man paused, arms crossed over his broad, barrel-shaped chest, a soft-plumed black Fascist headgear adorned his bullet-shaped skull. The crowd slowly quieted as Mussolini held out his arms and he resumed his speech.

"On October 05, I ordered our gallant air and ground forces to invade Ethiopia, a pestilence and disease ridden band of criminal vipers. It was done because it had to be done. For far too long a time Ethiopia has created an evil menace on our own colony of Eritrea. They have attacked our citizens there with a campaign of vicious lies and deceitful actions. This could not be allowed to stand, and so I have ordered our gallant forces to rid the Italian nation of this menace," Mussolini thundered on, chest turned out, chin thrust forward. The crowd again roared with more chants of "Duce! Duce! Duce! We love you!"

Again, the dictator paused, "Today Italy is continuing its march forward. Today, Italy is the envy of Europe. In fact, it is the envy of the world!"

"Duce! Duce! Duce!"

"But we cannot stop now. We must continue to go forward. *Avanti, avanti,* I say!"

More chants of "Duce! Duce! Duce!"

"Today our great nation is once again on the move. It is on the move toward the creation of a second Roman Empire. But… this is only the beginning. The whole world will be astounded and amazed at what Italy and Fascism will accomplish in the coming years!"

What Benito Mussolini failed to reveal from the most famous balcony in Rome was what the Italian forces would do to the poor, unfortunate people of Emperor Haille Selassie. Italy would conduct a vicious and brutal campaign, one that was punctuated by a massive aerial bombing campaign and the use of poison gas, which had been outlawed by the Geneva Convention. The Duce would make the Ethiopian people pay a fearsome price.

Del Bonis listened and closely watched his roommate and friend, as Leo Goncalo sat and occasionally shouted out, "Bravo, Duce! Bravo!: at the dictator's menacing speech. Del Bonis had long realized that he and Goncalo came from vastly different worlds, and different mindsets. It bothered him that someone like Goncalo could actually believe the bilge being spewed from the mouth of Benito Mussolini.

***

Mario Del Bonis had always marveled at the ease in which Leo Goncalo matriculated his way through his course work at the University of Palermo. Taking the usual pre-med course load, it seemed to Del Bonis, that his roommate never seemed to have to open a book. Little preparation and no cramming was ever required for Goncalo to pass his regular tests or mid- terms or finals. It all came so easily, so effortlessly to Leo.

At times, Leo provided tutoring services or assistance to Mario himself, who was majoring in Civil Engineering. But he had to apply himself diligently. There was no room for coasting. Del Bonis would have to prepare days in advance so as to pass all of his tests and examinations.

Goncalo was especially helpful to Mario when it came to prepping for oral arguments.

Mario Del Bonis also noticed that along with the seeming ease that Leo Goncalo possessed in getting through his course work, he was presented with the opportunity of more free time. But he would pay a price for this additional time on his hands.

And it came down to Leo Goncalo and the opposite sex. While not being overly boastful about his feminine conquests, Leo never held back in regaling to Del Bonis as to what he had done in bed with this or that girl. The price came due one day during the spring semester, nearly a year removed from the Gentile affair. One of his conquests, a bar maid at a local Palermo cantina, informed him with the news that she was carrying his child. This set off another panic within Leo, knowing full well he could never go back to his father with this news and then hope to garner his assistance on how to make the matter go away.

No, this time he could get the young woman to accede to an abortion or to remove herself from the environs of Palermo. Only this time, the young woman would bear the child, a baby boy, and Leo Goncalo would provide monetary support for it through the endowment he received on a monthly basis. Of course, this would necessitate Goncalo being forced to cut back on his freewheeling lifestyle, particularly with young women. But only by just a little. He just couldn't help himself.

Mario looked at the situation like this with disdain. How could someone, anyone, treat a young woman who was bearing his child, so cavalierly and, at times, so cruelly. Del Bonis would ruefully shake his head. Indeed, he and Leo were of very different natures and yet he never spoke a word of this to the man. It was true that Mario did not have a steady girlfriend, but did date occasionally. One of these young women was a girl from Siracusa by the name of Lilliana Mangano. The girl was of medium height with auburn-colored, flowing hair. She had soft brown eyes, a beautifully shaped nose with just a little bump mid-way down its length, and wide mouth with full lips. But it was Mangano's body that completely enthralled Mario Del Bonis. Armed with a lustful endowment and a slim hourglass waist, Lilliana had the most gorgeous pair of long legs he had ever seen. They seemed to him without end. He constantly envisioned in coitus with the girl, and those spectacular legs wrapped around his torso.

Chapter Three

The Plot Thickens

In the dark of night on November 10th three vehicles, two black Lancia sedans and one Fiat army truck, left Fascist headquarters in Mettuno and set out for the home of Umberto Mancini. Prefect Stefano Fanti had dispatched them with the order to arrest Mancini. An apprehension in the middle of the night was standard practice when a target would most likely be asleep and unaware that something sinister was afoot.

It was nearing 2:20 am when the vehicles arrived at the Mancini home, whereby eight police agents alighted and silently took off for the home. The army truck contained a squad of ten soldiers, their job was to form an outer cordon so as to prevent any of the Mancinis from escaping. Capitano Luigi Penta silently motioned with his right hand to the men gathered around him. The house was shrouded in darkness. Off in the distance a dog was heard howling at who knew what. Otherwise, everything looked set for Penta to be able to make a quick apprehension of Umberto Mancini.

Mancini and his wife had been asleep in their bed when they were awakened by a loud and persistent banging on their front door. Husband and wife groggily shook the cobwebs from their fog-enshrouded brains.

"What could that be?" muttered Berto. Maria was instantly filled with an inner dread. She had the distinct feeling that something very ominous was about to descend upon them. She never would have imagined the nightmare that was about to unfold upon the entire Mancini family.

"Umberto Mancini, open up in the name of the authority invested in me in the name of Prefect Stefano Fanti!" shouted the stern and commanding voice of Luigi Penta. Just a few short years before, he'd been a middling and unassuming mail carrier. Now, for the first time in his insignificant life he finally possessed some real power. He had become somebody.

Quickly throwing on a full-length nightshirt, Berto Mancini made his way to the front door. Maria stood off to one side, tears trickling down her drawn face.

Berto Mancini paused for a moment and smoothed out the sides of his head with his hands, for what reason he did not know. Taking the doorknob he slowly pulled it open, and before him stood Capitano Penta, along with the seven other police agents.

Penta addressed Mancini, pulling himself up to his 5' 9'' height and thrust forward a standardized form authorizing entry and search into his home.

"Umberto Mancini, I am hereby authorized to search your premises and to apprehend your person," growled Penta.

"But why…what have I done, Capitano?" croaked Berto Mancini, still hardly believing what he was seeing and hearing.

"You have committed crimes against the state. You will have ten minutes to pack some things and to dress yourself, and be ready to leave with us." As Penta said this, the agents fanned out and around the house. Drawers were opened and their contents dumped onto the floor.

Maria Mancini and their daughter, Monica, stood clutching to one another in abject fear and terror. Both were sobbing uncontrollably.

***

Umberto Mancini was seated in a straight-backed wooden chair, his arms tightly secured by rope to the chair. A powerful overhead incandescent light beamed down, causing Mancini to perspire heavily. Sweat trickled down his face, more poured down the small of his back and into the seat of his pants. He hadn't even time to put on a belt.

Prefect Stefano Fanti observed the prisoner through an opening in the door.

"He has not yet revealed anything to us, Prefect," revealed Tenente Mario Tonino, as he stood to the side of Fanti. "Of course, we have not yet subjected him to any intensive interrogation," sneered Tonino. He couldn't wait to commence the procedure.

"We shall see, Tonino. We shall see," said Fanti, who then opened the cell door and went in to confront Umberto Mancini.

"Please, Prefect, tell me what I have done. Why am I being treated like this...like a common criminal?" pleaded a desperate Mancini.

Fanti looked down at his prisoner and at first he did not reply. "First of all, my dear Mancini, you will not be the one to ask the questions. That is reserved for me or for one of my staff. Second, you are considered an enemy of the state and will have to answer to some serious accusations. Do you understand?"

Berto Mancini sat forlornly in his chair and slowly nodded his head to his interlocutor. He looked up and said, "*Si, si*, I understand. I understand perfectly."

"*Bene, bene*, then let us get down to business," said Fanti as he sat down across from Mancini. He then made an elaborate show of removing his calf-skinned gloves and tossing them onto the table. Fanti did not speak for what seemed to Mancini several minutes, when in fact not even 30 seconds had elapsed.

"As I was saying, Mancini, you are being charged with a series of very serious crimes: sedition, conspiracy to act in a manner so as to advocate for the overthrow of the government of Italy; statements critical of the Duce and other top Fascist officials; malfeasance in the manner and way in which you conduct your various businesses. You are to be subjected to questioning on each and every charge I have listed. And, let me warn you now, do not attempt to try my patience or the consequences will be even more severe than what you are currently experiencing," concluded Stefano Fanti. "Guards! Take him away back to his cell."

Fanti stood and again looked down at Mancini. "Mancini, you have made some terrible mistakes and for which you'll pay dearly." It sounded to Berto Mancini that Fanti already considered the case to be an open and shut one. How could they be refuted? How could he fight back?

***

Maria Mancini managed to gather her wits and was able to begin formulating a plan to help her husband. First thing, though, she contacted her daughter, Rosalie. Maria knew she was the one person she could and would have to rely on in any attempt to have Berto freed. Notwithstanding that traditionally Italian, and especially Sicilian, families had always relied on the eldest son to provide the necessary moral and practical guidance in a crisis of this magnitude. No, Rosalie was the one.

She and Franco Donato had tied the knot earlier in the year in a quiet wedding ceremony celebrated at the Church of Santa Infante in Mettuno. A small reception was then held in the town square. Rosalie had looked resplendent and regal in her white-laced white wedding gown. It had been the creation of Maria, an expert seamstress.

"Mother, please slow down. What has happened?" asked a perplexed Rosalie.

"Your father. They came for him in the middle of the night. Those bastards! He never had a chance," moaned Maria Mancini.

"Who came for him? I don't understand," said a now concerned and increasingly frightened Rosalie. She had seldom heard her mother say a curse word before.

"Stefano Fanti and his Fascist goons. They say he has committed crimes. But what crimes, I ask you?" continued Maria, as she began to sob again.

"All right, mother, what we have to do is to keep our heads. It won't help papa to come unglued. I will come over as soon as I can, but I have to take of a few things first." "Okay, Rosalie, but hurry. Please hurry," said Maria as she rang off.

Rosalie put down her phone and began to think. As she sat in her kitchen she started to feel a bit woozy. She had recently been wondering about how she was feeling, especially in the morning. Then, a cold sweat began to formulate on her face and she realized she might well be experiencing morning sickness, which could mean only one thing. She was pregnant with their first child. What a time for it to happen. Rosalie would have to soon see the local doctor, Dottore Vinagro. But that would have to wait. Right now she would have to contact a lawyer. The only one she knew was Advocate Roberto Rossini.

Rosalie began to scramble around the kitchen, looking in this drawer and that for the address book. The she was desperately hoping would contain Rossini's name. She barely noticed the beautiful morning that was unfolding outside. Radiant sunshine was cascading its way through the white lace curtains hung along the kitchen windows.

At last, her fingers dropped upon the black address notebook. Rosalie frantically began thumbing through the pages, past B, G, M, P, and at last R. Her index finger was wrapped in a band-aid courtesy of a cut she suffered in the garden, drawing down the Rs. There it was, R. Rossini- 82-4056. Rosalie reached for the phone and began to dial.

The following day saw Rosalie accompany her mother to the law office of Roberto Rossini in Mettuno. The office was located in an impressive looking stone and mason building along Via Moncada, the town's main thoroughfare.

Rossini was waiting for them at the pre-arranged time of 10:00 am. The lawyer was good looking handsome man of about 40 years of age. He had a full head of gray-tinged hair and a determined face. The man exuded confidence, dressed in a finely cut black pin-striped suit, adorned by gold cuff links. Rossini also wore a large college ring on his right hand. Rosalie had never seen one so big.

"*Buon giorno, Buon giorno*, ladies. Please come in and take a seat," greeted Rossini graciously. He wanted to make the women as comfortable as possible in view of the trauma they were undergoing.

Rosalie guided her mother to an oaken chair in front of Rossini's desk. She took a seat in the next chair over. Maria Mancini was sitting straight up, nervously clutching a set of rosary beads in her gnarled hands.

"Is there anything I can get for you? Perhaps some coffee or tea?" asked Rossini as he glided into his swivel backed chair.

"No, *signore*, we are fine. Well, you see, I tried yesterday to give you as much information as possible regarding the arrest of my father. I'm afraid I may have sounded a little disjointed. We have been devastated by what has happened," Rosalie began, who herself was beginning to knead her hands together.

"That is quite all right. In light of what has transpired it is perfectly understandable. Believe me, I do understand. You were saying, Rosalie, that your father was arrested in the middle of the night and for no apparent reason by Prefect Stefano Fanti, is that correct?" asked Rossini in a soothing tone of voice.

"Si, si, that is correct, sir. We don't ...we don't know for any reason. My father has no enemies that we know of. We are completely mystified as to why he was taken. We fear to think of what he may be going through at this very moment," said Rosalie, clearly in control of herself and the situation. Outside, the day which had begun so promisingly was beginning to cloud over.

"Mmm," murmured Rossini, as he sat back and steepled his fingers together. " I must say this is rather perplexing. Well, all right, I will contact the Prefect and try to get some additional information as to why Umberto was seized, and for what reasons. I will also bring in a private detective that I often use. He is quite good. I also want to assure the both of you that I will do all that I can to secure Umberto's release," said Roberto Rossini in his smooth and urbane manner.

Until now, Maria Mancini had not uttered a single word. She had continued with the massage of her hands and rosary beads. Most of the time she had spent looking down at the floor. "I believe I know who the man may be behind my husband's arrest. The man responsible for this sordid and despicable act."

"You do, *signora*? What can you tell me? Anything at all would be most helpful," replied a surprised Rossini.

Si, avocato. This has the fingerprints of Carlo Goncalo all over it. I know it, I just know it," replied Maria calmly and who was looking directly at Rossini. There was a fire in her eyes. A blazing fire that startled the usually imperturbable lawyer.

"*Signore*, how do you know this?"

"I know Carlo Goncalo has long wanted to get his slimy hands on some of our land. Berto has suspected this for a long time. As for me, I had always thought that my husband was imagining things. And he concocted a devilish scheme to do it. Of course, he needed the services of Prefect Fanti to assist him. Goncalo is a man who will stop at nothing to get what he wants. He would destroy anyone...anyone." Maria finished her damning statement and then proceeded to sit back in her chair. It was beginning to bother her aching back.

"Well, well, that is certainly something I can and will look into. I can promise you that," said a now highly intrigued Roberto Rossini.

Rosalie was completely shaken be what she had just heard. Privately, she suspected that her mother might be right. It was just the very thing a man like Goncalo would do. A cold dread began to fill her inner being right down to her soul.

"I should caution the both of you that this may take some time. You see we are living in what I would say are very challenging times. Very challenging, indeed."

"Why do you say that, sir?" asked Rosalie.

"I say that because justice now has a new face to it. A new face that is a reflection of the government in Rome. Fascist law has become rather unique."

Rosalie was now filled with a new sense of dread. A dread that may well result in her and her family never seeing her father again.

Rossini saw the women to the door and then immediately got down to work. This case would require him to use all of his skills and connections as a lawyer. Going head to head with Stefano Fanti and his henchmen would be difficult. Extremely difficult. If he weren't careful he might well find himself incarcerated by the authorities. First, he would contact his private detective, Massimo Indelicato. He would direct the man to begin digging up whatever Fanti had on Umberto Mancini.

***

It took Roberto Rosini more than two weeks to garner an interview with Police Prefect Stefano Fanti. In that time he had not been allowed to see nor to question Mancini, his client. It was as if a news blackout had been cast down upon the case.

On the day Roberto Rossini was able to sit down with Fanti it could well be characterized as being straight from the depths of hell itself. The sky was black, driving sheets of rain fell from the heavens on all that lay below. Rainwater had pooled itself virtually everywhere imaginable. Streets and alleys were basically impassable.

Roberto Rossini was a sodden mess of a figure as he entered the Prefect's office. His fedora had been beaten down into an unrecognizable shape. His raincoat had been completely soaked through. Rossini desperately hoped the contents of his briefcase had not been turned into a mask of illegible words. The lawyer was well aware that his task that day would not be an easy one. He hoped he would be granted a meeting, no matter how brief, with his client, so that could get Mancini's own personal account of what had transpired. He also wanted to assure Berto that he was not alone. His wife and family believed in him, and in his innocence. And that they loved him.

"All right, Rossini, I would like to make this quick. I have a pressing engagement. I may be able to grant you 20 to 30 minutes, no more," said Stefano Fanti imperiously. The man was dressed in an all-black Fascist uniform, one that this uncultured and deceitful man appear even more sinister than Rossini had already believed.

"I am representing Umberto Mancini at the request of his family, Prefect Fanti. I am entitled under the law to be allowed to consult with my client. *Signore* Mancini is entitled to a vigorous and thorough defense. And..." Rossini had been prepared to go on, but a commanding hand by Fanti stopped him in full stride.

"You are entitled you say? Who the hell do you think you are to come striding into my office and to act in such a manner? Mmmm?" sneered a vicious looking Fanti.

Roberto Rossini sat back in his chair and stared dumbfoundedly at the Fascist. Right then and there, he knew that he, or anyone else, would be unable to do a single thing to help Umberto Mancini in his case. He would not be allowed to provide any succor to his client. "Prefect, I do believe that should be afforded a modicum of respect from you. After all, I am an advocate of the law. I...I," once again Rossini was forced to halt as Stefano Fanti slammed down his right hand upon his glass-topped desk. A wooden elephant figurine toppled over onto its side from the blast.

"Listen to me, Advocate. I am the law here in Mettuno. Do you understand? I will determine what Umberto Mancini is entitled to and what kind of defense you, or anyone else can mount."

"Prefect, in the name of all that is decent and human, you should allow me to visit with my client. I should be able to see the evidence you have so as to have justified what has taken place. That is the law," pleaded Rossini. Beads of perspiration broke out on his face and he reached for his handkerchief to daub at them. Thunder and lightning crackled and boomed in the sky above Mettuno, adding to the figurative gloom already present in the foreboding room.

"The evidence is quite clear and overwhelming. This is an open and shut case. However, I will tell you that your client is being charged with sedition and false and damning statements against the state. Wait, Rossini, I have not finished. I will think about your requests, but I cannot promise you anything more at this point in time," summed up the Prefect. "And now my time with you is up. Good day to you, sir. Hail Duce!" said Fanti as he made the one-armed Fascist salute.

Rossini stood in doleful silence, a look of loathing set itself upon his visage as he stared at the vituperative Fascist.

***

"I do not know…I don't know anything. How can I tell you what I don't know. Please, I beg of you," pleaded an emaciated and tortured Berto Mancini. The prisoner was 55 years old and while in relatively good health he had never been a terribly robust individual. During his brief time in captivity he had begun to wear down, not only physically, but mentally as well.

"I don't believe you. Not one bit. Why don't you just confess? It will make things considerably easier for you," soothed Inspector Captain Luigi Penta. He spoke as if he were speaking with a young and petulant child who had run afoul of some minor school rule. "Come now, Mancini, we both know you are hiding something, and I know that you really want to tell me."

"No, no, there is nothing to say. I have never spoken ill of the Duce. You must believe me," continued Mancini, now having been driven beyond his point of endurance.

Penta nodded to Sergento Tommaso Buffo to push Mancini's head under the water in the basin. Buffo held the elder man's head under for nearly 30 seconds, although to Mancini it had felt more like five minutes. Buffo raised Berto's head. Coughing and spluttering, Berto thought he was about to die. He desperately tried to expel water from this throat and mouth. His ears began to ring when Buffo cuffed them with his hands.

The policemen continued with the treatment for nearly 30 minutes, until finally Penta grew tired of the exercise. He realized that Mancini was probably telling the truth, but Penta had his orders to extract a confession. Of course, there was a fine line to be observed. It would never be good to have Mancini's life extinguished during the course of the interrogation.

"All right, Mancini, have it your way. No confession is it? You are making things harder for yourself," sneered Penta with obvious disdain.

"Please, sir, when will I be able to speak with my wife, my family?" croaked Mancini.

"You can forget about that, Mancini. As long as you remain defiant and refuse to cooperate with us, you can forget it," replied Penta, who picked up his uniform jacket and threw it over his shoulders. "Take him away, Buffo." Penta looked around the desk and the darkened cell, which resided in the basement of the Prefect's headquarters building. The cell was not far below Stefano Fanti's office, where Umberto Mancini's lawyer, Roberto Rossini had sat and made his case to Fanti.

Penta observed to himself that some redecorating was definitely in order for the room. Definitely, the décor needed an upgrade. Who knew, perhaps new surroundings might make some prisoners more conducive to what was being asked of them. He would bring this up with Fanti in the future.

***

During this time, Benito Mussolini was tasting the greatest success of his amazing life. Here was a man who had defied the powers of Europe, had launched the Ethiopian War and won it. He was able to claim that, like some of the other major nations, Italy now had a foreign, albeit a small one, empire. The Duce was awarded the Cross of the Military Order of Savoy, Italy's highest decoration, by a grateful King Victor Emmanuel. And, what was more, the citizenry was behind him. The walls of Rome and other major cities such as Milan and Venice, sprouted posters with such proclamations as "Mussolini has conquered" and "the tricolor sheds its rays over Addis Ababa."

A price was paid by the nation for the Duce's hubris and grandiose dreams. The African campaign saw the country drained of $50 million dollars from its coffers and its armory of large quantities of arms and armaments. Mussolini had placed himself and the country in jeopardy for the looming international crisis that was building.

Shortly after he had proclaimed victory in Ethiopia, Mussolini further drained Italy's resources by pushing it into another conflict, the Spanish Civil War. Italy threw its support behind the right-wing insurgents of Generalissimo Francisco Franco. Unofficially a non-participant, it was expensive. Mussolini committed 70,000 soldiers, as well as large numbers of arms, aircraft, artillery, and other equipment in support of Franco's ultimately successful campaign.

And, though he could not possibly have perceived it at the time, Benito Mussolini had reached the apex of his career. For now he began an imperceptible, but precipitous slide into an alliance with the "violent man with no self-control," Adolf Hitler.

Of course, Hitler had already taken advantage of the Duce's Ethiopian victory to laud and lionize his Italian hero. In the summer of 1937 he invited the Italian leader to visit Germany that fall. The Fuhrer had taken note of his fellow Fascist and immediately recognized his susceptibility to flattery.

The visit began in Munich, where Mussolini was treated to numerous parades of the National Labor Service, Hitler Youth, and Nazi Party officials; all of them marching to the ridiculous goose step. The German tour then followed to Mecklinburg for army maneuvers, and on to Essen to take in the massive Krupp works.

Hitler then hosted the Duce during a lavish visit to Berlin. There Mussolini was treated to a grandiose marvel of pomp and ceremony designed to dazzle the man. Driving down the Unter den Linden, the broad boulevard leading to the city center, the two dictators passed an array of thousands of flags: the symbol of the Fascist rods was as prevalent as the swastika.

The climax of the visit was a joint appearance by Hitler and Mussolini in the field that adjoined the huge stadium built for the 1936 summer Olympics. Hitler introduced his guest to the crowd of more than 100,000, then turned the microphone over to his guest.

Benito Mussolini made a gallant effort to speak in German. Just then the skies opened up and driving rains turned the pages of his manuscript into a mashed pulp. The sound of his words were drowned out. When he left Germany on the following day, Mussolini carried with him a deep impression of the apparent might of the Third Reich and the deeper conviction that Hitler could be a powerful future ally. From that moment, Benito Mussolini was drawn into a net that would lash him and Italy firmly to Hitler's Germany. Up to this point, the German leader had followed the lead of Italy. But from now on, it would be Mussolini who would follow the Fuhrer's lead. And with disastrous results.

***

Leo Goncalo sailed through his remaining undergraduate courses at the University of Palermo to graduate with high honors: Magna Summa Cum Laude in fact. Leo's parents beamed with pride as they witnessed their son's graduation procession. At last, thought Leo, he could now go on to medical school at the University of Bologna where he had been almost immediately accepted upon submission of his application. He hadn't been quite sure whether it had been his outstanding academic record or the behind the scenes influence of his father. Nonetheless, he would now be on his way in the fall semester.

Something did trouble Goncalo the younger, and it had to do with the fact that not only was he from the south of Italy, he was from Sicily. It had never been a secret on how northerners, those from north of Rome, had always looked down their noses at their southern brethren. They had always viewed them as slow, slovenly, uncultured, dirty, and applied just about any other pejorative term one could think of. Northerners had long lamented that Italy should have been cut off at Rome when it had been created. The remainder could then have been cast adrift into the Mediterranean Sea.

Leo would have to keep his wits about him. He knew he could handle the course load, and he knew he was ready to take the next step in his ascension to becoming a member of the medical fraternity. Besides, his dashing good looks and his way with the opposite sex should keep him in good stead. Who knew, a sampling of some northern beauties, or even, perhaps, some fair-haired Germanic ones, might be availed to his services and skills in the boudoir.

Leo Goncalo would lose sight of his roommate and good friend, Mario Del Bonis. If and when they ran into one another again it might well be under vastly different circumstances. As to the present, Mario would take his degree and then head back to his family's groves around Anzio, south of Rome. Groves of lemons and limes, as well as oranges occupied much of the Del Bonis land around the famous summer resort town. Much of the lemon output was turned into the luscious alcoholic beverage, limoncello. Nearly half of which was exported to the United States.

***

After nearly three months of incarceration, Roberto Rossini was finally granted access to his client, Umberto Mancini. When the lawyer first took hold of the man a sense of cold dread seized him. Mancini appeared gaunt and haggard, and looked to have lost some 30 pounds. His hair was unwashed and greasy, and it hung down in spaghetti-like strands. The face was unshaven and was punctuated by red-splotches. Puffiness and fatigue outlined his sad and downcast eyes. Mancini's lips were bruised, as well as his nose. Lastly, Berto, who had always carried himself with dignity, could be seen to have stained and unbrushed clothes, He knew his breath smelled acidly.

Rossini also took in Berto Mancini's tattered and unwashed clothes, and the foul smell emanating from his unwashed body, nearly bowled Rossini over. He was shocked at what he saw before him. Clearly, Berto had been tortured, had not been fed properly, and was completely disheveled. Quickly gathering up his composure, Roberto Rossini sat down before Mancini. Nearby, a policeman stood guard, pretending not to be paying any attention, but Rossini well knew that the man had been instructed to listen in on every word he could possibly hear from the two men's discussion.

"Berto, I am glad to now have the opportunity to meet you. I wish it were under…under different circumstances. I want you to know that I am here to help you, and I will do all in my power to help secure your release," said Rossini in his most confident voice.

Berto Mancini slowly picked up his head and brought his red-rimmed eyes to meet Rossini's and shook his head dolefully. "No, Roberto, this is nothing at all. They have told me that I committed sedition. I barely know the meaning of the word. That I have spoken ill of the Duce. But they are lies. I have done nothing of what they say. I do not know what I can add," said a defeated Berto Mancini.

Rossini knew what he was up against in the matter of confronting Fascist justice. Many others had simply disappeared into the Mussolini gulag, never to be heard from again. His private detective had come up against a proverbial stone wall in his attempts to ferret out information from anyone who knew of, or was aware of, Berto Mancini. "I know things have been difficult for you, my friend, by try to have faith. Myself and your family are doing all that can be done."

"When will I be able to see Maria and my family? I miss them dearly," mumbled a nearly incoherent Mancini. His head was matted down into a mess of tangled hair, looking as if he had slept on the streets for weeks. Obviously it had never been washed from the time Berto had been held.

" I am working on that with the Prefect. I hope to have some news for you and Maria soon," said Rossini, who could now feel his anger and disgust building within himself. *Fanti is a bastard!* He thought to himself.

"*Bene, bene*, Roberto," whispered Mancini. He now bent his head toward the lawyer. "You know I cannot prove it, but I strongly suspect the hand of Carlo Goncalo. He has always coveted some of my land, if not all of it. And he has never been able to do it. This galls him. Perhaps you and your people could look into this."

Rossini nodded his now clammy feeling head. Mancini's words echoed those of his wife, Maria, when he had spoken with her and Rosalie.

***

Rosalie gave birth to a lively and enchanting baby girl during the time of her father's detention. She and Franco named her Rosanna. It was a desperate and trying time for the Mancinis and the Donatos. Rosalie spent her time between caring for the baby to being a wife to her husband, taking care of her mother, and then working to secure her father's release. After endless, and, often fruitless attempts Roberto Rossini had finally been able to get the authorities to allow for Maria and Rosalie to see Umberto Mancini.

The sight of the man stunned them both into a momentary silence. Rosalie bit her lip, but managed to maintain her composure for the sake of her mother. Maria sat before Berto and could say nothing, she could not bring herself to speak a single word. Maria did not feel a part of the real word. *How could this be happening? Some otherworldly power must be at play here.*

The meeting was brief, as Stefano Fanti only allowed them ten minutes. Rosalie did most of the talking with Berto. Maria maintained her silence, her hands busy at work on the rosary beads, handed down for several generations.

At last, the policeman in the interview room walked over and indicated that the meeting was at an end.

"Papa, we will do everything we can for you. Is there anything you need? "As she said the words, Rosalie felt a tinge of regret. *What did her father need? Of course, he needed his freedom from this dreadful and ghastly place, and the torture he was being put through,* she thought.

Berto shook his grizzled head slowly and looked to Maria. "Thank you for seeing me. I have missed you, my love. Do not lose hope, I have not, despite my appearance."

Maria so wanted to reach out and embrace her husband, but this had been forbidden by Fanti. No contact between parties was to be allowed. He said to Rosalie he was grateful that he could see them after being separated from them for so long. He joked that Fanti must have been in a good mood when he had decided to allow the Mancinis to meet. Rosalie had not laughed, and could not remember the last time she had had a laugh or even a grin. *Thank you, Duce, you have given us so much.* She looked at the pitiful and wretched state she found her father in, and it sent a wave of revulsion flooding throughout her body. She still couldn't figure out how her father was a part of this tragedy. Fanti, the bastard. Rosalie would one day see him roast in hell for this.

That night Rosalie lay naked in bed next to Franco, following some passionate lovemaking, the couple spoke about Berto Mancini's situation. Franco loved the presence of his wife's frontal endowment just touching the skin of his back. Rosalie was a determined and passionate lover. Every time they had made love in the previous months, she had displayed a fierceness to these amorous activities. The way she would close her eyes and bow her throat out as she sat atop Franco, humping away with a desperate intensity. Her large, well-shaped breasts would bounce and sway to the rhythm of her lower body as she took in Franco's manhood.

"I don't know what more we can do, Franco. I think things have now proceeded to the point of desperation," Rosalie moaned as she pressed herself more tightly against Franco's body.

"I know, my pet, I know. Can't Rossini do anything more? I mean, what exactly is the man doing? What is he being paid for?" asked an exasperated Franco, who by now was long past exhibiting any further patience. If he had his way, he would have organized a break-out operation to free Berto Mancini from his captivity. But, of course, there was never any practical or realistic way of carrying out such an idea.

"I'm afraid we may never see him again. At least, not as a free man, one who can rejoin his family," lamented Rosalie as tears began to fall down her cheeks onto Franco's back.

He turned to face Rosalie. "We have to keep faith, my love. What else do we have? We have to trust in God's divine mercy and love. He will not forsake your father in his hour of need, and he won't forsake us."

Franco leaned in toward Rosalie's face and brought his lips to hers. She inhaled the musk that emanated from Franco. She inserted her tongue into his mouth, and he responded in kind. The couple then engaged themselves in another session of passion. At the moment of Rosalie's climax, Franco ejaculated into her. Tears, unrestrained tears cascaded their way from the corners of her eyes. Their saltiness caused a slight sting on her tongue. She clamped her long, smooth legs around Franco's torso.

***

Rosanna was growing up before their eyes, She was a bright, vivacious child. Her curly blond hair resembled the looks of her mother. She possessed Rosalie's eyes, nose, and mouth. Only her ears, one of which contained a small birthmark on the lobe, that her father had. The little, adorable girl was approaching two years of age when Nazi Germany invaded Poland on September 1, 1939, kicking off the Second World War. The Germans quickly overwhelmed the brave Polish units deployed to meet them across the broad countryside. The situation went from bad to worse when the Soviet Union honored its commitment to Germany, as part of the Nazi-Soviet Pact, and invaded Poland from the east in late September.

Italy was a part of Adolf Hitler' plan and, on the surface, had been content to sit on the sidelines. But Benito Mussolini had never been a patient man, even in the best of circumstances. And now he had to watch as his Fascist counterpart garnered laurels and plaudits for having crushed Poland in mere weeks. The Duce dearly wanted to be able to display his armed forces. He wanted to show off his army, navy, and air force. And he was especially eager to shed the blood of Italian youth. For the time being, he would have to bide his time, although the general staff was breathing a sigh of relief. They well knew that the Italian armed forces were far from ready for a global challenge of war. And yet, they knew they could not put off Mussolini's fervor forever. When the great man's blood came up for conquest they would have to accede to the inevitable.

In the meantime, Franco and Rosalie Donato quietly raised their daughter, and enjoyed her and realized how precious each moment with her was.

***

Meanwhile, Leo Goncalo was finishing up his studies at the University of Bologna. He was now making the rounds as an intern. Part of this centered around his involvement with the military. Goncalo, upon permanently becoming a physician, was to be assigned to the 15th Corps in the Italian Army. He saw this as being particularly advantageous as it would allow him to get a leg up on many other aspiring young doctors. Assignment to a military branch carried significance and a noteworthiness with the government.

Leo also thought involvement with the army might allow him the chance to gain some laurels and awards and enhance his name and reputation. Who knew, perhaps this would show his father that the son was not completely dependent on Carlo Goncalo for his future. Now Leo would stand on his own two feet. He could swing out and away from the powerful centrifugal force of his father. The son would show his domineering father, that he, Leo, could and would attain his own sphere of influence and power, and, eventually wealth.

Chapter Four

War

At the start of the year 1940, Leo Goncalo was immersed in the daily activities of a medical intern of the 14th Corps Field Hospital located just outside of the city of Milan. This industrialized modern city of more than 600,000 was considered a gleaming jewel in the eyes of Benito Mussolini and his Black Shirt lapdogs. It was the capital of the province of Lombardy. Milan had always seen itself as a leading, global city, with strengths in art, commerce, design, education, entertainment, finance, and research. Its business district saw host to Italy's stock exchange and as headquarters of numerous national and international banks and companies.

The city had long been recognized as one of the world's four fashion capitals, in large part to several international events and fairs, such as the Milan Fashion Week and the Furniture Fair. Milan was also the home of many cultural institutions, academies, universities. Its varied and eclectic museums were home to works of art from such major artists as Leonardo da Vinci and Michelangelo.

Only a few remains of an ancient Roman colony, notably the well-preserved Colonne di San Lorenzo, were still to be seen in 1940 Milan. During the latter half of the fourth century, Saint Ambrose, Bishop of Milan had a strong influence on the layout of the city, reshaping the center and the building of some of the great basilicas at the city gates: Sant' Ambrogo and San Simpliciano.

Leo Goncalo stood at rigid attention in front of the desk of Colonello Paolo Cardelli, chief resident of the 14th Corps Army Hospital. Cardelli was reading through Goncalo's resume. "At ease, Goncalo, we are not yet on the parade ground. And I do allow for some degree of informality while in my office."

Leo looked down at the man who would be his superior for the foreseeable future, a man who would have a direct influence on Leo's future as a doctor, and as a man. Cardelli displayed a formidable presence: dark wavy hair, interspersed with flecks of gray; aquiline shaped nose; deep-set brown eyes; and a firm chin and mouth. One, thought Goncalo, of a boxer. The young intern did not realize that Paolo Cardelli had been a one-time amateur boxer in his youth, and had endured a couple of broken noses and numerous cuts and abrasions. Leo knew he would have to tread carefully, at least, for the immediate future. He did not want to get on Cardelli's bad side for whatever reason.

"All right, Goncalo, I will lay it out for you. I expect you to be prompt each and every day. I expect you to do whatever is assigned to you, no matter how trivial it may seem. You will, at all times, act and dress in a professional manner. I never want to see an unshaven face or coffee stains on your lab coat. I do not want to see a disheveled appearance. Is that clear?" Cardelli paused for a moment as Leo nodded. "You will see that I am really not that hard to get along with. I think you will find this hospital will provide you with a great learning experience, and will have been well worth your while."

***

"That is easy for you to say," argued Rosalie as she was engaged in a verbal stand-off with Franco. "He is not your father who is sitting and rotting in that God-damned jail, is it?"

Franco Donato was seated in his accustomed kitchen chair and was listening to his agitated wife accost him verbally. "Rosalie, Rosalie, what do you want me to say? What do you want me to do?" he pleaded.

"My father has been falsely imprisoned for nearly two years and all I keep hearing is to be patient, to trust in the Lord. Well, where is he? Where is this precious lord of the Church we are always praying to? Well?" Rosalie went on as she feverishly paced back and forth across the tiled floor. Franco thought the floor might well wear right out, but he kept his silence.

"Franco, I swear, I swear that this God in Heaven, that sometimes I think I will just burst." Rosalie felt herself begin to tear up.

Watching from the kitchen doorway stood little Rosanna. The child was trembling, she was not used to her parents arguing. What she could remember were the soft moans of her mother as she and Franco made love in the bedroom next to hers.

"Mommy, why are you shouting? I cannot sleep when you are angry," murmured Rosanna, clutching a soft pink- eared stuffed rabbit.

Rosalie looked over to see her daughter and instantly she was ashamed. She should have known better. How could she and Franco argue in front of Rosanna. Rosalie rushed over to the little girl and scooped her up into her arms, reigning a shower of kisses on Rosanna's head.

"Well, Rosanna. Mommy and daddy weren't really arguing. It was what we big people call a difference of opinion. And sometimes we can get very excited. We are sorry, very sorry, if we frightened you. It will not happen again," said Rosalie, looking at Franco, who slowly nodded his head. She was right, as the so-called big people, the two of them had been acting like children. Although, Franco knew and understood his wife's frustration and anger. He knew she had long been at the breaking point with concern over Umberto Mancini. In addition, they had now a visitor in the person of Maria Mancini. The older woman had been forced to vacate her home of decades as a result of the scheme cooked up by Carlo Goncalo. This had placed more tinder on the fire of the Donato home.

"Mommy, when is Nonno going to come home? I miss him," said Rosanna plaintively, as she pulled on her auburn haired locks.

Rosalie did not know what to say to her daughter. All of them missed the loving, sweet man. "We all miss him little one. We hope he will come home soon, very soon, to join us all again. Just like it used to be." It was a hope. A now apparently false and fading hope that Rosalie clung to every day. What else could she do? However, Rosalie had been thinking about an idea. A new idea she well-hoped might be able to obtain the release of her father.

***

Alberto Cardi knew why he had been summoned to the estate of Carlo Goncalo. He was to receive additional directives as to how he was to manage the land and property that had been shanghaied from Umberto Mancini. His blood pressure only went up when he saw Aldo Goncalo, the eldest of Goncalo's five sons, seated in the full leather couch of the study.

"And how are you today, my friend?" asked a genial Goncalo.

Cardi saw this for the obvious sham that it was. Goncalo couldn't have cared less about the health and welfare of him, or anyone else who didn't have the name of Goncalo.

"*Bene, bene*, Carlo, not too bad," said Alberto Cardi as he tilted his head to one side. He felt a nervous tick beginning to formulate around his right eye. This always happened when he knew his volatile blood pressure was beginning to rise. Cardi looked from Carlo to Aldo, who continued to say nothing but, to Cardi, seemed to curl up his upper lip into a semi-sneer. The oppressiveness of the oak-paneled room seemed as if it were closing in on him. Outside, what had started out as a pleasant and sunny autumn day was now clouding over. It matched Cardi's mood.

"I am so glad to hear it. I really am," enthused a smiling Carlo as he sat down into his chair. A slight groan was heard to emit from the bulk of Goncalo resting on it. "Now, let us get down to business. I must say you have been a fine job in your handling of the Mancini property. A fine job, indeed. You are to be commended," continued Carlo. "But there is the small matter of the Mancini home. Why have you not moved into the house? After all, you are the rightful owner, so to speak and you should be ensconced within the dwelling. Is it not larger and somewhat more, how should I say, endowed than what you are living in now?"

"Well, I…er, my family likes our own home and really do not want to move…to move into the Mancini home," replied Cardi, who had begun shifting his feet. He failed to mention that he and his wife believed it might bring bad karma to occupy someone else's house. Especially the way Mancini had been robbed of his home.

"Nonsense, nonsense, my friend. I really think you should move. Why delay?" said Goncalo. Only now he was no longer smiling. He was not the affable and amiable man he had earlier presented to Alberto. His fiery eyes were now ablaze with a look that figuratively told Cardi, "*You must do this. I will not tell you again.*"

"Well, I suppose, we can do it. I will tell my wife today. I am sure she will agree," said Cardi, who well knew that he would have a fight on his hands. Laura had never expressed any desire to move anywhere else from their comfortable home of more than thirty years.

"Eh, to change the subject a bit. What do you think of Adolf Hitler? I tell he has the right idea when it comes to those God-damned Jews. He has been rounding them up all over Germany and then sending them away," rhapsodized a now enthusiastic Carlo Goncalo.

"I think the Duce should pay a little more attention to what his colleague is doing within Germany," peeped up Aldo Goncalo, who, heretofore, had been a silent participant to the proceedings.

"Aldo, you should show more respect to our leader. After all, he knows what he is doing and has placed Italy on the right track at long last. Although, I have to say that Hitler has the right idea. The Jews have always been a gang of blood-suckers. They have stolen what was never rightfully theirs. These people have never done an honest day's work in their lives. And they have gotten rich off the backs and sweat of us Christians. It has been an outrage," thundered Carlo Goncalo.

Aldo Goncalo remained muted as he listened to his father's diatribe against the Jews. He was struck by the fact that his long-time physician, Pietro Colbi, had just had his medical license revoked by the government within the past week. Colbi had always been a caring and considerate doctor, a man who always seemed to have all the time in the world with his patient. And now, has practice had been closed down. He and his family had now been forced to live hand to mouth, one day to the next. And all because they were Jews.

***

Leo Goncalo dutifully performed his intern's tasks as required at the 14th Corps Field Hospital. His superior and mentor, Paolo Cardelli, had been very impressed with his protégé's medical knowledge and dedication to his patients. No task or assignment was too small or trivial for Goncalo, although, privately, Leo thought many of these so-called tasks were indeed too minute and beneath his status as an up and coming physician.

One day in early March, Leo was summoned to Cardelli's office, whereupon he was greeted by two things: one was Cardelli's stunningly beautiful blond-haired wife. She was clearly a good ten to fifteen years his junior. And the other surprise was the offer Cardelli presented to him.

"Leo, I have to say that I have been most impressed by your performance at the hospital for these past few months. Most impressed," Cardelli repeated. "Therefore I am going to make you an offer which I firmly believe you're ready for…" Paolo Cardelli let his words hang in the air like an ether.

Leo hung on, eager to know what this offer was, while trying desperately not to stare at Cardelli's wife's bosom being harnessed within a tight-fitting white sweater. *Now, those mounds are most impressive,* thought Leo. He would have dearly loved to have examined them in bed.

"Yes, well, my offer is to allow you to sit in and assist me tomorrow when I perform a surgery on an unfortunate young private. You see, Leo, this young man has had the misfortune to have had his right leg run over by a tank while in the midst of a training exercise, and…" Cardelli let his words drift off.

"And you will have to amputate the leg, is that not so, sir?" asked Leo. This was not at all what he had expected. True, he had observed and handled situations where blood had made its presence, but to actually participate in the removal of a major limb was something else. And truthfully, Leo was not sure he had the stomach for it. At least, not just yet.

"*Si, si, si,* my young and sometimes impatient colleague. Well, are you interested?" asked Cardelli, closely watching for Goncalo's reaction. He had observed a number of young and flashy interns who thought they knew all the answers and could talk a good game. But to see an actual amputation was something else entirely. Some of those hotshots had flat-out passed out on the operating room floor. This was a test which separated the men from the boys.

Leo did not immediately reply, and, this time, he did not bother to glance at Paula Cardelli. Her breasts couldn't help him at this moment. He had to appear decisive. He couldn't flinch in front of his superior. "*Si*, Dottore Cardelli, I am eager to take you up on your offer. When is the operation to be scheduled?"

"At 0630 hours be ready to scrub up. The surgery is to commence at 0800. At that time I will brief you on some of the details of the surgery. Eh, so you will be ready my friend?" asked Cardelli jokingly. He had noticed Goncalo's interest in his wife's bustline. It was, no doubt, what had lured and fascinated a thousand men before today. Cardelli had harbored some suspicions as to his wife's faithfulness to him, but had always looked past them. He did enjoy Paula's ability in bed. It was a far different experience than what he endured with his first wife. "Oh, Leo, how remiss of me, let me introduce you to my lovely wife Paula."

Leo took a hesitant step forward and extended his hand to Signora Cardelli. He light grip in return sent a cold shiver through his right arm. Ice water.

"Dottore Goncalo, a pleasure," the young woman responded, her cool, green eyes focused on his.

***

Leo Goncalo still was not sure as to whether he was really meant to be a physician. At least, not a practicing surgeon. He was almost transfixed as he stood next to Cardelli in the operating theater, assisting as best he could. The unfortunate young soldier was one Gilberto Olmi. He lay upon the operating table, put out by way of anesthesia.

Paolo Cardelli made an incision with his scalpel and then proceeded to continue the incision completely around the damaged limb. Blood was soaked up and contained by a nurse. Goncalo was standing slightly to the right of Cardelli. Above them sat a coterie of medical students and some curious bystanders, peering down intently at the proceedings below them. Some turned their heads away. The scene was repulsive. "Now, all of you pay close attention, especially you Dottore Goncalo, as to what I shall do next," said Cardelli.

Leo recoiled slightly at the mention of his name, as if he had been singled out by his mentor.

Cardelli was then handed a surgical bone saw, which to Goncalo, distinctly resembled the kind of saw a carpenter would use in the building of a house. The surgeon deftly began to saw through the dense femur bone of the patient's leg. The femur was the largest and toughest bone in the human body.

To Goncalo, it had seemed as if Cardelli had performed this kind of procedure many times before. The saw went smoothly back and forth in short, controlled strokes. And in seemingly no time at all, the task was completed. The mangled mass of the removed portion was separated from the patient. The hapless Olmi was oblivious as to what had just been done to him. He would awaken to a far different world. His soldiering days were over. If he were to be fitted with a prosthetic leg he might be able to return to the dance floor. Paolo Cardelli had his attending physicians tie off the blood vessels in the stump and then stitched Olmi up. Leo Goncalo was relieved when the surgery was completed. At no point did he perceive that he would pass out. But he did wonder if ever a situation arose and he was confronted with having to perform an amputation himself if he could truly do it. Being an army doctor and with Italy in the war it was a distinct possibility. Especially if he were posted to a frontline unit.

"Well, Goncalo, what do you think? I thought the whole procedure went rather well. There were no complications and the patient, one..." Cardelli paused as he looked down at the medical chart. "Private Gilberto Olmi is in good health. I expect him to make a full recovery and be able to resume a somewhat normal life. Of course, he'll no longer be in the army."

"*Si*, Dottore Cardelli, *si*," murmured Goncalo.

"And you didn't pass out on me," joked the surgeon as he emitted a short, cackled laugh. "Believe me, I've had some interns get laid-out cold as they took in an amputation. And some of them had been quite promising students. Eh, what can you do? Some people simply cannot stand the sight of blood. Not to mention seeing a leg or an arm hacked off."

"No, there would be no room for them as doctors," said Leo Goncalo, who suddenly began to feel somewhat faint as he mentally recalled the surgery he had just witnessed.

"One day in the not too distant future, I will allow you to perform an amputation of...of a hand or a finger so as to give you a little experience. What do you say, Goncalo?" asked Cardelli as he stared right at Leo, as if trying to gage his reaction.

"Eh, *si, si*, Dottore, that would be good. I look forward to the opportunity," said Leo, although privately he was not really eager at all to such a prospect.

***

The nine months from September of 1939 to June 1940 were frustrating ones for Benito Mussolini. He had to grimly watch as his former junior partner demolished Poland in a mere three weeks. He realized, that militarily, he was powerless to take part, but, nevertheless, he had felt ashamed to have had to sit on the sidelines. In his eyes Italy could not long remain neutral without losing her status around the world.

This feeling only intensified when Germany began to pressure Italy to enter the war. Of course, on her side. In October, Hitler informed Foreign Minister Galeazzo Ciano, who was on a state visit to the Reich: "If Germany and Italy went into battle together, England and France would so completely crushed that many of the still unsettled problems would be solved once and for all."

In March 1940, the Duce was given peremptory notice that Hitler would be going to the Brenner Pass to meet him. "These Germans are unbelievable," exclaimed an exasperated Mussolini. "They don't give us any time to breathe or to think matters over" Still, he agreed to meet with the Fuhrer.

The two had not met since the 1938 Munich Conference when the Duce had served in the role as mediator in the Sudeten question. Hitler now teased the vanity and pride of Mussolini by pointing out that if Italy was content to play second fiddle in the Mediterranean, then he, Mussolini, should go home and forget about the war. However, should he want to achieve the status of a great power, he should join with Germany in the fight against England and France. Hitler also revealed that Germany was preparing for a big attack on France in the near future.

This slap in the face was more than the man could bear, and he now took the step from which there would be no turning back. Mussolini now promised Hitler that the Italians would indeed join in the conflict.

Hitler left the Brenner Pass meeting with what he had wanted: a commitment from Mussolini. He could and would use this as leverage and influence on the high commands of Britain and France. They would have to face the prospect of having to fight on another front: the Mediterranean.

In short order in April 1940, Germany invaded and swiftly conquered Denmark and Norway. Mussolini duly declared his unwavering support of

Hitler's move. Although Mussolini gave the outward appearance of welcoming the news, he was stunned and resentful at having been kept in the dark once again by his friend.

On May 10th, German forces struck an overwhelming blow on the Low Countries of Holland, Belgium, and Luxembourg, and Germany's greatest foe, France. The time was growing near when Mussolini would have to keep his promise, and he grew increasingly fretful. When King Victor Emmanuel urged caution to Mussolini, the Duce scoffed: "The king would like to enter only to pick up the broken dishes." He rejected a peace overture from Great Britain's newly installed Prime Minister, Winston Churchill. The prime minister had asked in a letter, "Is it too late to stop a river of blood from flowing between the British and Italian peoples?"

It was too late; much too late. Benito Mussolini was more anxious for action, and on June 10th he boldly announced his intentions to the Italian people and to the world.

Italy's declaration of war was, at first, little beyond symbolic. The day after her declaration, the Italian submarine "Bagnolini" sank the British cruiser "Calypso" in the Med. The 32 army divisions that Mussolini had sent to the French border were so poorly equipped that they were barely able to maneuver. Some artillery batteries were grossly outdated. Even field kitchens lacked sufficient pots and pans to cook hot meals. Several days after Italy's entry into the war, the French asked for an armistice from Hitler.

Benito Mussolini had conceived visions of adding Nice, Corsica, and Tunisia to his perceived Italian empire. The Fuhrer would only concede to agreeing not to sign an armistice until France signed with Italy. That did allow Mussolini a brief grace period to press the French on his own to acquire whatever territory his troops could seize by force of arms.

The Italians were only able to grab very little. In the Alps, Italian soldiers attacked through the Little Saint Bernard Pass, but were stalled by a snowstorm. An attack on the Riviera near Nice ground to a halt only five miles beyond the Italian border. In the end, all Italy had secured were few scant acres of French soil.

It was only at this point that Mussolini realized what he had gotten himself, and Italy, into. Adolf Hitler hardly needed him. And now the Germans refused to confide in him as to the campaign that lay ahead.

***

Franco and Rosalie Donato had been keenly aware of the transpiring world events, political and military, for quite some time. Besides the obvious fact of Rosalie's father continuing to languish in prison, they were rightly concerned and alarmed by Italy's military adventures and the Duce's plans and intentions for the country. Franco had shaken his head in disgust and disbelief at the Italian invasion of Albania in April 1939. To provide an excuse for the invasion, Count Ciano's lackeys in Albania had trumped up a revolution, on the pretext of restoring order among the people.

Upon their entry into Albania, the Italians only encountered feeble resistance, and the poor, downtrodden country was quickly overrun. Franco well knew that had the Albanians been able to make any kind of a stand, the invasion could have been turned into a disaster. Green troops had been mobilized at the last minute. Men with no experience with motorcycles were, of course, assigned to operate...motorcycles. Signal units had not even been aware of the Morse code to be sent out. A number of the infantrymen had never even fired their weapons before the invasion. Franco had been made aware, from friends who had participated in the operation, that the conquest of Albania had actually been a showpiece of ineptitude. "If the Albanians had possessed even one well-armed fire brigade," said a member of Ciano's staff, "they could have driven us back into the sea." Franco and Rosalie well-remembered the headlines and newspaper articles that had presented a far different picture to the world—that of a well-oiled Fascist war machine rolling effortlessly over its Albanian opposition.

So when the mail carrier brought their mail to them on a hot and sultry early August day, both Donatos did not suspect their world would become anything earth-shattering when they opened their mail. They were soon in for a shock. Rosalie took the packet from Alfredo DeSimone, their long-time carrier and sauntered back into the kitchen. Normally, she would not open any mail addressed to Franco, but that changed on that day when she noticed the return address of the Army Department. Rosalie's hands began to tremble and she felt tears well up in her eyes. She briefly contemplated for a minute to open the envelope, but she just placed the offending piece back down on the table.

"What is it, Mama?" asked a wide-eyed Rosanna when she saw her mother shaking with the piece of paper in her hands.

Rosalie quickly glanced at her little daughter in her child-like innocence and said, "Oh dear, it is nothing. Nothing at all," she lied. She hated doing this to Rosanna. The child would never understand why her father would soon have to leave them and possibly be sent off to a foreign land to have to fight all because of the insatiable and unmitigated greed of Benito Mussolini and his Fascist lackeys and sycophants. And that her father might be seriously wounded or even die. No, the little girl did not have to be presented with such stark and unpleasant facts.

***

Franco Donato had just opened the envelope from the Italian Army. He sat immobile for what to Rosalie seemed to have been several minutes before he said, "It seems as if the Duce will require my services in his campaign against the enemies of Italy." The venom dripping from his lips with every word.

At first, Rosalie said nothing as she watched her husband continuing to stare at the notice. She had suspected the nature of the letter that afternoon. "What will we do, Franco? I…I…don't know what Rosanna and I will do," she said plaintively, her red-rimmed eyes pleading for something more from Franco.

He looked up at his wife, "It seems that I do not have to report until the end of September. At least this will enable me, they say, to get my affairs in order. And then …then I am to report to the military entrance processing station in Catania. It will be at that time that I will commence my military service for the greater glory of Italy and, of course, our beloved Duce," said Donato bitterly. He began to crumple up the notice when he suddenly stopped. He would have to present it at the time of his induction.

"I don't know, Franco. I don't know whether I will be able to hold up under the pressure. My father is in prison and you will be going off to the army. And then there is our life here with Rosanna and the home… and…" Rosalie's voice trailed off.

Franco got up from his chair and walked behind Rosalie. He bent down to lift her up and embrace her. "You will have to be strong, dearest. It will not only be for me, but for Rosanna as well. I know you can do it. I know you will be able to do it. You're one of the strongest persons I know of."

Rosalie looked up at her husband and began to feel weak-kneed, as if she could feel the air within her body slowly seeping away and until her skin would unfold and collapse to the floor. Tears again formed in her eyes and they began to run down her cheeks. One found its way to the corner of her mouth.

"There, there, my Rosalie. Do not worry. I will take care of myself, I promise you. I will do my duty and then I will return to you and Rosanna, and we shall pick up where we have left off," said Franco, who really didn't believe his own words. He feared he might well be entering a potential death trap, what with the pathetic nature and condition of Italy's armed forces, at least where the army was concerned. He was likely to become a casualty because of the lack of food, or water, or...who knew.

Rosalie took Franco's hand and led them to their bedroom. Rosanna had been tucked into some two hours before. Both slowly undressed and lay down upon their bed. Rosalie turned to her husband and presented her breasts to him. He took them into his mouth and suckled them until her nipples hardened. They would make love slowly and caressingly, both totally engrossed in their bodies. Who knew how many more times they would have together. As Franco entered Rosalie, she took him in and at the moment of her climax had more tears streaming down her face.

***

"All right, Goncalo, I have summoned you here because I have some good news," said Paolo Cardelli as he looked up from his desk. "Yes, and the news is that you are to be assigned to a unit in North Africa. As you know, our glorious forces have advanced into Egypt and are doing furious battle with our British enemies," continued Cardelli, who now stood before Leo in a marshal like pose.

Leo wasn't sure he'd heard correctly. *North Africa?* With its intense and all-pervading heat and the absolute desolation, its... its absolute bleakness. No, he had never bargained for this. But...

"Yes, North Africa. Come on man, don't tell me this wasn't what you ever wanted. This will give you the chance to show everyone, the world, what kind of doctor, what kind of man you truly are. All right, Goncalo, I'll admit that it might sound like the end of the world, and quite frankly…it is. But there it is. You knew, or you had to know, that this day might come. And now, it has. But I do know that you're a fine doctor. You have what it takes. And that is not always easy to see. You have an instinctive feel of what is at hand. You know what to do. Look upon this as an opportunity."

Leo Goncalo began to go over his thoughts as he left Cardelli's office. He well knew that Mussolini had ordered Marshal Rodolfo Graziani to launch Italy's 10th Army across the Egyptian frontier on September 13th. After four days, the offensive had been halted, with Graziani pleading a lack of supplies and arms. The Italians were 60 miles inside of Egypt, but still some 80 miles from the British defenses at Mersa Matruh. Foreign Minister Galeazzo Ciano noted, "Never has a military operation been conducted so much against the will of the commanders."

Benito Mussolini threatened and cajoled Graziani with a barrage of furious telegrams to get his 10th Army moving again, but without success. The Italian Navy had also been reluctant to engage British naval forces in the Mediterranean. The Duce bitterly dismissed all Italians as, "too fond of drink and incapable of making decisions."

It would be into this muddled and emerging disaster of a campaign that Leo Goncalo would be embarking upon. He would soon learn that he was to be assigned to a Berseglieri unit in Libya. The Berseglieris were the elite troops of the Italian Army. The equivalent of the German paratrooper units and the British commandos. These men were the best of the best, the bravest. Men who would give their all to accomplish their objectives.

Still, Goncalo had in the back of his mind the thought that considering the actual state of Italy's armed forces, and especially the army, being the best of the best may not have meant much for the Berseglieri corps.

***

Rosalie stood looking out from her front picture window, desperately hoping she would see Franco returning. Just a short time before Franco had kissed her and little Rosanna good-bye. He hadn't wanted for Rosalie to see him off in town, it would "be better to say their farewells at home."

She already missed him dearly and wanted to believe, feared otherwise, that she might never see him again. True, he would go through basic training somewhere in the Naples area. And it was likely he would get the chance to see her and Rosanna upon its completion. Who knew. maybe, just maybe he would be posted to some rear-echelon unit, somewhere nowhere near any of the fighting. Perhaps even somewhere right there on Sicily.

***

Franco Donato was appalled, without speech, and stunned by what he saw when he arrived at boot camp. There was virtually nothing available to conduct even a modicum of the basics that would be required for an infantryman or a tank man, or a signals specialist to carry out their tasks. Equipment was lacking everywhere. There were not even a sufficient number of rifles available for manual of arms training and, of course, target shooting. Recruits were forced to share those weapons available, passing them back and forth to one another. Donato looked at all this and ruefully shook his head. How could Mussolini and his Black Shirt lackeys expect Italian soldiers to carry out missions against the well-trained and toughened Australians, New Zealanders, South Africans, as well as British troops. The army's basic problems were both material and organizational, and these in turn had a devastating effect on the men's morale and attitudes. Donato didn't know of the high-level view of such matters, but he could clearly see for himself that things were beyond being somewhat amiss.

Prior to Italy going to war, Mussolini had boasted of being able to mobilize "eight million bayonets," which the high command had massaged to their envisioning an army of ten million men (Italy only had a population of 40 million) and, ultimately, 12 million. In fact, the Italian Army had only enough equipment, uniforms, and barracks to house, at most, one million men. This helped to explain why Italy had never declared a general mobilization.

Material furnished to Francisco Franco's Spanish republican forces—a quarter million rifles, 1900 artillery pieces, and more than seven hundred aircraft—had not yet been replaced. And much of the army's remaining equipment was obsolete; rifles were so old that many were downright useless and horse-drawn artillery dated back to the First World War. Benito Mussolini then came up with the idea for a reduction in the number of army divisions from three regiments to two. This enabled him to falsely claim eighty divisions. Such was the calamity of a nation which couldn't call more men to arms. Later during the war the Duce would forget about how badly he had over-estimated the strength of his forces.

***

"I tell you, Donato, he is the devil incarnate himself," said a disgusted Private Rodolfo Armbrusto, a ruddy looking, slightly portly recruit from Palermo. "You know what some of the other men call him? Behind his back, of course."

"No, what?" asked a bemused Franco Donato.

"Bastico the bastard. I hate the man. He seems to get inordinate pleasure at being able to grind his boot into a recruit. Some day, some day, Donato, I am going to get even with him," threatened Armbrusto.

"I would keep things under my hat if I were you Rodolfo. You never know who may be listening. Besides, there could be a method to Sergente Bastico's seeming madness," said Donato to Armbrusto patiently. Franco liked the outspoken, seemingly brash Armbrusto. He said what came to mind and took no shit from anyone. Still, he would be better served if he could keep some of his thoughts to himself.

"And what is his method, if I might ask?"

"Well, he is being tough on us because he figures this will help to save our lives when we enter combat against the British and Australians. Or perhaps the Greeks," replied Donato to his distracted listener, who was attempting to sharpen his bayonet.

"The Greeks? I hate the fuckin Greeks. I hear that some of their men like to take it up the ass. Did you know that, Donato?" offered a now smiling Armbrusto. Franco thought it more resembled a smirk.

"I didn't know that. Thank you for the tip, Rodolfo."

"Not at all, Donato. And, know what else?"

"No, I can hardly guess at this one."

"I hear that Bastico likes it up the ass, as well," heehawed Armbrusto.

Franco looked at his friend and discerned a distinct resemblance to a braying mule. He shook his head and replied, "You know Rodolfo, sometimes I have to wonder about you. Still, I would adopt a lower tone and watch what I said. If Bastico finds out what you have been saying about him, he may want to grind his boot into you much deeper than what he is doing right now," advised Franco.

The men had to pick up the pace, Sgt. Bastico wasn't pleased. Not by a long shot. He cursed them and then accused them of being soft-hearted assholes.

"Hey, know what else, Donato?" asked a slightly winded Armbrusto.

"I can hardly guess. What else?"

"Some of our Fascist brothers-in-arms are marching around with wooden toy rifles. They are carrying pieces of wood, and no bullets, and we have to hoist around the real thing," said a disgusted Armbrusto.

"Rodolfo, to make up for the difference in weight those men have to carry bricks in their knapsacks."

"Oh, I didn't know that," said a momentarily chastened Armbrusto.

"Just try and relax, Rodolfo. Don't let yourself get too agitated. It won't change anything and it won't help you in the long run," said Franco, who privately agreed with his friend's assessment of their drill sergeant. The man truly was a bastard.

***

"Mama, mama, it's time to get up," said Rosalie wearily. She was running late and still had to make sure that she got Rosanna over to the Rosatis for the day. She had to get to Mettuno to take care of some family business. Business that Franco was supposed to have taken care of. But with his draft notice into the army and all had entailed he had forgotten.

"Mama, please," Rosalie repeated, then shaking the older woman's arm. Maria lay supine on her stomach. Rosalie instantly felt the touch of lifelessness in her mother's body. "Oh, no! Oh, no!" she cried. She then began to turn over the inert body of Maria Mancini. A look of pure serenity and peacefulness was displayed by the old woman. All of her demons and bad thoughts, and all of the unhappiness and bitterness she had built up and stored within her mind had finally been expunged.

Rosalie knelt over Maria and then bent her head toward the woman's wrinkled face. No breath emerged from her nose or mouth. Her chest did not rise and fall. In that instant, at that moment, Rosalie knew what the cause of death had been. Of course the coroner would say it was from some high-sounding, long-winded scientific term. To Rosalie, Maria's death was a direct result of her having suffered from a broken heart. All of the months, all of the waiting for Berto Mancini to be released, all of it had finally caused Maria's shattered heart to give out. She had no more to give to life.

In the days ahead, Rosalie was assisted by her younger brother, Aldo, in making the funeral arrangements. Older brother Federico, who should have been the one to take over the reins, as head of the household, had acted as if he could not be bothered. During all of the time of Berto's incarceration, Federico had visited only once. And, at that, the son had barely uttered a word to his long suffering father. It was not as if Federico had held any sort of grudge against Berto. It was more like the eldest son just didn't know what words to form, so as to provide some comfort to his mother. He could not bestow any kind of support. Rosalie, who had been present, also noted virtually no discernible expression upon her brother's face. It almost seemed as if he had been going through the obligatory motions of having to visit his father.

From that moment, Rosalie knew that it would be her, and, her alone who would have to bear the burden of contending with the likes of Carlo Goncalo and his devious and disruptive designs. She would have to carry the torch for her father. And, of course, she would have to continue to raise little Rosanna. And, not least, she would have to continue on with the family business. At one time, Rosalie had actually believed in the old proverb: "God only gives me what he knows I can handle." But at that very moment she knew she was at her breaking point. A breaking point that could have devastating consequences for all concerned.

The night of Maria Mancini's funeral, Rosalie sat at her kitchen table and began to compose a letter to her husband, informing him of Maria's passing. She knew he would be quite saddened at receiving the news. Rosalie also knew that Franco had always liked, and loved his mother-in-law.

Chapter Five

North Africa

Imagine listening to a narration of the Western Desert by the famed British actor Michael Rennie of the desert of western Libya in 1941. His impressive and impeccable intonation, pitch, and timbre resonating as he described the bleak and forbidding landscape that characterizes this part of the world. The eye takes in thousands of square miles of dry and desolate sand; unending waves of undulating sand crested into breathtaking, sweeping dunes. Little, if any, water falls upon this bleak vista. Water, and its limited presence, is the lifeblood of the little human life that may find itself there.

Since June 1940, the Western Desert had been the scene of the armies of the British Western Desert Taskforce locked in a death struggle with the forces of Fascist Italy. The Italians would eventually gain the assistance of Nazi Germany in February of 1941 with the entry of the German general Erwin Rommel. But first, it is necessary to set the stage for which caused the necessity of the Germans to have to come to the aid of their Fascist brethren.

***

Fifty-eight year old Marshal Rodolfo Graziani had been chosen by Benito Mussolini to lead Italy's North African campaign. A multi-medaled veteran of several previous desert campaigns, mostly against outgunned Libyan natives, was known behind his back as the "Butcher."

The Marshal had expected his task to have been one primarily of a defensive nature- that is, to simply guard the Libyan frontier against British in-roads from Egypt. Mussolini ordered him to advance some 300 miles into Egypt, and to capture the large British naval base at Alexandria.

At this directive, Graziani flew back to Rome to plead with the Duce and chief-of-staff, Pietro Badoglio. He argued that the Italians were no match for the British. He had motor transport for less than five battalions; some of his weapons actually belonged in the scrap heap. Graziani further argued that he was short of modern weapons: planes, tanks, artillery, even land mines. At some places along the Egyptian border Italian soldiers had been forced to pilfer British mines in order to sow their own minefields.

This bleak and discouraging picture could hardly have been a surprise to Mussolini and Badoglio. As already noted, the country's military adventures in Ethiopia and Albania had sapped much of Italy's military strength.

Still, Benito Mussolini hungered for some sort of victory, desperate for anything in North Africa. Graziani only received from him the words: "I only ask you to attack the British forces opposing you." Egypt, he predicted would prove to be a rich prize and its seizure "the final blow to Great Britain.

Mussolini then forced Graziani, ready or not, to move his troops into Egypt. And it had to be by early September. Graziani would have two days or he would be replaced.

At first, Graziani's pessimism seemed unfounded. Within four days his soldiers advanced more than 60 miles inside of Egypt. His men held the coastal settlement of Sidi Barrani. Rome Radio lost no time in proclaiming victory. "Thanks to the skill of the Italian engineers," it fatuously announced, "the tramcars are once again running in Sidi Barrani."

What Italian listeners couldn't fathom was that British forces had been ordered to carefully withdraw to a fishermen's village known as Mersa Matruh. The site had once been called Paraetomium, where Marc Antony and Cleopatra had frolicked in the blue sea waves of the Mediterranean.

(Mersa Matruh was the terminus of a rail line that ran from Alexandria.) This gave the British an important advantage if the Italians continued to advance their supply lines, they would become overextended and exposed to attack. The British could now wait for the right moment to launch a counterattack.

Rodolfo Graziani was unwilling to attack at Mersa Matruh, and, instead, ordered his men to dig in around Sidi Barrani. Outposts took on a leisurely air of a peacetime cantonment, including such refinements as colognes and silver hairbrushes for officers. Wells and gateways were emblazoned with rallying cries from Mussolini's speeches, such as "He who hesitates is lost" and "ever forward!"

Meanwhile, British commanding General Archibald Wavell bided his time, waiting for troop and armored reinforcements. However, Wavell also knew he needed more than just weapons to prevail upon and overcome the parched and desolate wasteland of the Western Desert. This area had expanded from western Egypt alone to include eastern Libya, a land area approximately 500 miles long by 150 miles wide. Behind a sandy plain along the Mediterranean lay a high desert plateau, much of its brownish colored expanse strewn with boulders and rocks.

The worst part this desert was the lack of distinctive landmarks. Traveling across it, (with the exception of the coastal road,) was the equivalent of sailing on an uncharted ocean, navigable only by sun, stars, and compass. The analogy between sea and desert warfare was such that each tank or truck was as individual as a destroyer, and every squadron of tanks made great sweeps across the desert as a battle squadron at sea.

General Wavell never contemplated a major offensive against the Italians. He had planned only for a mere five day raid with an objective of 25 miles. He had only 30,000 men: an amalgam of British, Irish, Cameron Highlanders, Sikhs and Hindus.

On the morning of December 6th (1940), two divisions moved out; most of General Bernard O'Connor's men believed they were only on a routine training exercise. Early on the ninth the British attacked in full force against the Italians, who had been in the midst of breakfast preparations. A breakfast never to be eaten.

Rank upon rank of tanks came rumbling in, and riding on their flanks were Bren gun carriers, their machine guns tilted so as to maintain a high-angle of fire against the startled Italian sentries. Then followed a sound strange to the Italians' ears: the sound of bagpipes as the Cameron Highlanders joined in the attack. The rising sun shimmering from the glint of steel of their bayonets. Italian cavalry horses panicked and stampeded in a wild mass through the drifting and noxious smoke.

The Italians stood no chance. British Matilda tanks destroyed more than 20 Italian tanks within minutes. Defenders tried mightily to fight back as best they could with machine guns and hand grenades: many fell bloodily beneath the Matildas' tracks. The stench of bursting and burning creosote barrels; Italian officers, swathed in heavy blue cavalry cloaks, desperately tried to rally their men.

By December 12 th, three days after the attack had begun, more than 39,000 Italians had surrendered or been captured. Unending lines of weary and dejected Italian men in dusty green uniforms choked the road to Mersa Matruh. The British denoted an immediate disenchantment with Fascism and Mussolini. Captured engineers, seeing British gunners set to work on new forward gun emplacements, promptly brought picks and shovels and pitched in to help.

General Wavell quickly realized that his limited five day raid had acquired the irresistible momentum of a major campaign. By the 16th of December, the British had taken Sollum and Halfaya Pass, and then moved into Libya to take Fort Cappuzzo and Sidi Omar.

Meanwhile, the relationship between Mussolini and Graziani was worsening by the day. The marshal accused the Duce of never having listened to him. Mussolini blamed his fighting men, as he always had when faced with a military disaster.

As to the immediate future, the Duce was to turn to an old friend and fighter: Lt General Annibale Bergonzoli, the commandant at Bardia, whose flaming red beard had earned him the sobriquet "Electric Whiskers." The general had a dynamic personality as well; during action in the Spanish Civil War, Bergonzoli had eaten and drunk with his men, and had slept in a simple tent.

Mussolini felt certain that "Electric Whiskers" and his brave men would stand their ground at whatever the cost. The Italians felt the British would have a difficult time in trying to capture Bardia. The attack would be conducted by the tough and grizzled men of the 6th Australian Division.

Bergonzoli never had a chance at any kind of success and by January 4th of 1941. He ordered the Italian flag to be hauled down from the Government House. The British took control of more than 40,000 new prisoners of war.

Disaster followed upon disaster for Italian fortunes in Libya. Tobruk and Derna soon fell to the British . And O'Connor's men then drove across Libyan Cyrenaica to cut off the retreating Italian forces beyond Benghazi. By first light of 7th February, O'Connor received word that Marshal Graziani had decamped to Tripoli and the army he had abandoned was surrendering; it could fight no longer.

On Sunday, February 9th, 1941, Major General Enno von Rentelen, Germany's military attaché in Rome, brought news that delighted Benito Mussolini. The Duce had been the recipient of almost constant bad news for weeks. A panzer division and a light mechanized division were being sent from Germany to Libya to act as a blocking force in Tripolitania in the western part of the country.

Germany was at long last coming to the rescue of Italy's and the Duce's fortunes in North Africa.

***

The Ariete Division was occupying ground somewhere to the east of Mechili in the Libyan Desert. There, Corporale Franco Donato and Private Rodolfo Armbrusto sat in their just dug-in foxhole. Both men looked out over the hardscrabble of land before them. Small rocks and boulders and a constantly blowing sand were all that one could see. Hardly an animal could ever be seen flitting about. This was always true during the daylight hours; At night small rodents like the field mouse would emerge in a hunt for food in the cracks and crevices of the parched earth. It was a land so bleak that the famed German General Erwin Rommel was once heard to remark: "The men of these armies are spilling blood and sacrificing their bodies over land the poorest Arab wouldn't bother his head over."

***

"Do you love your wife, Donato?" asked a pensive Rodolfo Armbrusto of his superior. Although Franco outranked his comrade he didn't mind, and never took offence at being referred to by his last name.

"Of course I do, Armbrusto," responded Franco. *What a question,* he thought.

"I know you do. I have seen her picture. A lovely looking woman, I must say. Do you think of her, and do you think, or can you picture…how can I say it?...Do you remember of intimate things?"

Donato knew where his comrade was going with his line of reasoning, but, he, at first, did not respond. After only a minute, Franco said, "I think of her every day, and my little girl as well. Sometimes I have to block them out or I can't do what I am here for. You know, to look out for guys like you, Armbrusto. But yes, I do think of us together: the curl of her hair, its golden color, the curve of her mouth. I think and I can imagine the feel of her breasts, and when she clamps her legs around my body when we make love. Yes, I do remember," said Franco longingly, who quietly realized he may have said too much to his compatriot.

As to Armbrusto, he had been surprised to hear Donato talk of lovemaking with his wife and it was not with the same feeling as Donato had just related. "When I think of my wife, I think of nearly ten years of pain. And for the past few years, when we have attempted intimacy I have preferred to think of it as making pain. Not making love, but making pain," mused a wistful Armbrusto.

"I am sorry, Armbrusto. I really am."

"You know, when I received the Duce's draft notice, I practically jumped for joy. At last, I would be freed from the clutches and the bitching of Angelina. I would be released from the torment of my two boys. Boys who have caused almost nothing but trouble, whether in our home or at school. But one can one expect of children who see their parents engaged in daily conflict. Always bickering, always finding fault with the other." Armbrusto suddenly halted his diatribe. Donato looked at the man and thought he looked exhausted, not only physically, but spiritually as well.

"Well, Rodolfo, here you are in the middle of nowhere. Your Angelina cannot get at you from here, can she?" asked Franco, attempting to elicit a small laugh from his friend. He had no idea the man was being assaulted by so many inner demons. Franco had seen Armbrusto as a rather jovial person, someone who always seemed to be able to keep others around him loose. Apparently, this had all been a façade to mask a deep, inner pain.

"You know what, Donato?" Armbrusto suddenly asked.

"No, what?"

"When I get the chance, I am going to make a break for the other side. I mean it. I am going to do it. Just think, to spend the rest of the war in relative comfort in a British or Canadian prison camp."

Donato could not believe what he had just heard. His friend had simply gone mad. Maybe he hadn't received enough water. Or perhaps he had fallen off a truck and hit his head. "I would be careful if I were you, my friend. You may never know who may be listening."

"You mean Sergente Bastico. I don't care if he hears me. I've gotten long past caring. Look at us, not only you and me, but this so-called army of ours out here in this God forsaken wasteland. We are out here to die. To die, I tell you, Donato. Mussolini doesn't give three shits about us. Look about you, our weapons, our vehicles, everything. Look at us compared to our German allies. Do you see how they look at us? How they look down on us? I see them as sneering at us." Armbrusto had picked up steam again.

Franco reached over and gently patted Armbrusto's arm. He had to agree with the man's arguments. It was plain for all to see. The Italian Army, the air force, the navy, Italy herself had not been anywhere close to being ready when Benito Mussolini had cast his lot with Adolf Hitler. "Quiet down, my friend. Bastico is sure to hear us or maybe one of his lapdog lackeys who overhears you. I can just picture Carbone running to him with glee to inform on you."

And he was right. At that very moment, Luigi Carbone had heard virtually every word that had emerged from Rodolfo Armbrusto's mouth. At first chance, he went to Sergeant Bastico with his information. Carbone could not wait to see what kind of punishment the sergeant would mete out to the wayward and treacherous Rodolfo Armbrusto.

***

"Hey, hey, Donato. Donato?! Wake up, there is something out there," hissed an agitated Armbrusto to Franco.

"Haaa, what is it?" questioned the slumbering Donato.

"Donato, I tell you there is something out there," insisted Armbrusto as he vigorously shook Franco's arm.

"It's probably just a field mouse," replied Donato as he continued to shift his weight in the foxhole. Slowly, gradually be became awakened. Above him the night sky was clear and near perfect. Stars dotted the purplish stained background. He shivered as the desert's night chill encumbered his body. The great coat he was wearing afforded some warmth from the cold, but only to a minimum.

"A field mouse, you say? No, a field mouse doesn't make a scraping sound, unless one were to wear a size nine shoe," continued Armbrusto.

Fully awake, Franco looked out over the lunar landscape of the desert around Mechili. There, he saw something. Yes, Armbrusto had not been hallucinating, he had not seen a mirage.

"Yes, yes, I see, wait…one…two men. They must be Australians, a night patrol out to probe our lines." Franco quickly and quietly got to his feet and went off to find Sergeant Bastico.

"I know, Donato. I have seen them. Capelli, send up a flare directly of our position. Let's shed a little light on the subject," said Bastico in his clear and authoritative voice.

Capelli did as he had been ordered. The star shell flare burst high in the dark-tinted Libyan sky, resembling a firework one might well see at an amusement park. The light cascaded over the immediate front of the Italians. Instantly, four men, Australians, were exposed. They paused like the proverbial deer in the headlights. Franco could clearly make out that none of the enemy were wearing steel helmets, so as not to create any additional sounds as they moved about in the night.

Almost at once the Italians' guns, rifles and machine guns coughed into action. Two of the Australians went down almost immediately in a heap, as if they had been sacks of cement. Another managed to scamper off for a little before he, too, collapsed. The last man had been able to effect his escape as he disappeared off into the Libyan night. Then suddenly silence reigned.

"Donato, Armbrusto, check them out," ordered Bastico. "But be careful, take no chances."

"*Si, Sargente*," responded Franco. "Come on Armbrusto, let's go."

Armbrusto said nothing, but only gathered his Mannlicher-Carcano rifle, its bayonet attached, reflecting a glint off the moonlight cast down upon the scene.

Franco slowly approached the first Australian, kneeing the man to see whether he might still be alive. The inert body did not stir. Donato reached down to turn the man over. On his right temple appeared a bullet hole having made a clean entry. There was little blood around the wound, but a gurgle had emerged from the dead man's mouth. Franco reached over and felt his way into the soldier's smock pockets. From the right one he extracted a photograph of a young blond-haired woman. She appeared to be about 20 or 21 years old. Franco could see that the young woman was quite attractive in her white swimsuit. She had a gorgeous face, full lips, and long, smooth legs. Undoubtedly the man's wife or girlfriend. *Too bad,* mused Donato.

Franco replaced the picture back into the pocket and moved onto the next man. Only as Donato approached he could hear a soft moaning. This one was still alive. Franco would have to be very careful and circumspect in his inspection of this Australian. Who knew, the man could well be concealing a pistol or even a knife, or even possibly a hand grenade, willing to take himself and Donato to the promised land.

Franco and Armbrusto struggled with their Australian prisoner as they made their way back to their platoon's position. Once there, they gently deposited the man to the ground. The man was conscious, but clearly was in great pain from a leg wound and an abrasion to his right arm. He moaned while calling out the name Lisa, probably the wife or girlfriend back somewhere in Australia.

Sgt. Bastico stood over the man, assessing the situation. "All right, this man is clearly in distress. That leg wound looks bad. Capelli, get some bandages, something, and apply pressure to the wound," he ordered. Armbrusto, get over to the *Tenente* and inform him that we have a prisoner who has been badly wounded. *Subito*!"

"*Si, Sargente*," said Armbrusto as he snapped off a quick salute to his noncom.

"Now, my friend, ahhh, he is starting to come to," said Bastico. He then took out his field knife from its scabbard and knelt down over his prisoner. "Lisa, you say. Who is Lisa? Never mind. Donato, you translate, as you seem to be the most conversant in English."

Franco nodded and waited for Bastico to begin the interrogation.

"Ask him who he is and what he and his friends were doing?" directed Bastico.

"*Si, Sargente,* answered Franco as he translated the sergeant's question into English.

The Australian slowly turned his head toward Franco. "Go to hell, you Eyetie bastards," he spat out as if he had just been administered poison.

Franco hesitated.

"Never mind. I think I know what he said. Cheeky fellow. So, you don't want to cooperate. You choose to be a hard case. All right, have it your way," said Bastico, who then applied the flat of his bayonet to the Australian's leg wound.

That slightest of pressures caused the man to wince in pain. "Fuck you, you bastard. Torturing a prisoner. All of you can go straight to bloody hell!"

"All right, Donato. I can see that this man doesn't want to cooperate with us, so why waste any more time with him. We will wait to see what Lieutenant Montella wants to do with him. Probably send him back to battalion to see if they can get anything out of him. Meanwhile, let's see to it that the bugger doesn't die on us."

***

"Armbrusto, take Private Damiano with you and bring the prisoner over to battalion HQ. See if you guys can find a cart or something, that will make things easier for you. And, for God's sake, make sure he doesn't die on you. I think he may be able to provide some information," Bastico ordered.

Armbrusto and Damiano each took one end of the stretcher and lifted the Aussie off the ground. He didn't seem to be that big of a fellow, and that made it a little easier for the two men to get him over to the battalion.

While on the way, they passed by *Tenente* Montella where they were able to procure a two-wheeled cart. The Australian continued to moan and twist about as he was placed into its straw-lined body. Armbrusto noticed that the bleeding had subsided from a short time before.

"Eh, Armbrusto, good thing the battalion is only a short distance from here," commented Damiano

"I suppose, but this cart is not really making things any easier for us," complained the once jovial Armbrusto, who was beginning to perspire, despite the chill in the desert air. He stole a glance at the star-filled sky and for some unfathomable reason a picture of his Angelina appeared before him. At this he nearly dropped his end of the stretcher. *It couldn't be, could it? Why that ungrateful bitch and no good wife. Had he really meant what he had said to Donato? Did he?"* Yes, every word of it. He really hoped he would get the chance to go over to the English.

At long last, after grunting and groaning for what had seemed like hours, Privates Armbrusto and Damiano arrived at the battalion headquarters. The adjutant took one look at the Australian and directed that he be taken to the surgeon for treatment of his wounds.

"All right, men, I'll take it from here, said the handsome and urbane young surgeon. Armbrusto noticed his name tag identified the man as Goncalo. In any event, the doctor soon said, "*Bene*, you fellows did a fine job in getting this man here. I am Capitano Goncalo. Please, one of you has to sign this form signifying as having brought in a prisoner of war.

The pair were a little stunned to have heard a compliment directed at them, especially one from an officer. Armbrusto took hold of the offered pen from Goncalo and proceeded to scribble his name on it.

A short time later, Armbrusto and Damiano returned to their unit.

"I see that you accomplished your mission, Armbrusto," said Franco half-mockingly. He always took a small measure of enjoyment when he needled Armbrusto, who always seemed to take it good-naturedly. He really was, at least, a good egg, despite Bastico always seeming to take an opportunity to disparage him. Oh well, it was what seemed to come with the power of command, even it was only between a sergeant and a lowly private.

"Oh, you know how it is, Donato. Whatever it takes for us to help the Duce and his grand campaign here in North Africa, and the world, or, at the very least, his Libyan conquest," replied Armbrusto as he began to untie and loosen his boots. The transfer of the prisoner had nearly killed his already badly blistered and aching feet. "Well, we got the Aussie over to battalion and then deposited him with the doctor. A rather pleasant chap. He even gave us a compliment. A fellow by the name of Goncalo."

Armbrusto had hardly gotten the words out of his mouth when Franco's eyes opened wide and he snapped his head around toward Armbrusto.

"Did you say Goncalo?"

"*Si, si*, Goncalo. Why Donato?"

"Leo Goncalo?"

"I don't know, he only said he was Capitano Goncalo," replied a now mystified Armbrusto. Why?" Does he mean anything to you?"

"No, no, I'm not sure," said Franco. *Could it be? Was it possible?*

My dearest Rosalie,

I miss you and Rosanna each and every day. I wish I that I could be home with the two of you. Here in the Libyan Desert things are as to be expected. We had some action the other day, not much, but, at least, it broke up the boredom. Do not worry, I am safe. And so is my good friend, Rodolfo. He really is quite a character. To look at him you might not think very much of him. But he really is a good guy and I'm very lucky to be serving with him.

How is your father? I still cannot believe what has been done to him. Any news as to when he might be released? Oh, you would never believe what I came across the other day. As I said, we had a little action and we took one of the enemy as a prisoner. The man had been badly wounded. Armbrusto and another man took the prisoner to the battalion aid station for treatment. And who do you think was the attending doctor? You would never have guessed it, but it turned out to be a Dottore Goncalo. Yes, that's right, the son of that malicious bastard, Carlo Goncalo. I'm sure of it. I know I shouldn't speak in that way, but if I should ever come across this guy I may be unable to resist sticking a shiv into him. I know, I'm attributing guilt by association. But I can't help it, after what his father has done to you, and to us.

I am going to finish up now. I have to attend to some things for my men. Do not worry, I will try and stay safe. Give a big hug and kisses to Rosanna for me. And, I give, one, figuratively, to you. All my love.

Your everlasting love,
Franco

PS: Rodolfo Armbrusto is apparently in a loveless marriage. He simply cannot stand his wife, or his children. I know this could never happen to us. Again, all of my love.

***

Rosalie was seated by the window of the home she now shared with her brother Aldo and her sister. And, of course, there was little Rosanna. It was nighttime, rains that had poured down all day long had ceased for the moment. The weather had brought on a feeling of melancholia, something one tried desperately to shake, to no avail. When the postman delivered the mail, Rosalie felt a surge of adrenaline, especially when she saw that the mail packet included a letter from Franco.

Rosalie opened the envelope with a carving knife, a glass of Chianti on the table next to her. Of late, she had taken to drinking more of it. She didn't think it had gotten to the point where it should be a concern, but still she felt it was something for her to think about. Straightening out the letter, she noted her husband's distinctive handwriting, not quite a scrawl, but it never would have won any penmanship awards. Rosalie read with relief that her dearest was well and seemed to be in good spirits. It was something, a dread, that she lived with day to day. Lately, perhaps it had been due to her increased wine intake, she had been handling her anxiety better.

Rosalie stiffened in her seat when she read Franco's words describing about Capitano Goncalo. The son, the ardent Fascist. The offspring of that pig, Carlo Goncalo.

She did not share Franco's regret regarding his castigation of the son of the man they both hated. No, Rosalie now burned with an anger that Leo Goncalo was poisoned fruit. Poisoned fruit that fell from a poisoned tree. She then was brought back to her recent visit to her father. The poor man had seemed to wither from the time of her last visit. An air of hopelessness enveloped him, it was in his eyes and wrinkled face. Rosalie had barely been able to get him to speak. And worse, the Prefect, Fanti, had been hinting that Berto Mancini might be moved to another jail, perhaps even one on the mainland. Perhaps to a prison in Rome. If that happened she would not be able to see him. Rosalie would be unable to offer Berto any comfort, or love, even as little as what she had able to do thus far. She also thought that Fanti might just be teasing her or, more likely, just enjoying the fact he could torment her and her family. She well-remembered the Prefect denying her father the opportunity to attend his wife's funeral. He was still classified as an enemy of the state. The cold- hearted, ruthless bastard. The man would probably be willing to see his own mother or father classified as an enemy of the state, if Rome decreed it.

Rosalie put down the letter and proceeded to finish her wine. Then, and she knew she shouldn't do it, she went to the liquor cabinet and reached for the brandy. Pausing momentarily, she poured herself two fingers of the amber colored liquid and quickly downed it. Its warmth and fire coursing down her throat. Rosalie then sat down heavily. It was imperative that she keep her head. She couldn't allow her brain to become clouded because of her being inebriated. But the brandy had felt good. Shaking her head, Rosalie gave thought to Rosanna, now sleeping peacefully in her bed. Above it all, Rosalie had to protect, nurture, and love the child.

***

A thick and hazy fog had hung over Mettuno for the better part of two days, which only added to the fugue that Alberto Cardi's mind had settled into. How he wished he had never acceded to the evil designs and machinations of Carlo Goncalo. Today he had once again been summoned, as if he were a dutiful school-boy being ordered to report to the schoolmaster's office. He had had to admit to himself that his conscience had finally gotten the better of him. To know that a man, a decent and honorable man, was sitting and rotting in a jail cell on completely trumped up and false charges.

"You are looking well today, Alberto," remarked Carlo

Goncalo sat imperiously in his newly purchased oaken framed high-back chair. "I do hope that everything is going well. How is your lovely and charming wife by the way?" asked Goncalo in a barely believable tone.

Cardi knew that Goncalo had hardly ever bothered to ask about his wife before. "*Grazie*, Carlo, she is doing well and sends her best regards to you and your family," replied a deflated Cardi. He had almost called the man Don Carlo, as if were a Mafia don, which, in effect, he had become. The Mafia may well have been vanquished by Mussolini, but Carlo Goncalo had moved into the role smoothly and effortlessly.

"*Bene, bene*, I am so glad to hear it, Alberto," soothed Goncalo in an oily manner. "Now, to get down to business, Nando here has reported to me that some of the land you appropriated from the Mancinis has been lying fallow, completely unproductive. I assume you must have a good reason for this," said Goncalo, but it was no longer in a friendly or paternal way.

At first, Alberto Cardi said nothing, but his stomach was beginning to churn, and it wasn't just from having eaten some disagreeable food. Unconsciously, he was twisting his fingers together, a nervous tic causing his right eye to flutter. He well thought he might be on his way to a heart attack or, at the least, a severe panic attack.

"Well Alberto, I am waiting. Surely you must have some good reason for this. Come now, my old friend, you can speak to me, man to man," again soothed Goncalo, but the look on his sternly crossed face belied anything that could be construed as calmness.

Cardi looked over at Nando, seated quietly in a corner of the forbidding room. The youngest of Goncalo's sons, he was a man with a ruthless reputation, perhaps more so than his crocodilian father. It was common knowledge in and around Mettuno that young Nando and his gang of youthful toughs were to known to periodically rough up those who failed to heed warnings or show the proper respect to his father. A number of farmers and common people had been beaten, some so severely, as to have required medical attention. And this had been because some of them had been unable to pay tribute to Carlo Goncalo. The more Cardi thought of it, the more Nando resembled a crocodile in his own right. A young man who enjoyed and took pleasure in seeing someone beaten, or worse, bludgeoned to the point of death. Cardi began to tremble. "I promise you, Carlo, I will rectify the matter at once." It had been all Alberto Cardi had been able to bring himself to say.

"*Bene, bene,* my good friend," oozed Carlo Goncalo. And to help you along, I am going to delegate that my son Nando here be assigned to your operation. I have no doubt that he'll be able to greatly assist you, and to facilitate operations to our mutual satisfaction." And with that Carlo Goncalo sat back into his chair as if he had just digested a wonderful and filling meal of veal piccata.

"*Si, si,* that is most kind of you, Carlo. And thank you for providing the services of your son," replied a chastened and fearful Cardi. But in the back of his churning mind he was well aware of what would happen with Nando being on the scene. The books would be falsified, cooked beyond recognition. Nando Goncalo would secretively raid the piggybank. It wouldn't be beyond young Nando to conduct some of his well-known extortion schemes from Cardi's base. But Alberto Cardi was powerless to resist. He dearly wished he could dig a hole in his yard and jump into it. He knew he had never been meant to assume the role of a heavy. He was nothing at all like the ilk of Carlo Goncalo, or Nando Goncalo. Nothing at all like them.

***

By the approaching fall of 1941, Italian troops in Libya had gotten used to playing second fiddle to their erstwhile German allies. For the public in Italy, a brave and false front was put on about how fraternal and brotherly relations were between the forces of the two nations. Each of them had their men putting their proverbial shoulders to the wheel in the on-going campaign against the Allied infidels.

But in truth, there was little brotherhood between the Germans and Italians. There was little trustworthiness between the two. In fact, German officers and men openly spoke contemptuously about their supposed allies. Their poor and totally lacking equipment, the poor condition and attitude of the regular soldiers of the army, and the martinesque manner of the officer corps. Rommel himself had virtually no use for them and only utilized them to serve in the role of a blocking force, oftentimes, because he could not spare German troops.

In early September, the men of the Ariete Division found themselves somewhere in the vicinity of the Gazala Line in northern Cyrenaica in Libya. Darkness blanketed the open desert before Franco Donato and company. The welling darkness was of a shade slightly paler than pitch black. Donato and Armbrusto had settled themselves into a foxhole they had excavated that very day. Franco had made sure it was more than deep enough, just in case they were attacked. He had the watch. Franco didn't expect anything to happen, beyond perhaps a scouting mission of the Australians, or of Indian troops under British command. The enemy had almost never mounted a nighttime attack, at least, one that Franco could remember.

Just after midnight, the area in front of the battalion was suddenly lit up as one might expect to see during a fireworks display in mid-summer. Just then, the Italians began to receive artillery fire. To Franco this had all the makings of a major attack. He knew the front had been too quiet, there had been moments when there had been too much time to think: To think of home, and loved ones, like Rosalie and Rosanna, and friends. That was all over now. The night air was rent through with loud crashes and bangs, and swirling smoke. It was a world of the bizarre.

For a brief moment, Franco wasn't sure, but he thought he'd heard the grinding engine sounds of tanks. *Could they be Italian? Or German? No, you fool!* He thought to himself, *these are British tanks.* Most likely Matildas, the heaviest armor in the British arsenal. Slow-moving and under gunned, these beasts were nevertheless quite formidable because of their heavy, nearly impervious armor plating. Italian anti-tank guns were virtually useless against them, their projectiles would just bounce off the Matildas as if they were tennis balls.

Franco and Armbrusto lay next to one another, the ground beginning to quake and shake beneath them as the Matildas advanced inexorably toward them. One of the tanks discharged its main gun, the resulting explosion tore up the ground just to the front of Franco. Dust and smoke swirled around him, and his hearing departed him, a loud and persistent ringing permeated through his eardrums. As if in a daze, Franco checked to see if he had been wounded. A minute before he believed he may well have been dead. Quickly looking himself over he couldn't detect any obvious wounds. Franco then looked to his right and found the back of Armbrusto. He wasn't moving.

"Rodolfo, Rodolfo, are you all right?" shouted Franco, trying to be heard above the maelstrom. There was no answer or movement. He turned Armbrusto's body around so as to face him. But now there was no face to Rodolfo Armbrusto. Now there were only black holes where his eyes, nose, and mouth had once been. Shuddering with shock and revulsion, Franco let go of his friend and pushed Arnbrusto over, so he wouldn't have to look at the ghastly sight. Armbrusto was now at peace. He wouldn't have to go back his wife and her yammering and complaining. For a lingering moment, Franco conjured up a thought of Rosalie and Rosanna. He could barely picture their faces. The fleeting images of them went away. He now had to turn his attention to the matter at hand.

One of the Matildas, probably the one that had killed Armbrusto, was approaching the very spot where he was situated. Slowly, the British tank moved in Franco's direction. Desperately trying to clear his fog-enshrouded head, he tried to recall what his training had instructed him to do when faced with a tank about to roll over him. Franco scrunched his body into a near ball as he hugged the bare ground. He tried, as best he could, to allow for the tank to just roll over him. *Yes,* he thought, *the tank's treads will pass by me. I will be safe.*

Onward the flaming monster came. The noise from its roaring engine deafening Franco even more. Ever so slowly, too slowly for Franco, the machine eventually passed over him. Now, inevitably, would follow the infantry. But Franco was now faced with the fact that his rifle had been rendered useless, resembling a frayed matchstick. He desperately looked about him. There, about ten feet away lay a Beretta machine gun, a belt of ammunition attached to it. Franco slowly and cautiously crawled over to it and grabbed hold of it. All around him was a blaring cacophony of sound and fury. All of his time in North Africa had failed to prepare him for this. This was truly the end of the world-his world. Righting the gun, Franco took aim at the British infantrymen who had been following the tanks. At first, he could not make out very much, too much smoke wafted above the desert floor. To the right and the left of him, Franco began to pick out several of his buddies, including Sgt. Bastico, who was calmly trying to issue orders amidst the chaos.

As if he had been viewing the events out of an apparition, Franco at last saw a approaching men: bearing rifles with long bayonets attached. Bayonets meant to impale and slaughter him and his comrades. But not today, and not now. Franco checked his newly acquired firearm and then prepared to fire it at the enemy. He looked over to Bastico who had raised his right hand, indicating to await his command to fire. Just as Bastico swung his arm down, he was felled by a bullet that had found its way to the center of his forehead. It was right between his unseeing eyes.

Franco pressed the trigger of the MG which barked out a string of fire at the scattered British infantry. He could see the enemy being cut down as if a scythe had been employed. Arms, legs, and bits and pieces of brain matter and gore flew out from the enemy troopers. It was a scene out of Dante's Inferno. Franco kept his finger on the trigger until the barrel of the gun began to glow red. By this time, he had been joined by another soldier he didn't recognize. The man must have been from another company. He had brought with him an additional belt of machine gun ammo. Franco's new friend began to calmly feed the ammunition into the Beretta. The pair worked together seamlessly as a team. At least some of their basic training had kicked in at a critical time. After what had seemed an eternity, the roar of the battle began to subside. Franco's hearing had partially returned to its near normal state.

At the very moment as Franco had begun to believe that the fight was over, he was suddenly and violently heaved from the ground by a mighty explosion. He had become a victim, joining so many of his comrades, of an accurately placed Australian mortar round. Franco's world began to fade into blackness.

***

As if he were coming out of a fog, Franco Donato, was not quite sure as to where he was. *Was he still alive?* Of that he was uncertain. He felt like he was on a cloud floating above terra firma, and he was looking down upon the proceedings. His blurry eyes began to focus on the here and now, and as the fog began to lift he took in a man hovering over him. To Franco, it couldn't be, this man leaning over him was someone he had been familiar with back in Mettuno. But who was he? *No, it couldn't be him. Leo Goncalo?*

"I think our young friend is starting to come around," came the soothing words of Dottore-Capitano Leonardo Goncalo, to the attending nurse at his side, Francesca Gallo.

Gallo did not reply to Goncalo, but continued prepping Franco for surgery. He had taken shrapnel to his upper body and arms, courtesy of the Australians' mortar.

"Yes, my friend, you are quite lucky. Oh, things will be somewhat painful, at least, for a while. But you have what they call the lire dollar wound. Or is it the million dollar wound? I do not know, I get confused with the idioms of the Americans. In any event, your wounds are serious and not to be taken lightly. We are going to prepare you for surgery to remove some of that shrapnel. But don't worry you are in good hands. Eh, Francesca?" said Goncalo.

"*Si, si, Dottore,* in quite good hands," replied Francesca as she slyly eyed Goncalo. The young and comely young woman had been the doctor's consort for the past two months. With her dark, deep-set brown eyes, curvaceous mouth, buxom chest, and long slender legs, Francesca Gallo had become quite the catch for Leo Goncalo. Even now, he had begun to fantasize about the two of them in bed together, her legs fiercely gripping around his torso as he thundered away on her body.

For the moment, Goncalo had to place those lascivious thoughts to the side. After all, he had a gravely injured patient to attend to.

Franco heard the man prattle on and about his physical state, and there being some sort of preparation going on. And he was aware of the hovering presence of someone else. Then, he caught a glimpse of Francesca Gallo: her extraordinary beauty and the fulsomeness of her body.

"Leo Goncalo, who would have thought it possible? To be treated by you. I never in a million years could have conceived of it," said a consciously clearing Franco.

"I'm here to help you, Donato. I'm doing the job I have been entrusted with by the army. I do not carry any personal animus toward you, or to your family."

Franco continued to gaze up at Leo, his personal loathing of the man building within him. What his father had done to the Mancinis: Mancini senior, and Rosalie, he did not think he could ever forgive.

In the background, the sounds of battle had started to recede. Here and there, one could make out the occasional crump of an artillery or mortar detonation. But these were now off in the distance. The battalion hospital was safe. For the moment.

As if reading Franco's thoughts, Leo Goncalo said, "Do not worry my friend, I will not cut you up with my scalpel. I'm only my father's son. I am not like him or my brothers."

"But you're an ardent Fascist, just like your father. And my wife's own father continues to languish in one of il Duce's hell-hole jails. And for having done nothing wrong, except for the fact that he was a thorn in the side of your father's ambitions. Everyone knows that Alberto Cardi is just a stooge, a front man for your father's designs," Franco was becoming heated.

Goncalo placed his hands on Franco's heaving chest. "Now, now, my friend. You must calm down. It does you no good to become agitated and excited. When you come out of surgery, you and I can have an earnest discussion about our families."

Leo then placed an oxygen mask over Franco's nose and mouth and instructed his patient to breathe slowly and deeply. Franco Donato began to soon drift off into a deep and restful peace.

Chapter Six

The Englishman

In mid-November, on the eve of Operation Crusader, Lt. General Alan Cunningham and his fellow officers and men were buoyantly optimistic. On the surface, they had every reason to be. The British War Office had spared no effort nor expense to provide insurance to the operation's success. The new 8th Army was composed of 118,000 men, more than 700 tanks, 600 field guns, 200 anti-tank guns, and was equipped with a vast number of support vehicles and weapons. And, what was more, it had the close ground support of the newly strengthened Desert Air Force, which now would possess nearly 600 aircraft.

Meanwhile, on the Axis side of the ball, Erwin Rommel wasn't as nearly as well off as Cunningham. He had managed to create a new division—called the 90th Light Division—from smaller caballed units already in North Africa. But he hadn't received any reinforcements from Europe since June. His command had been redesignated a new name: Panzer Group Africa. It included the Africa Corps (15th and 21st Panzer Divisions and the 90th Light), and two Italian Corps, totaling six divisions. Rommel did have, in his possession, about 119,000 troops, but only 400 tanks (150 of them Italian relics).

Cunningham's ambitious attack plan called for the armored XXX Corps, under the command of Lt. General C.W.M. Norrie, to advance westward from 8th Army HQ at Fort Maddalena, about 50 miles from the coast, and then swing around the German defenses, which ran from Bardia on the coast to Sidi Omar.

Once XXX Corps outflanked the German lines, two of its units, 22nd and 7th armored brigades, would move northwest to Gabr Saleh. Cunningham was expecting Rommel to send his panzer units to Gabr Saleh, where the British tanks would then engage and destroy them. This would allow the British to be free to swing either northwest to Africa Corps HQ at Bardia or northwest toward the beleaguered fortress at Tobruk.

Erwin Rommel, however, had made plans of his own. He had finally been able to win a grudging assent from the German High Command for a renewed assault on Tobruk. The British fortress, occupied by Australian soldiers, had been invested by his own units and by Italian troops. By early November, Rommel had begun to move his own German divisions from the Egyptian frontier toward Tobruk. He then planned to strike at the British on November 21st.

Cunningham's British soldiers were ready for him. At dawn on November 18th the XXX Corps Brigades crossed the frontier at Fort Maddalena and fanned out across the desert.

Alan Cunningham didn't receive an immediate reaction from Rommel. He was still preoccupied with his planned assault on Tobruk, and he hadn't had any forewarning at all of the British attack. The British assault caught him off guard.

Meanwhile, Alan Cunningham, still hadn't had any reaction from the Germans. The next day sent columns probing west to Bir el Gubi and Sidi Rezegh. This caused Rommel to begin to doubt his original assessment of what the British were up to. He allowed some of his panzers to meet the British columns head on. The result was a series of intense, isolated engagements that cost the British some fifty tanks. And it was here that Lieutenant George Sloan found himself in battle for the first time in his life. To the young man from Oxted, England it was a most frightening baptism.

As far as George could see German tanks were everywhere, most likely Mark IIIs and Mark IVs, from what he had been previously able to discern from intelligence reports. Clouds of dust, interrupted by the occasional explosion, filled the choking air around him. As a precaution, George had tied a bandanna around his mouth and nose and pulled down his black-outlined goggles. But still, it was a nightmare. A nightmare that would only grow worse over the coming hours.

"Hold your positions! Hold your positions!" urged Sloan's company commander, Captain Andrew Dowell. Some of the 4th Brigade's men desperately tried to do so. Sloan still wasn't quite sure where most of the men of his platoon were. First squad, under Sergeant Jonathan Perry, was close by. Sloan had come to rely on the older and experienced Perry, being that he was relatively new to the desert; he'd arrived less than a month before. Perry, for his part, was able to hold his men steady. George Sloan had to admire the man as he stood erect with his Thompson submachinegun cradled in his large hands. The man had once been a dynamic and feared rugby player in England. In 1940, he had been voted to the All-England team.

"Sergeant Perry, don't you think you should take cover?" asked Sloan, having to shout at the top of his voice so as to be heard over the growling sounds of the panzers. George feared the man might well be blown to bits at any moment.

"Just trying to steady the lads, sir," replied Perry calmly. "You there, Comley, take aim carefully and squeeze off the rounds. Don't jerk your Enfield. It doesn't take kindly to that sort of treatment."

George Sloan began to discern the outline of the German infantry, accompanying the tanks. Careful and coordinated fire from the British ranks began to pick off this infantry.

Suddenly, great clumps of earth began to fall upon the advancing Germans. Supporting artillery from the 4th Brigade six pounder howitzers were finding their mark. Captain Dowell's request, or had it been an order ? had been right on the money. Dowell had risked the lives of his own men when he called in his coordinates virtually on top of his own. But it had been a risk he had been forced to make. It was one of the obligations and requirements of command.

Gradually, the German attack began to lose steam, the panzers, after seeing the loss of several of their tanks, started to fall back. German infantry hurriedly tried to jump onto the retreating tanks and scurry away from the battlefield.

George Sloan felt, at long last, as if he could breathe in again. It was over, for the moment, and he had survived. Despite having been in fear for his life, he felt as if he had carried himself quite well. He had been prepared to jump out of his skin, but he'd held steady and guided his men, as any good leader would have done.

Still, 4th Brigade's day could only be characterized as having been one of disaster. Rommel's 15th Panzer Division had practically driven it from the field. It overran the brigade's headquarters and captured the brigade commander. Overall, in the outcome of the day's fighting the British lost an airfield, more than 100 tanks, and some 300 men.

George Sloan and the men of his unit fell back as they had been ordered to. That night, George found himself in the back of a lorry, most likely a Bedford 6x6. He wasn't sure as to where his unit was heading, but only that it was away from the carnage of the day. Drifting in and out of consciousness, he began to recount some of the days he had experienced growing up in Oxted.

***

Low and scudding clouds danced their way across the nighttime sky over the campus grounds of Pembroke Public Preparatory School, some ten miles outside of greater London.

"Come on, come on, George, my man. We don't have all day," urged George Sloan's close and good friend, Archie Collins. The 15 year old youths were engaged in a prank that involved the headmaster of the school, Mr. Arthur Digginham Clarke III. A stern and pedantic man in his early forties, he was a man who didn't suffer fools gladly. He had never been known to possess a sense of humor. Some attenuated this to having twice survived poison gas attacks on the Western Front during the First World War. Clarke III had been a member of the British Expeditionary Force (BEF). In any event, any charges of his at Pembroke had always been warned to tread lightly in regard to the headman.

"Are you sure this is something we should be doing, Archie?" asked an increasingly fearful Georgie Sloan.

"Of course, it is. Don't tell me you're getting cold feet, old boy. It's just a harmless prank. Don't worry as much," assured Collins , the self-styled leader of this bunch.

At that moment, another one of their compatriots was leading a magnificent, black-toned stallion, with just a trace of a white streak down the middle of his formidable head, just between his wild and piercing eyes. David Brown, 16 years of age, had been tasked with the assignment of spiriting the animal out of its stall. The horse began to whinny and neigh quietly as Brown led him out of the stall. None of the conspirators had been quite sure how this beast would react to their presence, and about how he'd react to being led away from his paddock. But *Aleaxander* did not seem at all reluctant to be following David Brown.

"All right, all right, do you have it?" asked Archie Collins to Herbert Dunn Asquith, another conspirator.

"Of course I have it. Didn't you think I could pull it off?" asked an assured Asquith. At that, he pulled from his waistcoat a long-barreled black Browning revolver, the kind many British officers had carried in the trenches in Belgium. All involved in the caper knew the draconian rules of the prep school with regard to any sort of firearm. Immediate expulsion would be the penalty to anyone found to be in possession of one, and of any who'd been aiding and abetting said individual.

"David, please steady the great steed," teased Asquith. "This is my first time at this sort of thing, you know." He then took aim at *Alexander* with the Browning. At that moment, the horse took sight of the weapon, his eyes bulging, his nostrils flaring, and he began to stomp his hooves. A loud crack broke the night's silence, as Herbert Asquith pulled the trigger of the gun. But no bullet had emerged from its barrel. The Browning had been loaded with blanks. But *Alexander* hadn't known of this and promptly suffered what could be considered a myocardial infarction, or simply as a heart attack. The stallion suddenly buckled into a heap on the stable's grounds.

At first, the boys had been stunned. This wasn't what anyone of them had expected. It had just been meant to be some fun. Each of them felt their heart rates accelerate and cold, clammy sweats broke out on their faces.

"What the hell just happened? What do we bloody well do now?" shouted an hysterical Archie Collins. "I thought you said the gun had blanks in it."

"It did, it did, I tell you!" blurted out a quaking and shaking Herbert Dunn Asquith. "He must have…I don't know…He must have had a heart attack. It does happen, even for horses."

"Thank you, doctor, for that opinion," snorted David Brown. "I don't know about you guys, but I'm taking off right quick. They are not going to pin anything on me," Brown finished, but he did not feel as confident as he sounded.

Almost seemingly all at once, each of the boys took off at a run. As George Sloan was about to take flight, he cast a glance toward the fallen horse, and then saw the Browning lying about two feet away from the animal. Asquith must have dropped it in his excitement, or had it been panic? George continued to stare at the weapon. He realized it couldn't be left behind. George ran over and picked it up and started off at an awkward run. He desperately hoped no one had witnessed what had just transpired.

There was one witness, so to speak, and he was Elijah Jackson, a stable hand at the school. A tall, gentle giant of a black man. He was reminiscent of a headmaster's assistant, at least, as far as the horses were concerned. Jackson hadn't quite seen Asquith take aim at the horse, but at the sound of the firing he'd quickly come running. And he had been able to identify one of the pranksters, George Sloan. And Elijah Jackson had always had a great affinity and affection for *Alexander*.

Arriving at their new base camp , George Sloan and his fellow survivors, decamped and were allowed a brief moment of respite. Sloan resurrected his pseudo-dream of that nightmarish night at the prep school. A thorough and complete investigation of the *Alexander* incident, as it soon came to be called, was conducted by Headmaster Clarke and the Pembroke Board of Governors. Although nothing could be definitively proven, two of the boys, Archie Collins and David Brown, were found guilty of having violated the school's rules and regulations regarding conduct of the guidelines. The two boys were duly expelled forthwith and escorted off of the campus.

Elijah Jackson, although interviewed by Headmaster Clarke and the school's Officer of Compliance, remained mum. He never revealed his sighting of George Sloan. But George would forever feel the weight of his guilt. He should have stepped forward and taken his place beside Collins and Brown, and been expelled from the hallowed grounds of Pembroke. But he hadn't, he had remained silent.

George knew that had he been exposed in the horse's death he would have brought instant and everlasting shame upon, not only himself, but of his loving and supportive parents. They had sacrificed much to be able to send George to such a fine and well-respected school as Pembroke. It had been a luxury they couldn't extend to their other two boys, Wendell and Oliver. George had proven to be the most reliable and gifted academically.

Harold Sloan was a talented and dedicated machinist at the Wexford Tool and Die Ltd company. He had also been a survivor of the Great War where he had served in the trenches on the Belgian front. Victim of a poison gas attack at Ypres, he'd resolved to put the war and all of its bloody and gory horror behind him. He never once spoke of it to his children. The only one who an inkling of what he had experienced was his faithful and loving wife, Harriet.

Harriet Sloan was the youngest of five children of the Carter household. She had met Harold after the war when he'd been convalescing at a military outside London. Harriet had been serving as a volunteer to veterans and been engaged in providing what could be considered rudimentary support to the nursing staff. For George, it had been a virtual love at first sight. The young woman was bright and cheerful, a woman who always seemed to possess the right touch, be it to change a dressing or a bandage or merely to provide some comforting words. But Harold had been most struck by Harriet's attractiveness: golden flowing hair; bright blue sparkling eyes; a soft mouth; and a positively knock-out body. Although she typically dressed in uncomplimentary billowing clothing, George had been able to. quickly discern long, slim legs, and breasts he couldn't wait to get his hands on. He would often find himself becoming aroused at Harriet's mere touch.

***

At 8th Army Headquarters, Alan Cunningham waited anxiously for reports from the front. His own HQ radio having gone on the frits. When he learned of the enormity of the disaster that had befallen his forces, he became a shattered and broken man. Perhaps he should have ordered his forces to retreat back into Egypt, where he could, at least, reorganized his scattered and bewildered men into relative safety. Fighting his nerves and indecision, he requested of his commander, Claude Auchinleck in Cairo, that he come in person to see the collapsing front. Auchinleck flew out to

Fort Maddalena and conducted a swift appraisal. He believed that Erwin Rommel was probably in as bad a shape as the British . The Auk ordered for the offensive to continue and to "attack the enemy relentlessly using all of your resources, even to the last tank."

All of this was, of course, far above the pay grade of Left-tenant George Sloan. Soon after, 4th Brigade had regrouped and George was made aware of the possibility of joining up with an elite group of warriors. An organization that could range far and deep into the enemy's rearward areas. A force of men who would be virtually living off the land. Almost like a modern day version of nomadic pirates.

The Long Range Desert Group (LRDG) was a reconnaissance and raiding unit of the British Army, founded in Egypt in 1940 by Major Ralph Bagnold, under the direction of General Archibald Wavell. Its primary role was designated to conduct reconnaissance and intelligence gathering. Their vehicles were mostly used Chevrolets or Ford trucks. At first, the majority of its ranks were filled by New Zealanders, but they were soon joined by Rhodesians and British volunteers.

LRDG was formulated to carry out deep penetration reconnaissance patrols and recon missions from behind German

and Italian lines. Combat would sometimes be inevitable. It was during a rest and recuperation period for George Sloan

in December that he met up with an old friend of his Pembroke days, Archibald Collins no less. His old, one time confederate in the *Alexander* affair was himself a member of the LRDG.

"I tell you, Georgie boy, this outfit is the one for you. Now, tell me, would I ever steer you wrong?" asked Collins, who immediately knew he had just placed his proverbial foot in his mouth.

"Well, Archie, my old friend, I do seem to recall the *Alexander* affair. I distinctly remembered you and David said it would be quite simple. Piece of cake. Just a little fun," said George dead panned.

"I know, I know. But who would have figured the bloody horse would have a fucking heart attack. I mean, what would have been the odds? Anyway, I am sorry I talked you into it," said a downcast and chastened Archie Collins. "I'm truly sorry."

"It is me who should be the one to apologize, Archie," said George as he stared at his Tangueray and tonic in the Shepheard's Hotel bar. "I should've stepped forward and admitted to my part in the whole sordid caper. But I didn't. I let you and David take the rap. You wouldn't know the guilt I still feel." All about Sloan and Collins, the atmosphere in the bar was festive. One would never imagine about the precarious British position out in the Western Desert.

"You don't have to apologize, old boy. We were just a bunch of stupid schoolboy kids. Anyway, I surely don't hold a grudge against you. Never have. In any event, this group, the LRDG. is the boss. You should really look into it while you're here in Cairo," whispered Collins conspiratorially. "Riding off into the desert in those Chevy trucks, not humping around mindlessly, moving from here to there, and then back again. Always in a hurry and then to just wait. I tell you there is nothing else like it. You'll feel like a freelancing pirate on the high seas, only in this case it's the desert."

"Archie, I think I just might. Yeah...maybe," said George as he scratched his slightly stubbled chin. He had had enough of the mindless operations he had been assigned to thus far as a member of the 4th Brigade. "Who did you say was the contact?"

"Now, you're talking, my friend. You should see a chap named David Taylor. Captain David Taylor, that is, and you won't get much closer than you are right now. He's the one sitting at that table, holding some cards," said Collins as he pointed to the blond-haired, impressive looking fellow to their right. It looked like Taylor could handle himself quite nicely. He certainly could play cards as he was about to win his third straight hand.

***

Franco Donato's injuries took some time to recover from. At first, he was convalescing in an army hospital in Tripoli. He had been most fortunate to have not incurred any injuries to his face, or to a much more important area down below. His damage had largely been confined to his chest area. Franco had to acknowledge that Leo Goncalo had done an outstanding job during his initial surgery in the field. Still, there as a tiny sliver of steel that had lodged itself about one inch from Franco's heart. Goncalo had thought it to be too early to try and remove it. At least, that had been Goncalo's perspective. Franco would need additional work.

At the beginning of the new year of 1942, Franco Donato was transported to a dock along the waterfront in Tripoli. From here he would be taken via ship, in his case the *Moscolo*, to another army hospital in Palermo. Better yet, he would be closer to home. Home to Sicily. Sicilians had always regarded themselves as belonging in that category, before considering themselves Italian. Franco desperately hoped that Rosalie and Rosanna would be able to visit him there. He hoped it would be soon.

The Mediterranean crossing was one that had always been fraught with peril. British submarines were always lurking about and their torpedoes were deadly. Aircraft from the Desert Air Force also had to be contended with. because already they'd exacted a perilous toll on Italian warships and merchant vessels.

For these reasons, Franco's ship would be part of a mini-convoy of two transports, including the *Moscolo*, and one destroyer. It would set sail by dusk on January 3rd, 1942.

Franco and about 400 other wounded men, mostly army personnel were loaded aboard during the day of the 3rd. The entire process had been slow and laborious, not so much for Franco, who could walk unassisted, but for those ambulatory cases. Men who had lost limbs or had been horribly burned and disfigured. Franco felt himself to be among the lucky ones. His wounds were trifling in comparison with some of the men. One of them was brought onboard on a stretcher and placed next to him on the deck. Franco could tell by the shape of the blanket atop the man that his right leg had been amputated at the knee. The man lay there, conscious and uncomplaining.

"Excuse me, friend. Would you happen to have a cigarette to spare?" the soldier asked, a serene and pleasant look upon his face.

Franco looked down at the unfortunate man. "I think I might just have one, my friend," he said as he reached into his left-hand breast pocket for a packet of John Player cigarettes. He had been given the prized English cigarettes while he had been in Tripoli. They were a welcome and pleasant relief from some of the dreadful Italian brands passed out to the men. Franco, liked many of his countrymen, thought the Italian military was conducting chemical warfare, so to speak, by allowing its men to smoke such fiendish products.

Franco extracted a cigarette and handed it to the wounded man. He then struck a match to light it.

"*Grazie, mille grazie*, my newfound friend. By the way, my name is Mauro. Mauro Modigli, at your service," said the man as he took in several deep drafts of the cigarette. A cloud of smoke poured forth from his mouth.

"I'm Franco Donato. A pleasure to meet you."

For several awkward moments neither man spoke as Modigli kept on smoking. He was clearly enjoying himself. Finally he was finished and looked around for what to do with the butt. Franco kindly reached down and took it from Modigli and flicked it over the side.

"Where did you get your?" asked Modigli.

"Uh, uh…I was wounded over near Mechili. I took some shrapnel in the chest," said Franco.

"Hmm, I see, well that must have been tough. As for me, you have undoubtedly deduced, I gave a part of my right leg to the Duce near Sidi Rezegh. I do hope our great leader will appreciate my sacrifice," said Modigli, dripping sarcasm at the dictator.

"I'm sorry to hear about what you have gone through. At least, now you are going home," said Franco, looking away to the receding shoreline of Libya. The *Moscolo* was underway.

"Indeed, we are alive. And you, my friend, I didn't get your name."

"Oh, my name is Franco, Franco Donato from Sicily."

"Eh, *bene, bene*. From Sicily. I'm from Reggio di Calabria. So you see, we're practically related," cackled a not really joyful Mauro Modigli. "Eh, we shouldn't really be down in the dumps. As you say, we are on our way home. If I might ask, do you happen to have someone waiting for you?"

"I do have someone. My wife and my little girl. Here, let me show you a picture of them," said Franco as he reached for his wallet and removed the photo showing Rosalie and Rosanna. With great care he handed it to Modigli.

The man took hold of the picture and beamed a bright smile, "*Bene, molto bene*. Your wife is a beautiful woman and your little girl is simply adorable. You must miss them very much," said Modigli. He really had been quite taken with Rosalie. This Donato was one lucky man. A most attractive woman. Not stunning, but one who possessed an earthy, natural beauty.

"*Grazie, grazie,* I do, Modigli," said Franco as he took back the picture. "Do you have someone waiting on you?"

"No, no, I do not. I have my father, who is supposed to meet me in Palermo. My mother passed away last year…"

"I'm so sorry of that, Modigli," lamented Franco. He felt a deep sadness now for his newly found friend.

More than two days had elapsed before the *Moscolo* approached the harbor of Palermo. Great excitement filled the area around the port. For the wounded men aboard ship, some grievously so, they were at long last home. The smoke, death, and destruction of North Africa were behind them.

Franco was searching frantically for Mauro Modigli, but couldn't locate the man in the frenzied excitement. He had wanted to speak one last time with his new friend. In their short time together the two men had bonded, to the point where the men could almost read one another's mind. But no matter how hard Franco tried he just couldn't find Mauro Modigli. He hoped Mauro would be able to move on with his life, that the loss of his leg wouldn't hinder him or his future.

Once upon shore, Franco was directed to the 5th Corps Army Hospital on the outskirts of Palermo. He couldn't wait to get the chance to place a phone call to Rosalie in their village. He wanted desperately to see her again; to kiss her passionately once again; to feel the warmth curves of her luscious body. And, of course, to see and hold little Rosanna. *She must be so big now.*

***

Rosalie took Franco's call while she had been in the midst of processing some paperwork for the family's winemaking business. She could hardly believe that it really was Franco, and that he was finally home. Tears began to form in her eyes and run down her cheeks. But she was happy to cry; these were tears of happiness and joy. Her husband of whom she hadn't seen for nearly a year was home. He did tell her not to worry too much that he had been wounded in the chest. The wounds were not life threatening, but they would take some time to heal. And heal he would in the arms of his loving wife. Franco was pretty sure the army would allow him time to convalesce at home. The Duce could not deny him this courtesy. Franco Donato had done more than his fair share.

Rosalie quickly put down her work and contacted her brother Angelo; she would need his assistance and his Lancia sedan to make the trip from Mettuno to Palermo. She wasn't sure, but believed it make take more than five or six hours. Angelo would have to procure the requisite paperwork and gasoline for their excursion, as this was wartime and strict rationing had been in place since 1940. Rosalie would be forced to leave Rosanna with her sister and brother. Although she had wanted Franco see their little girl, she had finally decided the trip would be too long and arduous. Father and daughter would have to wait a little longer before they were reunited.

There were a million other things for Rosalie to do before she could set off on her journey to Palermo. She wanted to see her father in prison before she left. There was nothing she could do, but she wanted Berto to know that Franco had made it. He was alive and she was going to see him. Oh, and before she forgot, she had to contact Franco's parents This she would do in person; Rosalie would immediately set off on foot to Ottavino where Stefano and Maria Donato lived in their small, bricked home.

***

"I can't believe it, you're here!" cried Franco as he looked at Rosalie, who stood mutely in the doorway. "Well, come here, let me hold you…and…well, you know."

Rosalie dropped her handbag on the floor and ran to Franco's bed. They embraced one another and exchanged a furry of kisses. Rosalie's brother Angelo quietly left the couple to themselves.

"Well, I still look pretty good, don't you think? I mean the English got me in the chest, but left my beautiful and smiling face alone," continued Franco jovially. He now reached out and took hold of one of Rosalie's breasts.

She swatted his hand away. "Don't do that. Someone may be watching."

"Who cares. It's been a long time, don't you think my love?" Franco said in a scolding manner.

Rosalie looked at her husband and knew he was perturbed. But still, people shouldn't be carousing in a hospital ward. "Oh, I know, Franco. I guess that I'm still a little in shock at seeing you after all of these months," said Rosalie as she settled herself on Franco's bed. She leaned in closer and bent to kiss him. Their mouths closed on one another, and, then, she, Rosalie, inserted her tongue. Franco, surprised, responded in kind. He quickly felt himself stiffening. Rosalie noticed the growing bulge beneath the hospital gown.

"No, no, Franco, please. We cannot do that here…and now. When we're back home again I will surrender myself to you completely."

"Yes, you are right. I couldn't help myself for a moment," Franco replied.

And for the next two hours Rosalie and Franco talked mostly about themselves, Rosanna, her father, his parents, the war, the Duce.

***

The new year of 1942 had turned into an eventful one for Dottore Leo Goncalo. The army hospital in Tripoli was constantly besieged by a never ending flow of casualties from the front.

In late May, Erwin Rommel was once again ready to resume the offensive against the 8th Army. While Axis infantry, primarily Italian, and some tanks launched holding attacks against the northern part of the Gazala Line so as to preoccupy the enemy divisions there, Rommel directed the Afrika Korps and one Italian division to turn south around an old fortress at Bir Hacheim. He would then swing some of his forces around to grind down the British tanks and, then, attack the rest of the British line from the vulnerable rear. Following a successful result, Rommel could then plan a special treat for himself: The seizure of Tobruk.

Leo Goncalo was assigned to that Italian division, the Ariete and despite Rommel's flair and intuitive genius for battle, the Italians were bled white by the British. Casualties were too numerous to count, and never ending. Leo was literally up to his neck in the primitive operating theater located a few scant miles from the front lines of the Ariete. He had been performing several amputations of arms and legs, the severed limbs being piled up in barrels just outside the operating tent. Goncalo kept on working, oblivious to the constant and uninterrupted moaning of the battered men, alongside the other surgeons and nurses. Perhaps the non-stop work had acted as a buffer: a buffer to being overcome by nauseousness.

Finally, it must have been past midnight, when Leo was allowed a moment's respite, a brief moment to pause and reflect. He took out of his field smock pocket a pack of cigarettes, British cigarettes, and drew one. He lit it with a Ronson lighter. Another gift courtesy of the British. Serpentine clouds of smoke spiraled up and around Leo's head. The unending surgery had been long and arduous. He and the other doctors had done the best they could with what they had, considering the conditions. And yet, for some of the young Italian soldiers it had been too late. What was worse, they would in all probability be buried right there in the North African desert. They would never get the chance to rest on Italian native soil.

Leo reflected on this and on his increasing admiration of the Germans. Now, there was a force, a force of men who knew what they were doing. They were well equipped and well led, and they possessed the required ardor for war. There was something else that Leo had been unable to put his finger on for some time. The Germans possessed ruthlessness. No quarter or mercy was to be shown to the enemy, be they British, French, or the Russians. Furthermore, he agreed completely with their beliefs concerning the handling of the Jews. He agreed that this group of individuals possessed no loyalty to anyone other than themselves. Herr Hitler and his chief lieutenants, men such as Heinrich Himmler, Reinhard Heydrich, and Hermann Goering spoke the truth when it came to Jews: always profiting off the sweat and labor of others, such as Christians. Too good for anyone else. They always required to have services provided for them. And, everyone knew they controlled all of the money in the international markets.

Although Leo had heard some unbelievable stories about how Jews, especially in Russia, were being handled, he hadn't really believed them. Even the rumors of death camps having been set up in places in Poland, as well as in Germany.

By April of 1942, Leonardo Goncalo was back in Italy at a military hospital just outside of Rome. He was about to be promoted to the rank of *maggiore* for his great work and dedication as a surgeon in Libya. He couldn't recount how many casualties he'd treated in the desert. The number of amputations had been mind-numbing and, for lack of a better word, grisly. Blood and gore oozing out of torn abdomens. Men crying out for their mothers or their wives in the dying moments of their lives.

For the most part, this was now behind him. The immediate future would only require him perform routine physical examinations and to assist in some rehabilitative therapies. And for the next few months, Leo Goncalo could also become more active in Fascist Party activities. After all, he was now in the very heart of Fascism, he was in Rome.

Leo was able to stop by his home for a few days and visit his parents. His mother was so proud of her boy, she had been bragging and boasting to family members and friends of Leo's work in the army. Most neighbors would begin to scatter when they would see Maria Concalo approaching them.

Leo sat down in his father's study on the second day. Low scudding, nearly blackish, clouds peppered the sky above Mettuno. It looked like rain would soon be falling. This would provide a welcome respite for Sicilian farmers as conditions had been bone-dry and parched for quite some time. People and animals alike were in need of quenching their thirsts.

"Leo, my boy, we are quite proud of you," gushed Carlo Goncalo to his newly returned prodigal son. "You've brought great credit and dignity to yourself and to your family. I understand that the Duce is going to personally decorate you with a high medal some time this month."

"I was just doing what I'd been taught to do in medical school, and to what I felt obligated to do as a doctor and a soldier," said Leo self-deprecatingly. The young man had been brooding about what Franco Donato had said to him months before in Libya. He had to ask his father. He had to know the truth, although he secretly believed that Donato had probably been truthful.

Leo patiently listened to his father blather on about Leo's exploits, the Duce, the war, and so on. At what he deemed to be an appropriate moment Leo spoke. "Father, there is one thing I would like to speak with you about. Actually, it came about quite unexpectedly in Libya. You see I was treating a casualty and you wouldn't have believed it, who turned out to be Franco Donato from right here in Mettuno. And do you know what he said to me?" asked Leo, his head tilted to one side. Carlo had an underlying suspicion that he knew. "He said to me that you had framed Umberto Mancini and had swindled him of a considerable amount of his land.

Mancini is now languishing in jail on fake and trumped up charges. I naturally didn't think these accusations could possibly be true. That it was simply preposterous, just the ravings of a man out of his head."

Carlo Goncalo didn't address his son right away, he was looking downward, as if he were studying his reflection in the glass-topped desk. Seemingly on cue a great cloudburst opened in the sky above the two men. Darkness enveloped the room, lightning flashes danced their way across the crazed skies.

"You see Leo, a man in my position, one which means oftentimes a gathering of powers will sometimes bring about jealousies and untruths. No, my son, I didn't swindle Mancini out of any of his land. He is now sitting in jail because he spoke false and hateful things against not only his country, but the Duce as well. And for that he must suffer the consequences. Unfortunately, his daughter and son-in-law see things differently and so they've taken to blaming me."

"Father, we both know that when you want something you can be…uh, rather ruthless, and"

Carlo immediately cut off his son. "I'm your father, my business affairs are my own. You have no right…no right to come here and to question my motives or to discuss rumors or anything of that nature. I will not have it. I'll tell you once again that I had no hand into what happened involving Umberto Mancini. He has only himself to blame. That and his own big mouth. He should have kept it shut. And he couldn't, and therefore he is now rightfully where he belongs. And that is in jail. Is that clear?" harrumphed Goncalo senior as he stood imperiously in front of Leo.

"*Si, si,* it is perfectly clear, father. I did not mean to offend or to upset you," said a now chastened Leo.

"Anyway, I do want your opinion about what you think the Germans are doing with some of their…their undesirables," exclaimed Carlo.

"You mean the Jews?" questioned Leo.

"Hmm, among others," responded senior in a lowered tone voice. He sat down with a slight grimace which caused a measure of concern in Leo. Perhaps his father was just getting old and beginning to show his age. Leo just couldn't imagine his father as being anything less than dynamic and vigorous.

"Well, I have to say that I'm pretty much in agreement with them. And they are being pretty decisive about things," said Leo.

"You mean they're not dancing around the dance floor like the Duce and some of his comrades. Yes, you're quite right. Outwardly our leader says he is in agreement with Hitler concerning relations with the Jews, but in reality this is merely lip service."

"Father, there have been reports of the Nazis having set up concentration camps. These are not just labor camps. Some say they're outright death camps. The Nazis have established ghettoes in cities such as Warsaw and Cracow. And in them they're forcing Jews to live in them: poor food, little or no medical care, and so on…and…"

"Ahh, don't believe any of that nonsense. I think most of it is just trumped up propaganda being conjured up by the British. They're very clever and very good at spouting this kind of bullshit. And, anyway, if the Germans are indeed placing Jews and other undesirables, like Gypsies, into these so-called ghettoes I say good riddance to them," concluded Carlo Goncalo.

Father and son then settled down and fought over a two hour game of chess. Leo had selected white while father had black. Leo had to admit that his father was quite good at the game. He'd always had a difficult time at going head to head with the old man, and today would prove no different. Ruthlessness was how Carlo Goncalo played chess: take no prisoners, give no quarter. It reminded Leo of *Ben Hur* and the evil Roman nobleman Masala and his team of black horses and chariot. Ben Hur and his team of four magnificent whites. Good had triumphed over bad on that fictional day in history.

***

"Ohh, Leo, you are an absolute animal between the sheets. An absolute animal," cooed a perspiring Lina Pandolfo. She and her lover Leo Goncalo had just been engaged in rabid sex. And Lina had been up for it, she thought. However, when Leo had assaulted her body with an assortment of body blows she had been surprised. Lina was no neophyte and by no means inexperienced when it came to carnal relations, but on this night Leo had been more than an absolute bull of a man. It had seemed to Lina that at times during their lovemaking her partner had been possessed by some demonic power. As if he had been trying to exorcise something from within his soul. Lina had not actually been assaulted, it was just a figure of speech.

" I'm so glad that you've approved, my darling, Lina," leered Leo as he lay shoulder to shoulder with his paramour for the evening.

"Oh, I'm not complaining, mind you, but one time I thought you were going to drill right through me," responded Lina as she lightly patted his chest.

Leo remained silent as he contemplated the young woman. Long, dark, straight hair; beautiful face and luscious lips. Lina possessed long, not exactly slender, but still well-formed legs that expertly gripped his plunging body. The young woman was not enormously endowed, but she still possessed a formidable pair of breasts.

For Lina, Leo was an Adonis. She thought his body to be almost flawless, and his skill under the sheets was unsurpassed. Lina Pandolfo was no virgin, but Goncalo had been her best lover yet. There was one question which still lurked in the back of her mind. She knew Leo to be a restless soul, a man who tired quickly of women. A man who was always on to some new conquest. Lina Pandolfo wondered how long she would continue to hold Leo's interest before he moved on from her.

***

"My friend Archie Collins has informed me that you may be interested in joining our organization. Is that correct?" asked Captain David Taylor, his clear blue eyes settling on George Sloan.

"Yes, sir!" replied Sloan in his best parade ground voice. He stood stiffly at attention in front of Taylor's desk at LRDG headquarters in Cairo. Not a paper or a note could be found upon the mahogany topped piece of furniture. Sloan wondered if this were truly Taylor's office or just a place the captain was occupying just to impress Sloan. "Well, I've been reviewing your service record and..." Taylor looked up and noticed Sloan standing ramrod straight. "Er, Sloan, you can stand at ease. You're making me a trifle nervous."

"Thank you, sir. I mean I don't want to make you nervous..." as he now took a parade rest stance.

"Ah, yes. As I was saying, you have a rather impressive record here in the good old "Blue", I must say. As to your joining the LRDG, hmmm, that may well be another story. Do you happen to know what we do, and how we do it?" continued Taylor as a single overhead fan twirled slowly above their heads. It didn't seem to Sloan to be providing any semblance of relief to the suffocating heat and humidity filling the room.

"Just a bit from what Archie, er, Corporal Collins has told me, sir," responded Sloan as he continued looking straight ahead of him, never once glancing down at Taylor.

"Leftenant, would you please sit down. We aren't on the parade ground," said a seemingly perturbed Taylor who felt he could get a better measure and perspective of the man he was interviewing for the LRDG.

"Thank you, sir," said George as he took his seat. He felt himself beginning to calm down a bit from his previous nervousness over the entire situation he now found himself in. Perhaps he had or was about to get himself into something that would be over his head. "Yes, well…Ah, where was I? Do you happen to speak any language other than English?"

"Yes, sir, I do," said George who was now looking past Taylor and out the window at a good looking and most attractive young woman. An Englishwoman he presumed by her look and dress. She must have been a member of the nursing corps or, perhaps, one of the innumerable foreign service organizations seeming to overflow in Cairo.

"Leftenant Sloan, the primary reason that I asked you to take a seat is that we can engage and interact with one another in a more congenial and collegial manner. Now, what language would you be referring to?" asked David Taylor, who was clearly hoping he would hear German with just a trace of Bavarian or, perhaps, Italian. But what he heard wasn't only disappointing, but almost downright comical.

"Gaelic, sir. My last instructor said I was a dead-ringer for a native of Belfast," replied a now proud George Sloan.

"Yes, well, that is all well and good, but right now, here in the desert, we aren't in need of any Gaelic speakers, Belfastian or not. Not that it should be considered a black mark against you, Sloan. What I will tell you is that we're in need, desperate need, for young, keen, intelligent officers. Men who are quick-witted and not afraid to take the initiative. Men who are adaptable and can think outside the box. Sloan, the British Army, and the 8th Army in particular, is now in a desperate and rather precarious situation. Things aren't looking up at this moment. But the…the situation can be turned around to our advantage. Sloan, we need men such as yourself, not only in the British Army, but for the Long Range Desert Group. Welcome aboard." And with that exhortation David Taylor stood and extended his right toward George Sloan. Just as contact was made Taylor looked him straight in the eye and said, "Sloan, this will be no picnic, no lark. It will not be a walk in the park. You may find yourself out of the front line, not sitting in a foxhole. But what you will undergo in the next few weeks will be the most intense training you have ever undergone during your entire time in the army. I hope and trust you will be up to it."

"I will, sir. You'll be able to count on me," exclaimed a bursting with pride George Sloan. And he was quite proud, as he well should have been. He was now going to be a member of an elite fighting force. A unit that was the pride and envy of the entire 8th Army. And he, George Sloan, would have his name cast among the legendary heraldic names such as Ralph Bagnold and David Stirling.

As soon as George had been dismissed by Taylor he practically bolted down the steps of the headquarters building to the pedestrian laden sidewalk. He paused for a moment, wondering as to what he should do next. *How about a drink?* A drink to celebrate his acceptance into the LRDG. Yes, he would immediately contact his old buddy Archie Collins. Good ol' Archie, the man who had opened the door for him into the LRDG.

Chapter Seven

The LRDG

For George Sloan the next couple of months was a period of great intensity, in terms of the physical and mental preparation required in meeting the needs of the LRDG. It was also a time of what Sloan termed the inculcation of the philosophy of this unique organization. It was as if each and every man had to be imbued with the special spirit and the ferocity of being a long range desert warrior.

Sloan learned of the pre-war work performed by what had been termed an eclectic group which included two Englishmen. Men who would be destined to create and serve in the Long Range Desert Group: Ralph Bagnold and Patrick Clayton. The survey work conducted by these men consisted of the mapping out of the network of ancient trails, including nearly every feature in an otherwise barren landscape. The bones of escarpments, sunken depressions, oases, salt marshes, and dry wadis which could suddenly spring to life after rains were all shown to their full effect.

The work of these bold and dynamic pioneers help to lay the seeds of future operations across the great Western Desert by the LRDG. The outright audacity of conducting deep and wide-ranging penetrations of the enemy's rearward areas flouted and defied conventional military thinking. Among the hide-bound upper class men of the British General Staff, the very idea of a gang of eccentrics in uniform and operating out on a virtual limb, hundreds and perhaps thousands of miles from a formal command and control structure, was pure madness to the point of heresy.

George Sloan and other newcomers were briefed and imbued with an unofficial creed or doctrine as to how things would be conducted in the new unit. The LRDG raiders anticipated endeavors which were usually easier to grasp than the role of the ordinary British infantryman, or Tommy. LRDG troopers were always fully briefed on operations. Specialist units saw the normal distances of each operation shrunk exponentially for every member; officers and enlisted men were their very own specialists. Patrols carried with them highly proficient drivers, along with vehicle fitters, wireless operators, armorers, and paramedics. Each man's survival would depend on the rest. Patrols were to be conducted with no higher chain of command, no spit and polish. There was to be none of the "bullshit" of regular army life. In addition, Sloan would soon learn that there would be nowhere to run to, no one else to blame, as well as no room for any nonsense, and nobody to pass the buck to.

LRDG men also learned that they would have the primary role of gathering intelligence rather than attacking the enemy. Across the vast and limitless expanse of the desert, knowledge of the enemy's strength and likely intentions would be invaluable. For these objectives to be carried out successfully, both the right type of man and the right equipment were absolutely critical.

One day George Sloan and a couple of his mates had just concluded a series of calisthenics and were gathering around a vehicle, or lorry in British parlance. They were about to be lectured on the characteristics and capabilities of this rather remarkable vehicle.

"All right, gentlemen, if I could have your attention," said Captain Eric Dufford-Smith. "I would like to point out some of the unique features of the vehicle you see before you." Smith pointed with his swagger stick to the tan colored Chevrolet 30-cwt truck. Begged or borrowed from local dealers in the Nile Delta, these trucks had become the standard commercial vehicles which then had become heavily customized for the harsh conditions of desert warfare. The Chevies had been stripped down to their bare skeletons, their load carrying capacity beefed up to two tons through the addition of heavy springs.

"As you gentlemen can clearly see, these vehicles have been fitted out to carry any number of weapons and ammunition, wireless and medical gear. Rigs have been welded on so as to accommodate heavy and medium machine guns, such as the Browning .50 caliber, as seen here, or twin Vickers K machine guns," Smith continued to prattle on as if he had been reading the report card showing the outstanding grades of a ten year old child.

"And if you men would be so kind as to follow me around to the front of the vehicle I shall point out what I consider to be a most outstanding feature." The men dutifully followed Dufford-Smith to the front of the Chevy. "Now, here, our outstanding engineers have made an ingenious adaptation in the form of a radiator condenser. This little item will be of invaluable assistance to our vehicles as we go bounding about in the "Blue."

Following the demonstration, Captain Smith faced and then addressed George Sloan and his newly inducted LRDG troopers.

"Gentlemen, I have just shown you what I consider to be the pre-eminent vehicle for use in the desert. Along with this truck, and the weaponry, we now possess the necessary instruments; binoculars, sun compasses, and as up-to-date maps as we've been able to scrounge up. We have assembled the men needed, men of high caliber. Men such as yourselves. We have and will continue to provide you with the necessary training so as to enable you to go out and to knock about the Jerries and the Eyeties for six. And never forget, the 8th Army needs you. Great and congruent events are at this very moment taking place. I know that each and everyone of you will do your duty and account well of yourselves. That is all." And with that Eric Dufford Smith turned on his heel and walked off.

George Sloan would have sworn he'd just heard one of the most impressive pep talks ever. Smith was a man who had all of the qualities of an outstanding leader. Sloan wasn't sure about the some of the others, but to him, he felt as if could march out now and take it to the enemy.

***

That night Sloan was in his tent, along with fellow trooper, Stanley Stone. They were in the Fort Abbassiga Barracks just outside of Cairo.

Both of the men were breaking down and lubricating their Thompson submachineguns. The gun was a fearsome weapon in the hands of a trained soldier, capable of delivering a wallop from the 30 round magazine. It was superb for close-in fighting.

"So tell me, Stan, what exactly happened during the Tobruk raid?" asked Sloan somewhat cautiously. He pretended to be focusing on his weapon, but he cast a sidelong glance at Stone.

"Wrong? What went wrong? Practically everything, if you ask me. It was a total cock-up, that's what it was. Anything that could go wrong went wrong," said Stone who had now put the Thompson's stock down on the small table in front of him. "From what I heard, the plan started out small, but then various parties decided to put their two cents in, and before anyone knew it, we ended up with a plan that no way in the world would work . That's what happened." Stone sounded bitter and he'd every right to have been. He'd been on the raid and been lucky to have been able to be extricated after Operation Agreement had crashed and burned in flames.

"See, George, here's the thing. LRDG was originally designed to be a long range intelligence gathering operation, with an occasional foray into some demolition work. You know, if during the course of a scouting mission a patrol came across some aircraft the bad guys were neglecting, well, then why not blow them to kingdom come."

"And that's not what happened at Tobruk," said Sloan, who by now had too placed his weapon down.

Stanley Stone looked around the tent in a conspiratorial manner as if fearful of someone overhearing what he was about to say next. "You see, George, the plan began small, you know, LRDG would transport and guide in some commando chaps. It was our specialty. If the big boys in Cairo had kept it to that, then things might've turned out differently. By that I mean, the navy wouldn't have lost two destroyers and one light cruiser, and God knows how many ratings. And the marines wouldn't have gotten screwed either," finished Stone who now hung his head as if in shame at the memory of the debacle and the loss of men.

"But what about the LRDG? I mean how could things have gone differently for them?" pushed a now eager for details George Sloan.

"Well, if, as I said, they had kept things a little more simple, in other words, just to have been satisfied with getting the commandos into Tobruk and perhaps just going after some aircraft and such, it would've been different. But, as I've said, the first plan just kept getting bigger and bigger. And before anyone knew it the plan was totally unrecognizable. It was decided to have Royal Marines land from offshore, but the landing craft were totally unsuited for the job. Then, it was decided to have the Desert Air Force bombard the port before the commandos or the marines had done anything. So we now had a fully alerted enemy when things started to happen in Tobruk. I mean if some were Eyeties, we, the good guys, didn't have very good odds."

At this point in his soliloquy Stanley Stone paused, but only for a moment. He was eager to go on with his narrative, his tale of woe, lament, loss, and anger.

"What was that?" asked an alarmed George Sloan.

"Probably just a field mouse. You know, George, you can't be overly concerned with little piss-ant things, like some mice scurrying about. It won't make for a good show. Anyways, as I was saying, the plan was downright wrong, the equipment was wrong, the boats, everything went wrong. It wasn't what LRDG had been designed for. And you know, our new boss, good old Monty, was right quick to distance himself from the disaster. You can be sure that Fleet CNO Harwood must have been royally pissed off at the loss of his precious ships. But of course, heads had to roll. Not any of the big shots in Cairo mind you who had put this disaster together. No, sacrifices were found amongst the lower ranks. Surely someone had failed to possess the proper nerve at the decisive moment in time."

"I wonder what Rommel must've thought?" asked a passive George Sloan.

"Rommel? I imagine he must've laughed his arse off. So much expended for so little success. A typical British production," laughed Stanley Stone in abject bitterness.

***

For the moment George Sloan and his fellow LRDG troopers were to play a secondary role in the desert war. On October 23rd 1942, General Bernard Law Montgomery commenced the overwhelming attack by the 8th Army at El Alamein. As zero hour approached , Montgomery could count on a two to one superiority over his German opponent in nearly every respect. His troops outnumbered the Germans and Italians by 195,000 men to 105,000; in medium tanks by 1,029 to 500. The British also possessed a two to one advantage in anti-tank guns and artillery. Furthermore, Monty's 8th Army was very well-supplied. Rommel's forces, by contrast, were suffering greatly from critical shortages of everything imaginable.

Another compounding problem for the Germans was the fact that Rommel had fallen ill. Throughout the long and exhausting summer, Erwin Rommel had driven himself to a point beyond endurance. In late September, the man could hold out no longer. Stricken by a chronic stomach and intestinal catarrh, on top of pre-existing circulatory troubles and nasal diphtheria, he was to be airlifted out of North Africa to Austria for treatment. General Georg von Stumme, a veteran of fighting on the Russian Front, and afflicted by acute high blood pressure, took Rommel's place.

At 9:30 pm, a faint throbbing from overhead could be heard over the battlefront: British bombers were moving in to strike German and Italian positions and airfields in and around El Alamein.

At precisely 9:40, all along the British line, nine hundred guns spoke out with an earsplitting, earth-shaking roar, and the entire front erupted in smoke and flame. The largest barrage of the war poured out death and destruction onto the Axis positions. The explosions could be heard more than sixty miles away in Alexandria.

Confusion reigned along the entire Axis line. Officers of the German 164th Division had been consuming spirits in the dugout that served as tactical headquarters when the first explosions caused a soda siphon to roll and crash to the floor.

General von Stumme was more than confused and within minutes of the start of the barrage, shots had torn his communications to bits. Stumme was thus cut off from every division of his command. He immediately set off for the front early on the next morning, when his staff car came under a hail of fire from Australian gunners. Stumme then succumbed to a fatal heart attack. At the moment, Axis forces were leaderless—and the battle had been only a few hours old.

Over the ensuing days, the overwhelming British attack went slowly, but inexorably, over the Germans and Italians. Montgomery's forces suffered appalling casualties and the loss of a great many tanks. But he had many men and many more tanks that he was able to throw into the Alamein maelstrom. Erwin Rommel, still suffering physically, rushed back to the crumbling battlefield, only to find that the expected replacements and tanks, and fuel he'd been promised had not arrived.

Rommel was clearly able to read the proverbial tea leaves and, at long last, came to the sad and mournful conclusion that he would have to retreat. That is, if he hoped to be able to salvage some of his forces and live on to fight another day. Adolf Hitler, however, had other ideas in mind, and had expressly forbidden the Desert Fox to retreat as much as one millimeter. Rommel stood in disbelief when he was handed the Fuhrer's order: "The Afrika Korps is not to retreat as much one millimeter from its present position. It is to be victory or death."

***

In the wake of Rommel's retreat at El Alamein, Montgomery's 8th Army began a cautious advance. There was to be no way for the Englishman to allow for the wily Desert Fox to snap back at him. He'd be the one to dictate the tempo of the North African campaign.

As a result, the Long Range Desert Group was tasked to perform primarily what it had been originally envisioned to do: conduct long and far-ranging reconnaissance of the fleeing panzers of the Africa Corps. And George Sloan now found himself in the thick of the action, as it was. Moving out and around the Alamein battlefield, Sloan took in what could be casually called the detritus of war. Burned out hulks of tanks and armored cars, both German and domestic. Abandoned artillery pieces, some with their long barrels bent and twisted, or just haggardly broken off as if some monster had pulled and twisted them apart with its great hands.

What struck George and his fellow troopers the most were the various stages of the dead they saw. Bodies had been torn and mangled in a dreadful and despoiling manner. Men could clearly be seen as having been disemboweled, and some decapitated. Then there were the bodies that had become limbless. And then there were the sights and smells that ordinary people could never imagine in ordinary times. It was a sight that George Sloan knew he'd never get over for the rest of his life.

***

LRDG Troop A was gathered around Major Eric Snead, recently promoted for gallantry and heroism in the field. "All right, gentlemen. You've just been briefed as to what your assignment is. You are to gather as much intelligence as you can on the retreating elements of the Africa Corps. Remember, you are to primarily gather information regarding the enemy's troop strengths, and their order of battle. This is imperative to aiding and abetting 8th Army's objective of Mersa Matruh. You are not to become engaged in any combat operations that can be avoided. In other words, don't go looking for trouble. Are there any questions?" asked Smith as he looked out at his gathered men. He didn't expect any and would been surprised if any of the men had any. "Very well. I would advise all of you to check out your equipment and vehicle one last time. Also, your weaponry and kit, and food and provisions. All right, that's all. Good luck and as we always say in good ole England, Good Hunting!"

George Sloan left the briefing and went back to his tent. He checked out his own personal kit and equipment. He grasped the stock of the fabled Thompson in his increasingly calloused hands. He loved the feel of its wooden stock and the glint of the cold blue steel of the barrel and the ammo clip of 30 rounds. A real killing instrument, and he was going to get the opportunity of using it in action as a member of the Long Range Desert Group.

"I'm just going to make a last check on the men and the Chevy, sir," said Sergeant Michael Perry as he stood before Sloan at complete attention.

George looked at the weather-beaten man who stood before him. A man who had become more than simply Sloan's right-hand man. Perry seemed to possess an unerring and intuitive capacity to anticipate almost anything Sloan might happen to be thinking. A veritable sixth sense. It gave George an almost uncanny feeling that no matter what situation might arise, he, George Sloan, would be able to do what was required to accomplish any mission. "Very good, Sergeant, I'll be with you shortly to give a last once over to our objective."

"Very good, sir!" said Perry as snapped off a very correct British salute of the palm and fingers splayed flat.

The Chevy LRDG truck cruised just off the main tarmac road just off the Libyan coast. George Sloan's eyes had finally become adjusted to the nighttime. For some particular reason on this night it had taken George an abnormally longer period than he'd ever experienced previously. Just what he needed. Perhaps he should see the surgeon when he got back, if he got back, from the foray.

Long, low-scudding clouds filled the nighttime sky above the patrol group as it moved furtively across the forbidding desert. A heaviness seemed to hang in the cloying air. Sgt Perry was in the lead vehicle, along with Sloan, motioned with his right arm and said, "Excuse me, sir, but I think this might be a good place to stop and have the troop fan out. I have a feeling the Eyties may be lurking about. Nothing definite, mind you, but just a gut feeling."

George had known for quite some time to trust in any gut feelings Sgt Perry may have harbored. The man simply had an uncanny and unerring ability to sense, perhaps he could smell, any danger.

"All right, Sergeant, we'll have the patrol pull over to that lee along the drive. We'll start from there," said George, It made him feel, for some unknown reason, as if he'd made a command decision and that he was in command and not the sergeant.

The men filed out of the two Chevies silently, only the occasional clink of equipment disturbed the night. None of the men grumbled about having to bivouac at yet another unknown and virtually endless stop along the desert way. The men of the LRDG were all volunteers and the men totally dedicated to whatever mission that was assigned to them. They were there in the Libyan Desert because they wanted to be in the Libyan Desert. Sloan knew they would perform any task he assigned to them because they trusted him and his leadership implicitly. He desperately hoped he would live up to that trust. He would shortly find out.

Sloan spread out the map along the ground beside his Chevy truck. He covered a cone of light from his field torch as he scanned the map. The patrol was less than thirty miles from Mersa Matruh. Elements of the Italian Pavia Division had been rumored to be in the area. The Italians had been assigned to act as a screening unit for one of Rommel's panzer units, the 21st Panzer. It was, to the Italians, a typical assignment handed down by the imperious Desert Fox. One that implied that acting as a shield was about the only effective thing Italians could be trusted to do. It was just another demeaning task given to Il Duce's men by another high-ranking German commander who had little or no respect or expectation for Italians.

"All right, Sergeant, deploy the men along that berm," said Sloan as he pointed in the direction of it. "And make sure that everyone's reminded not to get the jitters. I don't want to see anyone firing on some phantom target, that in all likelihood turns out to be something no more than a field mouse. And Sergeant, make sure the flares are properly distributed."

"Very good, sir," responded Perry, who was now beginning to see a slight change, one for the better, in his commanding officer. Sloan was new to the unit, but Perry could clearly discern that the young man was rapidly catching on.

Less than two hours later, Sloan and his men could hear the low growl of an approaching vehicle. George wasn't sure if it might be friend or foe. He thought it couldn't be friendly as no other LRDG units were supposed to be in that area. He well knew that it couldn't possibly be an LRDG units that had gotten lost, that just couldn't happen. And he also was aware that it couldn't be a regular 8th Army troop, Sloan and his unit were too far forward of the main 8th. No, it must likely be an Italian vehicle. Maybe a Fiat-Ansaldo armored car. One of the few Italian weapons the British respected. It was a fast, speedy car that had enjoyed some measure of success in the Western Desert.

Slowly, inexorably, the sound grew closer and suddenly shut down. Voices could be heard. At first, Sloan couldn't decipher what tongue was being spoken in the near distance. Then, it became clear as to the identity of the mystery unit when a loud "*Jesu Christo*" was yelled out. The Bloody Eyeties were about. But was it just one vehicle they were confronting, or were there others?

"Sergeant Perry," Sloan hissed at his subordinate.

"Sir," responded Perry.

"Dispatch two men to reconnoiter the Italian position. We need to find out how many of them are out there. They are to use extreme caution," Sloan urged.

"Yes, sir. Very good, sir," whispered back Perry who knew that Sloan was aware of the LRDG men did not have to be told to be careful. It was something that was implicitly understood by all of the men.

Sergeant Perry dispatched Privates Murray and Dibwell to reconnoiter the Italian positions. The pair slowly emerged from their fighting hole, their Lee-Enfield rifles at the ready. Both advanced cautiously, silently over the barren desert floor. The men made sure their spacing was text-book, it wouldn't do to be too close to one another, and as one advanced the other provided covering fire if needed.

Andrew Murray, hailing from Aberdeen, Scotland, wondered how in the hell he now found himself in the midst of this vast, sprawling, moon-like environment. Being from Scotland he could hardly remember the temperature at any time in his life being above 70 degrees Fahrenheit, even during the high summer. It was far different from the scorching daytime highs that could be in excess of 100 degrees in July or August in Libya. And then the nighttime would descend to near freezing temps. Nevertheless, there he was and now as he approached the Italian position he stopped and paused. He could barely discern one lone Italian leaning against the Fiat-Ansaldo armored car smoking a cigarette. The man looked to be engaged in a conversation with another soldier, but their voices were too low for Murray to pick up any gist. Over the past year he'd been able to pick up the odd turn of phrase and some typical Italian vocabulary. He was no linguist by any means, but he could discern a thing or two.

Silently, Andy Murray signaled to Jim Dibwell to advance to his position. Stealthily, Dibwell did so until he was at Murray's elbow. "What's up, Andy?"

"Over there you can just pick out an Eyetie having a fag," said Murray. "He's apparently in conversation with one of his buddies. I can't make out how many of them are there," whispered Murray in frustration.

"What's our next move?" whispered back Dibwell.

"Well, I think our mission is to gather in how many we may be up against, And then, if we can, snatch a prisoner to bring back for questioning," continued Murray. "But for now, let's lay low right here and see what happens."

At that very moment, the Italian who'd been luxuriating in a brief smoke apparently decided he needed to relieve himself, and it would not be number one. Murray and Dibwell could see the man reach down and grab what looked like a rag. He then proceeded to walk almost directly in the direction of the LRDG men. When he had decided on a suitable enough spot, less than ten feet from Murray and Dibwell, the man dropped his drawers and proceeded to squat. A fart was emitted from the Italian's backside and then a turd duly followed.

Seizing the moment, Murray removed his bayonet from its scabbard and then rushed toward the Italian as he was still in dispose. Before the poor man knew what was upon him, he was seized by the back of his head by Murray and before he could raise any kind of alarm he was clubbed to the ground by Murray's bayonet handle. The LRDG man was immediately nauseated by the smell of the shit clinging to the Italian's ass. He nevertheless grabbed at the prone man and then hefted him onto his right shoulder. Looking right and left, Andy Murray scooted back to where Jim Dibwell was and dropped his smelly load.

"Good God, Andy, what the hell is this?" asked Dibwell, wrinkling his nose in abject disgust.

"The old boy had apparently been in the midst of relieving himself when I happened to stumble upon him. He was rather easy picking, if I must say," said Murray. "Let's tie up his trousers and make him somewhat presentable when we bring him to Captain Sloan."

"Rather!" prattled Dibwell.

"Well done, lads, even if he's in a rather disagreeable state," said George Sloan with a big smile across his face. "Let's bring the man to and see if he can tell us anything worthwhile." George then lightly slapped the Italian on the cheek and then tossed some of the contents of his canteen onto the man's face.

Slowly, the Italian became conscious and when he saw that he was in the presence of British soldiers his breathing rapidly proceeded to escalate.

"There, there, my friend," said Sloan in Italian. "You're among friends. Tell me, how many of your friends are out there?" as George waved a hand in the general direction of the armored car.

The Italian's eyes widened in fear. He thought these men might be commandoes and that they would slit his throat. And he'd once thought he might have a shot at the opera.

"Now, now, do not be afraid. We simply would like to know how many other Italians are with you?" Sloan continued with his questioning. It was likely the man would reveal nothing and they'd just take him with them when they returned to their base camp.

"Eh, six or seven. Three are with the armored car and the other four, including me, are attached as infantry," said the man, his breathing becoming more shallow.

George offered the man a sip of his canteen, which the Italian seized gratefully. "*Grazie, grazie.*"

"What is your unit? Are you with the Pavia Division?"

"Eh, *si*, sir. The Pavia Division," blurted out the prisoner, his eyes still bugged out in fear.

"All right, we know what we're up against," said George to his men. " I'd like to be able to get away from here without disturbing our Italian friends," continued Sloan.

"Sir, sir, it looks like the Eyeties may be stirring," said one of the troopers.

George stood up and looked in the direction his man was pointing to. A couple of the enemy were seen to be advancing, with fixed bayonets attached to their rifles. Just then, Andy Murray stumbled over an ammo cannister and a loud screeching noise was emitted. The Italians immediately dropped to the ground and commenced to firing wildly. There was no chance they would hit anything. Nevertheless, the jig was now obviously up. A loud cacophony of sound and fury erupted between the Brits and the Italians.

Sergeant Perry directed that the unit's PIAT (projectile infantry anti-tank) weapon be brought up. Private Debwell reached into the Chevy and pulled the weapon out. The PIAT was a single-shot, hollow charge weapon of dubious reliability. "All right, Debwell, I want you to get yourself into position and get off a good shot at the armored car. Wait for my command for covering fire before you move out to those low-lying rocks over on the right. Do you see them?"

Debwell in his excitement and rising nervousness could only nod his head.

"All right, men, on three. One...two...three. Covering fire!" shouted Perry at the top of his lungs. At that, every man unleashed a furious volley at the enemy positions. George Sloan noticed that the armored car was now buttoned-up and the turret containing its 37 mm gun was slowly turning to face Sloan and his men. He desperately hoped that Private Debwell would get his PIAT in position to take out the Italian vehicle before it was too late.

Jimmy Debwell did indeed manage to get himself into the proper position with the PIAT. Taking careful aim, as much as was possible in the chaotic situation, he lined up the Fiat-Ansaldo and pulled the shotgun styled trigger. The projectile fired straight and true toward its target. A loud explosion and following flame soon consumed the vehicle. Almost at once, the firing from the Italian infantrymen slackened off.

The LRDG looked on in awe at the pyrotechnical spectacle before them. It was like an apparition from the fingers of God.

"Right, right, continue firing. There can't be more than a few of them left," shouted George Sloan as he tried his best to be heard over the din. He then moved off a little to the right flank and before he even realized it he found himself staring face to face with an Italian, an officer no doubt from the fine cut of his uniform jacket. But the man's pants were smoking beneath him. Perhaps he had been the commander of the armored car and had managed to effect his escape before the blast had consumed it. In any event, the man was staggering toward George, a pistol gripped in his right hand. To Sloan, now less than 15 feet from the Italian could clearly make out that the man was not in his right mind. He reached for his own Webley service revolver and removed it from its holster. The gun was tethered to the holster with a corded string.

Sloan continued to stare at the man and his blackened face, and now that he looked more closely he could see that the Italian's hair was also smoking. The man resembled a walking Frankenstein. Sloan hesitated. Should he put the man out of his misery? Should he take him prisoner? Slowly the Italian officer started to raise his pistol, when suddenly a shot rang out. The bullet had penetrated the Italian dead center into his forehead. The man staggered and seemed to perform a little dance before he went down onto his knees. After pausing, as if in prayer, the Italian pitched forward onto the unforgiving and uncaring sand.

"Have to be a bit careful, sir," said Andrew Murray to Sloan, before he sauntered off to take in the two surrendering Italian survivors.

Chapter Eight

Battle of Sicily

The war groaned on slowly for Italy in 1943, its troops in North Africa were being reduced to pitiful remnants by the growing superiority of the Allies. Erwin Rommel and his Africa Corps were gradually pushed back into Tunisia by January. Italian units were amongst that Corps, but suffering mightily from a lack of practically everything: weapons, whether machine guns, artillery pieces, food, but mostly that most precious commodity of all, fuel. It wouldn't have shocked most Italians to have realized that during the war the Ford Motor Company had outproduced Italy.

Convoy after convoy from Italy was subjected to unmerciful and unending attacks, be it from British submarines or aircraft of the Desert Air Force. Tellingly, attack bombers and fighters based on Malta, scant miles from Sicily, were a significant part of the Allied air armada. Fuel tanker ships were especially prized by those submarines and many were sent to the bottom of the Mediterranean by their deadly torpedoes.

In the end, the battle of North Africa came to its inevitable conclusion in late May, when more than 400,000 Germans and Italians became prisoners of war to the Allies. During this time, Franco Donato had been recuperating from his war wounds. He was eventually discharged from the army hospital in Palermo in March, whereupon he was allowed to complete his convalescence at home with Rosalie by his side, and little Rosanna. Franco was flabbergasted by how much his little girl had grown while he'd been away. In his eyes she was now a proper little lady. How much he had missed his wife and daughter. He swore he'd never leave them again. To hell with *il Duce* and his braggadocious and stupid boasting. He'd always exclaimed he'd turn Italy into 20th century Roman Empire. Empty words, indeed.

"You know, Rosalie, I don't think I ever really appreciated the beauty of this part of Sicily before. It took being sent to that God forsaken desert for me to realize the true beauty we have here. I mean, there was always the beauty of you and Rosanna," mused Franco as he sat with his wife on the piazza of their home. They were seated on a wooden glider that Rosalie's father had constructed many years before when she had been just a young child herself. She ruefully thought back to the many happy and fun times she had spent with her father on that glider. He'd patiently try to describe for her the many trees and shrubs scattered around and about their home.

"Mmm, mmm," soothed Rosalie as she linked her arm around Franco's. These past couple of months of Franco's convalescence had also been a time of renewal for Rosalie, and her spirit. She vividly could recall the first time the couple had made love. It had been done slowly, almost languidly, by them. Rosalie had simply luxuriated in the feel of her skin gliding along with Franco's body. She'd always loved the way he would take in her breasts and nipples, as if were suckling them. And when he entered her, she would bring her full arsenal of lovemaking to him. She'd made Franco cry out in complete pleasure when she climaxed.

"Well, anyway, as they say, all good things must come to an end," Franco continued. He got up from the glider and slowly stretched out his suspenders hitched to his gray military pants.

"When will you have to report?" Rosalie asked tentatively. She knew their little soliloquy in the midst of the war would come to an end. But she didn't want for it to be just then. She desperately wanted the war to end. And she still held out hope that the Fascist bastards would one day finally release her father. In all this time, she still had been unable to free him, nor had she been able to see him for awhile. For all she knew, he might well be dead.

"I've been told I must report by June 30th," replied Franco.

"And where will you report, or to whom, will you report to?" asked Rosalie.

"The 51st Coastal Division, and at Gela on the coast."

"A static division, one with no transport whatsoever," continued Rosalie, a taste of pure venom in her voice.

"Listen to my wife, the general," scoffed an impressed Franco Donato.

"I have my sources of information, my love. I'm not just one of those cuckolded wives chained to their kitchens," said Rosalie as she turned to face Franco. There was a fire in her eyes. Italy is *finite*. The Duce should throw in the towel. What is the point of continuing this madness? Does he need the sacrifice of more dead to satisfy some base and inner need?" Rosalie bit off her words.

"Careful, my love, you never know who may be listening," said Franco in a calm and soothing tone.

"I don't give a damn! By this point, I simply do not care anymore. I want my father home. I want you home with Rosanna and me. And I want this wanton and cruel suffering pain that the Italian people have been put through to end once and for all!" And with that Rosalie released herself from her husband's grasp and stood.

Franco also stood up and approached his wife. He slowly placed his arms across her waist and then brought his hands up to cup her breasts. Rosalie turned herself to face Franco. She brought her head forward and took in the scent of the musk smell that emanated from his body. She brought her lips toward his. They kissed slowly, somewhat chastely. It was good to feel Rosalie's body again. He only hoped he wouldn't be going away for too long from her and Rosanna when he was sent off to Gela.

***

Less than two weeks before Franco would be required to report for duty, Rosalie watched in happiness, and with a touch of sadness, as Franco played in the backyard with Rosanna. The little girl was now five years old and fluttered about with seemingly unbounded happiness as she chased down a bright red rubber ball. Her pink cherubic cheeks glowed in the morning sunlight. Rosanna laughed and giggled as she tried to run down the elusive ball. Finally, at one point, she showed a trace of frustration and took to kicking at it as hard she could with her left foot. That was odd to Rosalie, her little one was left-footed. Not that it mattered.

"Rosanna, you shouldn't do that!" scolded Franco at his daughter. He pretended to be perturbed at her.

"Why not?" asked Rosanna innocently, now cradling the ball in her little hands.

"Well, well…it's not nice. It isn't something a little girl should do," said Franco as he reached down and picked up Rosanna.

"What about little boys? Are they allowed to kick a ball hard? I see them do it on the pitch all the time," said Rosanna as she picked at the collar tabs on Franco's shirt.

"Well…you see, Rosanna, what you have seen are the boys playing a football match. They are supposed to kick the ball and to kick it hard," continued Franco paternally. He had to admit the little girl had made a good point.

"But papa, what about when someone kicks the ball off of someone else's head? Isn't that wrong, too?"

Franco was about to give up, his little one was too smart for him. How he loved her, and how he never wanted to leave her. Her and her beautiful mother. Franco Donato couldn't believe that this might be the last time he would ever see them after he went away to his new assignment. The Americans and the British were coming. And they would be coming with a vengeance: untold numbers of ships and men, aircraft and tanks.

That night Rosalie lay in his arms. They had just concluded some passionate and extended lovemaking. Franco could never get enough of the sight of Rosalie's magnificent breasts heaving and swaying above him as she rode him hard, like a bucking bronco. And he luxuriated in the feel of her legs wrapped around his plunging torso when he mounted her.

"Are you sure the Allies will land in Sicily" Perhaps it will be Greece or Sardinia?" asked Rosalie hopefully, desperately.

"Who knows, my fearsome field marshal. It could be Sardinia, but I don't think so. Anyway, I have to report. And we can only hope that the war or, at least, our war will be over soon. But for now, let us try and forget about war," said Franco as he brought his musk-scented face toward Rosalie's waiting lips.

***

Leo Goncalo was a restless and increasingly angry young man by the time July 1st arrived. He'd been assigned, lampooned in his opinion, to a military hospital in Palermo. Goncalo, like many of his fellow doctors, and most of the military personnel around him, felt that Sicily would be the site of the next Allied attack. He, and they, could feel it in their bones. The German and Italian high commands did not necessarily share that thought. In their minds, the Allies were as likely to attack in Greece or Sardinia.

In fact, the Allies had staged an elaborate and rather intelligence gambit when they utilized the body of a dead naval rating and placed sensitive information on the body. A British submarine had then deposited the body of "The Man Who Never Was" in the waters off the coast of Spain. Spanish authorities had then duly inspected the documents and sent them on to German contacts. From there, the information was conveyed to the German High Command in Berlin. This convinced them and, more importantly, Adolf Hitler, that the Americans and British would more than likely begin a campaign against the Greek islands. This caused them to not reinforce the Italian and German garrisons already in Sicily.

Goncalo had arranged to secure an appointment with the chief SS/ SD officer in Rome, Oberstgruppenfuhrer Herbert Kappler in May.

"Tell me again why you'd like to be assigned to work…and study with Dr Mengele," said Kappler as he sat in his plush office in the heart of Rome.

Leo Goncalo knew he would have to choose his words carefully if he were to gain the confidence of this powerful man of the Third Reich. Kappler was perhaps the most feared man in Rome. He was in charge of all security matters throughout the Eternal City. One could say he possessed the most power amongst all German personnel. He would not be a man to suffer fools easily.

"Well, you see, Colonel, I've long held the same beliefs of many Germans. That is, Germans of the highest rank and order in regard to the Jews. I firmly believe that they are a pestilence and, as such, must be done away with. And the sooner the better," said Goncalo as he sat stiffly across from the SS man. He thought Kappler to be a rather handsome man with firm masculine features. He knew the German to also be a character who embraced ruthlessness. A man who'd stop at nothing in carrying out any orders from his superior, Heinrich Himmler and, of course, the Fuhrer. Leo began to feel his sweat glands disgorging their contents throughout his body. He desperately hoped that it wouldn't transpire onto his face.

"Hmm, I see. That is most admirable, doctor," said Kappler as he sat back, his hands steepled together. He held Goncalo's gaze in his crystal clear blue eyes. "I'm curious as to why you have chosen to work under...that is, to study under Dr Mengele. What do you know of his activities? I am most curious." At that, Kappler leaned forward, his forearms resting on his glass-topped desk.

Leo looked at the German in his full dress SS uniform of field gray, the imposing SS runes on his collar tab. He looked over at the man's cap, featuring the death head's skull. A cold chill manifested itself within Goncalo. "Colonel, I know of Dr Mengele and his study and his accomplishments in the field of genetics. It is something I've long admired. It is a subject I'd like to be a part of and what better way than to study under the direction and guidance of a man who is clearly a world leader in the field."

"I see, I see, Dottore. But I'm still curious as to why genetics. You are not a geneticist, are you? From your record you've been a surgeon," said Kappler as he now glanced over Goncalo's military record in the notes in his hand. "Why are you so intent on working with the doctor?"

Leo knew he'd arrived at the moment of truth. He'd have to be very careful, and convincing with the German. "Well, Colonel..." Leo hesitated. He would just have to continue and hope he'd be convincing enough with this man. "I don't believe that Italy has her heart in the war any longer. She is not fulfilling her obligations to Germany and to her crusade in Europe. Germany is the last, and only, bastion against the Bolshevik hordes. And, by extension, the Jews and their infernal aid and assistance to Bolshevism. I would like to be engaged more so in this effort And, I believe I can contribute something positive and good for the future," concluded Goncalo, who sat back in his chair after nearly rising out of it while he'd delivered his exhortation.

"I see, I see, Dottore," said Kappler. "I must say I'm very impressed with your beliefs. Most impressed. I'll tell you what I'll do. I will give my personal attention into seeing that your request be granted. I cannot guarantee you anything at this point in time. For the time being, I'd suggest you go back to your present posting and I'll be in touch with you should anything develop."

At that exact moment, the sky seemed to suddenly darken and, in the very next instant, a crashing thunder boomed out. Lightning bolts were hurled forth across the darkened sky. Leo Goncalo wondered as to whether he'd just concluded a pact with the devil.

***

On July 10th 1943, the great armada of Allied warships and transports arrived off the southern coast of Sicily. It was an enormous fleet that, on the horizon, resembled a distant city. The assault was code-named Operation Husky and involved more than 330 ships of all types. Seven Allied divisions were in the assault wave—two more than would make the initial landings in Normandy nearly a year into the future.

The Americans had been designated to land at the beaches of Licata, Gela, and Scoglitti. Meanwhile, the British would attack at several points to the southeast. From this, it was hoped they would soon take Syracuse and then proceed up the coastal road to Augusta and possibly even reach as far as Catania. The Germans would have other ideas.

The main thought was, according to Bernard Montgomery, commander of the British forces, to have the Americans protect the left flank of his famed 8th Army. After all, the British had been battle-tested, and the Americans were comparative neophytes to the war. Monty and his superior, General Sir Harold Alexander, had little confidence in the Americans' ability. Here, the American commander, George Patton, would soon reveal that he had his own theories and ideas as to how the Americans should conduct their campaign.

***

Sergeant Franco Donato was gathered with his squad in the coastal resort town of Gela. Donato and his men had been hastily attached to the Livorno Division, one of the few Italian mobile divisions available on Sicily.

"Hey, see here, you never know just who you may run into," bellowed Corporale Luigi Ferraro to Franco.

Donato had been looking down, checking his assault rifle. He looked up at the sound of Ferraro's voice and instantly recognized Rosalie's cousin. "*Si,* one never does. How are you, Luigi?"

"Eh, as well as can be expected, I suppose," said Ferraro as he stepped forward to embrace Franco. "You know, I lost touch with you after they posted me to the Syracuse area. But as you can plainly see our own high command has placed me where I can look after you for Rosalie," Ferraro continued, smiling broadly from ear to ear.

"No doubt, Luigi. In any event, I am glad to see you. I only wish it were under different circumstances," said Franco. "So, what do you think? As for me, I think we're soon going to be in the shit."

"I quite agree, but do not worry. Our great German ally is alongside of us. The Hermann Goering Division is deployed right over there," said Ferraro as he pointed in the general direction of the southeast. "That makes me totally confident that we can hold."

"Do you know if it will be the Americans or the British who will land here?"

"British, Americans, it will make no difference. They will be coming to annihilate us. As for me, the sooner one of them gets here the better, then we can get the whole thing over with," snarked Luigi Ferraro.

Franco could clearly discern the bitterness in Luigi's voice. In truth, he felt the same way. Only he'd not ever express his thoughts so openly. It just wasn't worth it.

"I'm tired of this war, my friend. All I want to do is to go home and sit and drink some wine. It could be some piss-ant poor home brew."

"I'd be careful, my friend. You never know who may be listening," said Franco.

"I don't give a damn, Franco. The Duce is finished, even though he doesn't know it yet. Italy is finished, and most Italians know it. Anyway, how is Rosalie and your little girl, Rosanna?"

"Oh, both of them are fine. I miss them already. The time I spent convalescing with them was the best time I've had in this whole bloody war," said Franco. He now looked out over at the clouds that had gathered above the coast of Gela. And before he could realize it, some of the Allied ships of the invasion force had hovered into view.

"I know, Franco. The hour of battle has arrived for us. May God have mercy on us," said Luigi Ferraro as he made the sign of the cross. "Well, my friend, I have to rejoin my platoon. Take care and I hope to see you soon."

"*Si*, Luigi, you too," said Franco. He watched Ferraro make his way back to his unit. He truly hoped both of them would live through the approaching apocalypse. The Allies appeared to have brought every ship they had. Personally, Franco thought the Italians had less than a 50-50 chance.

Shelling from the Allied heavy cruisers and destroyers cascaded down upon Franco Donato and his men. He'd never experienced anything like it before in his life. Compared to his time in North Africa this was simply beyond belief. Everywhere Franco looked, when he wasn't burrowed deep into his foxhole, was being obliterated. He couldn't imagine how one could possibly live through this hellish nightmare. It was Dante's Inferno, writ large.

Franco was now prepared to meet his maker. He'd never see Rosalie and Rosanna again. He was sure of it. He only hoped the end would come quickly, that he'd feel no pain. That he wouldn't linger in that purgatory between life and death. The explosions continued without let up.

Suddenly, after one loud burst, seemingly right by his ear, Franco heard a blood-curdling scream as the top half of Federico Mondali was hurled into the air above his head. Entrails from the poor man fell on top of Franco, coating him with a blend of blood and gore. He desperately tried to wipe away the gooey, sticky mess. How could it be? One moment Mondali had been a living, breathing, joke-telling character and in the next he was piece of chopped up meat. There would be no body to send home to parents in their tiny village outside of Naples.

Finally, the bombardment began to slow. Franco hesitatingly peered up from his fighting hole, the one he'd been burrowed into like a mole. Smoke and dust filled the air. He coughed as some of it had shifted into his nostrils and throat. Franco reached for his khaki colored handkerchief and blew out the contents from his nose. He then wiped his brow, removing some of the blood and brains that had once been part of Federico Mondali's body. When he brought his gaze out to the sea he was absolutely startled to see the approach of untold numbers of landing craft. Hundreds of them were headed straight for him, Franco Donato.

Unbeknownst to Franco, the commander of the Hermann Goering Panzer Division, Paul Conrath, had been alerted to the landings by his own reconnaissance patrols and by the Rome headquarters of Field Marshal Albert Kesselring. Conrath then made the decision to counterattack the Allied forces on his own immediately. Telephone communications with the Italian Guzzoni's headquarters had been disrupted by Allied bombing. Conrath never received any order from Guzzoni concerning any coordination with the Italians. Franco Donato and his men would be left on their own to confront the approaching might of General George Patton's force.

"Pull back, pull back! *Subito!*" commanded Tenente Giuseppe Trenti, Franco's platoon commander. "We have to move quickly or we'll become a permanent part of the landscape."

Franco allowed himself a small smile, despite the desperate situation they were in. Donato had great admiration and respect for Trenti, which was something he couldn't say for most of the Italian officers he'd seen. Many of them had been what he would've characterized as martinets; men more concerned about the cut of their uniforms, or the shine on their boots. Officers who were more interested in what food they would be consuming during their next meal or what vintage wine they'd be imbibing. These very men would, more often than not, be the first ones to cut out and run or cower in the ground like frightened dogs when things went bad.

***

Nearby, following a futile attack and withdrawal by a few Italian tanks against US Army Ranger units, under the command of Colonel William Darby, some 600 Italian infantrymen of the Livorno Division approached Gela. Marching in an impressive and brave parade ground formation, which would soon prove to be suicidal, they were savagely cut down by American small-arms and mortar fire. Not a single Italian reached the town. Their torn and bloody bodies gave stark evidence as to what had just happened.

The Hermann Goering Division also ran into heavy and determined resistance. Most of it the result of accurate naval gunfire support in the form of five and six inch shells. In addition, Tiger tanks which accompanied the German infantry attacking through olive groves to the east of Gela became hung up in the dense growths of the tough trees.

Albert Kesselring, upon receiving reports from the beachhead, was none too pleased with either the Italians or the Germans' performance. Another attack was ordered for the next day. This time the Hermann Goering would link up with designated Italian units. A column of Italian troops was spotted heading for Gela. The USS Savannah, mounting fifteen 6 inch guns cut loose on them. The Italians were decimated.

Meanwhile, Franco Donato and his decimated and demoralized unit became separated from their battalion and soon found themselves surrounded. Their lieutenant knew it would be futile to continue to show any kind of resistance and thereby ordered them to surrender.

While glad to be alive, and still in one piece, Franco was devastated. He wouldn't get to see Rosalie and Rosanna any time soon. Their warm home and the picturesque surroundings would not be seen again for how long he did not know.

Men were herded into wire enclosures across the open ground, just above the wind-swept surf along the beach at Gela. Franco Donato noted ironically that it wasn't very far from where he'd been taken prisoner by US Army Rangers. Some of the Italians seemed quite content and could be seen sitting or kneeling, talking and laughing with one another. Occasionally, long lost friends who may not have seen one another in who knew how long, ran into one another. There would be hugs, embraces, and backslapping and much animated chatter. In some cases, men from the same family would find themselves cast together with the same result.

Other men did not react this way and often could be found standing or sitting by themselves, and wouldn't engage or speak to anyone else. Those standing by fence-posts would sometimes bang their heads against them contentiously. On one occasion, one of these men impacted his head so hard that he gave himself a concussion. After lying in the dust, moaning and gripping his head, he was hauled away by amused MPs. One of the bystanders joked to his friends that that was one way to get themselves out of the compound, but it must have been a painful one he could well do without.

Franco Donato was on the fringe of a group of Italians when he felt a nudge in his back. He turned to find himself facing than none other than Luigi Ferraro, smiling broadly at him.

"Well, my friend, it seems like we've met again," said Ferraro as he removed a packet of cigarettes from his tunic. He slowly extracted one and handed it to Franco. He then removed one for himself. Ferraro then took a silver plated lighter and leaned forward to light Franco's cigarette. Franco cupped his hand around the cigarette to better catch the flame. Ferraro then stepped back to light his own.

"Grazie, my long lost friend. It seems as if we were just having a conversation not far from this very spot," said Franco. He paused to inhale on his cigarette. The taste of the tobacco and the exhalation of the smoke felt, initially, intoxicating.

"Indeed, I must say the most remarkable thing is that we have survived and, not only that, we are still in one piece," exclaimed a now pensive looking Luigi Ferraro.

Before Franco replied he looked about him at the conclave of prisoners, his fellow Italians. He then looked up to the sky, taking in some slow-moving, low-hanging clouds. Seagulls crisscrossed the blue sky, their wings extended to catch drafts of air. They had returned now that the battle had quieted and a degree of stillness reigned once again.

"On the one hand, I am glad to be alive, don't get me wrong. On the other hand, I think we're going to be sent on all paid expenses trip to England or America. As for me, I would just have soon paid my own way," noted Ferraro laconically, no longer seeming so jovial. "And, as for you, I don't think you will be seeing Rosalie or Rosanna for awhile."

The words stung Franco, not because he was angry at Ferraro, but because he knew them to be true. It would indeed be awhile, may be a long time, until he saw his loved ones again. He couldn't wait to be able to write them a letter conveying to them that he was safe and in good health.

After continuing with some more casual conversation both men fell into silence. Each lost in his own thoughts.

***

The hot and humid days of August limped into the weary and tired lives of virtually every citizen of Ottavino. Technically, Rosalie Donato and her family were not formally a part of the town, but still considered themselves full-fledged members of it. Rosalie had been closely following news of the Allied landings on the island. Inwardly, she was glad that the Americans and British had finally come to liberate the Sicilian people, and yet, she was terrified of what might've happened to Franco. The only news she had last heard from him was that he and his unit had been on the move somewhere south of Palermo.

Throughout July, Rosalie did her best to meet the needs of Rosanna. She was constantly amazed at how fast her little girl was growing, and how bright and quick-witted she was. No one, including Rosalie, could put a thing past the little one. Some of the townspeople of Ottavino thought they could slyly tease the little girl, but she would never have any of it. And Rosanna would push back by gently and subtly chastising the older citizen.

Rosalie knew she'd have to be very careful and circumspect whenever the little girl was around. She'd have to remind Franco when he returned, whenever he returned home.

The long, hot, and seemingly endless summer had seen the Donato family manage to hang onto to what they had, in terms of their land and financial holdings. But Carlo Goncalo had continued bearing down hard.

It was never direct or overt, but Rosalie knew that he was the master puppeteer pulling the strings of his front men.

On August 1st, Rosalie received word, by way of a cold-hearted telegram, that her beloved father had expired away during the night. "*Expired*?" That was how the Prefect had worded it. As if her father had been a metaphor for a license that had lapsed. She crumpled up the telegram, but didn't throw it away. She would take it with her when she went to Mettuno to confront the Prefect, the oily and despicable Stefano Fanti.

It took Rosalie several hours to make her way to the jail where her father had been held, and, in her view, murdered. The raging battle for Sicily, started on July 10th, was approaching its climax which come to an end at Messina. George Patton's American forces had been making their way along the northern coastal route, in a race against General Montgomery's British troops, which had been moving up along the east coast of the island.

Rosalie had left Rosanna in the care of her sister. She had instructed her to make sure that Rosanna stayed indoors, Allied planes had been occasionally seen flying about the area. One never knew when the Allies might make their final push to attack Messina, and secure the island from the Germans.

Roads had been choked, mostly with German vehicles scurrying about. Rosalie and her brother Aldo, had been able to painstakingly make their way by bicycle to the jail. Once there, Rosalie raised a scene. In past days she would have stayed at home and bitterly cursed out Stefano Fanti and Mussolini. But not now. On this day her blood was up.

"I am sorry, signora, but the Prefect is not available to see you, or anyone, at this time," claimed one of Fanti's minions.

"I know he is here. I know it. Let me in to see him. I have a right to confront Prefect Fanti about my father. He was murdered! Murdered! I tell you…you little worm!" screamed Rosalie, blood was in her eyes.

The diminutive corporal took a step backward.

Rosalie's brother placed an arm around her waist and gently tried to restrain her. He thought she might physically assault the man. He felt there was a good chance she could take the corporal down. Rosalie was a well-proportioned and solidly built Sicilian woman. And at that moment it was on full display as she sneered at Fascist authority.

"I know that worm, Fanti is in there," she pointed at the door to Stefano Fanti's office. "Murderer, murderer!" continued Rosalie, her brother having a hard time in restraining his sister.

"Rosalie, it will do you no good. You'll only end up in jail here. Fanti would just love to be able to act on the merest pretext to put you away. And then what, who would be there for Rosanna?" said Aldo.

Somehow, Rosalie managed to calm herself down. "*Corporale* you tell the Prefect that his day is coming. There will be a day of judgment. And that judgment of him will not be kind. It will be harsh. And I will pursue him to the ends of the earth so that he gets what he deserves. He will have to answer for what he has done to our father," glowered Rosalie Donato. With that, she turned on her heel and along with her brother strode from the jail.

Once they were outside in the mid-day sun, Rosalie and Aldo turned to one another and embraced. Rosalie couldn't restrain the tears that now fell down her face. Above her a flight of British bombers were on their way to bomb Messina.

***

It was inevitable that the Allies would conquer Sicily. The only question that remained was as to when. Most of the Italian troops on the island had long thrown in the towel. At best, they had offered only token resistance to the British and Americans. The German forces had presented another dimension entirely. Never mounting more than three divisions, they'd managed to force the Allies to fight and bleed for every yard of Sicilian soil. The topography of it lent itself to the perfect defense against any invading force.

To the objective observer of the campaign it would have seemed that the Allied men were working at cross purposes to one another. George Patton had chafed at his 7th Army's assignment at Gela to merely provide flank protection to Bernard Montgomery's 8th Army. The aggressive and brash American had resented the secondary job given to his men. He well knew that Montgomery and his superior, Harold Alexander, did not respect the fighting ability of the Americans. The main task of securing Sicily should fall to the battle-tested and experienced men who'd fought so long and so hard in the North African desert.

On his own authority, Patton directed the American 2nd Armored Division and 3rd Infantry Division for a drive on the city of Palermo. It was ripe for the plucking, and the lightning campaign that followed would pay a rich dividend in the clearing of the western half of Sicily. It would also deliver a major port into Allied hands. The Americans covered more than 100 miles in less than four days, encountering little resistance along the way. The worst enemies to confront the Americans were the steaming summer heat and the choking, cloying dust that rose from the parched gravel roads.

Once Palermo fell, Patton would then place his army at a full gallop across the northern coast to Messina. He was absolutely determined to beat Montgomery to the port city and bring the Sicilian campaign to a conclusion. It was as if Patton and Montgomery were engaged in their personal duel as to whom would get to Messina first. Casualties be damned. German forces trapped? Perhaps. "This is a horse race in which the prestige of the US Army is at stake," said Patton; "We must take Messina before the British!"

The American had in his possession two key roads, one of them led along the coast toward Messina, and the other sliced through the mountainous interior. The 7th Army would be a battering ram, operating in the north as an equal to the 8th Army, which was continuing to hammer away at the gates of Catania in the east.

The Americans faced a duel enemy: the terrain and the ever resourceful Germans. The roads of northern Sicily were narrow, twisting, and steep, punctuated by tunnels and bridges that could be easily defended, and then either blown up or face Germans with automatic weapons and demolition charges.

At one point, Patton, impatient at best, and always highly emotional, became extremely irritable. His temper would give rise to an ugly episode that would come to matter more in the United States than the capture of Palermo had been. It would nearly cost him his military career. One day, as was his habit, Patton visited an army field hospital near Nicosia to speak with some of the wounded soldiers. After congratulating some of the men for their bravery, Patton came upon one man who had no bandages and showed no sign of having been wounded. The general asked the soldier what was wrong, only to be told, "I guess I can't take it anymore," the soldier replied. Patton exploded in a rage and then proceeded to slap the hapless man across the face. He then shoved the sniveling soldier out of the tent, calling him a coward and a disgrace to the army. It later turned out that the man had been running a high fever caused by malaria and dysentery.

One week later, there was a similar episode when Patton knocked another soldier's helmet off his head and then waved a pistol in the man's face, threatening to shoot him right then and there.

Nevertheless, George Patton drove his men relentlessly toward Messina. During the course of one amphibious landing a regiment of American troops came dangerously close to being stranded and destroyed at a town called Brolo. Fortunately for them, other American units broke through and rescued them.

Meanwhile, the British had been slowly slogging their way up along Sicily's eastern coast. Montgomery, too, harbored visions of glory, and he, too, desired to be the first into Messina. He'd long been held up by the treacherous terrain in front of Catania, and also the pestilence of the mosquitoes in the region. Monty may well have hindered his own advance by what some commanders, mostly American, saw as an abnormal degree of caution. "Monty" had proven in the past to be the master of the set-piece battle: subscribing to the theories of having overwhelming ground forces and air support before beginning an offensive.

***

The Donato and Mancini families, along with the Goncalo clan, waited in trepidation and in some degree of fear, as the battle lines slowly drew closer to Ottavino and Mettuno. Daily could be heard the eruptions and sounds of artillery to the west and to the east. Allied planes could be seen roaming throughout the skies above. Cautious residents would try and catch a peek of the planes and their falling projectiles. Secretly, invariably they cheered as it meant they were getting closer to liberation. It was a price they would have to pay, even at the risk of their own lives.

Rosalie was prepared to take shelter in the make-shift below-ground cave her father had had dug out by her brothers. If the moment ever presented itself, she would hide there along with little Rosanna, and other family members. Of course, this was no guarantee they would be saved if a bomb were to fall on them.

When the end came, it was George Patton and the Americans who won the race to Messina. Montgomery 's hopes had been dashed. Lost in all of the hoopla was the fact most of the German forces, including their heavy tanks and artillery, had effected their escape to the Italian mainland. They would later exact a high toll of casualties at a quaint resort town by the name of Anzio.

***

Franco Donato found himself amongst some 1,500 fellow Italian prisoners of war who were now aboard the American transport ship *Ambrose Palmer*. The vessel took its name from some obscure Union Army general of the American Civil War. Franco could see that the ship wasn't in the most seaworthy condition. Numerous rust spots and rotting metal could be found throughout the ship. To Franco's untrained nautical eye the *Palmer* looked old and decrepit. His foremost hope was that it would convey him to its destination of Bizerte, Tunisia safely. Donato would pray that some of his Italian Air Force countrymen would not locate and sink the *Ambrose Palmer* in their SM-79 "Sparrowhawk" torpedo bombers.

From Gela to Bizerte would be a relatively short trip which would consume barely a day. Upon their arrival in Tunisia, Franco Donato and his fellow Italians were loaded onto US Army GMC 6 x 6 trucks for transport to a large POW enclosure. The camp was so large and there were be so many prisoners that not all of them could be housed under shelter. Franco was fortunate to be one of the lucky ones who would have a roof over his head.

"Look at them. Would you just look at them. The poor bastards," muttered Luigi Del Bonis from the shelter of his hut located along the edge of the compound. Straggly barbed wire hung loosely along the nearby perimeter. Del Bonis was alluding to the uncovered men on the other side of the camp and what they were being subjected to as a heavy rain pelted down on them. "Why, I say it's a bloody war crime. That's what it is," continued Del Bonis.

"You don't know what the hell you're talking about, *paisan*. I have been on the Russian Front and I tell you what I saw would make your head spin. You want to talk about war crimes? What the Germans did to some unfortunate civilians was beyond a crime. It was…it was…I tell you, you would not believe what I saw," said *Corporale* Emidio Cardelli.

"And so you're taking the side of the Americans are you?" spat out Del Bonis. "I think you're an asshole, my friend."

Cardelli took a step forward is if he would strike out at Del Bonis. At this point, Franco, who'd been standing nearby, decided to intervene. "That's right, why don't you two tough guys get into a fistfight. Then you can both show how tough you are. You guys should have shown a little more fortitude while you had the chance on Sicily."

"Ah, I still say he's an asshole," muttered Cardelli as he slowly faded away back to his bunk.

Franco Donato had composed several letters to Rosalie, but something was holding him back from sending them to her. For some unknown reason, the camp authorities wouldn't allow it. It was also more likely that it wasn't just feasible at the moment. Donato and his compatriots waited in the camp for several weeks before they learned of their fate. Nearly half of the camp would be shipped to North America, some going to the States and the rest to Canada. The other half would find themselves on their way to England.

Franco learned he would be going to the United States. It was a country he'd long heard about. A country that was bountiful and beautiful. A nation that was so much larger than Italy. Franco knew of many friends some from his own family members who'd packed up and left as they emigrated to the States. He had once heard that the streets were practically paved with gold. Franco realized that this was more likely grand hyperbole. There could be no place that was that good. But still, he'd heard that in America if one had drive and ambition there was no limit as to what one could do, what anyone could accomplish.

It took more than two weeks for Franco's ship to make its way across the Atlantic. Days and days went by when the POWs saw nothing but unending blue skies above them. No birds could be seen flittering about. The *Ambrose Palmer* took on the air of a floating mausoleum, its holds stuffy and dank. Men would often be found by the rails, puking their guts out. No doubt the abysmal food contributed to it immeasurably.

The days continued to drag on. At long last the men could discern that the coast of America must be near. Seagulls began flying over their heads. Excitement began to build and circulated throughout the ship.

To Franco, it was a welcome relief. It had been a hell of a long way to the New World. The *Ambrose Palmer* pulled up the quay at the port of Brooklyn. Donato and his companions would now be transported by train over the course of the next two weeks to prisoner of war camps in Texas. Perhaps when he arrived there, Franco would be able to post some of his letters to Rosalie.

Chapter Nine

Auschwitz

Standartenfuhrer Herbert Kappler was as good as his word to *Dottore* Leo Goncalo. He had indeed looked into the matter of Goncalo's request to work and study with the Germans, and more specifically with SS doctors, in some of the new and… unusual biological and hereditary research projects that had come of age. Kappler had contacted an SS colleague of his, one Doctor Albert Dornhoefer, and informed him of Leo Goncalo's interest and enthusiasm for what some Nazi doctors were engaged in.

On October 15th, 1943, Leo Goncalo found himself sitting in the office of SS Colonel Dornhoefer in Berlin. "I must say that I'm much impressed with your service record, doctor. Most impressed," said Dornhoefer as a cloud of cigarette smoke wreathed about the Nazi's head. Dornhoefer wore rimless spectacles, which in the pale light of the room cast a rather sinister look upon the man.

Leo Goncalo felt a cold shiver run through his body as he sat in the spartan looking office of Colonel Dornhoefer. Outside, a cold and gray, uncomfortable day could be observed. A heavy drizzle had been forecast for the day. It seemed to fit the mood in the leaden office, and the subject matter being discussed between the two men. For the moment, Leo remained rooted and immutable to his chair.

"Yes, yes, most impressive. But…I am curious as to why you would like to volunteer for what you've requested. After all, it isn't every day that I receive a request such as this. And that is from a German doctor, let alone an Italian. I do believe you may well be the first Italian doctor to have made such a request," continued Colonel Dornhoefer as he sat back in his seat.

The cold glare emanating from the German's face disarmed Leo, but he well knew he would have to carefully and craftily provide a fitting and believable response. "Colonel, I've long admired Germany and what she is doing for all of Europe. Furthermore, I sincerely believe in research that is presently being conducted by the SS medical staff. I believe that I could significantly contribute to this cause. I am willing to work in one of the camps that have been established. Perhaps one such as Auschwitz or Treblinka," said Leo, as he now sat back, an inward sign of relief evident on his face. He was able to conceal a sheen of perspiration from breaking out.

"What do you know of these camps, *Dottore*?" questioned Dornhoefer in a seemingly petulant and annoyed tone.

Leo knew he was now on shaky ground and so he tentatively offered, "Colonel, we both know some of what is going on in these camps, and…"

"These camps are merely resettlement camps, nothing more. I think you should be more careful in future as to what you're basing some of your conclusions on," said Dornhoefer, his tone softening to a degree.

"I meant no disrespect, sir. Nevertheless, SS doctors and researchers have been conducting certain medical experiments on subjects. And as I have said, I believe that I can be of significant assistance in this research."

Dornhoefer sat himself up, the smoke having cleared away, offering Leo a clear view of this austere man. "All right, *Dottore* Goncalo, I do believe that you are sincere. I will forward your request to the proper and cognizant authority here in Berlin. But I cannot promise you anything. However, there is one other matter I'd like to discuss with you."

"Certainly, sir, and what would that be?" asked Leo, feeling more relaxed and confident.

"I believe you mentioned to Colonel Kappler that you would like to work with Dr Mengele. As you know, the doctor is an expert researcher in the field of genetics, but he isn't that widely known. How did you happen to select him?" asked the SS man. That look, that cold, sinister, and calculating look had returned.

Leo's stomach started to tremble and turn over, it felt like butterflies were filling it at the same time. "Well, sir, although I'm or have been primarily a surgeon, Dr Mengele's field has always interested and intrigued me and…"

"Intrigued? How so?" asked Dornhoefer, who made a move to extract another cigarette from its silver-plated case, but then apparently abruptly changed his mind. He steepled his fingers together in an approximation of interest.

"The very idea that genetics can be used in a manner that has not, as far as I am aware, yet been used before is something for which the ramifications are unknown and therefore are limitless. This is something which just a short time ago was simply unheard of," concluded Leo. He hoped his answer had been sufficient. Truthfully, he had to admit to himself that it sounded like a bunch of gobbledy gook. He looked at Dornhoefer, hoping for the best that the Nazi believed him; privately fearing the worst.

"Good, good. Very good. I will pass on your earnest request to my superior. But again I can't promise you anything definite," said Dornhoefer as he held up his right hand. He now stood and extended his right hand toward Leo Goncalo, who shook it earnestly. He and the SS man looked steadily into one another's eyes. Leo felt more than assured he would be granted his wish.

***

30 Sep 43

Dear Dr Mengele,

I am writing to you, Herr Doctor, to express my fervent desire to join you and some of your associates in the research work you are now engaged in. Before I get into specifics, I'd like to express by heartfelt support and belief in Germany and her cause to date in this unfortunate war in which we now find ourselves in. A war entirely the fault of the Allies and those hiding behind the curtains. By that, I mean the accursed Jews of Europe. Indeed, of the entire world. The Fuhrer has been right all along. I only wish that our own leader, il Duce, were as forceful as the Fuhrer has been.

Be that as it may, I believe that I possess the requisite skills and knowledge as a physician so as to be able to assist you, and your associates, in the necessary medical research you're now conducting. I believe I possess, in addition, the correct attitude and desire that is needed in these trying times.

I have read and been most impressed by your dissertation in the ANTHROPOLIGICAL INSTITUTE at the University of Munich, which was entitled "Racial-Morphological Examination of the Anterior Portion of the Lower Jaw." I was most fascinated by your demonstration of structural differences in portions of the lower jaw in old Egyptians, Melanesians, short-skulled Europeans, and, of course, long-skulled Europeans, primarily of the Nordic races. Your conclusion that the anterior segments of the lower jaw showed clear differences well-suited for racial distinctions was absolutely brilliant.

I was also impressed by your publication "Hereditary Transmission of Fistulae Auris," an abnormal opening in the ear cartilage, The means of the LENZ-VERSHUER principle of irregular, dominant hereditary process has long been misunderstood by many researchers and clinicians. You, doctor, have been able to translate this process, into a readable and more easily understood phenomenon.

I do hope to be able to have the opportunity to join you and your associates in the not too distant future. I thank you for your time and your patience.

With Warmest Regards

Dottore Leonardo Goncalo

Leo read the letter over several times, making small corrections and additions, until he thought it looked just right. He would now contact his friend and colleague, Armando, to translate the letter into perfect German.

***

"Then my ruin is complete," said the defeated man who stood before King Victor Emmanuel III. The speaker was none other than Benito Mussolini. The King had just informed him that at that moment he was the most hated man in Italy. The recorder of the meeting was Field Marshal Pietro Badoglio, who on July 25th 1943, had just been appointed by the King to succeed Mussolini as head of the Italian government.

Following his dismissal by Victor Emmanuel, Mussolini went out to his automobile, but it had suddenly disappeared. A military officer then pointed in the direction he said the vehicle had been taken. As the Duce walked in the direction indicated he found himself surrounded by police. He was told to get into a waiting ambulance. The former leader of Fascist Italy now understood what he was confronted with. Benito Mussolini was then hustled off under arrest, and with it the twenty-one years of his dictatorship came to an end.

The Italians had long grown weary of the War and the twenty plus years of Fascist rule. The disintegration of the country's military position was matched by the demise of the home front. The economy was in shambles, industry had been crippled, and food rations were now down to a bare 900 calories per day. The measure had been taken so as to facilitate the shipment of more food to Germany. The summer of 1943 had presented a ripe opportunity for the overthrow of Benito Mussolini.

The Duce's sudden removal from power not only surprised the Allies, but also signaled to them that Italy wanted to up and quit the war entirely. Up to this moment, the British and Americans had been proceeding rather cautiously. General Dwight Eisenhower, Allied Commander in Chief, had been instructed to plan for an operation, after Sicily's fall, so as to remove Italy from the war. In addition to contain as many German divisions as possible.

The Allies hurried up with their plans to exploit Mussolini's fall. In the meantime, Field Marshal Badoglio, who had stated that Italy would continue in the war, sent emissaries on July 31st to make a separate peace deal with the Allies. Badoglio feared the degree of German retaliation when they learned of Italy's defection. It would undoubtedly be swift and cruel.

The Allies invasion plan called for Bernard Montgomery's 8th Army to cross the Strait of Messina some time before September 4th. On September 9th, the US Fifth Army, under the command of General Mark Clark, would land at Salerno. It was hoped that Monty could come to Clark's aid should the 5th Army run into trouble with the Germans at Salerno.

Montgomery's landing went off smoothly, but it soon was confronted with mountainous country, narrow and winding roads, many bridges, viaducts, culverts, and tunnels. A handful of German engineers skilled in the art of demolition could hold up an army indefinitely in that region.

Mark Clark's 5th Army's target of Salerno had once been described as one of the most beguiling spots in the world. Longfellow had once commented, "as the blue Salerno Bay with its sickle of white sand." The Gulf of Salerno presented the Allied invaders with some definite advantages. The steepness of the beaches would make it possible for landing craft to run themselves up on the sand and land troops directly onto the shore. The small harbor, if seized intact, could handle most of the supply tonnages.

The Germans, however, would have other ideas. In fact, the German divisions under Field Marshal Albert Kesselring and General Heinrich von Viettinghoff, would put up such a stiff challenge to the Allies that a withdrawal wouldn't have been considered beyond a reasonable decision.

***

The remaining months of 1943 were of great hardship to Rosalie and her family. They weren't as much for young Rosanna, who was too youthful and innocent to realize how bad things really were. How dire the entire situation was for the Donatos. Rosalie, at last, after more than three months, received her first letters from Franco. Naturally, she was glad and thankful that her husband had survived and was safe, albeit even if he were now in America. He was still far from home, further than he'd ever been before. But, he was safe, and he'd not been injured.

Rosalie was able to detect that Franco was in a good frame of mind. She could intuitively deduce his tone by his handwriting's legibility. The letters were flowing and not jammed together, as if he'd been in an agitated or angry state of mind. For that, she could breathe a sigh of relief. Rosalie now felt certain that Franco would return to her and Rosanna whenever this ungodly and seemingly unending war would cease.

Rosalie, of course, wrote many letters in reply, now that she knew where Franco was. Somewhere in some state called Texas. She tried, as desperately as she could, to convey that all was well, but she knew that Franco would not be fooled.

Rosalie wrote in one letter that Carlo Goncalo had developed some kind of respiratory problem and wished she had added how she secretly wished the "old bastard" would die an agonizing and slow death. But she couldn't, being the good Christian woman she still considered herself to be. Rosalie didn't want to take the chance that government censors wouldn't eavesdrop on her note. Then, she, too, might be spirited away in the dead of night. That would leave little Rosanna without her mother, and her father.

Life in Ottavino had begun to ease up somewhat for the citizenry. The Americans, for the most part, were now in charge. Rations were increased, as well as sundry items such as cooking oil and coal. Much to Rosalie's delight, the Americans had begun looking into some of Carlo Goncalo's business activities, and his ardent rapture of Mussolini and the Fascists. This, of course, had come too late for Rosalie's father, and, for her dearly departed and missed mother. Nevertheless, it presented to her a small degree of satisfaction. She vowed once again that she wouldn't falter in her continuing quest to bring Goncalo to justice once the war finally ended.

***

The shining black Mercedes touring car slowly approached the main gate of the most feared and notorious concentration camp in all of Europe. Inside the vehicle in the backseat sat Hauptsturmfuhrer Erik Kramer and Dottore Leonardo Goncalo. Despite the car's heater being set on the high level, Leo sat shivering in his seat. He looked over at Kramer, who maintained a muted face, an impassioned look. The ride to the camp had been one of virtual silence between the two men; Kramer was not one to engage in any kind of verbal discourse, with the exception of military or camp matters. As to conversing with this pretentious Italian doctor, forget it.

The Mercedes finally came to a stop. Leo looked out and up from his rear seat window. He struggled to make out the words located atop the gate, *Arbeit Macht Frei* (Work Makes You Free), almost as if denoting a department store. Not one announcing a death camp; one where thousands of individuals: men, women, children were being put to immediate death, or slowly being worked to a slow and agonizing expiration.

The date was December 15th, 1943, and in the sky above, there was a mix of blue and gray leaden clouds, seeming to capture to the exact degree the cold and frigid atmosphere surrounding the camp. After a brief check of papers, the Mercedes was admitted into Auschwitz formally. The vehicle then slowly made its way along an inclined track, passing an endless line of barracks on both sides. Goncalo could make out huddled individuals between the buildings; of what sex he could not determine, walking about in a slow and desultory fashion.

Eventually, the car carrying Goncalo and Kramer slowed as it neared the home of Kommandant Artur Liebehenschel. Leo knew the man's rank as that of Sturmbannfuhrer, or the equivalent of major in the German Army. Leo thought that a man of Liebehenschel's standing would have had a higher rank, but no matter, the Sturmbannfuhrer was the undisputed lord and master of Auschwitz. He was the man who held absolute power over the life and death of every prisoner in the camp.

Goncalo also took in the Gestapo's office, right next door to the Kommandant's home. Across the road was the SS Headquarters building. Leo shivered again, but this time not from the cold, but from an impending sense of dread, and something else he couldn't quite put his finger on.

"Well, Doctor, you are here at last. I trust you will make a good impression on the Kommandant," sneered a smug Erik Kramer, who reached for the door handle to exit the vehicle. Goncalo nodded and opened his own side door. Once outside, not only the cold assaulted him, but a smell hit him full in the face. It was of an odor he'd never encountered before.

"It is a pleasure to meet you at long last, *Dottore* Goncalo. An extreme pleasure," gushed Sturmbannfuhrer Arthur Liebehenschel to Leo. "I'm so glad to finally have the opportunity to meet you. I only wish that my wife could be here as well, but she's in the town of Oswiecim for some shopping. You know, woman things."

The commandant who only recently had replaced its former incumbent, the notorious, and some might have said the malodorous Rudolf Hoess. Liebehenschel stood before Leo in a spiffy field gray uniform, black jack boots gleaming. The man stood about six feet tall with an impressive military bearing. His once crew-cut blond hair had begun to gray, but it was Liebehenschel's face with its imposing set of ice-blue eyes set above a curvaceous mouth containing full red lips. The man's face appeared slightly flush, which to Leo might be indicative of perhaps a little too much to drink.

"Thank you, sir, that is most kind of you. I am most grateful for your acceptance to my request for admittance here to Auschwitz. I'm most anxious to learn of some of the research that is being conducted here," said Leo, perhaps at too much length. He thought he was beginning to ramble, which was a bad habit of his when confronted with an imposing situation.

"We're most glad to be able to accommodate a person of such renown as yourself. Although, I should add that you request being granted was really the result of my predecessor, Sturmbannfuhrer Hoess," continued Liebbehenschel. All the while observing this pretentious Italian doctor.

"I was surprised to hear that he is no longer in command here," said Leo, still feeling apprehensive. His attention was now focused on a massive grandfather clock behind and just to the left of the commandant's desk.

"Yes, yes, he has been promoted to a most important position in Berlin. Undoubtedly in recognition of his fine and upstanding work here at Auschwitz, " said Liebehenschel. "How remiss of me, would you care to sample some Riesling wine, Doctor?"

"*Si*, er, yes. I would be most appreciative, sir" gulped Leo in reply. He couldn't help it that the German commandant left him in an icy chill.

As Liebehenschel offered the wine to Leo he paused to say, "*Dottore*, this wine is some of the best we Germans have to offer. But seriously, I personally believe that Italian wine is the best. However, we shall keep that to ourselves."

"Certainly, sir. That is most kind of you,"

"I'd like to say," said Liebehenschel conspiratorially, "that some people have a misconception of this camp. By that I mean that some of these same individuals have called our camp a death camp or a concentration camp. It is nothing of the kind. I admit that we do have a concentration of a great number of people from all over Europe. But these people have been deemed enemies of the state by our Fuhrer, Adolf Hitler and by Reichsfuhrer Himmler. As a result, they have to be forced to pay for their crimes. Would you not agree?" asked Liebehenschel as to Leo for affirmation.

"I most certainly do, sir" agreed Leo Goncalo. Privately he was already having second thoughts. That there could be this many so- called enemies of the state in one place. To say nothing about the many other camps scattered about Germany and Poland. Leo held his silence.

"Good, good. I do hope that you'll be able to learn from what you see being conducted here. I understand that you've requested to work with one of our foremost medical associates, Dr Mengele. Is that not correct?"

"It is indeed, sir. Doctor Mengele and some of his associates," replied Leo enthusiastically. He was beginning to perspire once again from the heat being thrown off from the log fireplace just behind him.

"I believe that Dr Mengele is now presently involved with a selection process for some of our newly arrived...eh...newly arrived guests. Perhaps you'll be able to meet with him later today," offered Liebehenschel, in his most ingratiating manner.

To Leo, the German still made his blood run cold. He was desperately trying to conceal his discomfort, but he instinctively felt that Liebehenschel could sense it. "That would be fine, sir," said Leo.

"Good, good, very good. And now I will have Hauptsturmfuhrer Kramer escort you to your quarters."

***

It was early evening and Leo Goncalo had just finished a light supper in his quarters. He went to a window and looked up into the smoky haze of the frigid December night in southern Poland. Above the nearby barrack buildings he glimpsed a red glow that rose up into the sky, something akin to an effervescence. The scene mesmerized the young man and he was struck by the thought that he may well have been looking at a scene from out of Dante's Inferno. The Italian quickly realized that what he was gazing at were the destroyed remains of countless individuals. Individuals judged to have been unworthy. Unworthy of life. Of course, the Nazis had deemed these irredeemables as criminals.

Suddenly, Leo heard a knock at his door. He turned from the window and was about to ask who it was, when the doorknob turned and in stepped a short, rather unimpressive looking man.

"I understand you have been looking for me," said the stranger. I am Doctor Josef Mengele, at your service."

Leo continued to look at the man and judged him to be about 5' 9" in height. Dark, nearly blond, wavy hair danced upon the top of his head. Mengele's facial features were not those of what would be characterized as Aryan. In fact, to Goncalo, the German appeared to be more Romany (gypsy) than a member of the master race. Dark brown eyes were set into his open face, a gentle curve to the mouth. It wasn't anything like Leo had expected in the least. To him, Mengele was almost a disappointment, not that it really mattered. After all, Leo was there to learn and to put into practice what he fervently believed in. And Josef Mengele would be the perfect instrument.

"Dr Mengele, it is a great honor to finally meet you. I have followed your career and your research with great interest," said Leo, turning to face Mengele.

"Thank you, *Dottore* Goncalo. I must say I was most intrigued by your letter. In fact, I was quite flattered. A man in my position often receives, what I consider to be, fatuous and unconvincing agreement in regard to my work. That was not the case with your letter. In addition, I did some research of my own and found your own background to be rather impressive in its own right."

"*Grazie,* er, thank you, doctor. That is most kind of you," said an ingratiating Leo Goncalo. He remained rooted to his spot on the floor, as Mengele advanced a couple of steps. Goncalo thought he detected a whiff of some type of men's cologne. It seemed rather odd, given the location and the business of the camp.

"You're most welcome, *Dottore*. You know, I do think you should join me tomorrow morning. Say around 0930 hours. You see we are set to receive a shipment of Jews from Holland. I understand it to be a nice assortment of men, women, and kinder. Who knows, there may even be some twins? And from these I can make a selection for some of my own experimentation. As I'm sure you know, I've dedicated much of my time and resources to an intensive study of twinned individuals. Perhaps I'll even share with you some of my findings to date. What do you say?" asked Mengele as he looked directly at Leo.

To Leo, it seemed as if Mengele was trying to generate a reaction from him unspoken. As if the German could discern Leo's true feelings telepathically. Goncalo found this feeling unsettling. "That sounds fine, Dr Mengele. I shall meet you, uh, where, sir?"

"At the parade ground inside the main gate," responded Mengele.

"Is there anything I need? Anything I should bring with me?"

"*Nein*, just bring yourself. And be ready to witness something...something extraordinary. It will provide you with a rather unique perspective, perhaps and even a more honest view of human nature. One could say that people will do the most unfathomable things to live for just one more moment."

***

After Mengele had left Leo, the young man sat down heavily on his bed and reflected back on what he'd read about the German in his biography. He'd been 32 years old when he'd arrived at Auschwitz. Josef Mengele was the second son of a well-to-do Bavarian industrialist. The family could even have been considered *nouveau riche*. The Mengeles were considered to be strict Catholics, and Josef always identified himself as one on all of his official school forms. The young man was remembered as a serious student, a popular and enthusiastic friend in whom one could recognize a distinct ambition.

Mengele's early right-wing nationalism was reflected by his joining the *Steel Helmet* Association in 1931. He then joined the Nazi SA in 1934, and then applied for Party membership in 1937. Mengele went on and applied for SS membership the following year.

At universities in Bonn, Vienna, and Frankfort, Josef Mengele came to concentrate on the physical anthropology and genetics of the period. He came to work under Otmar von Vershuer and his quest for a biological society of means of a national system of files on individual genetic characteristics.

Leo Goncalo had been impressed by the three aforementioned publications of Mengele prior to his arrival at Auschwitz. It looked, at one time, as if the young man would one day be headed for an academic career of some renown.

In 1940, Josef Mengele served in the reserve medical corps, and then spent three years with a Waffen SS unit, mostly on the Russian Front. He was said to have acquitted well of himself in the face of the enemy and was promoted to the rank of captain (Hauptsturmfuhrer). He was the only doctor in Auschwitz with an array of medals.

Leo had also read that Mengele was highly admired as a doctor and researcher by many of his associates. However, there had been rumors about that the good doctor was not all of what he seemed to be. Some of his colleagues wondered at what Mengele actually did in the camp. Undoubtedly, these had to be jealous and envious individuals who were simply trying to place him in a bad light.

***

"You are right on-time," glibbed Josef Mengele to his new erstwhile pupil. "I hope you had a restful evening. I think you will find today's proceedings, uh…rather interesting. Yes, indeed," continued the German as he greeted Leo Goncalo on the parade ground.

Restful? thought Goncalo. No, he wouldn't have said that in the least. But Leo did not, or could not, reveal his true, inner feelings to Mengele. The man would judge him to be soft and might well have him tossed right out of the camp on his ear. Leo Goncalo had spent his night in abject mental anguish. It was true that he truly believed that what the Nazis were doing was right concerning race, culture, and what the future of mankind should be like. But he was suddenly less than certain about some of their methodologies, such as some of the very ones going on inside Auschwitz. And today, like the day before, there was that curious and indelible smell which assaulted his nostrils literally. And his brain figuratively.

"Yes, Dr Mengele, it was quite restful," lied Leo.

"Good, good, I'm glad to hear of it, said Mengele as he slapped his gloved hands together, trying to ward off the cold. "Now, we are expecting a transport of approximately 800 Dutch Jews. They're scheduled to arrive at 1000 hours. I know the shipment will be on-time. Your Mussolini may have succeeded in getting Italian trains to run on-time, but we Germans are a very punctilious and punctual lot in our own right."

For the next 30 minutes, the two men chatted amiably about a variety of topics, such as: the war, art, and human nature. At precisely 1000 hours, Leo Goncalo heard a distant train whistle and shortly thereafter the chuff-chuffing of a locomotive engine pull up and stop just outside the main gate of the camp. A white painted inscription was sprawled across the engine. "*Ein volk, todt krieg*" (One people, total war).

A retinue of SS guards, cradling MP-40 sub-machine guns, and holding back straining German shepherd police dogs, waited. White-striped clad prisoners stepped forward on cue and proceeded to unlock the boxcar doors. Bewildered and shaking men, women, and children peered out. The SS men immediately began screaming invective obscenities at their hapless victims who were scrambling and falling down from the cars.

Leo Goncalo and Josef Mengele stepped forward. Mengele proceeded to mount the few steps of a reviewing stand, riding crop gripped firmly under his right arm. Goncalo looked on in awe at the teeming mass of humanity set before him. He had never seen anything like it before in all of his life. SS men, and prisoners, he'd later learn called kapos, unleashed an assault to beggar the description. Snarling dogs, foaming at the mouth, were unleashed on untold numbers, mostly old men and women, who could barely carry themselves in any kind of erect posture. The train's passengers had been in transit for more than a week since their excursion began in distant Holland.

Leo looked up at Mengele, who stood calmly amidst the reigning chaos spread out before them. Slowly, lines were formed and then were marched past the waiting German. Mengele began to whistle the theme from the musical opera *Aida*. He then took the riding crop and began to move it about as if he were conducting the Berlin Philharmonic. Goncalo stood transfixed. He well thought he might be having an out of body experience. *Was he really here? Were these things actually happening?*

Mengele looked at the approaching procession. Most of these unfortunates were directed toward the left. Goncalo would later learn that these individuals would be told they were going to shower for disinfecting purposes. In truth, they were to be gassed immediately. The Nazis would have no use for them. Their bodies would then be submitted for inspection by teams of prisoner workers who would check for gold fillings in their teeth, and then extract them. The bodies would then be dispatched to the crematoriums and burned.

Mengele, meanwhile, periodically selected certain individuals, such as sets of twins, who were directed to the right. At one point in the process, when about half of the transport had already passed, Mengele pointed his crop at a young woman. Leo could see, despite her haggard and disheveled appearance, that underneath the grit and grime she was quite gorgeous. An older woman was bent at her side. Leo presumed her to be the younger woman's mother.

"Halt!" ordered Mengele, his crop now pointed directly at the girl. "You are to go to the right. Do you happen to have any particular skills?" he asked in German.

The young woman understood as she nodded her head. "Yes?" she said haltingly.

"What can you do?" Mengele asked imperiously. His gaze had softened as he discerned the girl's natural beauty.

"Well…I can do seamstress work. And I know several languages…and…"

"Stop, you don't have to go on. You can proceed to the right. And this , I assume is your mother?"

"Yes, sir. I'd like for her to remain with me. She needs me…," the girl looked down.

"Stop, miss. She cannot go on. She is old and has lived her life. She, I cannot help. But you can live, if you so choose. So, will you accept my offer?" asked Mengele patronizingly. But now his expression had hardened and his dark shadowed eyes gleamed a stone-cold black. Goncalo wondered if this were actually be possible. He was convinced that the German's eye color had turned black.

The young Dutch woman slowly looked up and brought her gaze to meet Mengele's. "No, sir. I do not accept your offer. I have to stay with my mother," The woman gripped her mother's hand more tightly, as if she instinctively knew what her and her mother's fates would be.

"Well then, I'm afraid there is nothing I can do for you, my dear," and with that Josef Mengele played God and pointed his riding crop to the left and then proceeded to resume his selection process.

Leo Goncalo watched in abject fascination as the Dutch mother and daughter made their way amongst the other struggling refugees. An SS man struck the older woman over the top of her head with the butt of his rifle. The woman collapsed to the ground as if she were a sack of potatoes. Leo surmised that it looked as if the head had been split open. The daughter dropped to her knees and began wailing a high-pitched scream. Another SS man tried to bring her to her feet, but she resisted his effort as she continued to cling to her mother's inert and lifeless body. The German who'd struck the mother then took aim with his Mauser and shot the young woman in the head. A geyser of crimson red blood shot out in an arc from the girl's skull as she collapsed to the ground in a heap.

Goncalo thought he would become physically sick and vomit from what he'd just seen. But he was able to hold himself together. He hoped that Mengele hadn't noticed.

***

The Christmas holiday season soon arrived, and Auschwitz would be decked out in the usual decorative fashion. Christmas trees were seen throughout the camp in every SS building, of course, including Kommandant Liebehenschel's home. To Leo Goncalo the entire holiday scene seemed otherworldly. On the one hand, the SS observed the yuletide holiday, despite their official rejection of anything resembling Christianity. In their jaded eyes the world of the SS was the lord high religion. There was no need for Catholicism or Lutheranism, etc.,. On the other hand, the prisoners were virtually all Jewish and they'd never be allowed to celebrate something as lowly and degraded as Hannukah.

Josef Mengele took the opportunity to visit Germany for a few days just before Christmas Day. He hadn't spoken a word of it to Leo. Rumors went out saying the doctor had left for somewhere unspecified in Germany. As to Leo, he would've liked to have spent the holiday season back in Sicily. But, of course, that had not been possible as he'd just arrived in Auschwitz.

Goncalo reflected on what Mengele had told him just days after Leo's witnessing of the Dutch women's demise. *I must say, Leo, that you conducted yourself rather well the other day. Some may have flinched at what they had observed, but you held your ground. You know, I once had a young apprentice from Stuttgart, who, on his very first day, absolutely panicked. The young man had had to be sedated and sent off back to Germany. It really was a pity."*

Leo hadn't responded at first, but gradually he was able to bring himself to say, "Thank you, Doctor Mengele, I appreciate your words."

"You're most welcome, Leo. You know, I really tried to help that young Dutch woman. I really did. But she couldn't see reason and...and there was nothing I could do. She decided to choose her fate and to remain with her mother. A pity...a true pity," said Mengele, who cast his look downward, as if he were really contemplating the tragedy of the loss of the two women. "In any event, a new year is approaching. And I believe you will find some very interesting things that we will be doing."

And with that, Mengele had left. Leo would spend the rest of December and early January administering basic healthcare needs to individuals in the camp sick-bay. At least there he would be practicing some basic medicine, if only for a brief while.

Days before Josef Mengele was due to arrive back at the camp, Leo received a visitor to his quarters one day. The stranger had knocked on Goncalo's door and made his own way in and announced himself.

"Excuse me, sir. I'd like to introduce myself. My name is Leonardo... Leonardo Levi, at your service," the man said. He stood before Goncalo in a soiled, prison-striped garment, holding his soil-stained cap in his slightly trembling hands.

"Yes, and what can I do for you?" asked Leo as he looked up from his desk. He'd been in the midst of writing a letter home to his father, and had been fumbling about on how best to describe the place he now found himself in.

"I know that you are Italian. I am also Italian, but I come from a region that is now a part of Yugoslavia. At one time it was considered Italian soil.

But in the settlement following the First World War it was awarded to the new Yugoslavian government."

And what does that have to do with me?" Leo answered, clearly disturbed at this interloper for having interrupted him. Besides, the man shouldn't have even entered his quarters. This was strictly *verboten*. Goncalo could have the man severely punished, or worse.

"Well, sir, I was hoping that I'd be able to speak frankly with you," said Levi, now fumbling excitedly with his cap. Once he nearly dropped it, but was able to catch it before it fell to the floor.

Goncalo was about to call out to one of the SS guards to have this…this uninvited visitor summarily removed, but for some reason he caught himself. There was something in the man's words, the timbre of his voice, and the haunting look in his eyes.

"I know you have been working with Dr Mengele, or maybe I should say, I have seen you in his company. And…I thought I should perhaps warn you…"

"Warn me?! What do you mean warn me? I don't even know you from Adam and you have the temerity to barge in here and interrupt me with what you say is a warning," blurted out Goncalo. Maybe he should call out the guard. Outside of Leo's room he could see the sun shining brightly, most unusual for a January day in Auschwitz.

Leonardo Levi realized he was on shaky ground and he'd have to parse his next words carefully. He'd wanted to ask Goncalo as to whatever had possessed him to volunteer to enter this house of bestial horror.

Leo, for his part, began to carefully study his visitor and now realized he'd seen the man on a couple of occasions moving about the operating theater rather surreptitiously.

"Yes, sir. I just thought I should at least speak to you and to tell you that the doctor is rather mercurial. That is, one day, or even at one moment, he can be the most personable, charming person in the world. And the next, well…it is as if he just flips a switch and he becomes someone…someone completely the opposite. I only say this so that you may be prepared if you should ever do or say something the doctor takes exception with." Levi abruptly stopped and looked down.

Leo took in the man's words and began to see him in a new light. Perhaps he should heed what he'd just heard from Levi and be prepared for the future. "I think that you should leave now, Mr. Levi. It wouldn't be a good thing for you to be discovered here by certain individuals."

In the days following Leonardo Levi's impromptu visit, Leo Goncalo had checked into the background of the erstwhile prisoner physician. He'd found out that Levi was an Italian Jew who indeed hailed from the section of Yugoslavia that was once considered Italian. In the aftermath of the First World War and the ensuing Treaty of Versailles, this disputed territory had been handed over to the newly created Yugoslav state by the victorious Allies, despite the fact Italy had been on the winning side. Italians of every political stripe considered this a betrayal on the part of the French and the English. It was quickly utilized by Benito Mussolini and his Black Shirts when they seized power in Rome in 1922.

Goncalo also discovered that Levi was considered to be an outstanding physician. He'd taken his medical training in the late 30s at the world-renowned University of Bologna. Levi's specialty was open heart surgery. But now the only medicine he practiced in Auschwitz was of a far different nature, courtesy of his SS overseers.

The cold only seemed to intensify from the start of the new year for Leo Goncalo. He often could hardly bring himself to emerge from his bed in the morning. He found the food rations to be desultory, often consisting of endless heads of cabbage or thinly gruelled soup. Even the bread, a staple and mainstay of any Italian's diet, was typically of a rock-hard crust. Leo sometimes had to force the ersatz material down his throat. Goncalo feared he might well break some teeth before he ever left the camp.

Goncalo did manage, despite all he'd seen and heard, to increase his dislikes, or was it a personal hatred, of the inmates. Somehow he'd been able to anesthetize himself so as to feel absolutely no pity, no empathy, for the poor, pathetic creatures who aimlessly meandered about. The Fuhrer, the SS, were right in that these so-called individuals were of no use and of no concern, and should be done away with as soon as possible.

***

Josef Mengele returned to Auschwitz on January 15th, 1944. The air temperature hovered just above 10 degrees Fahrenheit. People's breaths seemed to hang in mid-air. Leo Goncalo found that even the basic function of walking could be exhausting for his body. He couldn't begin to imagine what the prisoners in their threadbare and tattered dress were going through. Leo noticed a cart was being pushed about the camp by a couple of emaciated prisoners, the men pausing to pick up a body of someone who hadn't survived the bitter cold. The men picked up the bodies and would then swing them up and into the wagon, as if they were stacking firewood.

On one Saturday morning, that coincided with a day off for Leo Goncalo, the Italian observed Mengele sprint across the compound while in earnest discussion with an SS officer. This was a man Leo didn't know. Upon concluding his discussion with the officer, Mengele looked about and noticed Leo. He then quickly strode toward him.

"Goncalo, my friend, how are you? It's too bad you had to spend your holiday in this… this." Mengele paused and spread his hand outward from his body. "I'll bet you missed being home in Italy, didn't you?"

"Well, sir, I'd be lying if I said I didn't," mused Leo, who stood wrapping his arms across his body and stamping his feet up and down on the frozen ground. As if any of these futile gestures could somehow increase his body heat. And he being a physician should have known better.

"I'll bet, I'll bet," said Mengele. "I'll tell you what, I have something coming up, or I should say that Dr. Weber has something on the horizon. Something I do think you may well be interested in," continued Mengele, a sly smile crossing his face.

Leo waited for the German to continue and when apparently nothing more was to be forthcoming, he finally asked, "And what might that be, Doctor?"

Mengele softly pursed his slightly red lips together and said, "Doctor Weber is set to perform a castration on several pris…uh, patients. Rumor has it he may even practice conducting one procedure without the use of an anesthetic. That should be something, don't you think?" announced Mengele, as if the event were to be an athletic contest, and one not to be missed.

For some reason, Leo, not for the life of him that he could think of, could he find the proposal surprising or shocking. "I look forward to being able to witness the procedure, Dr Mengele. When, may I ask is this…this procedure scheduled to take place?"

"I'm not exactly sure, but I will notify you in advance. It might be within the next couple of days," Mengele paused, before adding, "You know Leo I honestly thought you might've told me to go shit in my hat when I mentioned a castration without anesthetic. Well, anyway, that is on the docket."

***

The center for virtually all of the castration experimental surgeries was the notorious Block 10, a place that could have well been considered the quintessential Auschwitz. Made up for the most part of women prisoners, it was strangely located in the men's camp. Its windows were always kept closed and shuttered or boarded up, so as to prevent any kind of communication with the outside. Leo Goncalo learned that one woman prisoner doctor who'd endured within its confines had described it as being a "place of horror" which distinctly resembled a combination of hell and a mental institution.

The block was divided into two research areas: those of Professor Clausberg and Dr Schumann, both men specialized in sterilization. Then there was a special area for studies performed by the Hygienic Institute. It was the Institute that sponsored some of the most sinister work of Dr Klaus Weber.

Leo thought Weber, upon first appearance, to be a rather unpleasant and cheerless man. A man who carried himself with a punctilious air. Prior to the war, Weber had been an internist in the city of Cologne. There he had been able to garner a close and special relationship with Josef Mengele.

On the day of the scheduled castration procedure Leo Goncalo was to witness, the sky above the camp had broken clear and the air temperature had even risen to a most tolerable 30 degrees Fahrenheit. Leo joined Mengele in the viewing section just above the operating theater. Weber, assisted by a coterie of prisoner doctors and prisoner nurses, would be on stage directly beneath the two men.

Suddenly, a bedraggled, unshaven man of, in Goncalo's estimation, to have been twenty years old was wheeled into the room. The patient's arms and legs were being secured by leather straps. The man turned and twisted his head, his body convulsing. He appeared to be under some form of drug-induced state, but still remained in a degree of semi-consciousness.

Weber spoke quietly to the prisoner doctor standing next to him. At first, Leo couldn't make out the doctor's identity. But then, as the man turned to the side, and to Leo's shocking dismay he could now see that it was none other than Leonardo Levi. Levi gave no sign that he recognized Leo Goncalo.

The patient's surgical gown, if one could call it that, was slipped down thereby exposing the groin area. A thin, washed-out coating of mercurochrome was spread out along the penis and gonads of the man. Then, almost at once, Weber took hold of a scalpel and, seizing the organ, snipped an incision along the scrotal sack. Deftly, the surgeon removed one of the gonads. Clamps and wads of gauze were quickly applied. In the meantime, the patient had been fully awakened out of his semi-comatose state and emitted a shrill and shrieking primordial scream. Two prisoners, who had been standing by, were now directed by Weber to move in and control the unfortunate patient. One of them stuffed a clump of cotton into the prisoner's mouth so as to stifle the unbearable screaming.

Leo sat next to Mengele open-mouthed and transfixed. He simply couldn't believe what he had just witnessed. It had happened, and yet, had appeared as surreal.

"What did I tell you, eh Leo, that Weber was one of the best. It was as if he had been handling marbles in the schoolyard," said Mengele as he nodded his head, a wide smile spread clear across his face.

***

Spring was slowly emerging by the time March rolled around. Leo Goncalo was in his quarters one mid-week afternoon, reflecting on his role in the state of affairs that was Auschwitz. The sky was clear, and nearly devoid of all clouds. It was a perfect harbinger, even in as desperate a place as this camp, for a renewed new year. Suddenly, Goncalo's reverie was broken by the cadence of several pairs of marching boots. Leo got up from his chair and looked out of his window. At least ten SS troopers were in lock-step as they marched across the compound. For some unknown reason, Leo Goncalo's curiosity got the better of him. He reached for his jacket hanging from the coatrack and put it on. He hurried out the door and moved after the SS men.

Leo hung back a bit and watched as the troopers stopped in front of a paneled wall. He looked about, as he wasn't sure the commandant would have approved at what he was about to witness. The SS men stood at attention, rifles at parade rest. From the right, several bedraggled women prisoners could be seen. Among them a teenaged blond girl. They were prodded before the wall by a kapo. Some were openly weeping, while others stood defiantly. The blond girl looked about and shook, her body quivering in fear, not only from the cold.

A scharffuhrer (sergeant) standing off from the assembled firing squad, gave the command. All of the SS men brought their weapons to present arms, then took aim at the quivering women. *"Feuer!",* shouted the scharffuhrer. Ten Mauser rifles barked and spat out their deadly volley. All of the women collapsed in heaps on the barren ground, with the exception of the teen-aged blond girl. She lay upon the ground moaning softly, perhaps for her mother, as her body rocked back and forth, her hair and face doused in the blood-spattered soil. The squad commander walked over and stood atop her body. He then removed his Walther PPK sidearm from its holster and, barely taking aim, fired a round directly into the girl's head. Her agonized body and cavorted movements abruptly ceased.

"You shouldn't be too alarmed, Doctor Goncalo. This is a normal occurrence in this facility," said a familiar voice.

Leo turned around only to see the grim-faced visage of Leonardo Levi.

"You must force yourself to not see what you have just seen here. Otherwise…you could well go mad."

"But why?...Why were those women executed?" questioned a still-shocked Leo Goncalo.

"Why? Why, indeed? Perhaps one of them stole some bread. Or perhaps one of them insulted a German. Who knows? It doesn't really matter in this world we call Auschwitz," said Levi in a perfectly level tone of voice.

***

The next day, after having completed his rounds of regular medical care, Leo found himself once again alone in his room. He distinctly remembered what had happened exactly one week ago. Leo had been operating on an elderly Hungarian Jew, with Doctor Weber by his side advising. The operation would be his tenth sterilization procedure. The entire process had been routine for Leo, and this time the patient had been truly sedated. There would be no moaning or thrashing about.

The castration process had just been completed, the patient's scrotal sac sewn up, when, without warning, the elderly man began to convulse. Leo was startled, but Weber merely looked on, completely dispassionate. He did intervene in front of Goncalo, but before any resuscitative measures could be taken, the Hungarian's body sagged and then went completely limp. He was gone.

Leo Goncalo looked on, not quite believing what had just happened. Weber had the countenance as if he couldn't have cared less.

"Well, Goncalo, you win some and you lose some. I wouldn't worry about it. After all, he was just an old Jew," said Weber, who then took a moment to pause and light a cigarette he'd removed from a silver-plated case. Rings of smoke curled their way into the operating room air. He then turned about on his heel and walked off without a further word.

Leo continued rooted to his seat, he truly wanted to believe what he'd been doing was justified, even necessary. After all, these so-called patients were not really people, in the sense of individuals that one should have compassion and understanding for. He knew that he had crossed that proverbial line, that precipice, that there would be no going back.

And then he recalled the words of Leonardo Levi, who had had ably assisted Leo during one of the castration procedures. *You know, Leo, you once took an oath, as we all once did, to do no harm as a physician. That path has now been obliterated. One day, you and I may be called to account for our actions."*

***

January morphed into February, which, in turn, made way for March. The days slowly became longer and winter began to relax its icy grip on all things Auschwitz. Leo Goncalo still felt himself plodding along, physically, as well as mentally. He'd been observing his supposed mentor, Josef Mengele, more closely. Goncalo found himself secretly in league with many of the camp's prisoner doctors in their internal struggles with Mengele's extraordinarily deep-seated convictions that was found in his overt doubling manifestation. Leo had asked himself: *Was he a kind man, good with children, good in general, who was only driven to do the things he did by his passion for research? Or was he a monster who only played a role with the children to hide his sinister and cruel game better, so as to get to his ends more easily?*

Goncalo began to suspect that a split personality was likely afoot regarding this strange and perplexing German. Sociologists would have characterized the Mengele persona as reflecting what was theorized as the doubling effect. The double man possessed all of the sentimental emotions, all of the human feeling, pity, and so on. He buried within his psyche a hermetically closed cell that was utterly impenetrable and indestructible, which, in turn, translated to blind obedience to the received order.

Leo also had learned that Mengele had once tried an experiment where he'd attempted to determine whether one twin was more susceptible to poison than the other twin. Goncalo thought the idea to be preposterous. It was the idea of a crazy man who really understood nothing about actual scientific problems, but… had the opportunity to experiment without any controls or restrictions.

In late April, Mengele approached Leo with his latest idea, one in which he would attempt to change the eye color of an individual. As Mengele explained the procedure to Leo, he said that he'd located a prisoner who had the unique feature of having one brown eye and the other one blue. He said he would have ideally liked to have had two individuals possessing the same feature, but he would just have to settle for the one.

The German then went to explain that he would inject a brown dye into the patient's blue eye. He reasoned that brown would be the dominant color and would take control over the blue eye's pigment. Leo had been aghast when he heard Mengele's proposed theory, but he kept his doubts to himself. He would never reveal to the great researcher that he thought the idea to be absurd and crazy. Leo would have to find a way to excuse himself from witnessing the operation.

Chapter Ten

Exodus

One day in April, Josef Mengele excitedly invited Leo to the camp's railroad siding. A transport of more than 1,000 Jews from Lublin, Poland was scheduled to arrive by 1000 hours.

"I'd like for you to see first-hand what the SS…what we are doing on a large scale. It is a task that is necessary if we Germans, and those who sympathize with us, are to survive. Yes, my friend, our very own survival is at stake," said Mengele as he stood next to Goncalo. The German was dressed in a field-gray uniform, not his usual white lab coat. Leo didn't bother to ask why Mengele was outfitted like this. It was a beautiful, picturesque spring day in southern Poland. A day, thought Leo, more suited to a stroll through a park, with a picnic basket in hand.

SS guards and their ever-present snarling shepherd guard dogs stood by waiting for the Lublin transport. At precisely 1000 hours a black-engined locomotive chuffed to a stop at the siding. As soon as the railcar doors were swung open, the SS men launched into their usual routine of shrilled whistles, harsh guttural commands, and frenzied whippings of the poor, unfortunate victims detraining.

Today was different in that Mengele wasn't performing his usual selection process, his place was taken by another SS doctor, Heinrich Hein.

The huddled and stumbling masses were pushed, prodded, shoved, and beaten along the way.

"Leo, come with me. It is almost time," said Mengele as he now led Goncalo to one of the ostensible shower buildings. Leo well knew that those selected for immediate showering would be getting something far different. *Well, it would be a shower of another kind: a shower of Zyklon B.* He'd never directly witnessed a gassing, having only heard of them.

Josef Mengele acted as if they were attending a soccer match and he was now looking for his seat. "Leo, over here," Mengele pointed to a wall containing a viewing port. "This will enable you to get a better view. A view of a special kind of shower," cackled Mengele with a maniacal glee.

Leo observed the last of the victims enter the shower room, the door closing and locking behind them. Then, a pair of SS men wearing gas masks moved along the roof and bent down. One man proceeded to remove the vent cover. He then took hold of the cannister he'd carried and pulled off its lid. The SS man then tilted the cannister's contents into the opened vent. He next replaced the vent cap.

Leo hesitatingly looked into the viewing port. And what he saw completely mesmerized him, and at the same time, fascinated him. He saw a morass of naked people: men, old men, women, children, some of them still clutching onto stuffed animals. It was pure chaos and, then, a slow motion dance began, accompanied by a building cacophony of screams and curses. Goncalo desperately wanted to tear himself away from the Dante's Inferno he was witnessing and to vomit and run off as fast as his shaking legs would take him. But he could not. The screams grew louder. Next, Leo saw a mound of people begin to take shape. The stronger among them were able to climb atop the weaker and commenced in a desperate and feeble attempt to reach the top of the pile. "Fantastic, simply fantastic," said Leo to the phantasmagoric sight before him.

After several minutes had elapsed, the screaming had ceased, a deathly silence reigned in the chamber. Sonderkommandoes, Jewish prisoners, who normally handled these tasks in the camp, pushed open the doors to the gas chamber. A strange and perceptible smell filled the outside air and assaulted Leo's nostrils.

"Leo, come with me. There is nothing more to see here. Oh, the sonderkommandoes will examine the dental work of the deceased and extract any teeth containing gold fillings. The Fuhrer must get his share, don't you think? Ha ha," chortled a clearly amused Josef Mengele.

Numbingly, Leo Goncalo followed in the wake of Josef Mengele.

***

As May of 1944 approached, Leo Goncalo knew he was approaching a crossroad: one was right there at Auschwitz, and the other was hidden within his own personal life. He'd once fervently believed in the philosophy of the Nazis, whom he thought were more thoroughly committed to racial identification among the masses than the Fascists of Italy ever had been. Leo had come to realize that Mussolini and his sycophantic lapdogs had only been going through the motions. Perhaps to merely flatter and satisfy the Duce's patron, Adolf Hitler. But at this very moment he, Leo Goncalo, didn't feel as if he were doing anything of importance or, more so, of significance.

The days of spring were warming and were turning to greater length than those of the winter season. The coldness in Leo's soul was...well... he had to admit to it that his inner being was itself beginning to warm. Almost as if he were undergoing an epiphany, Leo did not earnestly believe he could remain at Auschwitz much longer.

Leo Goncalo had performed several more castrations of prisoners during the previous two months. None of them involved patients not being fully sedated. And thankfully for him, none had expired. Nevertheless, Leo had decided he would have to leave the camp, and very soon, or he thought he might well lose his mind. He knew he'd have to find the most propitious moment for his exodus.

"Are you alright, Leo? You look troubled, my friend," said Josef Mengele, almost soothingly.

"Oh, yes, yes, Dr Mengele," replied a startled Goncalo.

"You seemed to be quite deep in thought," continued Mengele.

Leo had the uneasy feeling that the German was reading his mind. "Oh, no, sir. I am just fine,'' said Leo hurriedly.

"That's good. I'm glad to hear of it. You know, Dr Weber has been quite impressed by your work. Most impressed," continued Mengele, who'd taken to shining a button on his field-gray tunic.

"I'm glad to hear that, sir. It is most pleasing and rewarding to hear praise from such an exalted person as Dr Weber," said Leo, who strangely began to feel himself becoming immersed in a cold sweat. The German SS doctor could, at times, exert an unnatural coolness upon any person he might be talking to, be they prisoner or colleague.

That was it, Leo Goncalo knew that he never be quite like Josef Mengele. As hard as he might try, he knew he did not possess the inner constitution to be like the Nazi doctor. He'd never looked into Leo's eyes or displayed any sign of enjoyment while performing these operations. It as if he had something else on his mind other than what he was doing, even when he was speaking to Leo man to man.

Leo well believed that Mengele was able to numb himself to the grisly surgeries, the detestable and abominable camp conditions, everything. Leo realized that he himself had crossed that figurative bridge of no return and might well have to answer as to what he'd done at Auschwitz. He knew by now the Germans were clearly losing the war. And the Allies, after they were victorious, would in all probability decide to make who'd done unspeakable things account for their actions in a war crimes trial. *Well, so be it.* Leo Goncalo would have to face up to what he'd done. Secretly, he hoped that he might be able to find a way to disappear within the woodwork of a post-war chaos.

***

"Dottore Goncalo, would you have a minute?" asked Leonardo Levi as he stood in Leo's opened doorway.

Leo looked up from the letter he'd been reading from home. It was from his mother, and it was a troubling letter. Troubling in that the woman was struggling to convey her message to her son. Although his mother hadn't said it directly, Leo could tell that she was quite unsettled with some the actions of Leo's father. For virtually all of their married years together, the woman had never once been confided in by Carlo Goncalo. She'd been aware of some of his unsavory and questionable actions, but she'd never questioned her husband about them. But now in the midst of this desperate war, she'd finally been able to find her voice. The American Occupation authorities were investigating Carlo about some of his business practices, and about his Fascist association.

Leo looked up at his unexpected visitor while he simultaneously covered up the letter with a file folder. It had been as if he were afraid that Levi might discern something from it. "Ah, yes Leonardo. What is on your mind?"

Levi looked about in the corridor to see if someone might be lurking before he stepped into the room. Without asking for permission he turned and slowly closed the door. Levi then walked up to Leo's desk and stood looking down, his cap mashed within his now gnarled hands.

"Well, Leonardo, what is it?" questioned Goncalo. He had the distinct feeling the prisoner doctor would impart another word of wisdom. "Would you like to sit down?" offered Leo.

"Ah, yes, that is most kind of you, *Dottore,"* said Levi as he reached over and took hold of the dilapidated brown wooden chair and proceeded to drag it across the floor. The chair elicited a baying and scraping sound. Levi sat down heavily.

Leo continued to wait for the man to speak about something that must have been quite important to him. Levi appeared to be weighing something of profound import.

"*Dottore*, I have admired you for quite some time. And although I know it may be untoward for me to speak, I feel that I must do so...You see, *Dottore*, I think I know that you now realize that you...that you don't belong here. You may have come with certain intentions and expectations, but those have now changed. Well...I will just say it. I think what would be best for you would be to leave the camp. And to leave as soon as possible." Leonardo Levi again returned his gaze to the floor. He feared he may have just signed his own death sentence.

Outside, could be heard the usual sounds of the camp: SS men cursing and snarling, or marching in cadence to and fro; prisoners being ordered about, some dragging heavily laden wagons.

Leo stared at Levi in absolute astonishment and realized the man must possess some intuitive, inner sixth sense. Levi's words had been in his very thoughts for the past couple of months. And here it was now June in the year of 1944. Leo knew that Levi was right, and he must find a way to make his own escape from Auschwitz. Of course, he would have to try at a moment when Dr Mengele was away from the camp. Leo would make some obsequious and innocuous comments to the commandant, and then skedaddle his way back to Italy.

The time had come for him to exit this hellhole of humanity and to return to a place where there was, at least, a modicum of joy and happiness. A place where a person could blend in with his surroundings without causing a stir. A place where he, Leo Goncalo, could once again practice real medicine, not the dastardly things he'd been doing almost since he'd walked through Auschwitz's front gate.

***

Leo Goncalo effected his exodus from Auschwitz in the virtual dead of night in late June. After making a few perfunctory remarks to colleagues, such as Heinrich Weber and Max Verstaden, he left the camp in the very same black Mercedes touring car in which he'd arrived some months before. Goncalo hadn't bothered to say farewell to Leonardo Levi or to any of the other prisoner doctors. Leo had been able to persuade or, at least, convince Kommandant Liebehenschel, of his need to return to his native Italy. His family was in need of him at this most difficult and trying time in the war. It was almost an outright lie, but the SS man didn't need to know more.

The Italy Leo Goncalo returned to was at that very moment in the midst of what could only be described as total chaos. The Allies, following much bitter fighting at such venues as Monte Cassino and Anzio, had finally been able to push the Germans out from their entrenched positions. Rome, the Eternal City, was liberated by the Americans on June 4th, a mere two days before the D-Day landings in Normandy.

In the wake of Italy's defection from the Axis in September 1943, the Badoglio government and the monarchy of King Victor Emmanuel III, set up a new governing body in Brindisi, on the Adriatic coast of southern Italy. It was from here that they oddly mirrored the Salo Republic of Benito Mussolini's rump government in the north. Badoglio and his minions existed in a near state of limbo, exercising a limited authority under the direction of the Allied Control Commission, whose main function was to create an Allied military government in newly liberated locales.

Meanwhile, Mussolini had been going through his own trials and tribulations following his arrest on the order of the King and the Fascist Grand Council. The dictator had been languishing in confinement in the *Gran Sasso d'Italia*, a ski resort set high in the Apennine Mountains, northeast of Rome. The Duce had already been moved several times prior to this as the Fascists tried desperately to keep him hidden away, mostly from the Germans.

His captivity barely lasted 15 days. While there, he attempted suicide by slashing at his wrists rather than run the risk of being handed over to the Allies.

On the afternoon of September 12th, eight gliders carrying SS commando Colonel Otto Skorzeny and his detachment crash-landed near the resort and proceeded to exfiltrate the former dictator from his captors without having fired a shot. With Mussolini rescued, Skorzeny and his men flew off from the mountainside in a small Fieseler-Storch aircraft. The take-off could only have been carried off from a very short airstrip, a short downhill stretch of grass that ended at a precipice. The aircraft, heavily overloaded, barely clawed its way into the air.

The Germans then placed the Duce in the small, quaint town of Salo, quite near to the scenic Lake Garda. It was in this hidden, obscure place that Benito Mussolini proclaimed himself head of the Italian Social Republic.

In some respects Mussolini now found himself ensconced in one of the most luxurious villas on the western shore of the lake between Salo and the small town of Gargano. Surrounding him were the various ministries of the new republic. The restored Duce, along with his wife, Rachele, and family lived in the *Villa Feltrinelli*, a large, barren edifice that Mussolini himself considered "gloomy and unfriendly."

And it would be to Salo that Leonardo Goncalo would eventually be assigned to after his return from Auschwitz. He wouldn't be attending to the Duce himself, of course. There was already in place a retinue of physicians and specialists to attend personally to Mussolini and his family.

***

It was in January 1944 when Rosalie Donato received the news that Carlo Goncalo had been detained by American intelligence personnel. He was being held under armed guard, his case pending. Rosalie wanted to step outside into her front yard and shout to the heavens: "They've finally gotten the bastard!" Her neighbors be damned.

On a late Saturday morning, Rosalie gathered herself and proceeded to make her way to US Army's 52nd regiment's intelligence section located just outside of Messina. Her brother Aldo once again would accompany her. She was prepared to testify to the Americans against Goncalo. Rosalie had put together as much information and documentation as she could and would present it to the Americans.

Shortly before 11:00 am she and Aldo arrived at the 52nd headquarters building. They were directed to its entrance by helpful MPs. Once inside, they politely asked for assistance. Rosalie informed the soldiers that she had some very important information in her possession. She was certain the Americans would be most interested.

After having waited outside the office of Captain James Benedict for some 30 minutes, Rosalie and her brother were directed into the captain's office by a sergeant. The American had asked her if she and her brother would be in need of a translator. The man's name was DiDonato and he spoke more than passable Italian. Rosalie had thought the similarity of their names to be a little amusing.

Rosalie and Aldo stood mutely before Captain Benedict's desk. Aldo was clutching the paperwork and documents in a black leathered satchel close to his chest, as if he were hugging it. Rosalie took in the full measure of the American captain and had to admit she was impressed. Without having uttered a single word, she could tell the man possessed presence.

Benedict looked up at her and said, "Good morning, signora and signore. What can I do for you?"

Benedict had wavy brown hair and dark brown penetrating eyes. His face was open. He didn't appear to be a man who would want to waste time . The lines around his mouth were firm. The captain was smooth-shaven. His khaki-colored necktie was folded inside of his olive brown shirt.

"Thank you, Captain, for taking the time to see me and my brother. His name is Aldo," said Rosalie as she indicated her brother. "We realize that your time is most valuable and we shall try to be succinct."

Benedict looked directly at Rosalie, and he, in turn, was quite taken by this Italian woman's own presence. He thought her rather tall for an

Italian, estimating her height at 5' 8", and well put together. He could also discern that she was in possession of a good endowment. But it was her face and her hazel brown eyes, together with her frizzled, blond hair that he found especially beguiling and appealing. "I can assure you that you're not wasting my time. Won't you both please sit down," Benedict said soothingly, indicating the two wooden chairs. The more he looked at Rosalie the more intrigued he became. Or was it arousal?. He'd almost forgotten that Aldo was in the same room. Benedict then realized he'd have to disassociate himself from his present mesmerized state. After all, he was an officer in the United States Army.

"That is most kind of you, Captain. The reason we're here today has to do with a man we have learned is now in your custody. That man is Carlo Goncalo, and he has caused me and my family a great deal harm and loss, and a great deal of pain."

"How so, signora? Oh, by the way would you or your brother care for a cigarette or a beverage?" offered Benedict.

"Not for me, thank you, sir. Perhaps Aldo may like one," said Rosalie, who quickly translated into Italian for Aldo's benefit.

"Er, *si*, *si, grazie*," murmured Aldo, who then took the proffered cigarette from Benedict's fingers. The American then pulled out a silver-plated Ronson lighter and lit the cigarette. Aldo inhaled the Lucky Strike deeply into his lungs, exhaling a cloud of smoke into the office air. Benedict guided an ashtray on his desk over to the Italian.

"Well, Captain, as I was saying. This man, and please forgive me, this bastard has ruined my family. First, he had a lackey of his, a man by the name of Alberto Cardi, denounce my innocent father on false charges, that my father had denounced Mussolini. As a result, my father was then thrown into prison and we were never able to obtain his release. He died there. This, I have no doubt, led to the premature death of our beloved mother. Furthermore, this Goncalo swindled us out of much of our hard-earned land and holdings!" And with that, Rosalie slumped back into her chair.

Jim Benedict simply looked back at Rosalie in amazement. He and his staff had been looking into the affairs of Carlo Goncalo for some time. And now, this amazing and most attractive woman had shown up on his doorstep.

"In addition, *Capitano*, I have with me documentation and receipts, everything I could think of so as to provide to your office. I'd be willing to testify in a court of law," continued Rosalie.

Benedict was absolutely floored. This was precisely what he needed. And he couldn't but notice that Rosalie's English had gotten better the more agitated she had become. Most of the time, a foreign person's English would turn into a jumble and be almost unintelligible.

Rosalie signaled to Aldo for the briefcase, which he handed over to her. "Here, *Capitano,* this is the information. It is in Italian, but I'd be more than willing to help translate it for you."

"That would be most kind of you, signora."

"Rosalie, Captain," she said as she looked deeply into Benedict's eyes. She had the distinct feeling that the man's loins were being stirred by her presence. It would be foolish of her to think so, but it was something lingering in the air. It had been a long time since she had had carnal relations with Franco, and, she surmised, it had probably been a while since the captain had had any interaction with his wife or girlfriend. Still, it was probably silly of her to think in that vein. Well, she was still a woman, and every woman had needs. No, she should put that kind of thought away. Nevertheless, Rosalie could feel a vibe within her own body.

"Well, I appreciate this information. You also mentioned the name of another man a..."

"Alberto Cardi, sir," answered Rosalie. "You know, Captain, I think I'd like that cigarette now." Rosalie took hold of the one offered by Benedict. He duly lit it for her, the flame lighting up her golden face, making her even more seductive. As Rosalie inhaled, Benedict let his fingers brush against hers. As she continued smoking, the American thought at that very moment he was in the presence of one of the most attractive and intriguing women he'd ever met. He couldn't help himself either, his penis was now hardening rapidly. Benedict was glad the woman, and her brother were on the other side of his desk.

***

"I enjoyed our lovemaking, James," cooed Rosalie as she lay naked next to James Benedict. She and her lover were sharing drinks of Wild Turkey whiskey.

"It was good, Rosalie. You are a tremendous lover. You know how to make love to a man," replied Benedict as he swirled the whiskey around the cut-glass tumbler.

"*Grazie*, er, thank you. It has been a while. But they say it's like riding a bicycle." Rosalie snuggled herself closer to Benedict. She'd been assisting the American captain with translation of some of the documents she and Aldo had brought with them. The passion of the woman and the American had been immediate, something she'd the feeling would lead them inevitably to his bedroom. It could best be described as a spartan quarter right next to his office, but it was something they'd been forced to use; her own home was off-limits, what with Rosanna and her brother Aldo and his own wife.

As for Benedict, it had been an evening of unbridled and lustful sex. He'd found himself breathless when Rosalie had removed her blouse and bra, revealing her large and shapely breasts. He knew she'd given herself completely to him. He'd tried to conduct his foreplay slowly and carefully, but in the end he hadn't been able to restrain himself. And his entry into her inner sanctum had unleashed a primeval animal within him. Rosalie had kept up with Benedict's power and rhythm and had wrapped her shapely legs around his thrusting buttocks.

Rosalie herself had felt quite fulfilled and had climaxed at the exact moment of Benedict's release.

"Are you married, Rosalie?" asked Benedict tentatively.

"*Si*, ah, yes, I am. My husband is a prisoner of war somewhere in the U.S.. I think he was last in some place called Texas." She lay silent for a moment. "I think I am supposed to feel guilty, but for some strange reason I do not."

"It's funny, but I feel the same way. It just felt right, as if it were something we were both powerless to stop," said Benedict.

"Are you married, James?"

"Yes, yes, I am. My wife is really a wonderful girl. We've always been happy together. Only now it seems as if she's a million miles away," said Jim Benedict, his glass now drained of its amber content.

"What is her name?" Rosalie asked softly as she took Benedict's arm underneath her breasts.

"Allison. Allison Barber. I mean that was her maiden name."

"Mmm. I'm sure she's a very nice girl and you must miss her very much," said Rosalie as she now placed her empty tumbler down on the bedside crate that served as an end table. She turned to Benedict and asked, "James would you happen to have a cigarette? I'm so in the mood for one."

"Sure," said Benedict. He got out of bed and went to a makeshift dresser for a pack of Camels.

Rosalie admired his muscled back and his full buttocks as he stood up. As he turned around, she got a full-on view of his manhood. Simply put, James Benedict was a very well-endowed male specimen, and Rosalie had felt and pleasured in having taken receipt of it into her own body.

Benedict lit Rosalie's cigarette first and then placed the match to his.

"Thank you, James," said Rosalie huskily as she slowly inhaled the Camel. She released a small cloud of smoke, seductively. It oozed forth from seemingly every pore in her body.

"Rosalie, I just wanted to tell you that I've appreciated your translation assistance. It's been very helpful and will be useful to us in our investigation of Carlo Goncalo. I'd like to, but I can't promise you anything definitive. What I mean is we will gather all of the available evidence we can find. We will then present it to the military government authority, AMGOT. From there it will be up to them in terms of what they'll do to Goncalo and his associates."

"I know, James, but me, and my family will appreciate whatever you can do. I feel confident that you'll make Goncalo pay for the evil deeds he has done." Rosalie then snuffed out her cigarette. She did the same to Benedict's. She then turned out the light and went to the captain and mounted him. He was fully ready for her assault and lay back as Rosalie straddled him, her ample breasts heaving and swaying above him.

***

"You were with the American captain, weren't you?" demanded Aldo Donato. "How could you? How could you betray your husband? Your sordid act will bring shame down upon our family."

"Who do you think you're talking to, Aldo? I know what I have done, but you are not above reproach. You don't think I know what happened that time you were in Palermo. The time you had your own little fling with some floozy you'd only just met.. You think I didn't know?" snarled back Rosalie, who was nearly at the point of wanting to spit in Aldo's eye.

"How did you find out? Never mind, this was different," said Aldo defensively.

"Different? How was it different? Oh, I know, because you are a man and I'm a woman? I found out through my own sources. But do not lecture me on honor, trust, or betrayal. I know what I have done, and I know I will have to live with it."

"Are you going to see the American again" asked Aldo plaintively.

"That is my business, you're not my keeper."

"But you and your daughter share living quarters with us," said Aldo, beginning to feel the heat of burning anger build up once again.

"Look, Aldo, I am a grown woman. Do not try to threaten me or I may be forced to reveal what I know to your wife. Would you want that?"

Rosalie then walked abruptly out of the room, slamming the door shut behind her. The cooling Sicilian night air filled her lungs as she breathed it in. Standing by a porch post she asked herself: *Will I or should I go to bed again with James?* She knew she shouldn't, but the stirring he'd created within her body was like an irresistible and unyielding force had been released.

***

After the North African campaign, the war for George Sloan slowed down for a time. His LRDG unit didn't participate in the Sicilian operation. The unit rested and was refitted at an army camp roughly half-way between Alexandria and Cairo. One day while Sloan was on a holiday of his own in Cairo he came across one of the most beguiling and appealing women he'd ever laid eyes on.

"Well, now that we've won the war," declared the bright and vivacious blond woman to those gathered around her.

"Easy, Sal, easy. It might be more accurate to say that we've turned the corner," corrected one the male admirers of the young woman.

"As I was saying, now that we have turned the corner," mimicked the woman, to everyone's amusement.

Sloan noted the woman of his interest's accent. Definitely London. Probably one of those young society types, a debutante possibly, who'd joined the war effort out of some newly discovered patriotism, or because it just seemed to be some jolly good fun. Still, George couldn't take his eyes off of her, and in a short while the woman at last looked George's way. She smiled at him. He was so startled he quickly looked away, but just as rapidly returned his gaze to her. Only she was not in her seat, she was practically upon him at his barstool.

"I couldn't help but notice you staring at me, Lieutenant," the blond-haired woman addressed George Sloan.

"Er, well…I was. Guilty as charged," said George as he pantomimed a stop with his hands.

"Well, you know what that shows, don't you?" she questioned as she moved herself onto the barstool next to his.

"No…I'm not sure what it shows,"

"It shows me a man of good taste. My name is Sally, what's yours?" she said as she extended her right hand to Sloan.

"Ah, oh, my name is George. George Sloan, at your service."

Sally leaned her body against the bar, but Sloan could tell that she wasn't drunk. She hadn't slurred her words, even though presumably she'd imbibed some degree of alcohol.

"Can I buy you a drink, Sally?" offered George.

I believe that you can, kind sir. I would like a gin and tonic. And that would be Tanqueray," said Sally confidently.

Sloan passed the request to the barman. As he turned back to face Sally, he took in her face and body. She had a trimmed bob of blond hair, blazing blue eyes, a pert and rounded nose, and a full vivacious mouth. George gazed down at her shapely torso and long smooth legs beneath her uniform jacket. And despite the khaki shirt she had on, he could clearly discern an ample chest.

"Thank you, George," Sally said upon taking receipt of her drink. "Oh, I should say that my last name is Bedell."

George and Sally Bedell then engaged in a pleasant conversation, mostly over generalities, amidst the cloying, smoky air of the bar. The topic of weather was not brought up.

"Well, you see, my father works for Vickers-Armstrong. He's some sort of expeditor. My mum has been mostly a homemaker, but she has been doing some sewing at home. Since the start of the war, her work has mostly been of a repair nature. You know, workmen trying to make their work clothes last a bit longer."

Sloan filled her in, briefly, that is, on his background. But for the most part he just let this gorgeous, lovely, vivacious woman wax on and on.

"George, you must let me introduce you to my friends," Sally pleaded with Sloan.

"Well, I'm not..." George was hesitant. He really didn't want to meet Sally's friends.

"No, you simply must!" Sally insisted. "You'll love them, I just know it." And with that Sally Bedell dragged a reluctant George Sloan over to her friends. There was Simon: RAF pilot; Jane: War Office; Jim: army mechanic; Heather: Foreign Office. They all seemed to take an instant liking to George., especially when Sally let on that George was a member of the LRDG.

The couple became an almost instant item when they could make arrangements to meet. Sloan wasn't quite sure what Sally did at her posting, although he strongly suspected it had something to do with intelligence. Sally possessed a good grasp of German.

Nearly three weeks after George and Sally had met at that smoke-filled Cairo bar, George Sloan proposed to Sally Bedell. She eagerly and joyfully accepted. Both agreed the marriage should be done as quickly as possible. Therefore, on March 31st, 1944 the couple were married by an RAF Church of England chaplain at the LRDG base outside of Cairo. Several of George's fellow officers and men were in attendance. Sgt Perry served as the best man.

The couple were only able to enjoy a brief honeymoon in a seaside hotel in Alexandria. There George and Sally made mad and passionate love many times amidst the backdrop of pounding ocean waves. Soon after, George returned to his unit and began intensive training for what they all believed would be the bogged down Italian campaign.

Sally, meanwhile, was informed that she was to be transferred to an intelligence section near Reggio di Calabria. She along with several of her male and female colleagues boarded a transport, MS Quayle, at the port of Alexandria on April 30th. Low, scudding clouds greeted the group dockside. Sally thought the mood as ominous. She had a premonition of some kind of impending doom. No matter how hard she tried, she just couldn't shake it. She knew she was probably thinking too much, feeling silly. After all, the Allies now held complete control of the Mediterranean Sea.

Rain clouds had begun to gather above the mini- convoy, shortly after it had gotten underway. Unknown to any of the vessels within it, the U-571 was maneuvering its way amongst the transports and corvette escort ships. After taking bearings and obtaining the correct firing solution the U-571 proceeded to launch a spread of three torpedoes: its target the MS Quayle.

Two of the U-boat's deadly torpedoes struck home midway along the starboard side. The Quayle immediately took on a 20-30 degree list. It was clear to her captain that the ship was mortally wounded. He ordered everyone to abandon ship.

Sally (Bedell) Sloan had been below deck in the stateroom assigned to her and several other young women. One of the torpedoes had hit in virtually in that precise spot. Sally and her bunkmates were almost totally consumed. No trace of their bodies would ever be found. It was as if they'd simply disappeared.

***

In the meantime, George Sloan and his LRDG unit had been selected to take part in the Allies latest effort to oust the Germans from their stronghold at Monte Cassino. He wouldn't learn of his wife's death for another two weeks.

Sloan's unit's mission would be to gather intelligence for the men of the 8th Army, under the overall command of General Sir Harold Alexander. It had taken the general more than six weeks to complete all of his preparations, until finally on May 11th of 1944 he was ready. At 2300 hours the Allies unleashed the greatest cannonade the Italian campaign had yet seen. More than 1,600 guns along a 25 mile front had begun firing at virtually every known German position, covering the mountains with cascading flashes of fire. The valleys were filled with continuous reverberations and unyielding smoke. As the echoes died down the infantry moved forward.

Sloan's LRDG unit had provided valuable information that they'd gathered prior to the attack. And it was this very information that Lt General Wladyslav Anders and his Polish forces would utilize in their advance toward the dastardly objective of the monastery at Monte Cassino. The Poles were at the figurative crossroad, as being devout Catholics they were aiding and abetting in the continued destruction of one of the Catholic Church's most sacred and holy sites.

In any event, George Sloan and his compatriots had done their job and now watched as the Polish troops moved forward in the attack. In the background, a cacophony of sound and fury could be heard. George was only glad that he wasn't on the receiving end of the barrage.

By May 17th, after six days of heavy fighting, the British had advanced far enough from their Rapido River bridgehead into the Liri Valley so as to outflank the town of Cassino and the looming monastery above it. That night the Germans withdrew from both places. On the 18th, the Poles occupied the monastery and raised their national flag above it.

The next week saw the German 10th Army in full retreat all along the main front. It was time for the long-stalled Allied troops to break out from their lodgment at Anzio.

During a lull in the Allied advance, George was handed the note which informed him of Sally's death. At first, he did not, could not, believe it. How was it possible? He still hardly knew her. How could it be? But it was. George sat back against his backpack and, fighting back tears, slowly began to recount the short time he and Sally had spent together. He could clearly see her lovely and beautiful face, her infectious and never ending smile. He could feel the curves of her exquisite body in his hands once again. And, most of all, he could sense and smell her unique scent. The unmistakable influence of the pheromones each person's body sends out. Almost like DNA, this power was often the most dynamic attractive element between a man and a woman.

And now, it was all gone. It had been as if Sally Bedell had never existed. She was gone. George would not even be left with a body to mourn and to lay to rest. Oh, he would make sure a headstone would be placed at a cemetery in Britain, but still there would be no body of a beautiful young woman.

***

"Bloody war! Bloody fucking war!" cursed Captain Tom Lazenby as he read the note George Sloan had just handed to him. Softly, he went on, "I'm sorry, George, I truly am. I know there's nothing I can say or do for you at a time like this." He looked over at Sloan, of whom he thought might well burst out into tears. He'd taken an instant liking to George from the moment they were first introduced to one another. It had been about a week before the just recently concluded Monte Cassino attack. He remembered how George had practically gushed over about his "Sally." She was the woman of his dreams. He'd gone on about how he and Sally would grow old together. And now, this woman of his life was simply gone. It'd happened in a flash.

"Thank you, Tom. You've been a good and understanding friend to me. And in war that can be a bad thing. Some say you cannot or should not acquire friends as you can suddenly lose them, and..." lamented George plaintively.

"Maybe you can get some personal leave? You know, what do they call it? Compassionate leave?"

George didn't respond at first as he looked down at the barren ground. Suddenly, both men heard the distinct and unique sound of an artillery shell seemingly headed directly their way. Lazenby and Sloan leapt, or rather crawled and staggered to a nearby slit trench. They were glad they'd dug one earlier. The shell must have hit about 50 yards away. They could feel the concussive wave wash over them.

Tom and George slowly raised their heads, only to take in roiling smoke, flame, and dust rolling through the surrounding air.

"I'm not sure, Tom. I was thinking I might have been better off if it had bloody well killed me," muttered Sloan.

"Don't say that! Don't ever say that! I know you are angry and bitter, and have every right in the world to be, but your death will not bring Sally back," said Lazenby.

***

My Dearest,

I am writing to you to let you know that I am well. I don't want you to worry. I hope you and Rosanna are doing well. I miss the both of you more than I can say. As for me, things are pretty good. We dug a hole for a swimming pool last week. I tell you, I can't really say how much earth we dug out, but it was a lot. Anyway, I have to tell you that the people of Texas are pretty friendly. They all seem to greet everyone with, 'How y'all doing today?'

Me and your cousin, Luigi, have been together since we were taken prisoner on Sicily. He's a pretty good egg. He's always cracking jokes, even with some of the guards. I tell him he should be more careful at times with them, but he doesn't seem to care.

I do hope you and the little one are well. She must be getting big. I can still picture her, and you, my love, the last time I was home. I don't want to get maudlin in my letter. Oh, before I forget, could you send some of those anisette cookies you make? I think some of the men would like them.

I am going to close now. I, as always, give you and Rosanna all of my love. I miss you, Rosalie. I miss seeing you, the scent of your hair, your smile, and your body. That is all for now. We are about to fall out for assembly.

All my love,
Franco

Rosalie read the letter over and over, until she reached the point where she thought the paper might well wear out. She treasured every letter she received from Franco. In the back of her mind she remembered, fleetingly, her night with the American captain, James Benedict.

She well remembered Benedict recalling a funny story from his collegiate days, about how some of his friends had been gathered round one of their apartments and were engaged in a bout of drinking flaming *Wild Turkey* whiskey shots. Of course, Benedict just had to jump in and how he'd successfully downed three shots. It had been on the fourth, when the whiskey was set afire, that Mr. Benedict had run afoul of the Gods of Fate. When the inebriated Benedict had tossed back the shot it somehow missed most of his mouth and instead found its way to his nose, eyebrows, forehead, and some of his hair. His classmates had thought it to be absolute hoot and had laughed hysterically. A couple of them had even fallen to the floor, completely convulsed in laughter, peeing their pants.

After almost losing his head, Benedict had made his way to the school infirmary and gave them a lame excuse as to the root cause of the state of his face.

Rosalie, at first, had only made a sour face and shaken her head in amazement, or had it been disgust. She then had thrown her back in laughter at the sophomoric hijinks of Benedict and company.

Now, Rosalie was forced to banish further memories of the American to the recesses of her mind.

Rosalie then went to a drawer and removed some writing paper and set down to begin a letter to Franco. At first, she thought she knew just what she wanted to say to her husband, but struggled to begin. That blasted American captain kept entering and reentering her head. She had succumbed to temptation, to the man's body, and how she'd enjoyed the ribald and raw sex the pair had had together.

Rosalie's thoughts were suddenly interrupted by Rosanna as she burst into the kitchen, breathing hard with excitement.

"Mama, mama, look, isn't he the cutest thing you've ever seen?" crowed Rosanna, as she cradled a squirming black and white colored Jack Russell terrier.

Rosalie looked down at her daughter as she struggled to control the little animal. Standing next to her was Alberto, a friend of Rosanna's from a nearby farm.

"My, my, it seems as if you have found yourself a little friend," said an astonished and surprised Rosalie. She had to admit to herself that the little fellow was awfully cute.

"Can we keep him, mama? Oh, pleeease, he's so cute, isn't he?. Alberto said he has been wandering around. He is frightened by all of the soldiers and the big army trucks moving about. I have even named him Rudi. Oh, please, please, say yes!"

"*Si, signora*, what Rosanna has said is true. Even though the Americans have been giving him some food, there are still people around here who are still hungry. One of them could easily capture Rudi and then...well, you know," offered the boy.

There he stood, little Alberto, with his mop of unruly curly hair, soft brown eyes, and threadbare clothes. He resembled most of the children in this part of Sicily.

Rosalie had to acknowledge that what Alberto had said was true. There were indeed some people who would think of nothing of abducting a small and adorable little dog like Rudi and devouring what they could from his tiny, emaciated body. "Well...I don't know. Even though he is small, we'd still have to find a way to feed him and take care of him," hemmed Rosalie. The little dog whimpered little cries as he continued to struggle and squirm in Rosanna's arms. Rosalie was melting by the second as stared into the dog's soft brown eyes. "All right, I will tell you what we'll do, we'll keep him just for now. But I'll have to get the okay from your Uncle Aldo. I can't guarantee anything. I don't want you to get your hopes up, Rosanna."

"Oh, thank you, mama. Come Alberto, we'll get him some water and maybe some food. I think he may be hungry and thirsty," said Rosanna happily. She and Alberto then sprinted from the kitchen and out into the yard.

Rosalie sat down heavily, considering how she was ever going to talk her brother into agreeing to take in the dog. Well, that would come later. For now, she would turn her attention back to composing a letter to Franco.

***

"Absolutely not! Are you crazy, Rosalie?! A dog? You expect us to take in a dog?" muttered a disgusted Aldo Mancini. "You have all lost your minds."

"But Aldo the dog is so cute. And Rosanna adores him, and lord only knows she, as well as the rest of us, have not had much to be cheerful about," pleaded Rosalie. She was glad Aldo hadn't thrown into her face another crack about her affair with Captain Benedict.

"Cute, you say? Just another mouth to feed, albeit a small one," continued Aldo in disgust. "I honestly don't know where your head is at, sometimes, Rosalie. Have you no sense of… of what is practical?"

Rosalie now glared back at her brother.

"And, don't think I have forgotten our little discussion about your…well, you know what."

"There it is again. I'll just bet that you can't wait for Franco to return so you can tell him to his face about my affair!" threatened Rosalie. "Have you no sense of decency?"

Aldo took a step backward away from his enraged sister, momentarily frightened. He could clearly see the anger and the fire in Rosalie's blazing eyes. This was a woman who was normally quite calm and collected. But when her blood was up, as it now was, there was no telling what she might do.

"What's the matter, Aldo? Are you afraid that I might strike you? A demure and meek Sicilian woman would have the audacity to strike a man."

"There's no such thing as a weak Sicilian woman, Rosalie. I am sorry about what I said. It was wrong of me and I apologize."

"I accept your apology, Aldo. I think we'd all better cool down a little. I will speak to Rosanna about the dog. I will try and make her understand," said a downcast Rosalie.

"Don't bother. Forget about what I said about the dog. We'll just have to make do with what we have," said Aldo, who then turned to go out the door.

"Thank you, Aldo, that is most kind of you," soothed Rosalie, although she still wasn't quite sure that her brother might not try and spirit the dog away in the middle of the night.

***

"Duce, your blood pressure is a little on the high side," said Leo Goncalo to the leader of the Fascist rump state located in Salo. "I'll write out a prescription for it, but I would advise you to also watch your diet. Try to limit your salt content. I will speak with your cook about this." Goncalo was wrapping up his blood pressure kit. He looked over at the woman who was sitting languidly nearby. Mussolini had earlier introduced her as Claretta Petacci, his long-time lover. Leo thought the woman exhibited a sultriness and wasn't at all possessive of any kind of warmth or genteelness. All during the Duce's examination she had just sat and smoked one cigarette after another. Leo had always been aware about the dangers of smoking, or even being in the presence of a smoker, but decided against it. It could only have turned him into an instant enemy of the woman.

"And Duce, try and get some relaxation," advised Goncalo.

"Relax he says, Claretta. Did you hear him? He tells me to find some relaxation. Goncalo, I appreciate your being able to attend to me on such short notice. I know that you come from a fine Sicilian family. But you don't seem to realize what kind of pressure I'm under. I swear that one-half of the people, conservatively speaking, want my head on a platter, and the other half may have some lukewarm support for me," said the one-time fearsome strongman of all Italy. Mussolini sat in front of Leo slumped into a settee as he slowly buttoned his shirt.

Leo had initially been somewhat shocked when he'd first been introduced to the man. His face seemed to reflect a pasty, grayish color, and his body appeared somewhat shrunken. Mussolini had once been so proud of his robust, masculine form. He no longer looked as if he were a man to be feared. Still, looks could be deceiving. Leo knew that his patient consumed or, at least, he had, a 1940s male-enhancement drug, undoubtedly to assist him in trying to meet Signorina Petacci's carnal demands. The combination of poor diet, stress, and the drug could well have led the man to his present condition.

"I understand, Duce. I was only trying to provide you with a suggestion. While I'm here, I would like to tell you that I have long admired you and your leadership. You have been, I'd say, Italy's greatest leader," said Leo heartfully. He'd really meant what he'd just said.

"I do not think there are many in this country who'd agree with you, Goncalo, but I thank you for the kind words. That is most thoughtful of you."

Leo tilted his head to one side in acknowledgment of the compliment.

"By the way, how is your father these days? I have long admired him and his support of me and Fascism," said Mussolini.

"At present, Duce, he is being held by the Americans on several charges. But I thank you for your asking," said Goncalo.

"Bastards! Your father is a good man. I imagine that the Americans and the British are digging up all sorts of false charges. There are all kinds of people who will want to get in on the act when a man is down. I am a perfect example of this, wouldn't you agree, Claretta?" Mussolini called out to his paramour.

Petacci was now leafing through a fashion magazine, still smoking. She looked over at the Duce through a cloud of smoke wreathed around her head, and, at first, did not look as is if she'd bother to reply. Leo thought her the picture of complete and unmitigated arrogance. *What the Duce see in her, beyond the obvious?*

"Mmm, I suppose you are right, Duce. But there will always be all kinds of little people sniping away at people like us. Especially a great man like you. I think it is pure jealousy and envy." said the woman through the vail of smoke.

Petacci's voice was of a husky nature, but to Goncalo somewhat alluring. She put down the magazine and crossed her nylon stockinged legs. Leo thought her long smooth legs as quite shapely, and appealing. For a brief instant, he could envision them wrapped around Mussolini's torso as he fornicated with the woman. He imagined her rich brown eyes calling to him. Now he realized what Mussolini undoubtedly saw, and what would cause his loins to stir.

Outside, the once pleasant and sunny day had begun to darken. Soon, the darkness would intensify and jagged bolts of lightning, interspersed with rolling sounds of thunder, would fill the air. A heavy rain would follow. It would be a match for Leo's own darkening mood. He'd return to his staid and mundane medical duties. It would be a mood to also match Italy's continuing declining fortunes as the relentless Allied armies inexorably moved on in their campaign against the Germans, and their remaining Fascist lackeys.

Chapter Eleven

Italy's Agony

The war in Italy pressed on relentlessly. On August 4th , two months after the liberation of Rome, with Field Marshal Albert Kesselring grudgingly withdrew the German forces into a new line of defense, called the Arno Line . It ran from the Arno in Pisa to Florence and then over the Apennines to the Adriatic Sea.

Kesselring held little hope of being able to hold the Arno Line, but just 20 miles to the north was a mountain location, called the Gothic Line. It would be here where the Field Marshal would make his stand against the Allied forces.

On August 15th, American and British troops landed on the Riviera coast of southern France as part of the Allied campaign in France. This had forced the withdrawal of men of seven Allied divisions from Italy. The Allies were then left with 20 divisions in which to oppose 22 German divisions. And the Germans continued to have the advantage of being on the defensive.

Bitter fighting took place, either on the Arno Line or the Gothic. On September 13th, the US Fifth Army arrived at the well-prepared defenses of the Gothic Line 15 miles to the north of Florence. They immediately ran into determined opposition: Heavy casualties ensued. There turned out to be only two mountain passes through which the Americans could continue moving toward Bologna. The two passes were the Futa Pass and the Giogo Pass. American general Mark Clark chose to attack toward *il Giogo.*

The route through this treacherous pass was no wider than a two-lane rural road. It contained many sharp curves that were under direct German observation on the heights above. The terrain and the tenacious defense made it virtually impossible for the attacking Americans to deploy large numbers of soldiers.

The withdrawal of the Allied divisions to France, along with surprisingly stiffening German resistance would see the prolongment of the Italian campaign throughout the late fall of 1944 and into 1945. As spring arrived, American and British aircraft bombed and strafed without opposition in the Po Valley and the northern Alpine passes.

In the meantime, Italian partisans struck out at German positions with increasing boldness. Some 50,000 strong, armed largely with captured weapons taken from the Germans or dropped by Allied aircraft. They were trained and organized by Allied officers who'd penetrated enemy lines. Partisan units cut telephone wires, ambushed enemy troops, and dynamited culverts, bridges, roads, and railroad tracks. There was a price paid for these attacks. For every German soldier killed or wounded by partisans, the Germans routinely executed ten civilians, regardless of whether they were old men, or women, or even children. Still, this grim realization did not put a stop to Italian guerilla actions. In the northern part of the country many partisans were controlled by the Communist Party. They attacked German units, and often waylaid and killed Fascist Black shirts (Mussolini's hardcore supporters), and their own political opponents. Be they of the left or the right of center. Parisans would pin labels on the bodies marked *"Spia Tedesca"* (German spy).

***

It is at this point in the narrative that the author wishes to interject two true-to-life horrific events that took place in 1944 in northern Italy. They underscore the sheer brutality and inhumanity of the war, and it involved innocent men, women, and children. Ordinary citizens just trying to get by from one day to the next. Innocent people who had no stake in the war. Ordinary individuals who merely wanted to be allowed to live.

The first event occurred on August 12th, 1944 in the hill village of *Sant' Anna di Stazzema* in Tuscany. Waffen SS troopers were in the midst of an operation against the Italian resistance. The SS men assisted by the Fascist *Brigate Nere* (Black Brigade) unit began rounding up villagers and refugees during the early morning hours. They then proceeded to lock up several hundred of them in a number of barns and stables. The SS men began shooting people down with their machine guns. Some of the terrified citizenry had been herded down into basements and other enclosed spaces. The SS men then tossed hand grenades into them.

At the 16th century church, the parish priest, Fiore Menguzzo, was shot at point- blank range, after which machine guns were then turned on some 100 people gathered there. In all, the total number of victims included at least 107 children (the youngest of whom, Anna Paradini, was only 20 days old); as well as eight pregnant women. One of whom, Eveline Berretti, had her stomach slit open with a bayonet and her baby pulled out and killed separately.

Following the killing of several more individuals in the village, the corpses were piled up and set on fire. At the church, SS men dismantled some of the pews and used the wood for a bonfire to dispose of more bodies. All of the livestock of Sant' Anna were exterminated and the entire village was burned to the ground. The operation was over within three hours. The SS troopers and the men of *Brigate Nera* then sat down outside of the burning village and proceeded to have a leisurely lunch for themselves.

One may ask what could have caused these people to have suffered such a fate. The SS and the *Brigate Nera* men claimed it had been because of the village's collaborating and assisting partisan units in the area. Surely, one could see their argument in the dispatch of small children and infants.

The second incident occurred in the town of Marzalotto in the mountainous area south of Bologna during the period of September 29th to October 5th, 1944. It would turn out to be the largest massacre of civilians committed by the Waffen SS in western Europe during the entire war.

In retaliation for attacks on German soldiers by partisans of the Resistance, SS-Sturmbannfuhrer Walter Reder led troopers of the 16th SS Panzergrenadier Division in a systematic and brutal killing of several hundred people in the aforementioned Marzalotto. Many of the civilians of the nearby villages of Grizzana, Morandi, and Monzuno also perished.

Many historians and researchers have struggled to accurately determine the total number of victims. Some sources have reported that perhaps upward of 1,830 victims were killed, while others have estimated the number of dead at 955. Sturmbannfuhrer Reder, himself, figured the total dead at 770 criminals. One hundred and fifty-five of them had been under the age of 10, 95 had been aged 10 to 16, and 142 had been over 60 years old. And five of the victims had been priests.

Giovanni Farnarini, a parish priest and a member of the Resistance, risked his own life to protect some of the population of Marzalotto from the Nazis during the massacre. Fornarini escaped immediate death, but was later discovered by an SS officer of burying some of the bodies. This had been forbidden by the Germans. The officer accused the priest of having committed crimes against the authorities. When Fornarini confessed to having assisted villagers escape execution, the SS man shot and killed the man.

There were other mass killings by SS men and their Fascist Blackshirted allies as the fighting raged on north of Rome: 200 people killed here; 300 people gunned down in some other locality. It didn't matter, the killings would go on…and on.

***

Rosalie Donato read of these killings in the newspapers, and silently raged. It was madness, sheer and pointless madness. What had the Italian people done to deserve these outrages. Oh, yes, the country had hitched its figurative wagon to Benito Mussolini. And it was when he'd joined with that evil charlatan from the north, Adolf Hitler, that the page of doom was written. None of this would have happened without the presence of their great German allies.

Near the end of 1944, Rosalie took receipt of a letter the postman had dropped off. It was from Franco. She opened the envelope slowly and carefully, almost reverentially, anxious to read its contents. Rosanna was off playing with Rudi and some of her friends. They were all excited, Christmas was fast approaching. And even though the war was still going on, there was an expectancy of hope in the air. Everyone knew the conflict had to be approaching its climax. The Americans and British were almost at the Rhine River in Germany. It was true the Germans had initially surprised them in Belgium in what would be called the Battle of the Bulge, but the Allies were now slowly beating them back. In the east, the Russians were now in Polish territory. The Nazis had suffered grievous losses in just the past few months. Losses they could ill afford.

Rosalie read that Franco had been moved from the prison camp in Texas to one in an area called New England. He was now in a camp called Fort Miles Standish in Taunton, MA. More to the point, now that Italy was out of the war, and officially on the side of the Allies, selected groups of Italian POWs were now being allowed out on weekends. Men, such as himself, would be accompanied by an American officer or sergeant, usually of Italian descent were being invited to Sunday dinners in the home of a local Italian family. Franco had already been to several of these dinners at the home of a family with the name of Campanella, who lived in the city of Woonsocket, Rhode Island. It was largely a mill-working town composed, for the most part, of French-Canadians originating from Quebec, Canada.

Franco described for Rosalie of captivating and large meals of lasagna, veal cutlets, chicken cacciatore of such quantity as he'd never seen before. And, of course, there were the mouthwatering desserts of sup inglese and tiramisu. He also mentioned consuming well-crafted home-made wine. At the last dinner, Franco had to practically carry his chaperone, one *Tenente* Cardillo, back to the Miles Standish camp. After all, one of them had to be at least moderately sober.

Franco finished up his letter by wishing Rosalie and Rosanna all his love and he was sure they would all be reunited soon. The war was coming to a close. And he could hardly wait.

Rosalie put down the letter and silently knew that the war would soon end. Not soon enough for her, but soon.

***

"I would like to help you, Leo, but I'm afraid there's not much I can do," lamented Gregorio Lanza as he eased back into his leather armchair. Outside Lanza's cramped office the surrounding winter presented an ominous backdrop. A light snow on the previous evening had dropped a coating throughout the Salo countryside.

"Surely, Gregorio, there must be something that can be done. I have to help my father, I just have to," croaked an anguished and pained Leo Goncalo. He could feel his blood pressure rising. The predatory weather only adding to his depressed mental state.

"I know how you feel, I really do," continued Lanza. "But we have to face the facts. Your father is being held in Sicily. There are not, what could be called, normal diplomatic relations between Italy, under Allied control, and the Republic of Salo," Lanza went on. "Look, Leo, the war is approaching its end. We all know it, despite the braggadocious talk of the Duce. He's a mere shell of a man. He is only a puppet of the Germans. My suggestion is for you to wait for the war to end. I don't think the Ameri cans will have much of a case and in all likelihood release him. I really feel this way."

This was not what Leo had wanted to hear and his frustration and helplessness was only increasing. "That is easy for you to say, Gregorio, he is not your father," said Goncalo, who immediately regretted his choice of words. He knew Lanza was a trusted friend of his. He had been a man he'd become friends with over the past few months. And he was still a true Fascist. "I'm sorry Gregorio, I didn't mean it. It's…it's just that I feel so helpless. My father is sitting and rotting there in jail and I can do nothing to help him. It is not fair." And with that, Leo Goncalo slumped back into his chair. How he hated the absolute futility of it all.

"You don't have to apologize to me, Leo. Believe me, I do understand. Look, there may be a way. I do have contacts in Sicily. Men I can rely on, who before the war were dedicated Fascists. I'll try and get word through to them about your father, and his situation. However, I cannot promise you anything. I don't want you to get your hopes up."

"No, no, Gregorio, I understand. I'll pay you whatever it takes. I know you are a man who can get things done." Leo felt a momentary uplifting of his spirits at Lanza's mention of contacts in Sicily. The looming gray sky outside began to lighten as if in figurative support of his rejuvenated mood. Perhaps, all was not lost.

"Leo, as you are well aware, we are living in difficult times, but I feel confident that we'll come through it. There will be a tomorrow, I can assure you," a self-confident Gregorio Lanza concluded with a note of triumph. He began to lift his frame up from his chair, a slow, groaning sound being emitted.

Leo knew this was the signal that Lanza wished to conclude the consultation. He was grateful the lawyer had agreed to meet with him and to hear his case. "Gregorio, I am most appreciative for you having given your time to see me today on such short notice. I'll await word on what may develop." Leo stood and shook the hand of his advocate.

After Goncalo had left, Gregorio Lanza had once again begun to contemplate his own precarious future. He was about to put into place his own plan for extradition from the collapsing Republic of Salo. He would make an earnest attempt to help Leo Goncalo and his father. If at all possible, he would not fail him.

***

After resting and refitting over the winter of 1944, the Allied armies were poised to launch a new offensive in the spring of 1945. The American 10th Mountain Division had been added to the ranks. More than half of its soldiers were college students or graduates. A number had been signed up by the National Ski Patrol, a civilian organization that had been tasked by the War Department to recruit volunteers. In addition, new equipment and weapons, as well as ammunition and supplies had been stockpiled. Some of the equipment consisted of flame-throwing Crocodile tanks, amphibious troop carriers, and armored bridging equipment.

The battle plan for the spring campaign was the brain-child of General Sir Harold Alexander and would be in the familiar pattern used by the Allies throughout the Italian campaign. It would be another one-two punch, with one army group attacking first so as to fix the Germans' attention, while the second group delivered its blow on another front several days later. The British 8th Army struck first on April 9th in the direction of Lake Comacchio. The US 5th Army attacked near Bologna several days later.

On April 14th, the 5th Army unleashed the second punch. Led by the 10th Mountain Division, it sliced its way through the mass of the Germans' Gothic Line defenses in front of Bologna. General von Vietinghoff, now in command of the German forces, requested permission from Hitler to withdraw. He was refused and told to have his troops stand fast. There would be no retreat.

On the 21st of April, the 5th and 8th Armies had linked up just past Bologna, and the Germans were sent fleeing in disorder across the Po Valley. Armored spearheads, moving at high speed, had encircled them. In two days, the American 88th Infantry Division alone took more than 11,000 prisoners. Allied warplanes constantly swooped down on the German units, leaving the dust-filled roads clogged with destroyed and burning wreckage. All across northern Italy partisan units continued rising up. Railway workers sabotaged tracks in numerous provinces, so as to prevent or, at least, hinder the movements of German troops and supplies. In Genoa, partisans cut-off the water supplies and electrical service to German barracks. They also set up roadblocks to stop enemy troops from escaping.

It was now clear that the German armies in Italy were disintegrating. Exhausted and discouraged soldiers were surrendering by the thousands.

***

This now brings us to the final chapter in the fate of Benito Mussolini. In March of 1945 he was faced with the ever tightening circle of Allied armies and Italian partisans. Like his old friend and comrade-in-arms, Adolf Hitler, Mussolini had clung to the hope that Franklin Roosevelt's death on April 12th would somehow end the war in the Axis's favor.

On April 15th, Mussolini sent his son Vittorio to confer with Cardinal Schuster, Archbishop of Milan, in the vain hope of striking a deal with the Allies allowing him to surrender directly to them, and thereby keeping him out of the clutches of the partisans. No one was found willing to bargain with the young man. Benito Mussolini next tried to negotiate with the Committee for National Liberation, recognized by the Allies as the legal government in the north. The committee had earlier decreed that all Fascist leaders would get the death penalty. The Duce met with the committee in a face-to face encounter, but in the end amounted to nothing: Mussolini wanted to negotiate, the partisans demanded his unconditional surrender.

Upon his leaving the meeting, Mussolini composed some of his thoughts in a farewell note to his wife, Rachele. "I ask you forgiveness for all of the harm that I've done to you without meaning to," he wrote. Suddenly, a vehicle pulled up to his quarters carrying his long-time mistress, Claretta Petacci, who'd once again refused to be separated from her lover.

The pair set out on April 27th and soon joined up with a German motorized column that was heading north. About 45 miles from the tunnel that would've taken Mussolini and Petacci through the Alps and into Austria, the convoy was halted by a group of partisans. The leader offered to allow the Germans to pass, but insisted that no Italians be permitted through, and that each vehicle be searched. Mussolini had meanwhile tried to conceal himself in the back of one of the trucks. He wore a German greatcoat and helmet. Pretending to be a soldier sleeping off a drunkenness. The Duce was uncovered and then hustled off to the local partisan headquarters. Once there, he was interrogated and then locked in an abandoned room. He was soon joined by Petacci.

On orders from the subcommittee of Leftist partisan officials, one Colonel Valerio, raced to where Mussolini was being held and demanded custody of him. The partisans who'd been holding the Duce knew what this would mean, as Valerio had immediately made known his intentions.

Valerio burst into the room containing Mussolini and proceeded to shout: "I've come to liberate you!" He then led Mussolini and Petacci to a waiting vehicle and drove off with them for about a mile before stopping. Valerio ordered them out at gunpoint. They were then placed in front of a stone wall. The partisan leader then proclaimed: "By order of the High Command of the Corps of Volunteers for Freedom, I am instructed to do justice for the Italian people."

In the last moments of his life, Benito Mussolini was able to rise above his fear. He ordered Valerio to shoot him in the chest. Two volleys rang out in the cool, crisp air. The Duce and his mistress were now dead. Their bodies were then taken to Milan where they were ignominiously displayed to the world hanging from their heels from the girders of a filling station.

***

Six months later (December 1945)

Scurrying her way home in great excitement, Rosanna nearly skidded her way through the kitchen when she finally arrived there. Her boots, coated in moisture from the recently fallen rain, gave the little girl almost no purchase on the stone flooring underfoot.

"Oh, oh, Rosanna, hold on. You know that you shouldn't be so reckless. How many times have I told you that is no way for a young lady to behave?" Rosalie mockingly scolded her daughter. "What is it that has you so excited?"

"Mama, mama, my schoolmate Laura just told everyone that her father is supposed to be released from cust… cust…"

"Custody?" corrected Rosalie. She knew where the little girl was going.

"*Si, si*, custody. He has been a prisoner of the Americans, just like papa. Well, Laura has been told by her mama that he's to be released by them in the next two months. Isn't that exciting? That must mean that they will release Papa soon, doesn't it?" The little girl concluded breathlessly. Her little chest was rising and falling in her enthusiasm.

Rosalie looked down at Rosanna and reached for her with her muscled arms, courtesy of her hard and untiring work on the Donato land. She held the little girl close to her, nuzzling her curly blond hair. Hair just like her own. She brought her face close to Rosanna's and spoke softly with tenderness and heart. "Rosanna, I know you're excited, but that doesn't necessarily mean that Papa is going to be released soon as well. It.. it…"

"He has to, Mama! He has to!" said the little girl defiantly. She stiffened in her mother's grasp, a frown forming on her cherubic little face. Rosanna was doing her best to act like a grown-up.

"I know, I know, my little one. Well, you see, Laura's father is probably being held in another part of the United States. After all, it's a very big country, much bigger than Italy. And… and…well, I don't think every man…er, prisoner, like your father is going to be released at the same time," Rosalie's words began to fail her. She desperately wanted to say what she knew Rosanna wanted to hear, but she also knew she couldn't raise her child's hopes and then only to have them dashed.

" I was hoping he would be home with us by Christmas. This will be another year without him. Why are the Americans still holding him? What has he done to them? I think they are being very mean. I don't like the Americans!" huffed a defiant Rosanna, who now stamped her feet to emphasize her unhappiness and anger.

"I know how you feel. But sometimes things aren't as simple as they appear. The Americans are not angry with your father. They are just holding him for his protection. Things are still bad here in Sicily, and all over Italy. They don't want to send him back to a place that is still not safe. You'll just have to be a little more patient. Your Papa will be back home with us soon," Rosalie finished her bending of the truth.

"But if it is safe for us to live here, why isn't safe for Papa?" questioned Rosanna as she looked down at the floor. A scowl now crossed her face. She wouldn't be easy to placate. Rosalie knew the little girl was quite intelligent and advanced for her age. She possessed a degree of maturity far beyond her juvenile years.

"I still hate the Americans, Mama. They have no right to hold Papa anymore. I hate them! I hate them!" screamed Rosanna.

"Do not hate, Rosanna. There has been far too much of that in Italy and for far too long. You shouldn't hate anyone. I know that it's hard for you to see it now, but Papa being with the Americans now might be the best thing in the world. He could be held by people who are far, far worse than them. Like the ...I don't..." Rosalie soothed. She gently stroked Rosanna's golden locks.

Outside, the sky had suddenly grown much darker, as if reflective of the mood within the home.

"Who could be worse, Mama? Who?"

"Oh, people just to the north of Italy. People who said for many, many years that they were our friends. They urged Italy to join them. They said they were the future and our leader believed them. Now, our country has been defeated, and lies broken. Many people have suffered far, far worse than you and me, and your father have suffered. Trust me, my little one, you father will be home with us soon. You have to believe me... and to trust me."

***

The war's end saw *Dottore* Leo Goncalo cut adrift. There was no Italian Army, and he no longer had a practice to attend to in Salo. In fact, the longer he remained in the former Italian Socialist Republic the greater the possibility he would be apprehended, either by the Americans or the British. A worse alternative would be to fall into the hands of the roving bands of partisans, who, despite the war ending, still roamed the countryside in search of former Black Shirts, or other members of the Fascist Party.

Once again, Leo turned to his legal advocate, Gregorio Lanza. Goncalo had been able to track down the wily and elusive lawyer in the town of Cerveteri. It was located about 30 miles northwest of Rome, near the coast of the Tyrrhenian Sea. The office Lanza had holed himself up in contained a magnificent and breathtaking view of the sea. White and grayish plumed gulls fluttered above Cerveteri's beaches. Goncalo, however, was in no mood for sky gazing of any kind when he trod up the stairs of the ramshackle building where the lawyer was now practicing. Upon reaching the door of Lanza's office, Leo stood for a moment as he heard the lawyer's voice and that of a woman. From his guess, it was the lilting and soft voice of a young woman. Goncalo imagined the woman was probably a flirt Lanza had just picked up. The man had always had the reputation for being a ladies man. A real raconteur.

Unable to wait a moment longer, he wrapped three times on the faded and peeling green door of the office.

"Who is it? Who is there? I am conducting urgent business and cannot be disturbed. Please come back another time," said the startled voice of Advocate Gregorio Lanza.

"I cannot wait for another appointment, counselor. I need to see you right now. There is not a moment to waste," said an exasperated Leo Goncalo, his blood pressure rising and he could feel perspiration seeping through under his shirt collar. This was despite the fact that it was mid-October.

"Goncalo, is that you?" questioned Lanza.

Leo was able to hear things, as if they were on a desk being moved about, or, as if Lanza had been rearranging objects necessitated by some initial sexual foreplay.

"Just a minute, I will be with you shortly," said Lanza, his voice sounding slightly hoarse.

"*Yes*, thought Leo, *I've caught the rascal with a young woman about to engage in some afternoon sex.*

Finally, after what had seemed like several minutes had passed, but in actuality hadn't been more than two minutes, Gregorio Lanza slowly opened his door to Leo. "Eh, it is my old friend, Leo Goncalo. My, my, you are sight for sore eyes. Let me look at you," said Lanza in feigned exaggeration. From his harried look he plainly wasn't glad to see Leo, or anyone at that time.

Leo thought the lawyer's greeting had been a little over the top, forced. "I'll bet you are, *Avocato* Lanza. I'll bet you are," remarked Leo laconically.

"Oh, where are my manners? Leo, let me introduce you to Signorina Maria Bella. We were just going over some of her paperwork and…" said Lanza as he leaned forward conspiratorially. "She is going through a rather difficult divorce. And, well, you know how it is,"

"No, Gregorio, I do not know," said Goncalo with a cold sneer. He looked over at the young woman, who couldn't have been more than 19 or 20. He didn't notice any wedding ring, either. Bella was about 5' 6" tall, with curly brown hair and a soft, almost angelic face. From what Leo could see the girl's greatest assets appeared to be her long legs and impressive frontal endowment, which she did little to conceal. Maria Bella was dressed in a black skirt, cut just the knee. He could discern the length of her legs by the way she sat with them crossed. Her top was a white cotton knit which displayed her cleavage to the maximum effect. As if she needed even more enhancement, a heart-shaped diamond hung seductively between her breasts.

The girl stood and smoothed out the folds of her skirt, eying Leo at the same time. "I will be going now, Gregorio. I expect to be hearing from you soon," said Bella coquettishly. She batted her brown eyes at Lanza and quietly strode to the door. She looked at Leo and said, "You have placed yourself in the hands of one of the finest advocates this side of Rome, signore." And with that Maria Bella left. She left in her wake a slight scent of an appealing perfume.

***

In the backdrop of Italy's history for the period of 1945 to 1950 the following is of note. Towards the end of the Second World War, Victor Emmanuel III, the now discredited king, attempted to bring up the status of the Italian kingdom when he nominated his son to be head of government. Victor Emmanuel had promised the people that after the war they would be given the opportunity to choose the form of government they wanted by way of a referendum.

The term Italian kingdom was removed on June 2nd, 1946, and on January 1st, 1948 new foundations were put into place for a new democracy as a new Constitution was crafted.

The first elections were held in Italy in 1946: The main political parties were the Christian Democrats, the Italian Socialist Party, and the Communist Party. The Christian Democrats won the election, but the other two parties were allotted ministerial positions in the new coalition cabinet. Palmiro Togiatti, a Communist, was selected as the Minister of Justice. The Communists greatest strength was in the northern cities of Milan and Turin.

Worries among Italian voters about a possible Communist takeover proved vital in the electoral results when the election was held on April 18th, 1948. Rosalie Donato remembered well that some people she knew went to the polls that day and voted Communist, and later they proceeded to lay awake all that night fearing a Communist takeover of the government.

Aleide De Gaspari, leader of the Christian Democrats, won the election with 48% of the vote. The Communist Party performed well against the Socialist Party during the distribution process of seats in the assembly. They'd attained a solid place as the main opposition party in the country.

The famed Peace Treaty of 1947 saw a few adjustments made at the Italian and French border. The border area to the east turned out to be much less tranquil. Territory had been given to Yugoslavia and the region around Trieste was proclaimed a free territory. Its jurisdiction fell under the control of British and American forces in the region, and was divided between Yugoslavia and Italy.

***

The crowd at the dock in Naples was loud and boisterous. The cacophony would only grow as the US troopship *Magellan* slowly came into view. Rosalie Donato, along with Rosanna, and her brother Aldo were standing amongst the throng of people. Rosalie had already gathered up Rosanna in her arms. The Donatos could feel the surge and electricity of the crowd. Most of these people hadn't seen their loved ones for several years. Some of the women had given birth to sons and daughters of the returning men. Rosalie had to take care that she and Rosanna not get crushed in the enthusiasm of those gathered.

Slowly, ever so slowly, the *Magellan* glided to a stop, assisted by three tugboats. At long last the ship was secured by several thick ropes. The waiting, teeming crowd still had to wait for another two interminable hours before the disembarkation could commence. Finally, as the hour approached 4:00 pm, the Italian prisoners were released to their waiting relatives and friends. The men descended from the vessel from two points: one at the bow and the other at the stern.

For more than 20 minutes Rosalie waited. To her it seemed as if an hour, at least, had transpired. Desperately she searched for some sign of Franco. At one point she turned to Aldo, as if for assistance, but her brother could only shrug his shoulders in his own bewilderment. For the past several months, perhaps longer, Rosalie had come to increasingly rely on him for guidance and support. The two had come to grow much closer to one another than they had ever before. Something that had not been the case in prior years.

At last, Aldo pointed to the stern of the *Magellan* and gave out a shout. He simultaneously nudged Rosalie's shoulder to draw her attention to the sight of Franco Donato moving down the gangplank

Rosalie took sight of him at last and began shouting and waving at her husband, while she excitedly pushed Rosanna up and down. "There is your daddy, Rosanna! There he is! He has come home to us, just like I said he would!" she shouted into the little girl's ear.

Rosalie and Aldo made their laborious way through the bedlam toward where they'd last seen Franco.

He saw them first and ran to his wife and child. It was June 7th, 1946. Franco Donato had not seen them for nearly three years. He nearly couldn't contain himself as he swept them into his arms. Franco and

Rosalie exchanged sloppy kisses to one another, they did not care. Franco then smothered Rosanna with a flurry of his own hurried smooches. Aldo Mancini stood to one side after embracing Franco. This was a moment for the Donatos. Aldo took Rosanna's hand, so that Franco and Rosalie could more suitably embrace one another.

It took the Donatos two days before they returned to their home near Ottavino. On the first day back, Franco visited with his parents, family members, and some neighbors. When Franco returned home in the early evening, Rosalie noticed that he seemed drawn and tired. She didn't think much of it at the time.

That evening she and Franco made love for the first time in nearly three years. As he entered Rosalie, she experienced a brief flashback to the American captain, but the apparition quickly vanished from her mind. She now had her man back with her, and with their growing daughter. It would be the first night of lovemaking for them for years to come. Her dream of Franco's safe return had come true. Still, there in the recess of her mind lay the bitter and tender memories of her beloved mother and father. Then there were the memories of the devastation throughout Sicily and Italy. It would take years of rebuilding and recovery. Many shoulders would have to be put to the proverbial wheel.

***

"It seems as if you have a problem, eh?" asked Alberto Cardi as he glanced down at the business card on his desk. *Signore Alfonso DeBurri*

"You had ambitions and desires as a young man, and you pursued them. In addition, you became an ardent Fascist and complete admirer of the Duce. Of course, we cannot speak too loudly in that vein today..." Cardi continued as he sat in front of Leo Goncalo. The man now paused to reach for a dark cigarillo that was lying unattended upon the desk. Cardi placed the diminutive cigar in his mouth and lit it with his gold-plated lighter. He offered a cigarillo to Leo, who politely declined.

Leo wondered where the tenor of this discussion was heading. He hated the fact that he'd had to come crawling back on his hands and knees to this slippery, oily character. He knew full well that Alberto Cardi had served as his father's front man for his varied nefarious purposes. Leo had been aware of the role Cardi had played in his father's swindling of the Mancini properties. How the elder Mancini had endured a vicious and false prison sentence and then died alone without his family. Leo Goncalo knew all of it. But he now had no other choice. Cardi represented just about his last and best chance to slip back into the woodwork in some nearby, obscure town. A place where he could blend in seamlessly amongst the locals and thereby resume, albeit on a limited scale, his profession of medical doctor.

"I am sure that you realize master Leo that the Allies have placed a price on your head. A rather considerable price, I might add. From what I hear the Russians and even the Poles would love to get their hands on you. That is based on what you are alleged to have done at some place called Auschwitz. That is a little of what I've heard. Could I be wrong? Could this just be some malicious gossip?" Alberto Cardi stood and glanced at Leo, making him seem quite small.

Goncalo wished at that very moment he was possessed with the power to permeate his way through the very floor he now stood upon.

"All right, Signore Cardi, what do you want me to do? I stand before you Alberto, my proverbial hat in my hand. Do you wish me to beg on my hands and knees?"

"You know my young and learned friend, I do believe you should always address me as *Signore*. After all, one should always show a modicum of respect to one's elders," said a now half-smiling Cardi as he sat back down into his leather armchair. A slight grown was elicited from it.

"You are so right, *Signore* Cardi. It seems as if I have indeed forgotten some of my manners. You have to understand that I have been away for quite some time, and..." Leo hesitated for a moment in front of his father's former lackey. The Alberto Cardi he was now facing was a far different creature that the one he'd previously known. This Cardi had emerged from the shadows with the Americans arrest of Carlo Goncalo. He was the one who now ran the show for all Goncalo business interests. Outwardly he presented the appearance of trying to hold Carlo's fortune and empire together. And should Carlo never see the light of freedom again, well, so much the better.

Of course, none of this could be revealed to Leo, or this so-called Alfonso DeBurri. Still, Alberto thought to himself, *maybe this young and wanted man could be utilized for my own benefit.*

"All right, Leo, I'll do what I can to assist you in the new life you seek."

***

George Sloan's role as a combat soldier came to an end with his participation in the Italian campaign. He'd had to acknowledge that he'd been lucky. He'd only some suffered scratch wounds. Many of the men he'd served with in the desert and Sicily had either been killed in action or else gravely wounded. No, he realized, that a merciful and beneficent God had watched over him. Still, there was a wound that lay deep within his heart, the loss of his beloved Sally. He thought he would never get over it, never be able to absolve it from the furthest recesses of his mind.

The British Army decided, in its infinite wisdom, to send George back to England, to largely perform boring and bland staff work. Sloan was eventually to be directly involved with the planning and execution of Operation Overlord, the Allied invasion of northern France in June 1944.

Following the successful landings at the British beaches of Gold and Sword, George was joined up with General Bernard Montgomery's staff on the mainland.

Heavy fighting would ensue at such places as Caen and Falaise, but the Allies would inexorably and inevitably grind down the resisting German forces in France. Together with the Americans, the western Allies were placing a hammerlock on Nazi Germany. From the east, massive Soviet tank, infantry, and air formations virtually annihilated any German units in their path.

V-E Day, Victory Day in Europe, rang out on May 8th, 1945. The guns, at long last, fell silent, a peaceful silence ensued. It was time to pause and reflect, and to contemplate the future. For George Sloan, he would return to France and to Germany, after he'd spent a brief sojourn back home in Britain. This gave him some time to spend with his parents. It allowed for him to describe to them his brief marriage to Sally Bedell.

The British Army, for some unfathomable reason, decided to assign Captain George Sloan to what was designated the British Army of the Rhine's Judge Advocate General's Office. Its mission seemed to ring true. To seek out and bring to justice war criminals: The bludgeoning and bayoneting of small children, sometimes still clutching dolls at the time of their grisly deaths. Old men and women gathered together and then ruthlessly machine-gunned into oblivion. No, these were, plain and simple, war crimes, crimes committed by men who'd clearly had a blood lust to fill.

The cases George Sloan came to investigate soon filled him with an incredible passion, a drive, a sense of mission, to help bring justice to those innocent lives who'd been cold-bloodedly murdered, and often, for no reason at all. German soldiers, which often turned to have been SS men, were constantly crossing his desk. So when a file arrived on his desk in early June of 1948 he was brought to attention at his new JAG office in Rome. This was a case in which an Italian, a doctor no less, had been alleged to have perpetrated criminal medical acts at the death camp of Auschwitz.

As George read on in the file, the case concerned an Italian Army doctor by the name of Leonardo Goncalo. The young man hailed from some town called Ottavino in northeast Sicily. The report had gone on to state that Goncalo had compiled a sterling and exemplary record while serving as a surgeon with the army in North Africa. The narrative also indicated that Goncalo, for some unknown and implausible reason, had volunteered for admission to Auschwitz. Sloan knew the death camp was located near the Polish town of Oswiecim, not far from the city of Cracow.

The reading fascinated Sloan, who'd proceeded to light and consume one John Player cigarette after another as he continued his perusal. He noted that the young Italian physician had always been known to be an inveterate and dedicated Fascist. The man had always held Benito Mussolini in the highest esteem.

A further note indicated that young Goncalo's father, Carlo, had been incarcerated by the Americans for alleged illegal financial activities. Some involved extortion of some neighboring landholders. In fact, the elder Goncalo now sat in an Italian jail just outside of Naples.

George Sloan had been, at first, a little shocked at what the BAOR investigations had turned up in their rooting out and hunting down

German, and some Italian soldiers. These people had committed savage war crimes against soldiers of the Allied armies and civilians.

The search for war criminals by Sloan's unit also encompassed Italian territory. In fact, George had already been intimately involved in the tracking down and apprehension of Obersturmbannfuhrer Herbert Kappler. It had been Kappler who was intractably connected to the notorious Ardeatine Cave massacre in the outskirts of Rome in 1944. Less than two months before the liberation of the Eternal City by the Allies, the Italian Resistance had detonated a bomb amongst a company of marching SS troopers. More than 30 men had been killed, and an unknown number had been gravely wounded. In a brutal reprisal action, it had been Herbert Kappler who organized the roundup of more than 300 Italian civilians, most already being held in numerous Roman jails. These unfortunate souls were eventually taken up to the Ardeatine Cave complex, on Rome's outskirts, and then gunned down in cold blood by the SS. Kappler himself was responsible for the personal execution of several men during the course of the bloodshed.

It had been one of George Sloan's most satisfying moments when he'd been able to assist in Kappler's apprehension and his being brought to justice in a military tribunal.

George had also been part of the JAG's sections who'd investigated an alleged killing of a British officer in Italy in 1944. This one had been carried out from September 1947 to June 1948.

It made Sloan's blood run cold when he read some of the transcripts of German soldiers and the SS, concerning their roles during these killings. Most said they had only been following orders. They'd had no choice. But to Sloan, the words never had the ring of truth to them.

***

"Now, now, my dear Leo. Let us not be so melodramatic. We are both adults here. We're not actors in some playwright's scene on the stage at the local playhouse," expanded Alberto Cardi as he sat once again before Leo Goncalo. It was mid-1947 and Cardi had indeed helped Leo to assume a new identity and to take up practicing medicine once again. But Leo now was in need of the elder man's assistance, it had become urgently necessary for the physician to move again.

Albero Cardi resumed his dialogue, "You need a new place to go to. Another location where you can once again blend in with the local populace. You need to ameliorate yourself with the local scenery, in the metaphorical sense. And I think I have just the place and it's not very far from here. It is a small village by the name of Nettullo. But you are well aware of how suspicious many Sicilians are. Many do not even know their practically next door neighbors in villages right next to theirs."

Leo stood there like a mute, blandly taking in Cardi's blather. How he hated once again having to crawl in front of this…this unctuous toad. But once again, he'd been left with little choice, and Alberto Cardi knew it. He was reveling in the moment. "*Grazie, Signore* Alberto. *Mille grazie.* Once again I am in your debt.

"You are quite welcome," soothed back Cardi. "Yes, well then…There is one more thing I'd like to tell you. I have been really trying to secure your father's release. You have to believe me," said Alberto Cardi.

"*Grazie,* Don Alberto, once again I am in your debt," said Leo, who did not believe a word of Cardi.

Chapter Twelve

Pursuit of Justice

"This is simply unbelievable, George. Simply unbelievable," groaned a shaken Captain Jay Crawford, a fellow JAG officer.

"Isn't it?" lamented Sloan in agreement. "It's all there in the file. I mean I could understand German officials, and the sort, volunteering for such ghastly duty, and, of course, Jewish prisoner doctors being forced into it. But here, we have an Italian, of previous good reputation as a doctor and a surgeon," Sloan went on. "I'm not in agreement, Jay, that it was considered acceptable for German physicians to want to participate in such disgusting and degrading work."

"No, no, of course not," said Crawford as he continued leafing through the damning documents.

"It's all there. I mean this guy Goncalo, not only volunteered to go into Auschwitz, but apparently he was eager to perform multiple surgeries on these hapless people."

"Yes, it says here that Leo Goncalo operated on a number of male prisoners. And apparently his specialty was castration," continued Crawford, a haze of smoke curled up from the cigarette he was cradling in his right hand. The smoke cast a ghastly hue in the dimming light of the day.

"Not only that, my dear fellow, Goncalo appeared to have performed some of these surgeries without the use of an anesthetic. Can you imagine?

What sort of deranged human being could ever do such a thing? It is quite simply inhuman and barbaric," said Sloan, anger smoldering within himself. An anger he could do little to quell at that moment.

"Yes, well, my good man, what are you proposing to do?"

"Well, to start with I'm going to head back to Rome, and then, possibly Sicily, where the bastard has presumably gone into hiding."

"Who will you take with you?" asked Crawford.

"Beside you of course. Well, I was thinking of Sergeant Pepper," said Sloan. He had worked with Barry Pepper on two previous occasions. A dogged and determined ex-policeman from Coventry.

"Yes, a good man," agreed Crawford. "And since these alleged crimes occurred in Poland, do you think you may have to go there?"

"I don't know at this point. Perhaps me or someone may have to. You know how skeptical and suspicious the Russians are right now. But we'll cross that bridge when we come to it."

Both men then fell into a pensive silence. George looked out the office window into the dying haze of the day. The ruins of the once great port city of Hamburg lay stretched out in all directions before his unseeing eyes. Carcasses, the crushed and pulverized buildings reminded him of animal carcasses, gutted and now uninhabitable. Sloan and Crawford's office lay on the outskirts of this once great German city of the north.

It had been designated *Operation Gomorrah*, and during a week in July 1943 it created one of the largest firestorms raised by the Royal Air Force in World War II. It was estimated that more than 42,000 civilians may have perished, and another 125,000 more wounded. The city was virtually destroyed. Adding to the firestorm was the fact that there had been little rain for some time and just about everything was dry. The unusually warm weather and combustible conditions meant that the bombing was highly concentrated around the bombers' intended targets. This created a vortex and whirling updraft of super-heated air which, in turn, resulted in a more than thousand foot high tornado of fire.

The RAF's onslaught went on for eight days and seven nights. It would later be called the Hiroshima of Germany. And not to be outdone, the US Army Air Force joined in when they conducted a daylight raid on July 25th. Problems in the assembling of the American force resulted in only 90 B-17s reaching Hamburg.

The firestorm created by the nearly week-long bombing spawned an uncontrollable inferno with winds of up to 150 miles per hour. This incinerated more than eight square miles of the city. Asphalted streets burst openly into flame, and fuel oil from damaged and destroyed ships, barges, and storage tanks spilled their contents into the waters of the canals and harbor, causing them to ignite as well.

No other city in Germany was as shaken. German officials became thoroughly alarmed. Adolf Hitler was reported to have said that additional raids like the one on Hamburg would force Germany out of the war. More than 600 industrial concerns and armaments works had been damaged or completely destroyed. Local transport systems, such as buses, subways, and trolleys had been totally disrupted. More than half of inhabited dwellings had been destroyed. There was the lingering smell of natural gas that wafted its way throughout the city.

This was the venue of the JAG unit of Captains George Sloan and Jay Crawford. It would be from this vantage point their effort would go forth to bring Leonardo Goncalo to justice.

***

It hadn't taken long for Franco and Rosalie Donato to settle back into their old routine, to a point. Rosalie still desperately missed her parents, but she and Franco had their little Rosanna, who was now growing up rapidly before their very eyes. Franco swore to himself that a little woman was taking shape before them. Franco's parents were still alive, and living close by. Alberto and Nadia watched over the little one for them on those evenings when Franco and Rosalie wished to engage in some passionate lovemaking.

Just when it seemed that their lives could not be more idyllic, Rosalie began to notice Franco, and something wasn't quite right. At first, she couldn't put her finger on it. But then, Franco began to complain of intense stomach pains. This had always been a man who had never scared easily. Rosalie urged her husband to see a doctor. At her suggestion, he, at first, resisted. But she kept insisting.

Finally, one day, one of their hired hands, Rodolfo, brought into the house a staggering and wheezing Franco from the field they'd been working in. The helper half-carried, half-dragged the exhausted and sweating Franco into the living room and deposited him into the well-worn leather sofa.

Rosalie, hearing of the commotion from the bedroom ran in only to see her husband red-faced and sweating profusely over his entire body. His face looked absolutely ghastly, as if he'd been held over a blazing fire. Streams of sweat continued to pour forth from every crevice of his face.

This time Rosalie acted swiftly, ignoring Franco's protestations that he was fine. She told Rodolfo to continue looking after Franco, while she'd run for help. Thank God Rosanna was safely away at school. At least, she wouldn't have to worry about her for the moment.

Not bothering to go to the local doctor, *Dottore* Ribello, who, no doubt, was probably into his second or third glass of Chianti by now. The old physician would, in all probability, be in over his balding head if he'd tried to diagnose Franco's condition. Instead, Rosalie was able to get Aldo to drive them over to the American compound. There she was sure they would be able to get competent and professional medical personnel who could properly attend to her husband.

Two days later, Rosalie Donato sat before Dr Robert Clifford. The man was actually a captain in the US Army. Rosalie judged him to be about 35 to 40 years old, with a receding hairline. He possessed a firm mouth which was set below an aquiline shaped nose. Piercing blue eyes gave the army physician a determined, no-nonsense look. Rosalie had the distinct feeling she was in the presence of someone who knew his business. And yet, Dr Clifford seemed to possess a gentle and forgiving bedside manner.

"Please, *Dottore*, I would appreciate it if you just gave me the news straight. I have a feeling it is not going to be what I want to hear," Rosalie heard herself say, but for some strange reason it had sounded like an echo in her head. Remarkably, she'd spoken the words in a calm and level tone of voice. The past two days had been absolutely frantic for not only her, but for Rosanna as well. Rosalie knew, just knew that something had been dreadfully wrong with Franco all along. There could be no downplaying of what was affecting a clearly sick man.

"I wish that I could tell you what you'd like to hear," Captain Clifford cautiously began as he crafted his response to this forthright and steadfast woman who sat before him. There were no tears, only a steely determination. "I am afraid that your husband's is quite...quite grave... and."

"What is exactly wrong with Franco? You can tell me, *Dottore*, " Rosalie said as her hazel colored eyes focused straight into Dr Clifford's.

"Your husband has pancreatic cancer. And I'm afraid there is no cure. I am so sorry to have to tell you this, *Signora* Donato," said Clifford. The doctor over the course of his practice had previously informed many other families and loved ones of similar grim news. But for some strange reason for Clifford, this time it felt especially difficult. Here before him sat a remarkably attractive woman who'd taken in this devastating news with a stoicism that would have astonished Job himself. In all probability, she had already endured much hardship and loss from the war. Now, she would be losing her husband.

"How much time does he have left, *Dottore*?"

The words sounded leaden to Clifford's ears. "I would estimate your husband has about six months, perhaps."

"I see. And there is nothing that can be done?" asked Rosalie pitifully.

"Nothing outside of trying to make him as comfortable as possible. I can assure..."

"You may call me Rosalie, Doctor."

"I can assure you, Rosalie, that myself and my staff will do everything in our power to provide your husband the best medical care possible," continued Clifford.

Rosalie sat quietly as she half-listened to Captain Clifford. Some of his words went in one ear and right out the other. As she tried to process what she was hearing, she began to recount the years she and Franco had spent together. The years of toil and travail, the birth of their daughter, their love for one another, the war, the imprisonment of her father, and so many other things. A lifetime spent with her family and her husband. And it was all coming to a close in a blinding flash.

***

There was no other way for Leo Goncalo to look at the trajectory his life had taken. He'd once been a prominent and well-respected doctor, a notable surgeon no less. He had served with great pride and distinction with the Italian Army in North Africa. He had even, albeit briefly, tendered his service to Benito Mussolini, the former strong man and Duce of Italy. He now found himself hiding out in this small, non-descript hovel of a town. Hiding? It felt more like he was cowering. That was what his life and now come down to. Cowering.

It was now summer 1947, and Leo Goncalo, aka DeBurri was practicing medicine, if one could call it that, in a small backwater in Sicily. Despite his having taken an assumed name, Goncalo, always had the sneaking suspicion that he wasn't completely safe. Perhaps he never would be. The Allies, he knew, and their inveterate and unrelenting war crimes investigators were looking for him. They were after him because of his actions at Auschwitz. The investigators were not only after Leo, but many others as well. Men who, in their words, had committed unspeakable and brutal crimes against humanity. Leo had been cast, along with such brutal medical practitioners as Josef Mengele, as a war criminal. The Allies and thousands of victims and their families and friends were out for more than justice. Each and every one seemed as if they wanted to exact their pound of flesh.

At the mere thought of Leo being brought to this so-called justice, a clammy feeling would encase his body. Perhaps he should turn himself in and just submit himself to the designs of his pursuers. And yet he truly felt as if he'd done nothing especially wrong. After all, hadn't a good number of Germans and Italians, and others, possessed the very same thoughts.

Perhaps Leo should make himself disappear once again. This time he could seek refuge on the mainland. But deep down he knew he couldn't do it. Sicily was in his DNA, his roots, his very soul. He could not leave the land, this land, despite the fear which gripped him each and every day.

Every day he saw a litany of patients, most of whom were poor fainthearted individuals who were trying mightily to eke out a living in this hard-scrabbled, unforgiving land. Yes, his land. In the recesses of his ever probing and restive mind, Leo Goncalo felt he was surely destined for more. It was true, that presently he was depressed, and, perhaps, he felt as low as he'd ever been. His time in this small town of Borolino was only one of biding.

One day Leo had had to smile to himself when he recounted the episode of one Rigoberto Napoli, an elderly peasant farmer who had chosen to visit his surgery. The man had blithely informed Leo that he'd never once experienced a sick day in his life, and, yet, there he was. Napoli was insisting to Goncalo that he wasn't feeling well, that he knew he had a high fever. He might well have the flu. He told Leo of his memory of the great influenza epidemic that had broken out throughout the world in the wake of the Great War.

Leo patiently examined Rigoberto as the man sat quietly on the examination table. He informed the elderly man that he had nothing resembling the flu. In fact, Napoli had nothing more than a mild fever. Leo prescribed 20 mg of penicillin and some cough medicine and the man on his way.

A simple man among simple people. A people resigned to their poor and inevitable fate. People who had so little to look forward to every day. But Leo would not relegate himself to this ill-fated outlook on life.

***

The calendar turned to 1948 and Leo Goncalo once again found himself on the move. He didn't quite know why but he now felt that he had to move closer to Nettuno or Ottavino. He found himself fantasizing about Rosalie Donato, and wasn't quite sure why. He still thought her to be ravishing, what with her flowing, curled blond locks and the gentle curve of her inviting mouth. But it was the woman's body that really enthralled him. A full body with a frontal endowment second to no other woman he'd ever known. She possessed absolutely gorgeous and long legs which gave her walk that unmistakable feminine gait.

Leo quickly broke his reverie as he began to focus as to how he would conduct his next getaway. He decided he would secrete himself in the small town of Umbro, some three miles from Ottavino. It was nothing more than a glorified village, a place he'd once journeyed to as a young man. It had been a day when he'd had nothing in particular to do. Umbro was both quaint and charming in its own peculiar and unique way. His research had revealed that the town did not have a doctor in residence. Surely its citizens would gladly welcome someone like himself. Of course, he would hang his shingle with his new name of DeBurri. Leo didn't think it would present much of a problem, and he might be able to better spy on Rosalie Donato. He didn't quite know it but the woman would soon be a widow. Well, at this point in time it was still only a fantasy.

***

Rosalie knew it was only a matter of time before Franco would succumb to his suffering. In the meantime, she would do everything possible to make his world as comfortable as possible. Franco did his best to engage himself with Rosanna. Al least, as much as he was physically able to. The little girl hadn't spoken much about how much she saw her father in pain. It was very clear to all that she sensed something was very wrong with her father.

It had been pitiful to see the few times Franco had tried to make love to Rosalie, how much he was in pain. Rosalie did her best to make her husband feel as if he were still a robust and virile man, but, in truth there was always the element of futility to it all. Still, Rosalie tried to look on the bright side, especially when Rosanna was concerned. Their little girl was approaching her tenth birthday in 1948 and almost before their eyes their little princess was turning into a fine young woman. She shared her mother's flowing blond hair, but it was in her face that one could clearly see her father Franco, from her soft auburn colored eyes to her gently shaped mouth and beautifully pointed nose. She was indeed the apple of his eye.

Franco tried mightily, despite his continuous discomfort, in trying to play with Rosanna. This had become increasingly more difficult by the day.

Rosalie, for her part, did everything she could to spare Franco any evident humiliation as she was always interacting with Rosanna in playing card games and jacks. She'd even taking to skipping rope. To her surprise she had proven to be a quick study.

Franco, despite his debilitating condition, always found himself enjoying seeing his wife jumping rope, her ample breasts swaying underneath her blouse. He desperately tried to arouse himself, but he quickly realized this was a desire of the past.

Rosalie would occasionally spy her husband ogling her, she was glad he could still glimpse some of her sexiness.

As April approached it became clear to Rosalie that Franco could no longer remain at home. She'd done all she could to provide some succor and comfort, and, of course, love to him, but his pain threshold was diminishing by the day. She or an American medic would dispense pain-killing opium drugs, but she couldn't handle Franco in his own struggles to the bathroom for his bodily functions. Aldo would help her when he could, but he was tied up with the family business. And it had been more than once when Franco had soiled his bed and Rosalie had had to clean it up. Until one day when Franco leaned in toward Rosalie: "My dearest, I know you are doing your best, but I think it might be better for all if I were to be placed in the hospital." Franco cast a pleading look on his weary and drawn face. The threat of showers hung in the air outside the Donato home. Dark, luminous clouds limned their way across the darkening skies.

"Oh, it is all right, dear. I don't mind," replied Rosalie unconvincingly. She knew that the weary look she wore on her face told an otherwise truth. She could no longer mask the mental agony she was faced with. Perhaps Franco was right. He'd have to go away from his home…their home.

"We both know that it is the right thing to do in the time I have left. And you and Rosanna can always visit me at any time. I'm sure the doctors would not object."

Rosalie turned her head away from Franco so he couldn't see the tears forming in her eyes. She slumped her shoulders as in defeat, and used a handkerchief to daub away her tears. When she tried to face him she found that he'd fallen asleep. Silently, Rosalie wept again. She was slowly losing the only man she'd ever truly loved. She knew he would be better off in a hospital, and that he would no longer be in pain when at last he succumbed. It was only selfish of her to want him to hang on any longer. She would have to let him go. Rosalie clasped her grieving hands together and prayed Franco would pass on soon.

Franco Donato passed from this life at 3:15 in the morning. Doctors notified Rosalie immediately and she hurriedly dressed and then made her way to the hospital.

Rosalie was left alone with Franco's body for as much time as she needed, the hospital staff had said to her. She silently knelt beside her husband's bedside and reached for his stiffened hand. She whispered the Lord's Prayer and the Hail Mary. Rosalie thanked him for all of the love and comfort he'd provided to her and to Rosanna. She did not shed any tears, she had vowed not to on this day.

Franco Donato was buried next to the family plot just outside of Mettuno. A soft and lilting wind gently blew through most of the funeral service. Many attended from the town and from the surrounding area in a fitting tribute to a man nearly all had considered possessed of good, not malice. Standing next to Rosalie, dressed in somber black, was Rosanna, and brothers Aldo and Alberto. Her other brothers and sisters stood mutely in back. Rosalie, for some odd reason, was unsure as to whether she could only dress this way for the remainder of her life. Franco's parents stood nearby.

Not far away stood her cousin, Luigi Ferraro, a man she hadn't been that close to, but she had known that Franco had served with him and had said that Ferraro was a good egg. Or something to that effect. The local parish priest said final prayers and then Franco's casket was slowly lowered into his grave. Shovelfuls of dirt were then tossed on the box. And then, it was over.

As Rosalie walked away, carefully shepherding Rosanna, who'd been an absolute rock during the service, she felt a burning, a burning flaring up within her body. It was the burning of revenge. Rosalie burned with the desire to see the Goncalos roasted in hell. Carlo, the elder, was at that very moment rotting away in a prison cell nearby. His bastard son, Leonardo, was hiding out somewhere, perhaps in Sicily. Who knew, he might be close by as well. Rosalie had the sneaking feeling that the son would be unable to stay away for long from Sicilian soil. She would now invest herself to an even greater degree in bringing both Goncalos to justice. Rosalie was going to seek out the British and American investigators and assist them in any way she could. Rosalie Donato would make the Goncalos have to answer for her father, her mother, and now her husband. And Leo would have to account for what he'd done at some place called Auschwitz. Rosalie was well aware that there was a hefty price on the head of Leo Goncalo.

***

After settling into their quarters in Rome Captain George Sloan and Sgt Barry Pepper quickly set to work into their investigation of Leo Goncalo. Jay Crawford was set to join them shortly.

"I think we may have to journey to Trieste, Barry. We are going to need to interview this Dr Levi. In my opinion, he may be the key to any success we hope to achieve in getting the goods on our *Dottore* Goncalo."

"I think you're right, Captain. All indications seem to point to Levi being a key in regard to Goncalo. The file says he not only assisted Goncalo on some of these neutering operations, but was some sort of confidante to the good doctor," replied a pensive Pepper, holding a case file in his hand. A lit John Player in the other.

"Indeed, of course, that might be difficult to arrange what with the events going on in the northeast of Italy. Trieste has been the focal point of increasing tensions and intrigue between Italy and the newly formed Communist state of Yugoslavia." Sloan was referring to a Yugoslavia now under the firm thumb of Josep Broz Tito, a man not at all trusted by any of the Allied governments in the area. And although Tito had broken with Josef Stalin's Soviet Russia, his government was still, in its own unique way, Communist.

In addition to this, Sloan and his fellow Allied investigators had to contend with the increasing tension building between Britain and the Unites States on one side and the Soviet Union on the other. It was April 1948 and in less than two months this tension would culminate in the Russians closing off the Allied controlled sectors of Berlin to any and all land supplies to the city. Both Britain and America would then commence the great Berlin Airlift, whereby all food, lubricants, and supplies would be provided to Berlin by an immense airlift effort on a 24 hour a day basis. For the next year, the fate of all free Berliners would hang on this large-scale unparalleled and unequalled effort of a band of intrepid and determined aviators, largely flying in these aforementioned supplies in C-46 and C-47 transports.

"Well, we're going to have to make our way to Trieste and sit down with this Dr Levi and see if we can convince him to relate more information on our friend, Dr Goncalo," ruminated Sloan in the fading light of day. He, too, had now lit and was smoking his own John Player cigarette. Smoke from both men curled its way in the dying twilight.

"Sir, we are investigating Goncalo, any trial of him would undoubtedly have to take place under Polish auspices. After all, they would have first dibs on him. And, of course, this would probably mean the Russians would have a hand in the proceedings," said Barry Pepper.

"Indeed, Sergeant, indeed," agreed Sloan. "All right, let's begin by making arrangements to go to Trieste and to secure an interview with Dr Levi."

***

The Trieste Sloan and Pepper entered was seething with political intrigue. Nestled in the far northeastern part of Italy it abutted directly against the Yugoslavian Republic of Slovenia. It had been fought over between the two governments, its citizenry had long held to the belief that the city was Italian and must always remain a part of Italy. Throughout its history it had been influenced by its location at the crossroads of Latin, Slavic, and German culture.

The history of Trieste began with the formation of a modest town in pre-Roman times, which then acquired a proper urban connotation only after its conquest in the 2nd century B.C. and colonization by Rome. After the imperial run Trieste declined in the wake of the barbarian invasions. It flourished once again as part of the Austro-Hungarian Empire from 1382 until 1918. It was considered one of the most prosperous Mediterranean seaports, as well as a capital of literature and music.

The British investigators settled themselves into their hotel, the *Metropole*, together with an absolutely splendid and gorgeous view of the Gulf of Trieste. Its shining blue waters were mesmerizing to George as he gazed at them from his room window. A bright and shining sun shone down upon the city on this 10th day of April 1948. He and Barry Pepper anxiously awaited the expected arrival of *Dottore* Levi. Sloan desperately hoped the doctor would be willing to provide testimony and depth to the questions they had concerning Leo Goncalo.

At precisely 1300 hours George heard a soft knock on his hotel room door. When he opened it he was greeted by the sight of a graying and elderly appearing man accompanied by a smartly dressed and handsome younger man.

"Dr Levi, I am so glad to meet you at long last. I appreciate your having agreed to meet with me and my associate," said George Sloan in his most amiable manner.

"It is my pleasure, Captain Sloan. I would like to introduce you to my nephew, Gregorio Stanza. He is my escort and my driver," responded Levi as he gripped Sloan's extended right hand.

"Of course, well, welcome. Please, *Dottore,* won't you sit down. Can I get anything for you, perhaps some coffee, tea, or a libation?" asked Sloan, taking more of the measure of the man. George thought to himself that the doctor possessed great dignity and presence.

"At the moment, no, thank you. I am fine."

"Well, *Dottore*, let me introduce you to my assistant, Sergeant Barry Pepper, who is providing me with invaluable help in our investigation," continued Sloan.

"*Sergente*, it is my pleasure," said Levi as he in turn shook Pepper's hand.

"The pleasure is all mine, Doctor Levi," replied Pepper, who stood more than a head taller than Levi. He, too, felt a presence emanating from the smaller man.

After Levi and his nephew had been seated, George Sloan looked down at his prepared notes set before him on the dark walnut table. He then placed his reading glasses on and then looked at Levi. The older man sat impassively and waited for the interview to begin. He gave off the air of one who hadn't a care in the world. George hoped he would be able to probe the recesses of the man's memory and be able to sift out the information he needed to know relating to Levi's time at Auschwitz. Also his involvement with Leo Goncalo.

"*Dottore*, you were at the Auschwitz camp for approximately two years, is that correct?" asked Sloan, cautiously.

"That is correct, Captain. I was there from December 10th, 1942 to January of 1945 when the was liberated by the Russians," Levi responded. He was looking directly at Sloan, his gaze unwavering.

Sloan moved on to his next question as Sgt Pepper dutifully took notes, an ever-present cigarette resting between his fingers. "*Dottore*, did you have any personal observations of *Dottore* Goncalo and the procedures he performed on prisoners in the camp?"

"Yes, I did. I observed and, in some cases, I directly assisted the doctor," responded Levi coolly.

"Did you ever witness Doctor Goncalo perform a neutering procedure without the use of an anesthetic on a patient?" Sloan knew he would have to proceed with caution at this point in the interview. There was no way of knowing whether a particular question might cause Levi to simply shut down the interview and simply walk away.

"I did not assist Dr Goncalo on any of those particular surgeries. I did, however, on two occasions, witness these…these procedures. On those surgeries in which I did assist *Dottore* Goncalo, the patient had been sedated. They had been, how would you say? They were put under."

"Did any of these surgeries need to be performed? What I mean is, were any of these procedures medically necessary?" continued Sloan. Sgt Pepper continued with his notetaking, never once lifting his eyes as Levi gave his unvarnished and riveting testimony.

"To the best of my knowledge, no, none of these operations needed to be done."

"Why were they performed?" asked Sloan, who now paused to light a cigarette. "Do you mind if I smoke, Dr Levi?"

"No, no, I do not mind, Captain. They were performed, in my opinion, because the Germans were interested in seeing what the results would be. They wanted to see how these patients, as they put it, would react. In other words, they deemed it important to observe if there would be any difference between those who were sedated and those who'd not been."

"I see. Tell me, Doctor, did *Dottore* Goncalo willingly participate in any of these…these procedures? Do you believe that Goncalo may have been coerced into performing any of these surgeries?"

At first, Levi didn't respond, but eventually after what had seemed like an hour had passed, but in actuality had been only a minute, he finally answered Sloan's question. "No, Captain, I do not believe he was coerced. You see, I once thought that Leo Goncalo might be a caring individual, but I suppose that deep down he really believed…"

"Really believed? What did he believe, in your opinion?"

"He believed in the Germans and their theory of a master race. The unwilling patients he operated on were simply, how would you say…?"

"Guinea pigs?"

"Yes, yes. To him they were not really humans, but merely specimens. You know, as if they were something one could place under a microscope lens," finished Levi.

"I see, Doctor."

At this point, Levi's nephew interposed a question. "Captain, will my uncle's testimony jeopardize his freedom in such a way that he could be charged with a war crime?"

George Sloan took a moment to sit back: *That is a good question.* "I don't believe so, Signore Stanza. You see this interview is only in the exploratory phase. We are simply trying to gather facts at this stage. And based on what your uncle has been through I don't believe there is any court which would try and bring charges against him," concluded Sloan.

"But you are not absolutely certain, Captain. Are you?"

"No, but again I can only reiterate that I don't feel that Dr Levi would ever be charged. Signore, during the course of the Nuremberg Trials in 1946 and 1947 no prisoner doctor was ever charged with having committed crimes against humanity for their testimony. I myself would put in the record a firm recommendation against it."

Over the next hour Sloan asked more questions, more of what one would consider background information. Questions that pertained to Levi's upbringing, his medical education and training, his family, and so on.

"Dr Levi, if you were to be called to testify in court...would you?"

"Yes, yes, I would, Captain Sloan."

"I have to add that this would in all probability be at a trial held in Poland. After all, this is where the alleged crimes took place. Would you be willing to go there? I can assure you that His Majesty's government would take all the necessary precautions regarding your safety and well-being."

Levi sat up in his chair and looked directly at Sloan. His deep penetrative eyes were of those who'd seen so much over his long lifetime. "Captain, I'd be willing to go anywhere on God's green earth to see that justice is done. Men like Leo Goncalo should not be allowed to commit monstrous crimes against their fellow man and then be allowed to slink away to live the rest of their lives in peace and tranquility."

***

Once Sloan and Pepper returned to Rome they contemplated their next course of action. By this time they had been joined by Jay Crawford. It was decided they would travel to Sicily, by way of rail, ferry, and then jeep. The trio eventually arrived at Mettuno. It was now late April of 1948 and spring was definitely in the air. The skies were almost always an aqua blue, many days had not a cloud in the sky.

George Sloan quickly learned about, not only Leo Goncalo, but also his autocratic and domineering father, Carlo. The elder Goncalo was being held in a jail cell, having been convicted of numerous crimes: extortion, witness intimidation, misappropriation of other people's funds, tax evasion, and other crimes.

It was by mere happenstance that one day Sloan crossed paths with Luigi Ferraro. Ferraro had been in the British Headquarters building where Sloan and company had been working out of, when Ferraro overheard Sloan talking about none other than the Goncalos. "I did not mean to eavesdrop, sir," said Ferraro.

"Not at all. And to whom may I ask do I have the pleasure of speaking to?" asked George, one eye cocked upward.

"Luigi Ferraro at your service, sir. I happen to live in the area, and I have knowledge of the Goncalos."

"Indeed," said Sloan as he began to look the Sicilian over a little more closely. About average in height with a tanned skin, reminiscent of many Sicilians, and deep penetrating brown eyes. The eyes of a man who'd seen much over the course of a lifetime. "Would you mind stepping into my office?" he asked.

"No, not at all, sir," said Ferraro as he followed Sloan down the hall.

For the next half hour, Luigi Ferraro told Sloan of how Carlo Goncalo had cheated and swindled many Sicilians out of their land or money, or both. He became especially incensed when he mentioned what had happened to his cousin, Rosalie Donato. How the elder Goncalo had had her father incarcerated on false charges, and how he'd appropriated most of the Mancini holdings. Unfortunately, he couldn't relate much concerning Leo Goncalo. But he did drop a bombshell to Sloan when he mentioned he knew of Goncalo's hiding place.

"You're sure it is nearby, Signore?" asked George, barely able to contain himself at this breathtaking news.

"*Si,* er, yes, I know. I also know he is wanted by the Allies, your people, in connection with some alleged war crimes he was said to have committed at one of the death camps."

"I see, well. Do you know where he is now and can you take me there?" asked an increasingly excited Sloan. He was doing his best to contain his mounting excitement. This was the breakthrough he and Pepper, and Crawford had been desperately hoping for, but had never expected to happen.

"Yes, yes, I can take you there if you'd like. Perhaps we can go there tomorrow evening. He is hiding in a small village not far from here and he is operating under an assumed name. DeBurri."

"Good, good, very good. Yes, well, tomorrow night it will be," said Sloan. For the next 15 minutes the two men laid out the plan whereby George Sloan would have the opportunity of finally bringing Leo Goncalo in to face justice.

***

"Your cousin, you say?" asked Sloan as he slowly sipped on his espresso.

"Yes, yes, although I am not sure she can relate anything concerning Leo Goncalo's work at the camp, she can tell you a great deal about the father and his nefarious activities. What is more, she may be able to help you in ferreting out Goncalo so that you can then apprehend him."

Sloan looked across at Ferraro and had to admit to himself that the man was no ordinary Sicilian peasant. Here was a man who was clearly educated and spoke well, and was one who possessed an inner character. "All right. Do you think you can arrange for me to meet with Rosalie?" asked Sloan.

"Yes, I will make the arrangement. I will contact you in the next couple of days. I cannot guarantee you anything. After all, Rosalie may wish to have nothing to do with this matter. She has been through quite a lot over the years."

"I understand. All right, Luigi, I will wait for you to contact me."

***

Two days later, George Sloan found himself sitting in the very same café he'd been in with Luigi Ferraro. Only now it was 10:00 am, the sun shining brightly on what would be the start of a gorgeous and beautiful day in Ottavino. Moments later, a tall, blondish, statuesque woman strode into the café. Sloan knew it was her. It had to be her. The woman was dressed in white linen blouse, a gold chain with a turquoise colored amulet nestled within her bosom. She had on a black skirt cut at the knees. She wore aviator styled sunglasses that gave off an air of intrigue and mysteriousness.

George gulped as he took in the woman as she slowly made her way toward his table. Taking off her glasses she looked down at him and said, *"Capitano Sloan?"*

"Yes…yes," semi-croaked Sloan as he stood to greet Rosalie.

"*Bene,* I am Rosalie Donato. May I sit down?" she asked with a coolheadedness.

"Yes, yes, of course. I am so sorry, where are my manners?" said an embarrassed Sloan, who could feel his face coloring.

"That is quite all right," said Rosalie as she turned her head to one side.

"Would you like some coffee?" asked George politely.

"*Si, si*, er, yes, an espresso would be fine," she replied as she had now returned her gaze to Sloan. She thought she detected a slight tremor in his right hand. Perhaps the result of a war wound. Or perhaps he might be nervous in her presence.

Sloan would've had to admit that he was a bit nervous, and it was funny as normally the roles are reversed, the interviewee is left in the unsettled position. But with this woman, well she was not the average Sicilian peasant woman. Sloan signaled for the attention of a waiter to place their order.

"*Capitano*. I understand from my cousin that you'd like to ask me some questions, but I think I know what you may really be after…" Rosalie let her words linger.

"And what would that be, Signora?" asked Sloan, eying the woman closely. Her eyes enthralled him.

"That you would like to enlist my services in the apprehension of *Dottore* Leo Goncalo. Luigi didn't exactly come out and say it, but is that not correct?"

Sloan was glad he was sitting down. Rosalie Donato had cut to the chase. "Well…that is true, but…"

"*Capitano*, I only know what Leo Goncalo is alleged to have done. I am more aware of and have knowledge of what his evil father has done to me and my family. I blame Carlo Goncalo, and with good reason, for having my innocent father imprisoned on false and unsubstantiated charges. My father was never able to regain his freedom, and I know this killed my mother. But you feel you need me so that you can bring Leo Goncalo to face justice." Rosalie finished and then looked around the room. She began to fidget. She was letting her guard down.

In the meantime, the waiter had returned and set down Rosalie's espresso. She took hold of the small demitasse spoon and gently stirred her coffee, her luminous hazel eyes returning to George Sloan's.

"Well, yes, that is true. I just didn't expect to hear from you just now," said Sloan.

"As my cousin told you, Goncalo is in the area," Rosalie resumed.

"Do you mind if I call you Rosalie?" George asked gently.

"I would prefer that you do," Rosalie hinted seductively. "May I call you George?"

"Please."

"*Bene,* good. I know where he is because I've spied him observing me on at least two occasions. He thinks that I do not know. You see…George, at one time, Leo's father came up with a half-baked idea that he could put his son and me together. It never came to pass, thank God. I am not sure, but perhaps that may have led Carlo Goncalo to seek retribution against my father. And, there is the possibility that Carlo would like to get his hands on my body. My husband has passed away and maybe in Goncalo's mind I am once again a free woman."

"I'm so sorry on the loss of your husband, Rosalie. Luigi did not tell me," George offered.

"Thank you…George. He had been suffering greatly…well, anyway…" Rosalie then lapsed into silence. Suddenly, she perked up and said to George, " I know where Leo Goncalo has ensconced himself, and it not far from here."

The longer George Sloan listened to Rosalie Donato, the more impressed he became. "Rosalie, I have to tell you that I'm most impressed with your command of English."

"Thank you, George. I've always thought that English is an important language to know and will become more so in the coming years. I hope to one go to England or America."

"To visit?" asked Sloan.

"No, to live. I want to take my daughter to a place where there is peace and tranquility. In Italy, and especially Sicily, it is all intrigue, petty jealousies, getting even and *venetta*…revenge."

"I see, I see," said George. He then made arrangements with Rosalie to meet again over dinner so as to better plan on how they would bring about Leo Goncalo's apprehension. And because Sloan wanted to be in Rosalie's presence as soon as possible. He'd been clearly smitten with this intriguing woman.

Rosalie met up with Sloan for dinner on a warm and lovely April evening, a Saturday, at a restaurant named Attilio's. The establishment had been in existence for nearly a hundred years: what with its dark baroque woodwork and a bright shining mirror set just above the bar. All pictures and mementoes reflective of the Fascist era had long been removed. Its patrons were mostly from among the cognoscenti and well-heeled set.

Sloan had been impressed with the level of effort and determination that had been put forth by the citizens of this part of Sicily. Slowly, ever so slowly, the people had been rebuilding their villages and towns, and their lives.

The day before their dinner, Sloan had been in contact with the local Carabinieri, the elite Italian national police force, and its commander, *Colonello* Niccolo Guidi. The man had agreed to provide the Carabinieri's services to Sloan for the arrest of Leo Goncalo. George felt sure he could place his trust in these men and their commander. Guidi had an impeccable reputation and he, too, burned with a desire to bring in a lowly bastard like Leo Goncalo.

George and Rosalie repasted during the evening meal over a dinner of veal saltimbocca. A dish that had only recently returned to menus, due to the still prevalent food shortages.

Rosalie suggested that she make contact with Goncalo and to arrange for a meeting. She would falsely admit to him that she'd always harbored an admiration for him, that he wasn't at all like his father. She would say she would like to see him again. The meet-up would be at Attilio's.

Three days later, Rosalie hurried to Sloan's office with the news.

"I suggested to him that we should meet at Attilio's some time in the mid-week, a time when the restaurant wouldn't be too crowded," Rosalie said breathlessly. She could barely control her excitement.

"Good, good, that's good news, Rosalie. Did he seem suspicious?" asked George.

"No, I don't think so. He sounded very excited to have heard from me."

"Good. I am going to have *Colonello* Guidi's men in attendance for back-up. I have already gotten the okay from my superiors and from the Italian authorities."

"*Bene, bene,* George. You know I almost became sick to my stomach when I had to tell Goncalo that I still had feelings for him, uhh," she gasped.

"So, you do think he went for it?"

"Oh, yes, he went for it. I could hear him starting to breathe hard over the line. It was as if he couldn't believe what he was hearing."

On the following Wednesday at 7:00 pm Rosalie Donato quietly waited for her date to arrive. She felt a slight tremor course its way through her body. Rosalie took out a pack of cigarettes from her purse and lit one with a box match. She inhaled deeply into her lungs. She knew that Sloan and the Carabinieri men were around her, but she still felt an unease.

Rosalie had taken great care in her preparation for the evening. She had chosen to wear a silver silken blouse containing a deep vee neck which displayed to their fullest her breasts. She had also selected a beige skirt which when she crossed her legs they presented a revealing look.

The time had turned to 7:20 and still no sign of Leo Goncalo. *Perhaps he has decided to back out*, thought a now fidgeting Rosalie. *Maybe he suspects a trap.* Just as Rosalie was about to light another cigarette, in walked Leo Goncalo, a man she hadn't seen in years. A man she'd never expected to lay eyes on again. Goncalo was dressed smartly in a well-tailored black Brioni suit. He even wore a white carnation tucked into his right lapel. The silk tie was a bright flaming red.

"Good evening, Rosalie. It is so good to see you once again. It has been a long time," gushed Goncalo as he stood before Rosalie. He extended his right hand to her as he bowed from the waist.

Rosalie took Goncalo's hand and immediately felt a wave of revulsion wash over her. But she quickly remembered she had a role to play. "It is good to see you to again, Leo. It has been awhile," said Rosalie as she looked down at the floor for a moment.

Rosalie managed to engage Goncalo in light conversation about the past, the war, and themselves. He regaled her with stories of how he'd always liked and admired her. He did not mention much about his past, and nothing at all concerning his time at Auschwitz.

Both ordered drinks and dinner. Just at the moment when Goncalo appeared to have reached the point of being completely relaxed, and he began to drool over the sight of Rosalie's breasts, four Carabinieri men emerged from the shadows of the restaurant and stood around their table. Just behind them stood George Sloan. Goncalo's face had turned to a pasty and pale shade of white. Rosalie thought he looked as if he would faint just straightaway. A smile of distaste crossed her face, as if to say: *Take that you bastard. How does it feel? And now you will get what you deserve.*

"Leo Goncalo, in the name of His Majesty's Government and on behalf of the Allied War Crimes Commission, I am placing you under arrest for crimes against humanity. Please, sir, I would advise you not to resist. I would suggest that you come with us quietly," concluded George Sloan.

Just as he was about to pass from sight, Goncalo turned toward Rosalie and spat out: "You bitch, my father always said you were a whore. I did not believe him, but now…' He was then pushed forward violently by one of the Carabinieri where he was then handcuffed and taken to the local jail. Goncalo tried mightily to regain some degree of dignity as he was led away, but Rosalie only felt a deep bitterness.

***

In the days following the arrest of Leo Goncalo George and Rosalie began spending more and more time with one another. At first, it had been under the pretense of tying up some loose ends concerning the Goncalo case, but it soon became clear that the couple had fallen for one another. When he was alone Sloan would find himself fantasizing about Rosalie. He could picture her frizzled blond hair, her beguiling hazel eyes, and, perhaps, most of all, he pictured her body. She was voluptuous and possessed a pair of spectacular legs. He could envision them wrapped around his torso as he made mad and ravenous love to her. And yet, there was something more than he could see. It was the woman's presence, the way she made him feel deep within his own soul. No other woman, save Sally Bedell, had ever stirred such feelings in him.

George and Rosalie often took long walks together out into the countryside where she would point out particular things of interest. There were picnics where they took Rosanna along with them, the little girl squealing with delight. Sloan would meet Rosalie over coffee. This went on until the night, following a sumptuous meal, they found themselves alone in George's quarters. No one else was around. It couldn't be helped any longer and both of them knew it, and they helped themselves to one another.

Clothes were hurriedly abandoned, and then, George and Rosalie eyed one another. There she stood in absolute splendor, her breasts heaving and beckoning to him. For her it was his toned and well-muscled body, and his now hardening and throbbing penis. Soon George was all over Rosalie and she welcomed his assault. His mouth lingered with her tongue and then went to her breasts. He moved down to enter her vault. Finally, George brought himself back up her body, her hand deftly guiding him into her. He then thrusted and pounded away until Rosalie reached the moment of her climax. She thought she was floating along in space. Rosalie wanted the lovemaking to go on and on. Electricity had coursed its way through her body.

Moments later, George's head lay nestled upon her breasts. Both then fell into a deep and restful sleep.

Epilogue

Oswiecim Courthouse stood as an imposing three story blackish edifice, a yellow patina covered the outer walls, and light green accented its windows. The main courtroom was located on the third floor, where the Polish War Crimes Tribunal would hold session. The date was February 1st, 1949 and the courtroom reflected the gray dour weather to be found outside the building. A heavy clinging cloud cover blocked any sunlight from penetrating. The outside thermometer registered a freezing reading of 25 degrees Fahrenheit.

It would be a crowded courtroom #1 for the first day's proceedings. The trial had already garnered much of the attention of Poles throughout the nation. It had even been widely reported in many of the European countries, especially those which adjoined Poland.

The day would see the commencement of the trial of Leo Goncalo for the commission of war crimes during the period of time he had spent at the Auschwitz concentration camp. Present in the gallery were assembled newspapermen, and some women, and some political observers from several nations, including the recently established nation of Israel. Photographers and radio commentators had been barred. The three man judicial tribunal were not going to allow the court to be turned into a circus.

A most interested observer was also in attendance, Captain George Sloan. After all, it had been his team's investigative efforts, along with

Doctor Levi's testimony, that had provided the crucial material for the prosecution's case. Sloan was quite keen in being able to observe the Polish system of jurisprudence. Stirring in the back of his mind were thoughts of what and how much influence the Russians may have been exerting on the case behind the scenes.

Sloan's gaze swept around the courtroom until it settled upon the defendant, Leo Goncalo. The man already wore a look of defeat on his drawn and haggard face. It was as if he knew what his fate would be. He was dressed in the same suit he'd worn on the night Sloan and the Carabinieri had arrested him in Sicily.

Goncalo was being represented by his Polish appointed attorney. George had not gotten the man's name and he knew nothing of the barrister's background or qualifications. He appeared to be young, probably not even 30 years of age. Sloan doubted whether the man had much experience inside of a courtroom, not to mention that his client was on trial for his very life.

At precisely 10:00 am , the three men who would preside over the trial entered the courtroom and took their seats on the raised dais which was elevated a couple of feet above the main floor. Chief Justice Anton Cernak sat in the middle chair, flanked by Associate Justices, Peter Klimak and Walter Nehrinski. These would be the men who would judge the fate of Leo Goncalo.

Chief Justice Cernak was fifty years of age, who before the war had been a prominent defense attorney. Not a Communist, he was allowed on the court by the authorities because of his impeccable and incorruptible record. Cernak possessed a stern and imperturbable look: his close-cropped graying hair highlighting his blue-eyed, angular face. He would not tolerate anything untoward in his courtroom.

Almost immediately, just before the court was to be called to order, mayhem broke out, when several men and women began shouting invectives toward the defendant: "Murderer! Swine! You should roast in hell!" rang out. Cernak swung down his gavel viciously, as if it were a sledgehammer.

"There will be no further outbursts in this courtroom! This is not a circus! Any further disruptions or outbursts and we will have the courtroom cleared." And with that Cernak indicated to the chief prosecutor to begin his opening argument.

Advocate Stefan Wisniewski, stood up from his chair and commenced his preamble. He was about six feet tall, and, although not yet 30 he was already showing signs of premature balding. Wisniewski was most capable and for the next 30 minutes outlined the case against Leo Goncalo. During the course of his opening statement, several individuals, mostly older women, wept from the gallery.

George Sloan, through a Polish translator seated next to him, thought Wisniewski's statement and oratory had been brilliant. He'd clearly laid out the crimes Goncalo was being accused of having committed and how he now must be called to account for his actions.

Next, it was the turn of Leo Goncalo's defense attorney, Marek Gonkowski, to make his opening argument to the three judge panel. At first, Gonkowski could hardly be heard. And after Justice Cernak had requested the lawyer speak louder, his words were nothing remotely resembling brilliance. This was reflected in the downcast and defeated look on Leo Goncalo's visage. It had been so weak that Sloan thought Leo would drop his head into his hands. Gonkowski seemed in a hurry to conclude his remarks, and, as a result, took only about 10 to 15 minutes.

The prosecution called forth only one witness, *Dottore* Leonardo Levi. The former prisoner doctor stood resolutely in the witness box and was duly sworn in by the court reporter. Prosecutor Wisniewski welcomed Levi and quickly began his questioning.

Levi grimly recounted much of the testimony he'd already provided to George Sloan. Yes, he had participated in surgeries involving castration alongside Doctor Goncalo. It was true that these operations had been performed on anesthetized prisoner patients. And it was also true that he'd directly observed Leo Goncalo conduct surgery on unanesthetized patients.

Dottore Levi recounted his testimony in a clear and distinct voice, with virtually no hesitations. The man never faltered. George Sloan had been more than impressed and sat in admiration of the man. There could have been no doubt that the effort Levi had put forth had to have been most trying and painful for him. It was a pain in the rhetorical sense.

Defense Counsel Marek Gonkowski tried mightily, but, ultimately, vainly to poke holes in Levi's testimony, but with little effect. There was this one notable exchange.

"*Dottore* Levi, you have stated in your testimony that you readily participated in providing assistance to *Dottore* Goncalo during the course of these so-called castration procedures, is that not correct?" asked Gonkowski as he languidly leaned against the court room bench.

"First of all, I did not readily participate in these procedures as I was a prisoner doctor. We never had the option as to whether we could perform, assist, or provide whatever service, or not. Second of all, I would never have volunteered, as *Dottore* Goncalo did, to have conducted any of these ghastly and inhuman procedures on any human beings," said Levi, his voice rising in indignation.

"Objection, if it please the court, *Dottore* Levi cannot make such an assertion as to *Dottore* Goncalo volunteering to practice any forced procedures," stammered Gonkowski as he rose to his feet.

"Objection is sustained. The witness is to restrain from making any references as to whether *Dottore* Goncalo volunteered any services of his to the camp," said Justice Cermak. He then banged his gavel down at the sound of disagreeable murmurs from the assembly.

The defense attorney then called for his client to take the stand. For the most part, Leo Goncalo only brought forth more general Information regarding his past. How he'd always tried to be a caring and compassionate physician, always trying to do what was best for his patients.

Stefan Wisniewski, on cross-examination, asked Goncalo as to how the castrations could ever have been considered as humane and was this the right thing. Goncalo could offer little in rebuttal.

The entire proceeding took less than a day.

It was brought to its conclusion by the prosecutor stating that Leo Goncalo must be convicted of crimes against humanity for callous and dastardly, and inhuman work at Auschwitz.

Marek Gonkowski essentially requested that the court take mercy on his client. Leo Goncalo had not behaved in any way inhumanely. That, in essence, Goncalo was a decent and understanding human being.

Court was then adjourned for the day. Sentencing would be pronounced the following morning.

The next day, a bright sun made its appearance and gave forth a brief relief from the gripping and forbidding winter weather. At precisely 10:00 am the three tribunal judges filed into the courtroom and took their seats. Chief Justice Anton Cermak called the court to order and informed it that the panel was ready to pass sentence.

Leo Goncalo and his attorney stood. Leo began to feel his knees knock together. He thought he might well pass out, as the tension built within his body.

"As to the charge of crimes against humanity in the causation of having conducted undue, cruel, and inhuman suffering, the court finds the defendant, Leo Concalo…Guilty!" Cermak announced in a clear and stentorian voice.

There was a brief outburst from the visitors' gallery. Cheering and foot stomping ensued.

"There will be order in this court!" thundered Cermak.

Gradually, order was restored and only then did Anton Cermak proceed. "It is the judgment of this court that punishment is to be meted out as death by hanging. It is to be carried out at Luganski Prison one week from today. May God have mercy on your wretched soul, Comrade Goncalo. These proceedings are now closed." Cermak then banged his gavel down.

Leo Goncalo then collapsed in a heap on the courtroom floor. He would have to be revived and then be removed by two burly police guards. There would be no appeal to the judgment by Leo Goncalo's defense team. This was not at all like the court proceedings in America. Leonardo Levi stood and looked up at George Sloan. The two men acknowledged one another, a silent agreement on the satisfactory judgment rendered that day.

***

One week to the day from when sentence had been pronounced on Leo Goncalo, the time had arrived for the man to be called to account for what he had done. At the hour of 6:00 am, Leo was rousted from his bed by guards at Luganski Prison. The jail was an imposing and forbidding stone edifice, and to Goncalo it had seemed even more imposing than Auschwitz had been. Leo was in such a state that he could not consume even a morsel of food for his last meal.

Finally, at 1100 hours the moment of truth came to be. Prison Kommandant Stanislaw Wishek appeared before Goncalo's cell and informed him that the moment had arrived for his execution. Accompanying Wishek was a local parish priest who'd been summoned to Luganski should Goncalo wish to make a last confession. He had not, so the priest stood by to utter a prayer as the condemned man was led out of his cell. Leo Goncalo was brought out to the prison courtyard where the execution scaffold stood. He looked up at the looped rope and felt a lump form in this throat. Without further ceremony, he was led up the steps to the platform on which he would stand.

Sergeant Kliment Woroshowski, the Chief Executioner of the prison, stood by a wooden handled lever protruding up from the oaken platform. Leo was guided to the rope by two prison guards and made to stand upon a trapdoor. His hands had been tied together behind his back. One guard then fastened a black blindfold around Leo Goncalo's weeping eyes.

A moment before Woroshowski would activate the lever, Leo Goncalo yelled out his final words: "Long live Italy!"

At the command of Kommandant Wishek, Sergeant Woroshowski yanked back on the lever, causing the trapdoor to open and Goncalo's body to drop through. Wishek thought he distinctly heard the bones of the prisoner's neck snap.

Leo Goncalo briefly struggled in the last moment of his life, but his body soon stilled. The prison doctor stepped forward and checked for a pulse. There was none. The doctor pronounced Leo Goncalo dead at 1130 hours.

***

George and Rosalie were enjoying a light breakfast of buttered croissants and Lavazza espresso coffee. Lavazza was a brand that had been in the Mancini and Donato households for decades. In a short while they would be quietly married in Sant' Agata Church in Messina, and they, along with Rosanna, would journey to Rome. Sloan had to attend to some final details and then he and Rosalie and Rosanna would leave Sicily forever and settle in England. Rosalie had long desperately desired to escape from the twisted and decadent Sicilian lifestyle, and its so-called code of honor and *omerta;* its blood feuds, and ever present and clinging death. She wanted something clean and new and proper for her to raise Rosanna.

Rosalie had known of Goncalo's conviction as soon as George had informed her. She was sipping on her espresso with the newspaper in her other hand. When she turned to page two her attention was drawn to an article at the bottom of the page.

"Sicilian doctor executed in Poland!" Rosalie quickly read through the brief two column report. "George, Leo Goncalo was executed two days ago. It's right here in the paper."

Sloan looked over at Rosalie as he grasped her hand in one of his. Both looked at one another in that knowing and unstated way which said: "It's over. It is now truly over."

About the Author

Gary Benassi was employed for more than 30 years by the Defense Department as an analyst of private defense contractors. He has degrees from the University of Rhode Island and Michigan State University. The subject of World War II and, in particular the Italian campaign have long held his interest. Gary is also the author of *The Monsignor* and *The Woman Who Swam In The Nude*. He resides in the Cranston, RI area.

Made in the USA
Middletown, DE
02 April 2024

52283441R00146